AF589174
STAFF APARTMEN
HOLLIS'S BUNGALOW
ELI'S APARTMENT
STAFF PARKING
PICKLEBALL & TENNIS COURTS
POOL
STARLIGHT PALMS
SECURITY

VERA STEIN IS FINE

VERA STEIN IS FINE

A NOVEL

Julie Murphy

An Imprint of HarperCollins*Publishers*

 For information, address HarperCollins Publishers, 195 Broadway, New York, NY 10007. In Europe, HarperCollins Publishers, Macken House, 39/40 Mayor Street Upper, Dublin 1, D01 C9W8, Ireland.

HarperCollins books may be purchased for educational, business, or sales promotional use. For information, please email the Special Markets Department at SPsales@harpercollins.com.

hc.com

FIRST EDITION

Interior text design by Diahann Sturge-Campbell

Chapter opener graphic illustration © Galyna_P/Stock.Adobe.com
Interstitial poster art © Ezakiell/Stock.Adobe.com
Flamingo illustration © Never look back/Stock.Adobe.com
Front endpaper by Ruby Taylor
Back endpaper by Chloé ZG

Library of Congress Cataloging-in-Publication Data has been applied for.

ISBN 978-0-06-338683-9

Printed in the United States of America

26 27 28 29 30 LBC 5 4 3 2 1

To everyone who ever woke up to a birthday, looked back on their life, and thought, "Who the hell am I and how did I get here?"

And to the caretakers. It's okay to let someone take care of you too.

"It's no use going back to yesterday, because I was a different person then."
—Lewis Carroll, *Alice's Adventures in Wonderland*

If it doesn't scare you, you're already dead!
—Tagline for George A. Romero's *Night of the Living Dead*, 1968

PRIMARY CAST OF CHARACTERS

VERA STEIN
40 years old. She has been caretaking for her ill mother and working full time. Once aspiring screenwriter. Late bloomer.

RUBY STEIN
82 years old. Vera's grandmother. A woman of many caftans. Former creature feature scream queen. Tastefully vulgar.

TESS MELLER
40 years old. Entertainment lawyer. Perpetually renovating her home. Mother of five. Reckless abuser of speakerphone.

BRODY TURNER
40 years old. Vera's boss with benefits. Hollywood himbo. Good intentions with poor execution.

HOLLIS WHITMORE
80 years old. An unapologetically queer, Katharine Hepburn type. She doesn't wear clothes. They wear her. Headstrong.

DR. ELIAS BUCKLEY
42 years old. A bit of a poor little rich boy. Serious on the surface with a dry sense of humor. Owner of an excellent beard.

LEONARD MARVIS
81 years old. Prolific screenwriter. Flamboyant oddball with the fashion sensibilities of Elton John. Parakeet enthusiast.

June

Ending up at The Ivy with my grandmother was not how I planned on mourning the death of my mother. My grandmother and I sat down across from each other at The Ivy.

I did not want to be here. I didn't want to leave the house at all, and for the last week, I hadn't.

But this morning, Ruby was persistent.

She was visibly delighted as the hostess shook out the napkin and placed it in her lap. Her silk caftan–covered shoulders shimmied with excitement as the menu was handed to her. "Oooh, this limited menu is enticing. Though I don't understand this newfound obsession with grapefruit. Is it the new avocado? But pomegranate! Could we give pomegranate a moment, please?"

"I think I'll have the Southwest omelet with no Hatch chiles," I said without looking at the menu.

Ruby tsked. Nothing I did was ever adventurous enough for my grandmother. Eating, traveling, dating. It was all met with *tsk*s. But not all of us had the luxury of being spontaneous. Some of us had been taking care of ailing mothers since the year after college graduation.

It wasn't that Ruby didn't also take care of Mom, but it never came as naturally to her. She didn't know how to change an ostomy bag without grimacing. It didn't occur to her that spoon-fed ice chips were the best way to stay hydrated when the nausea made swallowing water too difficult.

"I'd hardly say this was the precipice." Ruby pouted as she considered our table location. "But I suppose it'll do."

I tipped my menu down and looked around. When I called for a last-minute reservation this morning, Ruby had insisted that I ask for a table with a view of the patio. Not on the actual patio, but the *precipice* of the patio. She wanted to look *upon* the outdoors without being in the outdoors.

We were definitely a few tables from a patio view, but it was better than sitting outside on this sweltering Sunday afternoon in June. Just parking the car left me with swamp ass. (I did not have expendable valet income.)

The Ivy wasn't really a financially sound decision. Ruby had caviar taste on a tuna salad budget. But my grandmother needed her fancy Sunday brunch like I needed to sit in a dark room with peppermint tea and a heating pad after a wild night of eating too much soft cheese. *This* was how Ruby needed to be cared for as we both grieved. With forty-eight-dollar eggs Benedict. And I'd promised Mom we'd take care of each other. We both had.

"Did you mention my name to the hostess?" Ruby whispered. "I could feel her staring."

"Rubes, I'm pretty sure the first Marvel movie came out before the hostess was even born." I'd name-dropped to get the reservation, but it hadn't been Ruby's name.

My grandmother's tight-lipped, all-knowing grin, the same one she'd carried since she was a teenager, faltered slightly.

"But you know," I added, "maybe she's seen *In the Family*. Or now that the creature movies are streaming, there's no telling. She could have recognized your red hair."

Ruby's "natural" color was a concoction of two Revlon box dyes. I'd seen a few pictures from when she was a kid and had that same murky brown hair that came naturally to me and Mom, but my own memories were of her fiery red perm.

After a moment, she nodded before peering over and then through her Iris Apfel–esque glasses until the words on the menu came into focus.

While she perused, I attempted the day's Wordle. I'd missed a few days when Mom died and felt unnecessarily bitter about my broken streak. Just as I hit enter on my personal favorite starting word (*roast*), a text from Brody appeared at the top of my screen.

Brody:
Hi! I know that I'm not supposed to be texting you because you're on garievement leave, but do you remember the password to my Hulu account?

Not only was I the assistant to Hollywood's favorite himbo, but I was also the keeper of his passwords.

Vera:
The first girl you kissed and the year you graduated high school.

I also nearly added: *And it's bereavement. Not garievement.* But there was no need for Brody to be the victim of my scorn. I tucked my phone into my purse with a smile. Did I *miss* work? Was I actually missing *work*? Or was it Brody who I missed?

My phone chirped again and I pulled it back out.

Brody:
Miss you more than I missed Taco Bell's Mexican Pizza when they took it off the menu that one time.

I laughed silently, something resembling glee swelling in my chest, and typed back:

Vera:
Miss you more than I miss *The West Wing*.

"What's got you smiling?" Ruby asked suspiciously.

Ruby had opinions about my screenwriting degree gathering dust for the last eighteen years and I didn't need any more of her opinions right now, especially when it came to working for Brody.

"Well, are you going to share your big news?" I asked in an attempt to deflect.

"Not until we have something to toast with," she said. "Oooh, is that Gillian Anderson over there? My god, that woman knows how to wear a silk blouse. Clothing really drapes so nicely over her breasts. Do you think they're natural?"

I glanced over my shoulder. "Uh, she's two tables away. Can you not talk about clothing draping her breasts while we're in earshot?"

"I'm sure she would take it as a compliment," Ruby said as she considered me.

When the waiter arrived, Ruby ordered us both some sort of superfood green juice and champagne while I stuck with my usual omelet, and she opted for the anchovy eggs Benedict.

I waited patiently for our bubbles to arrive, before holding up my glass in anticipation. Good news could mean anything with Ruby.

When I was a little girl, she and her friends hosted a "going away" party because a producer with a reputation for scummy behavior passed away. The dress code for the party was To Die For. Then there was the incident three years ago when she invested in some sort of crypto scam that was sure to change our lives. (To this day, she still couldn't explain cryptocurrency to me. But to be fair, I couldn't explain it to her without reading the Wiki page three times in a row and then promptly forgetting it all. We both walked away with many unanswered questions.)

Ruby scooted to the edge of her seat and raised her glass in a toast, her red-painted nails curled around the stem like talons. "To new beginnings," she said.

Slowly, I began to nod. "Um, not really how I think of my mother's death."

She took a sip from her glass and narrowed her gaze in disappointment at me for so obviously misunderstanding the moment. "I'm going to choose not to be offended by that comment."

"Okay, then, of what new beginnings do you speak, Grandmama?" I asked like a future lady of the house on *Downton Abbey*.

Ruby rolled her eyes briefly before leaning in excitedly. "I sold the house," she declared. "I sold Primrose!"

My heart stilled and those three words floated down softly like feathers on a breeze, taking me what felt like hours to comprehend. I stared at Ruby, completely dumbfounded, grasping for a thought or a word—or anything.

"The house," I finally managed to say. "You sold our home? The place where we live?" A suffocating heat flooded my chest and then clawed up my throat.

Primrose was the name my mom gave the three-bedroom West Hollywood two-story cottage Ruby bought forty-five years ago. The home where I'd lived for nearly my entire life. (Well, except for college and the year after, when Tess and I were roommates before she abandoned me to get married.) Mom had named it because she always loved houses having names, and even though the name was much more regal than the cottage would ever be, it stuck.

"What—what about— Where will we live?"

"Well . . ." Ruby paused, and I could see the actual war within her as she tried to hide her own personal glee while still allowing me to process this information. "Well, if you'll remember, my plan has always been to move into a retirement community. Surely you remember Starlight Palms."

Her timing was awful. I hated to ask. It felt silly and childish, and I was nearly forty years old, but I had to. "What about me?"

"Vera, honey. Sometimes when a baby bird fails to launch, it just needs a little push out of the nest. A nudge!"

The clank of metal on ceramic sounded as I dropped the butter knife. "A *nudge* is going to look at apartments with me. A *nudge* is asking me what my future plans look like. A *nudge* is encouraging me to start dating again. Not dumping me into one of the most volatile real estate markets in the country!" I could feel the level of my voice climbing with every syllable and the heat in my chest spreading up across my cheeks, turning them red next. (This involuntary bodily reaction brought to you by rosacea, thank you very much.)

And I hadn't failed to launch! I'd been—I'd been held back. God, I hated to even think of it that way. But I moved home for Mom because Ruby couldn't take care of her alone. I stayed at the same job for them. I skipped out on the social life that would have given me networking opportunities. My writing went from a future career to a weekend hobby to a forgotten past. It was all for *them*. And this was how Ruby repaid me.

I didn't ask for this life. I was supposed to fall in love and live in a nice house with an updated kitchen backsplash and go out with friends for happy hour. I wasn't supposed to be in a position where my grandmother selling her home would absolutely devastate me. But here I was.

"We'll sort something out," she said, reaching across the table as though her touch might ground me. "Breathe." She inhaled deeply through her nose and out through her mouth several times until I mimicked her, just like she used to do with her acting warm-up breathing exercises when she dropped me off for my first days of school, full of nerves and peppered with stress-induced acne.

"Can I get you two a few slices of our house-made banana bread?" the waiter asked.

Ruby looked up at him with a venomous gaze and said, "Shoo. Now."

"You can't just *shoo* people away," I told her after he'd backpedaled. I somehow had it in me to rein Ruby in even though it felt like my entire world was being broken down like a defunct production set. "Gillian Anderson will hear you and then she'll think we're the type of people who treat service workers like shit and she won't care what nice things you have to say about her . . . chest."

I blinked rapidly as my eyes began to well with tears. This could not be happening.

Ruby squeezed my hands. "Vera, dear, Starlight Palms has been my retirement plan since before you were born."

Years ago, when *colon cancer* were two words I'd only ever heard on chirpy pharmaceutical commercials, Mom, Ruby, and I had gone on several weekend trips to Palm Springs—always on a budget, of course, but every time, Ruby would have Mom drive us past Starlight Palms, an old resort that had been transformed into a retirement community and assisted living center. It was genius, honestly. A place for an aging generation to relive their youth.

"Mom died *two* weeks ago," I reminded her. "Her ashes are still cooling. We've barely had any time to grieve."

Her grip tightened. "I am eighty-two years old. Time isn't something I have an abundance of. Now, stuff, on the other hand, I do. Which is why I have an estate sale agency coming in on Tuesday afternoon to assess the situation."

"But the house never even went on the market," I said, still trying to piece the logistics together. She didn't even offer to sell it to me. Though I could never afford market price and this house was likely part of Ruby's retirement fund.

"Janice next door bought it for her son."

"Her son? Her son is like a human comments section! He's the worst." My voice began to escalate in volume. Sorry, Gillian Anderson.

Ruby chuckled and sat back in her seat before taking a pull from her glass of champagne and calling out to our waiter. "About that banana bread, young man!"

"Her son once stole her checkbook to write himself checks. Janice had a meltdown because she thought her identity had been stolen."

Ruby sighed. "Well, that wasn't ideal behavior, I'll admit, but he did write funny notes on the description line. I believe one of them said 'for wearing the clothes Mom buys me for Christmas.' The way Janice tells it now, the whole ordeal was nothing more than a practical joke."

The waiter returned with two decadent slices of banana bread and scoops of honey butter on the side.

"He better not ruin the place," I said bitterly.

It wasn't that Ruby owed me Primrose or that I ever expected her to leave it to me, but I had never imagined my future anywhere else. At least not for a very long time now.

"Well, thankfully," Ruby said, "those faulty pipes and cracked foundation are no longer our problem." She smeared the butter across the bread and took a bite. "Divine," she said as she covered her full mouth and pushed the basket to me. "You must try."

I glanced down at the bread, champagne, and green juice. Suddenly the smells of sickly-sweet syrup and sounds of silverware scratching against plates were all too much.

My head was too full.

Over the last seventeen years, I'd paid property taxes on the house, mostly covered the utilities, and kept the place out of disrepair. And now I had nothing to show for it.

This wasn't just about a house, though.

I was being left. I was still Mom's caretaker. I was tethered to her. No matter how gone she really was.

But suddenly Ruby was free, like she'd had this whole life planned and waiting for her the moment Mom died.

And I was cut loose.

August

"Just move out to the 'burbs," Tess said with a groan. "Fuck, have you eaten at a Chili's lately? Max ordered us an appetizer feast for dinner, and I forgot how hard their Southwestern eggrolls slap."

"They *slap*?" I asked. "Are we saying that now?"

Tess shrugged on the screen of my phone. "My assistant said it the other day and she has her nipples pierced, so I trust her."

I thought about that for a moment. Admittedly, the owner of two pierced nipples seemed like the exact right person to trust on something like this. "Okay, yeah. That makes sense. How's the renovation going?"

She rolled her eyes. "I'd rather be living in Brody's pool house at this point, TBH."

"I don't think we're saying abbreviations like that out loud, FYI."

"You just said 'FYI.'" She wiped ranch from the corner of her mouth.

"FYI is evergreen," I explained to her.

"Whatever. You sneaking any hotties into that pool house while Brody's out of town? Maybe you should let him see them on the security footage. Make him a little jealous."

"He's my *boss*," I reminded her, even if I had secretly fantasized about how far a little jealousy would go with Brody.

"Uh, your boss who doubles as your sometimes fuck buddy and who you've been infatuated with since college."

"You know I couldn't make any commitments when Mom was alive. There was no point in letting anything get serious enough to where someone would want to take the next step and live together—plus, Brody and I have always been purposefully casual," I said, as though I were a goddamn adult who knew what she wanted and got it too. "That's the only way this works. For both of us." That's what I'd told myself for the last few years. The convenient arrangement with Brody was as much for his sake as it was for mine.

I flopped back in bed and let the phone fall to my side so that Tess's view was of the ceiling fan. The very *sleek* ceiling fan.

Brody's pool house was nicer than my own home. Well, my former home.

He'd insisted I stay here after he found me crying in his walk-in closet the day of Ruby's estate sale. Tess had offered too, but she, Max, and their five kids were down to one bathroom and two bedrooms during their renovation.

In the moment, I'd wanted to be a martyr and refuse Brody's help, but the truth was I had nowhere to go. It would have been the perfect time for me to tell him that maybe I wouldn't be so on edge if he paid me enough to have my own place in a twenty-five-mile radius of my job or maybe if he'd just finally give me that long-promised promotion, but a small, pitiful part of me wondered if moving into his backyard would be the start of something more for us. Finally.

What it had turned out to mean was that I never actually went home from work.

Some nights were good. We'd stay up late in his media room and watch movies we had always tried to convince each other to like. (The fact that he didn't see the cinematic value in the 1991 classic horse-jumping movie *Wild Hearts Can't Be Broken* had and always would be Brody's number one red flag.) And then there were nights when he was getting home late and needed someone to run lines with him and sometimes that ended with us in bed and me tiptoeing back over to the pool house in the morning before the rest of the staff arrived.

Brody had left for a research trip to Scotland for his next feature three days ago, and I was nearly certain he planned on surprising me with a ticket to join him. It was my fortieth birthday today, and he had witnessed *both* of my *Outlander* phases. (When I discovered the first book in college and then again when the TV series began airing a few years ago. Brody was hooked too, though, and even watched a few episodes with me. I never told him I was actually rewatching each episode with him, because Mom and I always watched together when they dropped at midnight.)

So up until the moment Ruben, his driver, pulled out of the front gates with Brody in tow for the airport, I thought I was for sure about to *Eat, Pray, Love* my way through Scotland. But instead, I was here in the Hollywood Hills, signing for packages and fielding maintenance people on my fortieth birthday.

"I'm sorry we couldn't go out for your birthday tonight," Tess said. "Next week, though."

I picked the phone back up so she could see me again. "We're forty," I said, unable to hide the creeping dread in my voice.

"Babe, I've *been* forty. Don't make it a thing. Don't be one of those people who gets hung up on it. Graceful aging, et cetera, et cetera." She turned her head from the screen. "Did you put the kids down?"

Max said something I couldn't decipher in the background and then Tess said, "I'll talk to Chloe." She shoved a chip in her mouth and turned back to me. "Okay, I gotta run. But did you get the succulent I sent?"

"Yes," I said. "I look forward to killing it."

"Give it a name. That will make it harder to kill."

"Or worse when it finally does die. Love you. I'll talk to you later. Tell Chloe I support whatever form of civil disobedience she's currently participating in." I loved Tess's kids, but after years of caretaking for Mom and assisting for Brody, I had no desire to be a mother. Of all the things in my life that made me second-guess myself, the decision to stay childless was not one of them.

"Then you can come and deal with her tantrum tomorrow, when she hasn't slept in twenty-four hours," Max called off-screen.

"Love you, Max!" I said.

"Happy birthday, V!" he responded.

"Wait, wait," Tess said. "Did you finish your read-through of *The Wunderkind* for that agent with the Nelson Group?"

Ah, yes. Two months ago, just after Ruby's big announcement, I'd accidentally gotten tipsy at an after-party Brody was hosting and pitched the two-decade-old script I'd been nursing since college to some rando who turned out to be Simon Shah, a budding junior agent who'd just been featured in *The Hollywood Reporter*. I woke up to a text that he wanted to see my screenplay as soon as it was ready. (Spoiler: The damn thing would never be ready.)

Since then, I'd barely been able to bring myself to crack open my laptop. The thought that someone could say no to something I'd worked on for so long was suddenly very real.

"Yes!" I lied. "Totally. Just one last read for typos."

"Perfect. Okay, good. I'm here if you need eyes." Tess blew me a kiss and the screen went dark.

God, she and Max were fucking perfect. They were good friends to me *and* they made pretty babies. Tess was a fierce entertainment lawyer while Max was her ideal match and completely happy in his role as a stay-at-home dad. Sometimes they were too much to look at because they just complemented each other so well.

And I was forty. All of a sudden. Out of nowhere.

Forty didn't *sound* old. But I was feeling it. It was like I'd suddenly become the human form of the "over the hill" aisle at a party store. I was used to being a certain degree of invisible. All the body positivity in the world couldn't penetrate what it felt like to be a fat woman in this industry. But forty was a level up on the scale of insignificance. On the bright side, with this level of obscurity, I could probably commit a heinous crime and get away with it.

As much it seemed like it, though, tonight wasn't a pity party. A party required attendees. (*Ba-dum-tss!*)

This, however, was a cozy night with a bottle and a half of cheap rosé and a rewatch of the final season of *Boy Meets World*. And then maybe the last episode of *Six Feet Under* if I felt like I still needed to exorcise some emotional demons. I was a chronic rewatcher. It was comforting. The stakes were low.

In a way, it felt like unraveling a puzzle and doing a deep dive on why my favorites were my favorites. My Intro to Creative Writing professor, a romance author who refused to share her pen name, always said that the best writers were natural observers, but sometimes I felt like I observed more than I experienced. If I couldn't bring experience to the table, at least I could consume. That was something I could do while I took care of Mom or reorganized Brody's pantry.

As the credits on the final episode rolled, I began scrolling through channels until I stumbled upon a Brody classic, *Forever Yours.* Brody didn't do many rom-coms anymore, but this one had really resonated and became a bit of a moment. He played a widower who matched on a dating app with the woman who happened to be the funeral director for his late wife's funeral years before. I'd studied the script back and forth and liked it quite a bit. I always read scripts before he signed on, and this one had felt solid. It was funny, yet weighty. But then after some rewrites and with only a week left on set, I found a gaping plot hole everyone else had seemingly missed. I pitched Brody a fix and he got the studio to extend production by a few days for a reshoot. People still quoted lines back to him in the streets. Lines from the reshot scenes—many that I wrote word for word.

That wasn't the first time and it certainly wasn't the last time I'd helped Brody out on set. So even though this movie would never have my name in the credits, I couldn't help but feel a little proud whenever I saw it replaying on TV for the millionth time.

As Brody made his big gesture at the end of the movie, showing up to a national funeral director convention to win his lady back, my vision began to blur as my eyes grew heavier and heavier.

Marlon, my thirteen-year-old Pomeranian, curled up on the pillow next to my head. God, this bedding was elite. Money really could buy happiness. *And* good sleep. I needed to check the label on this pillow. Then I could google it and calculate how many hours' worth of work Brody would have to pay me so I could afford a set for myself.

Just as sleep was within reach, my phone chirped from where it dangled in my fingers. With a groan, I fumbled through my alerts until I noticed one from my bank.

ACCOUNT BALANCE: -$274.22

"Fuck," I whispered, as I sat up, the blood rushing to my head.

CHAPTER TWO

"Did my health insurance go through early?" A negative balance did not feel like it should be a forty-year-old woman's problem. That was like a twenty-six-year-old-eating-three-day-old-Thai-food problem.

I'd get paid tomorrow, but the bank gods had no mercy when it came to the order of posted charges, and I wasn't about to give up forty bucks for an overdraft fee on my birthday.

This is what emergency funds are for, I told myself in an attempt to calm my tits. I opened my banking app to transfer only enough to cover any overages, but the stupid loading wheel spun and spun until it froze.

Marlon let out a squeaky howl in his sleep as I rolled forward onto my stomach to reach for my laptop at the foot of the bed.

Dead. Of course it was. The thing was ancient and could barely hold a charge.

Rather than dig out the charger and wait for it to reboot, I decided to slither out of bed and into the main house to use Brody's computer in his office. And maybe even dig through his stocked snack pantry. The man loved Pop-Tarts, and at the moment, a s'mores two-pack could fix me.

Brody's house was modern but warm thanks to the celebrity interior designer we'd hired on the recommendation of Jon Hamm. We'd viewed so many properties and they all looked the same. Stark white walls. Sharp lines. Sterile. The Realtor was about ready to murder Brody and use his head as a trophy to ward off future potentially picky clients when I suggested we tour the properties at night to scope out the best twilight view, which ultimately did the trick.

Inside, I grabbed a pack of Pop-Tarts and heated them both in the toaster—which was more expensive than the newest fully loaded iPhone—before heading up to his office. I let my fingertips drag along the walls of the hallway past his bedroom, lingering for just a moment in the doorframe.

I sat down with my Pop-Tarts and typed in his password. The name of his first dog and the first year the Kansas City Royals won the World Series.

As the bank's website loaded, I opened the drawers of his desk to thumb through the contents. Of course, there wasn't a lot there. Brody never actually spent much time in this room. In fact, the only reason the office was finished was for the 73 Questions with *Vogue* segment he filmed last year.

I polished off a Pop-Tart and logged in to move funds from the tiny savings I had accrued. Crisis averted. Ruby had given me some money from the sale of the house to get on my feet, but before then, my account held only a few hundred dollars at a time because Mom's medical bills were never-ending and she died a year shy of Medicare eligibility. So, I was a little paranoid about what limited money I had in savings now. It felt like something could happen at any moment to empty my coffers.

I closed out of the window I was using to see that the tab with Brody's email address was already open.

It wouldn't hurt to look.

I'd read plenty of his emails before. Mostly the ones I was cc'ed on. But still. I knew everything there was to know about Brody. We'd been friends since college. He was a Kansas transplant with a disjointed relationship to his parents. I'd seen him cry. I knew that he liked his underwear folded and not rolled. I once drove him home after he had Botox done on a hemorrhoid. I even knew that a psychic once told him that he was a best-in-show-winning dachshund in a past life and he fully believed it.

I couldn't imagine I'd find anything remotely surprising.

Feeling justified, I pulled the chair back up to the desk and began to scroll. It was mostly unopened emails from his agent, Erin, or his manager, Savannah. And several opened emails from Arby's. The man loved a roast beef sandwich.

It was reckless, I knew, but my fingers danced across the keyboard as I typed my name into the inbox search bar.

Doesn't everyone want to know if they're being talked about? Even in the most monotonous ways.

There were heaps of calendar invites from me and scheduling emails I was already on. A delivery confirmation for flowers he'd sent me and Ruby after Mom died.

My chest tightened. They had been beautiful, but the thing I'd never considered about flowers and funerals is that eventually the flowers die too and throwing them away is depressing as hell.

Then I spotted an email from his business manager/professional leech and former fraternity brother, Dalton.

Subject: Q4 Reorganization Plan
From: Dalton@VPLFinance.net

B-man,

I've got Mallory contacting the staffing agency re: assistants. Moving on from Vera and hiring two or three part-time twenty-somethings will cut some costs on the overhead and eliminate the need for employee health insurance if we can get everyone on a part-time payroll. (I'll make sure they send over some cute girls too.) If we want to move forward with this production company plan, we need to keep looking for ways to cut corners and keep things a little lean for the first few years. Also, this won't affect your monthly take home, which is ideal.

Subject: Re: Q4 Reorganization Plan
From: Brody@BrodyTurner.com

Let's hit pause. V's mom isn't doing great, but we can follow through once things settle. Maybe before I leave for *Warbringer* filming. I hate to lose her, but she'll understand. Vera's a good girl.

My second Pop-Tart crumbled in my fist. Brody had plans to *fire* me? Me? The most consistent and stable person in his life. The person who often took pity on him and invited him over for holidays when the thought of going home to Kansas was too much. The same person he'd been fucking on again and off again since college.

Vera is a good girl? A good girl, really?

The blood in my veins was steaming. Sizzling. How could he? How *dare* he?

I'd been there for Brody from the very beginning when he dropped out of school after landing his first big role. I found him having a panic attack outside of the registrar's office. We were good friends before then, but it was at that moment when I stopped and crouched down on the floor next to him to help him breathe through the panic of dropping out before senior year and disappointing his family when things between us changed. He *needed* me suddenly, and being needed was an absolute drug. Especially after the fallout of that disastrous trip to Vegas just a few months prior. We were both adrift and found that clinging to each other could afford us each some amount of solidity.

But now? I was just some disposable "good girl" who was nothing more than a line item.

I let the anger consume me, because if it didn't, I might feel the deep embarrassment and shame burrowing under my skin. The number of times I'd hooked up with Brody in a trailer on set only for me to run over to craft services and get his lunch when we were done, or the times he'd gone out to be publicly seen with a female costar only for him to text me on the way home to see if I was awake. The delusion of what we could have been was quickly falling away and now all I could see was the reality of what we were.

I took the carcass of my Pop-Tart and hauled ass back over to the pool house before digging around for my charger and plugging in my laptop.

Ruby, my own *grandmother*, had dumped me, and I wasn't about to let Brody do the same. I refused to let him see me as pathetic. Somehow the fact that he'd drawn this out for months and let me move into his backyard made this all so much worse. What must he think of me?

Never mind. I knew what he thought. *Poor Vera and her sad little life living with her dying mom and has-been grandmother. Poor Vera tinkering with the same screenplay for years.*

I was promising once. I was the student professors doted on.

Beside me, Marlon stood, turned in a tight circle, and sat back down in his exact same spot with a huff, like he could and never would know comfort.

"I know, buddy," I whispered, feeling restless. Like it was impossible to ever feel fully settled.

I opened my laptop and began to type my formal and immediate resignation.

CHAPTER THREE

Should I have waited to quit my job until the next morning? Or maybe even a few days later? Yes. Would I have chickened out if I hadn't just done the damn thing? Also, yes.

So, when I woke up, I was immediately grateful to my former rash self while simultaneously freaking the fuck out over hitting the self-destruct button on my whole life with zero backup plan.

While I double-checked and triple-checked the pool house for any last-minute things I might have left behind, Marlon snoozed in the backyard. The gardener, Sammy, tended to the raised vegetable beds that Brody had envisioned but never actually maintained himself.

I eyed the comforter and the pillows once more.

Brody had outfitted the place with his parents in mind, but they rarely came to visit. They were farming people and had Brody late in middle age. They never really had a grasp on him or his life out here. I had probably been the first person to actually sleep on these sheets. In fact, without me and Marlon, this bed would be collecting dust. We'd done him a favor in a sense.

I reached under the bathroom sink for a trash bag.

"For Marlon," I whispered under my breath as I stuffed the sheets into the trash bag to take with me.

Slinging the bag over my shoulder and with my laptop tucked under my arm, I locked the pool house door behind me.

Sammy, a Deadhead whose long silver braid reached down the length of her spine, tossed a piece of lettuce to Marlon. "I can't believe you're really leaving."

"It's time," I said in a cool tone, like I wasn't smuggling obscenely high-thread-count sheets on my back and making the rashest decision I'd made . . . well, ever. "Going to drop the bedding off to be laundered on my way out."

Sammy turned back to her work with a shrug. I could have a sack full of cash and she wouldn't care.

After putting the trash bag in my front seat, I ran inside to leave the pool house key on the kitchen island for Brody's future army of hot little part-time assistants.

Because old habits die hard, I sifted through the mail on the counter and organized it into the usual piles before opening a box marked *FRAGILE*.

Under layers of Bubble Wrap and tissue paper and encased in foam was a tall cylindrical glass award. The shiny gold plaque was engraved with Brody's name and below that: *The Outstanding Ally Award*.

I snorted. Sure.

A small white card inside read:

Brody,

Thank you for your tireless efforts on behalf of menstrual equity. We know you're a busy man, and understand you couldn't accept this award in person, but please know how much we value you as a humanitarian and ally.

–The EveryBODY Project

I repacked the award with a grunt. Brody never would have won this award if I hadn't organized the period product fund and drive for him after he got dragged for laughing when a podcast host asked him if his moody costar was constantly on "the rag."

The man just signed the checks! I was the one who saved the day.

My brain didn't even need to process the decision. I left the pool house keys on the counter and took the box with me before scooping up Marlon. This was *my* award.

I waved goodbye to Sammy and buckled Marlon into his car seat in the back of my car.

Stealing the award meant reorganizing the floorboard contents a bit, so I pulled out a stack of things and set them on the trunk of my car in order to fit the box in the back seat.

"Are you really leaving without giving me a hug?" Sammy asked.

I wasn't a touchy person. Not because it made me claustrophobic, but because, as much as I hated myself for it, I had a hard time not overthinking about what it felt like for other people to touch my body and feel the lumps and rolls that I told myself my clothing disguised.

Even with Brody, he had to fight me to leave the lights on at times. I recoiled a little at the thought. What if Brody had just been a chubby chaser? Maybe I was just a dirty little secret kink to him.

God, why couldn't my brain just shut the hell up? I knew better than to buy into any of that.

Sammy stood there with a basket full of freshly picked produce. "Take this. At least you won't have to run out to the grocery store first thing at your new place."

"Thanks," I said, and wedged the basket on top of the box. I didn't have the heart to tell her that there was no new place. Yet.

Sammy held out her arms and I stepped toward her with the intention of a one-armed hug. People weren't always good at hugging fat bodies. There was lots of patting or half-hearted efforts, but not with Sammy. I never knew her that well other than that she always smelled like soil and weed, and she had two pet ferrets named Ben and Jerry, but damn, she gave great hugs.

"Brody will be lost without you," she said. "But I'm so happy for you. On to bigger things, kiddo! Such great news about that script of yours. You must be delighted."

My gut twisted. On to bigger things. *Right.* "Yeah, I'm pretty excited. I better get going," I told her. "The pear tree you ordered should be here next Tuesday."

She gave me a thumbs-up as I got into the car and drove down the driveway.

I watched in the rearview mirror as she waved her hands over her head. One last goodbye. So sweet. If I weren't such a mess at the moment, I might have regretted not getting to know her better, because *wow,* was she sad to see me go.

The Wunderkind

Written by Vera Stein

DRAFT 1

October 8, 2007

Advanced Screenwriting

Dr. Von Jacques

INT. COFFEE SHOP—DAY

He's not just making coffee—he's conducting symphonies in steamed milk. He is an awful and chaotic barista.

POPPY (V.O.)

I didn't believe in fate until he misspelled my name on a cup and made it sound better.

According to the GPS on my phone, Starlight Palms was just over three hours away, located on the outskirts of Palm Springs. The About page on the website explained that the place was once one of the most hopping resorts of the fifties and sixties for young Hollywood weekenders. Sometime in the late sixties the place shuttered and then sat for a few years before some nostalgic studio exec bought the property and turned it into a retirement community. While not explicitly so, it had become a favorite among the aging entertainment industry population.

The perfect place for those who weren't quite wealthy enough to maintain huge estates with full staffs, it was still ostentatious enough to signal status—and it was a solid plan for industry folks who had a pension through the Screen Actors Guild. Ruby had put her deposit down on her own one-room apartment here when it first opened, but with Mom's health, she'd deferred her move for over a decade.

The community was heavily gated with a security guard booth. Since I hadn't actually told Ruby I was coming, she wouldn't have me on her list, so Marlon and I sat in the car, sharing a cheeseburger and waiting for our moment.

"Here we go," I whispered as a moving truck pulled up followed by a caravan of cars. It looked like move-in day for a new resident, and with my car packed with stuff, I could easily pass for one of their family members.

I drove past the security booth and let out a squeal once I was in the clear. "Call me Jason fucking Bourne," I said to Marlon.

The property inside was soothingly crisp and clean with a mid-century modern aesthetic so well done you couldn't tell the difference between the original buildings and the newer ones. There were interconnected walkways between bungalows and very fancy-looking golf carts zipping on their own paths running alongside the road. Blooming cacti, manicured grass, and evenly spaced palm trees lined every bit of pavement. The buildings were low and sprawling, a true nod to the original resort, which was at the center of the property. According to the pamphlet Ruby had showed me, those who needed the most assistance resided there, near the offices.

Just before turning down her street, Saguaro Crossing, I passed the stunning rectangle-shaped pool with a huge flamingo fountain at the very center. I could definitely see myself melting into that pool.

Ahead of me, a man who looked to be in his late seventies, dressed in tiny little swimming shorts and an unbuttoned terry cloth shirt, crossed the street, each arm around a lady of a similar age on either side of him. His hands rested on their hips in a way that seemed more than friendly. One of the women laughed loudly as he pinched her butt and they disappeared behind a cluster of palm trees.

Well, *that* was saucy.

I parked in the closest visitor spot across from Ruby's unit and looked over at Marlon. "Let the impromptu family reunion begin."

This hadn't been my only option. I could have gone to Tess's house. I knew that, but I somehow felt like Ruby owed me this. At the very least. And with the ongoing renovations, Tess didn't have much of a house for me to go to anyway.

Double-checking the address in my phone as I followed the walkway, I knew I was in the right place as soon as I saw the doormat. In a beautiful elegant cursive font, it read: *This isn't a whorehouse. It's a whorehome.*

I sucked it up like a big girl and scooped Marlon into my arms before knocking on the door. This was temporary, I told myself. A night. Maybe two. Three, tops.

But there was no answer.

"Hello?" I checked the doorknob to find it unlocked. "Ruby?"

"Oh, she's home," someone called.

I looked over to find a thin, older man in a denim jumpsuit sitting on an iron bench with his legs crossed, a curling paperback in his hand and bright green readers perched on the tip of his nose.

"Thanks," I said as I opened the door.

"Just doing the neighborly thing," the man said before returning to his book.

I was immediately greeted with Ruby's signature Elizabeth Arden perfume, Red Door. Yup, this was definitely the place.

The living room held the velvet chaise longue and matching sofa she'd kept from Primrose. Both felt disproportionate and out of place in the way that furniture from a previous dwelling always seemed to. Some of her favorite art and self-portraits, including a framed photo of me, her, and Mom from a very curated photoshoot Ruby had organized, hung on the wall. In this particular photo, Ruby had asked that we not smile. The assigned theme was powerful matriarchs. (Well, except for Marlon, who sat on my lap wearing a pink silk bow tie.) My grandmother lived for a theme, and it was something I loved about growing up with her too. She would suddenly declare an average Tuesday dinner floral headpiece or statement sleeves and pearls night.

"Rubes?" I sat Marlon down on the familiar chaise longue, where he was immediately back at home.

The unit was small but efficient with very modern kitchen appliances and an attached breakfast nook. There were only two doors: one to the bathroom, which was open and unoccupied, and the other to what I assumed was the bedroom.

"Ruby, it's me," I called more loudly this time.

Maybe she'd gone off to the pool or shopping and had accidentally left her unit unlocked.

I opened the bedroom door, because the same part of my brain that constantly checked to make sure Marlon was still breathing during an exceptionally deep snooze needed to ensure that Ruby wasn't just dead in her bedroom. Morbid? Sure. Possible? Yes.

The curtains were drawn, and the room was dark, but that didn't stop my ears from being immediately assaulted with the sound of moaning.

Sensual. Moaning.

I let out a scream that rivaled Ruby's signature vocals and immediately covered my eyes, even though all I'd seen was a naked back and silk bedding. And legs. Multiple legs. At least five.

Behind me, Marlon yelped.

"Vera!" Ruby gasped as I slammed the door shut.

Okay. Well, that was awful.

Quickly, I went for the front door but doubled back when I realized that I really and truly had nowhere else to go. Marlon tottered back and forth across the chaise longue and occasionally barked in response to my panic.

Ruby had always been very . . . uh . . . active, but thankfully her room at Primrose was downstairs, and I only ran into her suitors a handful of times over an awkward breakfast or a midnight kitchen sojourn.

I sat down like I was in trouble and pulled Marlon into my lap as a shield.

And I waited.

After a few torturously long moments, Ruby exited her bedroom in a red silk robe trimmed in turquoise ostrich feathers.

"I suppose it would have been too much for you to call first," she said as she whisked into the kitchen and turned on her antique espresso machine that sounded like a Model T shitting its pants.

"I didn't think I'd catch you fornicating at two in the afternoon on a Wednesday."

"Espresso?" she asked.

"You know it makes me gassy."

Ruby sighed and opened a cabinet to pull out what she referred to as my "pedestrian coffee maker."

"I've been looking for that," I told her even though that wasn't true. Brody's pool house coffee machine was basically powered by AI and even included all the fancy flavors and syrups they had at Starbucks.

"I didn't realize I packed it, but it has come in handy. You'd be surprised how many people don't appreciate fresh espresso."

The bedroom door opened again and a woman with a very close-cut silver pixie walked out in one of Ruby's kimonos.

Wait.

A *woman*. That was new for Ruby . . . as far as I knew, at least.

"You must be Vera," the woman said, her voice smooth and husky.

"Vera, this is Hollis," Ruby told me as she handed Hollis an espresso.

"So nice to meet you finally." Hollis took a sip and waved to me before stepping back into the bedroom. "Excuse me while I get changed and attempt to retain some sense of dignity."

Ruby chuckled and just as she said, "So what brings you here?" I also asked, "So a woman, huh?"

Ruby came to sit down beside me and Marlon immediately jumped into her lap.

Four-legged traitor.

"Don't be such a stiff," Ruby said.

"I'm not being a stiff. I'm curious if this means you're gay or bisexual or pansexual or whatever identity speaks to you or if this is a onetime thing."

She shot back her espresso all at once and set the cup on her end table, which was a gold crane with a glass circle balanced on its wings. "What is it with young people and all these labels and types? Hollis is . . . an old, old friend from another life."

"And she lives here now?"

Ruby nodded. "In her own apartment."

"And you two are . . . ?"

She turned to me as she began to stroke Marlon between his ears. "My turn for answers."

"I need a place to stay," I blurted as the coffee machine dripped into the pot in the kitchen. "*Very* temporarily."

Vera's tattooed brows furrowed, and her spine straightened. "Well, I'm not technically allowed to have overnight guests here without putting in a request months in advance."

"You know I hate breaking rules," I told her.

"Just like Annie," she whispered, her expression softening at Mom's name.

I didn't have the energy for dead-mom feelings right now, so I swallowed back the thought of Mom and powered on. "But *you* love breaking the rules, and you know I wouldn't ask if I weren't in a seriously tough spot." I hated this. It felt too much like begging, and I was a little angry at her for even making me ask. Wouldn't literally any other grandmother in the world offer to shelter their own flesh and blood?

She looked down to Marlon, who she'd always had a soft spot for. "Temporarily," she said, repeating my own word back to me.

Just then Hollis stepped out of the bedroom in cream wide-leg linen trousers and a matching knit tank top with no bra. Her chest was minimal and nearly flat, but her nipples were still visibly sloped. The thought of someone simply *perceiving* the outline of my nipple through my shirt gave me premenopausal hot flashes. But Hollis looked cooler and more collected than most starlets I'd seen on Brody's arm. Her whole Katharine Hepburn vibe was very foxy. I could see how Ruby might find that hard to resist.

She nodded to me and then to Ruby. "Still on for tonight?"

"I'll ring you and let you know," Ruby told her.

Hollis leaned down to give Ruby a kiss on the temple, and I looked away. It felt oddly intimate and like I was twelve years old all over again.

"She won't tell people that I'm staying here, will she?" I asked.

No sooner had the door shut behind Hollis than another woman and a man shuffled out of Ruby's room looking disheveled, the man fumbling with the buttons on his silk bowling shirt.

"Thanks for hosting today, Ruby," the woman said as she led the grinning man out behind her.

I turned to my grandmother, my jaw hanging wide open. "Is your room a fucking clown car?" I asked. "How many more do you have in there?"

Ruby put her arm over my shoulder. "That was just Morty and Willa here for a little afternoon gathering."

I waited for her to further explain, not even slightly satisfied with that answer.

"Swinging is an evolved lifestyle," she said simply.

I'd heard of seniors letting loose in retirement communities, and I didn't want to be judgy, but I was still in a bit of shock. "So does everyone at Starlight Palms . . . swing?" I asked.

"Just because something's on the menu doesn't mean everyone's ordering it, but it's fair to say that Starlight Palms has a progressive reputation."

"It seems like a lot for an aging population," I said. "No offense."

"Oh, honey." Vera grinned. "There are cases of Viagra. *Cases.* And the lube. Did you know they have lube these days for cooling *and* warming?"

Well, good for them, I supposed. But I could think of no lonelier place on earth than being surrounded by a community of constantly boning elderly. I needed a plan to get back on my feet and I needed it yesterday.

"Now, if you're going to stay here," Ruby said, "there are rules. Obviously, lie low since you're not an approved guest. And second, I've waited a long time for this chapter of my life, and while I'm happy to share my home with you again, I would appreciate it if you didn't get in the way of my . . . recreational activities. I plan on reaping the rewards of a lifetime of sacrifice and hard work with as many partners as I please."

I glanced toward the door, where my grandmother's three bed partners had just exited.

"Don't worry. There are lots of snoops and gossips at Starlight Palms, but none of *my* friends are going to tattle on you. Just be discreet when you're unpacking your car."

"Thanks, Rubes," I said, still mentally recovering from what I'd just witnessed. "I promise not to get in the way of your . . . sexcapades."

She put Marlon back in my lap and went to pour my cup of coffee. She even pulled out my favorite caramel creamer and the exact right amount of sugar. "All right, now tell me exactly what happened."

I'd give Ruby this: She was a great audience to share my story with. She hissed and gasped at all the appropriate moments and practically cheered when I told her about the souvenirs I'd taken before leaving.

That night, we ordered shahi paneer and veggie pakora and Ruby insisted I display the ally award on the mantel. She also made me watch her latest obsession, *Vanderpump Rules*, with her while she filled me in on all the context I needed. Then she went to bed (alone, surprisingly) and I partially unpacked the car under the cover of night.

I made up the chaise longue with the bedding from the pool house and severely regretted my decision not to strap the mattress to the roof of my car. Marlon cuddled up at my feet while I finally brought myself to reread my resignation, which was time-stamped at 2:42 a.m. Surely nothing about that or the run-on sentences looked unhinged.

Next were all the texts I'd received from Brody throughout the day and managed to ignore.

Brody:

I just got your email. Let's talk about this when I get back. But are you sure this is what you want?

I rolled my eyes at the thought of him secretly being relieved that he didn't have to fire me himself.

Brody:

Sammy said you left today. Like for real. Are you serious, Vera? Can you please call me? Please?

A sick little part of me took glee in his panic.

Of course, I hadn't left things a mess for him, but Brody barely knew how to function without me. I'd been his assistant since college and went full time as soon as he could afford me. He didn't even have numbers saved in his phone beyond mine and a few others'. The guy couldn't figure out how to make a dentist appointment without me, let alone access his own calendar.

Brody:

You're not answering and we're off the grid camping for the next few days. Please get in touch with Erin or Savannah when you can. We need to talk.

Brody:

That's great about *The Wunderkind*, though. I know you've been working on that thing forever.

Brody:

Hey, I just checked in with Erin and she'd love to talk to you before you follow through with the sale. Her assistant should be sending over some times to meet with you.

My script. Uh. Oops.

I may have possibly told a white lie in my resignation and said that *The Wunderkind* had sold . . . at auction. And that I needed to dedicate time to editing immediately.

Fuck. Brody's agent, Erin, was an absolute shark. The kind of person who fought viciously on her client's behalf and had studios saying "Thank you, Mommy. May I have another?" She was an agent I'd absolutely die to have in my corner, but also one I definitely didn't want to cross. (For example: with a made-up offer from a made-up studio on a dusty old script that had sat like a fossil in my computer outside of a few adult-beverage-induced partial rereads.)

I sat up and took a sip from my emotional support water bottle, a huge metal cup some influencer had convinced me would change my life. (It hadn't, but I was more hydrated, and I finally had a place to put all the incredibly niche stickers I could not stop buying from Etsy.)

I needed to look at the script. Now. Right this moment. It was the same urgency I felt when I'd walk past a pile of laundry for days on end and would suddenly out of the blue decide that it had to be dealt with at that exact (and usually inappropriate) moment.

A part of me thought that maybe I actually could send this script to Simon Shah and sell it in some perfect Cinderella moment and Brody would be none the wiser. Or maybe I could take the meeting with Erin and say my original deal had fallen through. She'd offer to look at the script and maybe see the potential there. (First, I would have to edit with potential in mind and, god, that was a daunting prospect.)

But hey, maybe I could salvage this lapse in judgment and turn it into opportunity. For the first time in a very long time, something that felt eerily similar to determination ignited in my belly. What would Brody do in my shoes? He'd charm and woo and distract.

After slipping my flip-flops on and leaving Marlon to snooze, I snuck out to my car. The property was quiet except for the fountains from the pool and the occasional applause from a late-night television show. I'd left most of my things in the car. Somehow, bringing my belongings in meant I'd be here for longer than Ruby or I intended.

Thankfully, I had taken the produce from Sammy inside this afternoon, which Ruby had been impressed by. With the light of my cell phone, I sifted through the back seat full of bins and bags, looking for the pile of notebooks that I'd wedged my laptop in.

But it wasn't there.

Forget being discreet. I began to unload everything in the car into the empty parking lot spot beside me like I was shaking out a shoebox full of receipts and movie ticket stubs. But nothing.

There were loose socks. A daisy-printed cardigan with mismatched buttons I'd replaced over the years. A bag of snacks I'd lifted from the pantry. The massage gun I bought myself for Christmas. The vibrator I'd splurged on for Valentine's Day after it went viral for its hilarious but convincing reviews. (Sadly, it was still in the box.) And the blue hydrangea fascinator I'd worn to the Kentucky Derby party Brody hosted last year.

I even peeked inside my small jewelry pouch and found everything accounted for. Including the delicate gold band I found myself sometimes rubbing like a worry stone.

But no notebooks. No laptop.

I sat down in the back seat, my feet dangling out the car door.

No. No, no, no, no. It couldn't just be *gone.*

I didn't have money for a new laptop, but more importantly: my screenplay.

Surely it was in the cloud . . . or something. What was the cloud, anyway? Was it one specific place? Did it just hover? Surely, I'd emailed it to myself at some point.

Oh god.

I couldn't sell a script that didn't exist. Or only half existed.

Mentally, I began to retrace my steps earlier that day. This morning, I had the car all packed. Then I opened the package containing the award and I took it to the car. I put it on the floorboard . . .

But first I removed a pile of things from the car.

A pile of things that I placed on top of the trunk.

And left it there.

Oh, fuck me.

No.

The memory of Sammy waving her arms over her head as I drove away flashed through my head. I thought she was being especially emotive! Not that she was trying to flag me down and stop me from splattering my most precious possession somewhere on the road between Palm Springs and I-10 like roadkill.

This was bad. This was lie-face-down-in-a-pool-and-hold-your-breath-for-too-long-until-you're-gasping-for-air *bad.*

My stomach tightened and then that same gripping heat spread to my chest. I lay across the back seat. I would *know* if I'd backed up my documents, right? Or maybe the laptop just did that for me. Aren't electronics supposed to be getting more and more intuitive? Wouldn't it *know* that I wanted to back up my work?

Oh my god. I was a sad old person who barely knew how to work a computer. I was the kind of person who should be taking Computing for Beginners at the public library. I might as well open up all my junk emails and send the contents of my bank account to the first Nigerian prince I came across.

I needed a plan. Smart people had plans. Plans led to solutions.

Tomorrow I would call Sammy or maybe Ruben. Maybe the laptop landed gently on the steep, steep incline of Brody's driveway and it was perfectly fine. Maybe it wasn't flung off the back of my car as I sped down the hills toward the highway.

Tears began to prickle at the corners of my eyes and then rolled down the side of my face, wetting the hair I hadn't brushed in two days.

My mother knew how she wanted to die.

Ruby knew how she wanted to live.

And somewhere in between the two of them, I'd spent the last eighteen years in a holding pattern, waiting for something to happen to me. Waiting for my life to begin. To become the person I was meant to be—whoever the hell she was. And now the one thing I'd carried with me for all of these years, the one thing I could point to as something I'd done—something I'd completed—was gone.

But it wasn't just the script. I didn't just want to be a person with a job. There was a whole life that had unfolded behind me full of stops and detours that I never got to take. Instead, I'd kept my head down and never even bothered to become the type of person who would demand a raise or send a script off to an agent or put herself out there enough to meet someone who wanted a bona fide relationship that included a healthy sex life and dates in public and ordering takeout and going on weekend getaways and shopping at flea markets.

Instead, I'd let myself become the person who took care of everyone else, and that was it.

That was Vera.

She was a good girl.

CHAPTER SIX

Crashing on Ruby's couch for three nights straight had permanently altered the construction of my spinal cord, but that still hadn't stopped me from sleeping harder than I'd slept in months. I'd only gone outside to walk Marlon.

My eyes still crusty with sleep, I checked my phone for the time. It was twelve thirty-four in the afternoon. When I worked for Brody, I left my house every morning at six thirty. I was not a late riser. And yet, over the course of the last few days, I'd discovered that the more I slept, the less time there was in a day to be awake. The fewer hours I spent awake, the less time I had to live with the reality of whatever my life had turned into.

At the metallic sound of the key entering the front doorknob, I dropped my phone and closed my eyes again. By this time, Ruby would have had a breakfast with friends, gone to a water ballet class, and maybe even hit up a resale boutique. When she saw me lying here, she would definitely have *opinions* and I didn't want to be awake for them.

The door opened and the key hit the counter with a clatter. Heavy footsteps dropped closer and closer and I instinctively squeezed my eyes shut before realizing I probably looked constipated and then forced my face to relax, even letting my mouth fall open into a snore for good measure.

Ruby cleared her throat.

Nope. I wasn't falling for that trap. If she was going to lecture me, I would at least be showered and wearing a bra. So until she disappeared into her room, I'd play dead.

"Vera?" asked a deep, baffled voice. A voice much too deep to belong to Ruby or even Hollis.

I opened one single eye as I squinted up at the tall, broad figure hovering above me.

This was a dream. A depression-induced stress dream.

Against my will, I opened my other eye.

Because no way in hell was *Elias Buckley* standing in Ruby's living room, holding a stack of light bulbs.

I closed my eyes again and begged myself to wake up from this dream within a dream. "You're not real," I said to the dream version of Eli. A hypnagogic hallucination or a waking dream. Maybe with a side of sleep paralysis. Or something like that. I'd read about this before, but never experienced it myself. Stress could do weird things to a body, though.

"I assure you," the Eli-shaped hallucination said, "I am real."

I opened one eye again and then, to prove his point, he tapped his index finger to my nose.

Okay. I felt that.

"Uhhh . . ." As I sat up, my blanket fell away, and I was suddenly aware of my braless forty-year-old boobs, nipples pointing to the ground like a pair of *You Are Here* arrows on a shopping center map.

"Not to be a bad hostess," I said as he leaned on the arm of the chaise longue, "but what the fuck are you doing in my grandmother's apartment? Are you even real?"

He held up the boxes of light bulbs, and then, like *I* was the one out of place here, said, "Changing light bulbs. And yes, I hope that I am real."

"Are you a maintenance man?" My head felt like one of those shape-matching kids' toys and not a damn thing about this scene fit in the shapes of my brain.

He shook his head. "I just play one on TV."

I blinked at him. Did Eli Buckley make a . . . joke? I recalled many things about Eli, but his humor was not among them.

In fact, the last time we saw each other was deeply unfunny.

"I don't understand," I finally said.

He set the boxes down and proceeded to unbutton the cuffs of his sleeves and roll them up, thick blond hair coursing over his forearms. A single vein wound along the back of one of his arms and disappeared into his shirt. He had always been so hairy. I'd been so oddly mesmerized by that. Hair poking out the collar of his T-shirts. Trailing down the front of his belly. There were no men in my house growing up and something about being surrounded by so much testosterone in college left me fascinated in an anthropological sort of way.

Or maybe I was just super horny.

So much about him was the same as it was eighteen—no, *nineteen*—years ago, but the manicured beard on his face was a departure from the clean-shaven treasurer of Sigma Chi I remembered. He was softer now too and had a few creases at the corners of his green eyes. Yet he was still just as barrel-chested and capable of filling up a room without ever saying a word. And his clothing . . . it was less frat boy with his parents' credit card and more tailored and sleeker with a nod to Palm Springs in the 1950s. He was . . . stylish. And thoughtfully so.

"The maintenance guy ran off with a resident's grandson to Venezuela a few weeks ago, and we haven't found a replacement. Ruby needed help changing out some lights. Obviously, we prefer the residents not get on ladders."

"So you work here, then?" I asked, fidgeting with the ring on my right hand that once belonged to my mother.

He nodded, his green eyes briefly glancing down at my hands. "You could say that. I'm the head geriatric physician on staff."

I folded my arms over my chest, tucking my hands away. Geriatric? From what I recalled, Eli had big plans of following his father's footsteps into cardiovascular medicine. He once said that it was the type of medicine that attracted adrenaline-fueled fuckboys.

Eli had never really seemed like a fuckboy, but he was, however, annoyingly good at everything. Not only did he never seem to try, but he hardly seemed to care and I found that most frustrating of all.

And now he *worked* here. I knew I needed to get out of Ruby's hair immediately, but this was definitely a reason to expedite the process.

"I guess I should ask what you're doing here." He cocked his head to the side, scratching his chin. "You know, residents have to get special permission for long-term guests, so if you're crashing on Ruby's—"

The front door swung open and Ruby stepped inside followed by Hollis.

"Dr. Buckley," Ruby said, trying to mask her shock immediately followed by dismay at the sight of me still in the clothes I fell asleep in. "What a nice surprise!"

"I said I could change those bulbs for you," Hollis told Ruby.

"I don't need any of my residents needlessly climbing ladders," Eli said. "Even you, Hollis."

Hollis rolled her eyes.

"Well, I see you've met my granddaughter," Ruby said as she dropped a few shopping bags on the kitchen table. "I see she didn't go out of her way to dress for the occasion."

Low blow there, Rubes.

"We are previously acquainted," Eli said. "Isn't that right, honey?"

My nostrils flared at the pet name. Could I at least put a bra on before shit hit the fan?

"Is that so?" Ruby said, patiently waiting for the story there.

"Honey," Eli said again, his tone dry. "Should I tell them or would you rather?"

Well, shit. This was going to be a doozy. Might as well get it over with. Bra be damned. "Uh, Rubes. Meet Elias Buckley. My ex-husband."

Ruby froze. She was so still that had we been on a video call, I would have told her we should hang up and try again. For the first time in my life, I had left Ruby Stein speechless. Sadly, it was due to one of the worst mistakes I'd ever made, but it was satisfying, nevertheless.

And then the silence was gone, and her eyes lit up. "A doctor!" she exclaimed. "You secretly married a doctor and I am just now finding out?"

"He wasn't a doctor at the time," I muttered.

Hollis grinned as she leaned against the counter. "Well, I'm glad I decided to help bring the bags inside."

"It was . . . very brief," I told them.

Eli backed me up with a nod.

Ruby smirked, but before she could ask another question, there was a knock at the door, which was then immediately swung open without waiting for an answer.

"There you are!" said a young girl. No, not a girl. A woman in her twenties, who felt extremely girl-ish and yet quietly intimidating, like she was cataloging every cringey thing about me. "Doc B, I've been looking for you everywhere."

He held up the light bulbs, like they were an obvious explanation.

The girl looked to me, confused by my presence.

"This is my granddaughter," Ruby said. "She stopped over last night on her way through to . . . Where is it you were going?"

"Yeah," Eli chimed in unhelpfully. "Where is it that you said you were heading, Vera?"

I saw what was happening here. Ruby wanted me out, and Eli was a little too entertained by the thought of me getting caught breaking a rule.

I stood and let my blanket drop from my lap. "Hi, I'm Vera. I was visiting, but I stayed for a little longer than expected and Eli here was just telling me about the visitor policy, so—"

The woman held her hand up. "Morgan," she said curtly. "Residential director." She turned to Eli. "Josephine quit."

"What?" he asked. "How could she quit? She hadn't even started."

Morgan shook her head. "She quit. She called and said she couldn't leave behind her job on the high seas, so now I'm down a maintenance tech and an activities coordinator."

"We've been down an activities coordinator for a while," Eli reminded her.

Behind Morgan, Ruby rolled her eyes, which I took to mean she had thoughts on the activities calendar here at Starlight Palms.

"The people are revolting, Eli—I mean, Dr. Buckley."

"Morgan, I've told you several times. You can call me Eli."

She shook her head. "It's too weird. You're old. Basically old enough to be my dad."

"Maybe if I had been a teenage father," he said.

But Morgan had already moved on. "Someone pinned an activities calendar to my door with the words *do better* written across it."

"It is all rather boring," Ruby muttered.

"My numbers for knitting circle this morning were negative three residents," Morgan said.

"Negative three?" I asked. It wasn't really my place, but I had to know how that was mathematically sound. "How is that even possible?"

"Three people showed, but when they found out I didn't have a pattern for beer coozies they left," she explained.

Marlon trotted around my feet. I was wearing the gym shorts I'd stolen from Brody's giveaway pile and the free blood donation T-shirt that I had washed precisely enough times for it to be exactly threadbare enough. I had nowhere to go and no form of income. It was a real no-money-no-prospects-*Pride-and-Prejudice* moment. I couldn't bear the thought of heading back to LA with my tail between my legs. There was so much I needed to do, but none of it could happen without a job.

"I can plan activities," I blurted.

Ruby shook her head. "Vera, you do not have a social bone in your body."

I waved Ruby off and walked over to Morgan, who had turned her focus on me. We both smelled of desperation.

"I was a celebrity assistant for nearly two decades," I told her. "For Brody Turner. I planned charity events and parties and did so much creative problem-solving. And egos! I am so good at gently managing egos, which I'm sure you have in bulk at a place like this."

Eli crossed his arms over his chest and looked up to the ceiling, like he had something to say but was literally biting his tongue.

Morgan glanced to Ruby and then back to me. "We do have . . . personalities." She mulled over her options for a moment, before saying, "Come see me in my office this afternoon."

"Where's your—" I started, but I could already see her brain moving on to the next crisis.

"We might have the start of a chlamydia outbreak on our hands," she told Eli. "We need to get on this before it gets worse." She began to head for the door and then whispered, "I suspect patient zero is Louise."

Eli furiously shook his head. "Have you never heard of discretion? Doctor-patient confidentiality?" he asked her.

She shrugged. "I'm not a doctor."

"Obviously," he muttered as the door shut behind her.

"Louise." Ruby tapped her chin thoughtfully. "Hasn't she been with Martin, who's been with Rita? And who you have also been with?"

"You're thinking of Louise P.," Hollis told her. "And Louise P. actually died in her sleep two weeks ago, so we should be in the clear."

"I heard she was a good lay," Ruby said.

"Put that on my headstone," I muttered.

Eli grinned to himself and opened the boxes of bulbs. He was so at ease. So comfortable. Like my sudden appearance hadn't even rattled him.

Meanwhile, being in the same room with him right now was nothing short of a mindfuck.

"Well," Ruby shouted, so I could hear, "I guess you better get ready for your job interview today. Do you want me to run lines with you?"

I shook my head and started for the bathroom. "It's not an audition."

"It sort of is," Eli said quietly.

From over my shoulder, I gave him the kind of glare that made your lungs freeze. Or at least I hoped so, but something told me I just looked like a feral raccoon.

INT. YOU SCREAM ICE CREAM SHOP—AFTERNOON

She hands him a cone. He forgot his money. Again.

POPPY

Here. Just have it.

ARLO

(tips an imaginary hat)

Milady.

POPPY

Next time you'll have to pay with something other than charm.

LOS ANGELES
CALIFORNIA

ELIAS BUCKLEY

NINETEEN YEARS AGO

HI, VERA STEIN

Halloween was the goddamn Olympics of the Greek system, and the men of Sigma Chi were the reigning gold medalists. I stood leaning over the balcony of my bedroom, watching the debauchery unfold on the front lawn.

I wasn't a fraternity guy naturally. My circle of friends back home was more like a triangle. I didn't like noise. The traditions and unnecessary secrecy felt like playing dress-up. But Sigma Chi was a family tradition. Just like Stanford Med. Just like becoming an interventional cardiologist.

My roommate, Brody, had joined Sigma Chi with pure intentions a year after me. He wanted the family that joining a fraternity could bring you. I chose him as my little brother and roommate because he showed up to rush wearing a jacket and bow tie with no shirt under and it made me laugh. My friendship with Brody was simple and uncomplicated. He needed someone to keep him in line, and I needed someone to remind me to just fucking *breathe*. When alumni came to visit and you'd hear them spouting off about the bonds of brotherhood, the relationship I had with Brody was what they were talking about. Simple and familiar.

Then a mousy girl with riotous brown hair that was neither curly nor straight and glasses as round as her hips showed up on Halloween and ruined everything.

Well, not everything. Just me.

I watched from the balcony as she stood in line wearing black jeans and a black-and-white striped T-shirt with cat ears and a black mask over just her eyes. A cat burglar. It was the kind of costume that didn't commit but was clever enough for me to appreciate. The girl next to her I recognized from a philosophy class I took last semester. She had long auburn hair and I remembered her taking everything incredibly seriously. They stood out against the scantily clad throngs of girls.

The two of them waited, their arms looped together. I took a sip of beer as I watched them make it to the front of the line. The cat burglar swayed on her feet a little, attempting to pull away from the line, but her friend held her firmly in place. She was uncomfortable. I could relate.

I hated parties, but more than that, I hated myself at parties. I hated that I couldn't hear anything, and the only way to avoid feeling awkward was to get so wasted that you woke up with a sense of regret for things you couldn't even remember.

Dalton, a freshman from Redwood, stood at the door. He was supposed to be checking IDs and marking anyone under the age of twenty-one with a frowny face stamp on their hand, but really he was there to let the hot girls in . . . and keep the less than hot girls out. It was gross, but what had I done in the last three years—two of those as treasurer—to change shit?

Behind me, in my room, a few people stumbled in—presumably to use my or Brody's bed—and then stumbled right back out when they saw me on the balcony.

The cat burglar and her friend made it up to Dalton and he looked at their IDs closely with his flashlight. "I don't know," I heard him say. "Looks a little fake to me."

"Tess, can we just go?" the cat burglar asked.

"They're not fake, you dick hole," Tess, the girl I recognized from last year, said.

He shook his head. "Sorry, ladies. Can't get caught with fake IDs in the Sigma Chi house. That's bad for business. You get it."

Behind them, a group of first-year girls from Tri Pi laughed.

My grip on my beer can tightened, making a small crunching sound.

Then Brody came bounding around from the backyard in a Jack Sparrow costume that he'd borrowed from the drama department after he'd hooked up with someone who worked in costumes. "Vera!"

Dalton's shoulders slumped a little as he realized he was about to be overruled by an upperclassman.

"Fuck off, Dalty baby," Brody said as he hauled himself over the railing of the porch and opened the nearest beer cooler. "These two are with me."

Brody stamped both girls' hands with a red Sigma Chi logo, which meant they were allowed to be here and could legally drink.

He took the cat burglar's hand and pulled her out to the front lawn with the other girl following behind, before calling up to me. "Eli, there the fuck you are! Meet Vera Stein. She's so smart. Like, as smart as you. But way nicer and prettier too."

Vera looked over her shoulder, trying to hide the sweet blush gathering on her cheeks.

I couldn't explain why, but she made me feel like a bad person. Maybe because I should have gone down there and been the one to tell Dalton and the Tri Pi girls to fuck off. Or maybe because I couldn't stop staring at her body, even if her plain clothes in a sea of costume lingerie sent the clear signal that she didn't want to be gawked at.

"Say hi to Vera Stein, Eli!" Brody said with a slight slur. "Where are your manners?"

"Hi, Vera Stein," I finally ground out.

"Hi," she squeaked.

CHAPTER SEVEN

I still hadn't unpacked my car at all, but I had my toiletries and was able to find the black shirt and black pants that I regularly wore to more casual red carpets and press junkets. Surprisingly I enjoyed clothing. I liked colors and patterns and shapes that made me feel like someone's eccentric art teacher. But as Brody's assistant, my job was to be so good at assisting that I was practically invisible. If you were an assistant and someone noticed you, it usually meant you'd fucked up in a big way. So black on black was a necessary wardrobe staple for industry events, and over time, I found that corner of my wardrobe felt a bit like armor. Which was something I definitely needed to get through this interview today.

I walked out of Ruby's bedroom, teasing up my curls a bit with my fingers.

"You look like you work as a hostess at a TGI Fridays," she said.

"I guarantee you've never even been to a TGI Fridays," I told her as I poured some dry food into a bowl for Marlon.

"Yes, but I once saw one on television and I've seen all I need to see."

"Marlon should be fine while I'm gone, but if he needs to go out, I left his leash on the kitchen table. You just attach it to his little harness—"

"I remember how to walk a dog," she said dryly as she scooped Marlon up in her arms. He was unfazed, happy even. And I had to say, an aging Pomeranian who preferred to be carried everywhere rather than to walk himself really did fit Ruby's aesthetic.

"Okay, right," I said. "Wish me good luck!"

She held up Marlon's paw and they both waved. "Break a leg!"

"Salary is nonnegotiable," Morgan said flatly. "Which is sort of a bummer, because I am pro friendly confrontation. I'm a Scorpio sun and a Leo moon," she added as though that explained everything.

"Okay." Considering this was my only potential job, I didn't really have room to negotiate.

Morgan's hair was perfectly wavy and impressively healthy. It was hard to argue with people who had good hair. She shrugged as she browsed her computer and based on the reflection of the framed photo of the original Starlight Palms behind her, it appeared she was currently toggling between bidding on a Garfield cookie jar on eBay and reading an article about a British girl who interviews celebrities in fried chicken restaurants. "You give up fast."

"So it *is* negotiable?" I asked.

She shook her head. "Definitely not. Normally I would be able to offer you staff housing, but we're totally full at the moment."

That was a bummer, but I definitely hadn't expected free or discounted housing, so I supposed that wasn't really anything worth shedding a tear over. "So does this mean I'll get a housing allowance in the meantime?"

She sputtered out a laugh, but kept her eyes on the screen. "So *now* you're negotiating?"

"Is that okay?" I asked.

"My dad was in the car business. Everything is negotiable."

"Except my salary?"

"I like you." She nodded. "So you can start tomorrow."

"That's it?" I asked, relieved that she liked me. I'd never had a little sister, but I had been around a handful of actors around Morgan's age and the need to be liked by her generation was daunting. "No background check or probationary period?"

"Yes on the background check and meh on the probationary period.

This job requires you to essentially be a human complaint box, so if you can just last long enough for me to get your replacement lined up, I'll be happy." She spun around and reached into the cabinet behind her. "Here's a four-year-old laptop and an iPad that can only be used when it's charging. I'll see about getting you a replacement, but the last girl never returned her tech."

"Well, considering I accidentally left my personal laptop on my car before driving off earlier this week, this is an upgrade."

Morgan grimaced a little. "Tragic." Then she handed me a thick Starlight Palms–branded binder. "These are the activities calendars for the last two years along with what we have on the books currently. You can change anything you want except Tuesday night book club with Dr. Buckley. It's shockingly popular, which doesn't make sense because he's so boring and old. Lastly . . . the residents can smell weakness. It's really impressive, actually."

I found myself sniffing, like I might smell it on myself, but all I got was a whiff of the partially melted deodorant I had liberally applied before walking over. Probably not liberally enough, though . . .

"I'll need to get some documents together for you, but for now, sign this background check release."

She slid a tablet across her desk and I used the stylus to sign without examining too closely for fear of looking uncool by being worried about silly things like legally binding documents.

I gave the paper back and then waited for her next instructions, but she had already turned back to her eBay auction.

"I guess I'll see you tomorrow, then?" I asked.

"Unless you change your mind. Oh, and Vera, until we have any housing open up, you'll have to find a place of your own. Residents really aren't allowed to have long-term guests and even though I definitely have oppositional defiance disorder, and love breaking rules—especially my own—this is one rule I am pretty strict on. Otherwise, I'll have a whole slew of residents with grandchildren leeching on couches. Not that you're a leech," she added quickly. "As far as I can tell."

Well, that sucked, but I needed to get off Ruby's couch anyway. "It might take me a few weeks, but I definitely don't want you bending the rules for me, and who knows? Maybe some employee housing will open up?"

She laughed and then coughed into her fist when she realized I didn't get whatever the joke was. "Oh hey, before you go: What's the deal with you and Dr. B?"

"We were friends in college . . . I guess."

She nodded.

I stood up to leave but turned back to her and said, "It's sort of a wild story, actually. I can't believe he works here. It's so random, but back in college, he was . . ."

But Morgan was already locked on to her screen and totally tuned out.

"See you tomorrow," I said, and then headed back to Ruby's.

As I walked through the maze of palm trees, step stones, and crosswalks, my phone chimed.

Brody:

Did I do something? Haven't heard from you at all.

How could it take him nearly five days to come to the conclusion that just maybe I'd up and left because of something *he* had done?

My life would look so different if it took me days instead of seconds to consider that something could be my fault.

Ruby and Hollis were sipping gin and tonics on the couch/my bed when I got back. Marlon was curled into Hollis's lap as she gave him the most delicate head massage and his eyes were little slits as he leaned into her touch. He didn't even flinch when I walked in.

"Well, how'd it go?" Ruby asked.

"You are looking at an employed woman," I told them.

Hollis hooted and Ruby lifted her glass before throwing back a sip.

"The good news is that there is staff housing," I said.

Ruby slapped her thigh. "The good news? That sounds like *the* news!"

"Well, the bad news is that they're full up, so I'll start looking for a place." With money I definitely didn't have. "And maybe employee housing will open up soon."

Ruby's smile twitched.

"Still great news," Hollis chimed in. "We're going out for happy hour. My treat!"

I eyed them both, wondering how many gin and tonics deep they were. "I'm driving."

"Oh no, no," Ruby said. "We'll take the minibus."

CHAPTER EIGHT

The minibus was just that. A miniature bus that residents could use as transportation. I had a feeling it was meant for those who were unable to drive, but it seemed that Ruby, Hollis, and many other residents used the minibus as a designated driver, because the thing was more like a party bus at happy hour.

We filed in and Ruby pointed to the bus driver. "Phil, this is my granddaughter, Vera. She's the new activities coordinator, so I'm sure you'll be seeing plenty more of her."

The older man with curly black hair held his hand out for me. "My chariot is your chariot."

"Did someone say a new activities coordinator?" a voice called.

"Gwen, turn your damn hearing aid down," Hollis said. "Just because you can eavesdrop now with that little thing in your ear doesn't mean you should."

I turned and waved to the crowded bus of residents. "I guess this is my unofficial introduction," I said. "I'm Vera, the new activities coordinator."

"I've been requesting a nonfiction World War Two book club for the last year," one man with tight round tortoiseshell glasses said. "Maybe this one'll wise up and give the people what they want."

"Could we get a second night of celebrity memoir book club?" asked a woman, her hair covered with a handkerchief to protect it from the desert wind. "That Eli is just cute enough to pinch."

"His name is Dr. Buckley, you horndog," Gwen snapped back.

And before I could say anything or receive one more request, Phil got on his intercom and said, "The wheels don't roll until you're in your seats, people."

Ruby grabbed my hand and tugged me down beside her. "If we get seated before four o'clock, we can take advantage of happy hour *and* the Tuesday night half-off appetizers special."

The man behind us sitting next to Hollis leaned forward and said, "Honey, do you have any experience with Facebook Marketplace?"

Ruby shook her head without turning around, but the man seemed so kind and sweet and had called me honey and I was an easy target when it came to pet names. I also recognized him as the man on the bench outside of Ruby's apartment.

"I sold a couch online once. And I bought an office chair from some guy named Todd last summer, so I guess I have some experience."

The man squeezed my shoulder, a gold ring on every finger. "I'll be in your office bright and early tomorrow morning."

Ruby gave me a look that said, *Well, you did that to yourself.*

When we arrived at Ta Molly's, a restaurant that claimed to have the cheesiest tamale in the desert, it took about ten minutes to unload all the residents, wheelchairs and all. But the restaurant staff was more than prepared for the crowd and Ruby was even on a first-name basis with our adorable waiter, Tally.

"Tally uses they/them pronouns," Ruby explained as she introduced us, as though my grandmother even knew what that meant a few months ago.

"Sounds good," I said, hoping this didn't quickly veer into awkward territory for poor Tally.

"Thanks, Rubes," Tally said.

"You tell me if that dick Ralph forgets," Ruby said. "I tried to convince our driver to leave before he showed up, but no dice."

I felt weirdly jealous of this waiter and the easy relationship they seemed to have with my grandmother. It was baffling, actually.

Tally smiled. "Pitcher of margaritas for you three?" they asked.

"I'll actually have a sangria swirl if that's okay," I said.

Ruby turned to me, her brows arched impressively.

I shrugged. "I'm celebrating, right?"

"Indeed. Sangria swirls for the whole table!" Ruby said, and those of them that could hear her cheered loudly. And then to Tally, she whispered, "Put those on Ralph's tab, would ya?"

The rest of my night was spent doing more listening than talking, and I wasn't bothered by that at all. In fact, listening to Ruby's lore was something I was very familiar with.

Ruby broke out onto the scene in the sixties as a scream queen in creature features. She had Mom in 1967 and then kept on working through the seventies in mostly slasher films that were more concerned with her willingness to go topless than her acting chops.

It was the early eighties before she got her big break with *In the Family*. Critics called it the feminist response to *The Godfather*, which at the time was not a selling point. Ruby played the matriarch of an Irish crime family when her husband fell ill and she continued to run the family business behind closed doors.

Industry talking heads were sure she'd sweep awards season, but in the end, the only nominees from the film were for the actors playing her ailing husband and one of her meathead sons. Since then, there had been a handful of guest spots or cameos, but it seemed that no one was interested in seeing a sometimes-topless horror starlet having a Hollywood Cinderella story of her own.

And so, Ruby's face hadn't graced a movie poster in over thirty-five years, but I wasn't about to be the one to remind my grandmother of that. Or of the fact that she was a grandmother at all.

The moment Ruby found out that Mom was pregnant with me, the first thing out of her mouth was "*No one* is calling me Grandma." The second thing was "Who's the father?" My mother's answer was "Not someone who plans on sticking around."

Anyway, I never did call Ruby by any other honorific than her name. Unless I was trying to annoy her or make a point. The word *grandma* invoked the same response as calling someone by their full name.

But for the most part, Ruby had always simply been Ruby.

CHAPTER NINE

My office had no windows and smelled like chlorine. I was the first room from the indoor pool. The smell was oddly comforting and reminded me of the indoor community pool where Mom used to do water aerobics when I was a kid.

"The outdoor pool is basically boiling in the summer," Morgan explained. "So, the indoor pool is a hot commodity while temps are in the hundreds. We get some slips and falls in the hallway, so if you hear one of the fall alarms go off, just pop your head out and make sure everyone's breathing. An orderly should be there soon."

I nodded. "Breathing. Got it."

"A lot of the residents split for the summer, so the ones that are here are the ones who don't have second residences or really involved families. You've got to keep an eye out for heat exhaustion. Through the summer, we prefer the residents to only walk outside after dark and will have golf carts with misters running from their bungalows to the main building."

"Smart," I said with a nod, and managed not to tell her how I was a fragile LA flower and didn't handle fluctuation in weather well. Or at all.

"And that's your name tag. You don't actually have to wear it, but sometimes no matter how many times you tell a resident your name, they'll call you whatever they've decided your name is. One former resident called me Lydia for a year. She even left some of her designer costume jewelry to me, but no one knew who Lydia was so it took the family a while to figure that one out."

"Lydia isn't even close to Morgan," I said as I began to shuffle through the paperwork left behind from the previous coordinator.

Morgan shrugged, and I expected her to respond with something snarky, but all she said was "Brains are funny things." She hovered in the doorway for a moment. "I'm glad you ditched the black trash bag aesthetic."

"Uh, thanks?" Today, I had indeed ditched the black clothes, though I would have hardly described my black tunic yesterday as a trash bag. I opted for wide-leg teal pants and a brown belt with a white sleeveless shirt that I'd doctored from a men's vintage button-up, because the severely pointed collar was too good to say no to.

"Word has spread fast about the new activities coordinator," she continued, "so I'm sure you'll have a revolving door of opinionated residents all morning. But come see me later and we can talk budget."

"Hey, have you seen that email I sent over about the new ambulance contract?" a deep voice asked from just beyond my doorframe.

I knew who the voice belonged to without looking up, but I couldn't stop myself from looking. I had pushed every thought of Eli as far away as I could, but the question of when I might see him next still danced in the recesses of my mind.

He stepped forward into my sight line and his gaze swept my office and paused on the one thing I'd brought to decorate with, the award I'd stolen from Brody as a parting gift.

"Yes," Morgan told him. "And I have thoughts."

Eli swallowed and smiled half-heartedly. He'd always been a deeply efficient person and I was certain that Morgan having *thoughts* was slowing down his process.

Morgan spun on her heel and beckoned for him to follow. "And Vera, good luck with the apartment hunting!"

I swallowed, trying to push back the encroaching panic.

Eli lingered for a minute and then finally said to me, "I've got some sexual health clinics I'd like to get on your calendar."

"I'll see what we can make work." I came off a little more abrasive than I'd meant to, but it was hard to reconcile the current Eli, who seemed to be nice-ish if a little bit of a smart-ass still, with the Eli I knew years ago who looked like he couldn't breathe around me without becoming nauseous.

He studied me curiously before nodding and walking down the hallway in the direction Morgan had come in.

It wasn't long before the first knock on my door sounded and my Facebook Marketplace friend from last night walked in with a tortoiseshell cane decorated with gold filigree, a baby-blue silk button-down shirt, and bright red glasses. "I told you I'd be your first customer."

"Bright and early," I said, already regretting my decision to fess up to what minimal social media bartering knowledge I had. "And I was thinking . . ." I searched for his name.

"Leonard, honey." He blinked slowly like a cat. "You can call me Leonard."

"Leonard," I said with a smile. "I was thinking I might not be the right person for this specific job—"

"You are the activities director, are you not?" he asked in a sharp voice as he sat down. His tone reminded me of the child-hating acting coach Ruby had hired for me when I was eight years old and she was still determined to get me into commercials. "Well, this is an *activity* I would like to do."

Ruby was right. I should not have said yes, and now I would have to learn my lesson. "How about you bring your item by tomorrow morning and we'll see what we can do?"

He stood with a grin that bordered on terrifying. "Tomorrow morning is perfect. But you'll have to come to me. I'm in one thirty-one. Right next door to Ruby."

I jotted it down and by the time he was gone, the next resident was slipping in.

The first few hours of my day were endless requests and complaints. Requests came in the form of more water ballet class times or even a sourdough bread–making class. The complaints ranged from highly specific (the woman who teaches pottery classes every other week smells like cat pee) to broad and difficult to diagnose (the events lineup is uninspiring).

Just as I was about to close my door for lunch and crawl under my desk to play Wordle while I questioned every choice that had brought me to this moment, a familiar face appeared.

"First days are always shitty," Hollis said as she stepped inside and leaned against the short filing cabinet near the far wall. She wore white pleated linen shorts, a matching vest, and Ray-Bans tucked into her tousle of cropped silver hair.

"Who said I was having a shitty day?" I asked, my voice falsely bright.

She stood there quietly, and something about the way she was willing to indefinitely wait out a long and awkward silence reminded me of Eli.

"Well," I finally relented, "it seems like your crowd is a tough audience."

She nodded. "Well, I suppose you spend every day of your life working and it's hard not to feel like you're owed a certain kind of life at the end. For some people, that's a daily knitting group and food that's easily chewable, but for a lot of us . . . well, it's a time when we can finally let ourselves indulge in everything we resisted."

"Is that what you're doing with Ruby?" I asked. "Indulging?"

She chuckled at my hard-hitting question. "Or is that what Ruby's doing with me?"

"Sorry." I shook my head. I liked Hollis. A lot. "It's not my business, but I . . . I was surprised to see her . . ."

"With a woman?" she asked. "There's a lot more about Ruby that might surprise you."

Yeah, I didn't think I needed to learn any more surprises about my own grandmother anytime soon. "Some stones are best left unturned. So, you got any tips for how I can liven things up around here without getting fired?"

"The residents are . . . curious. And horny. Nostalgic too."

"Well, maybe we could look at doing some themed events, but I don't think they'll let me host a Starlight Palms–sanctioned orgy."

"Of course not," Hollis said with a laugh. "But there are things you can do to give them—us . . . agency. To remind us that we're adults.

You know, there are people here like me and Ruby who have chosen to be here, but a lot of the residents you'll meet were brought here by loved ones who couldn't physically take care of an aging family member, which is understandable. Or they were brought here because there's no real guide on what to do with the aging people in your life. It's easy to forget that we're just as alive . . . even though we're closer to death than the rest of you."

I nodded and only then did I notice my eyes beginning to water. Had I ever done that to my mother? Forgotten that she was still alive even when she was so close to the end?

Hollis reached over my desk to catch a single tear with her thumb. She smirked. "In the end, we're all sluts and then we die."

"Words to live by."

"You're going to do great. Sign me and Ruby up for your events," she called over her shoulder as she walked out the door.

"Which ones?" I asked.

"All of them!"

I snorted. Ruby was going to *love* that.

After crawling under my desk for my promised Wordle time and a few panicked texts to Tess, I dove into the colossal binder and began to brainstorm. I wrote down anything that came to mind no matter how impossible it felt. Some of my ideas were very adult in nature and others were nostalgic or practical.

cooking with marijuana
sex toy shopping party
synchronized swimming
understanding social media and social media etiquette
monologue workshop
movie screenings for residents' old films
navigating cell phones
entertainment memorabilia swap meet
speed dating
field trips!

By the time Morgan came around to discuss my budget, I was buzzing with possibilities and I was surprised to learn that my budget wasn't . . . nothing. And this was coming from someone who used to have to run out to pick up two-hundred-dollar undershirts for her boss every three weeks.

Whether these residents were choosing to be here or this place was their only option, I could at least try to make it worth their money and time . . . because time certainly was not on their side.

THE WUNDERKIND (FIRST DRAFT)
"PILOT" 10/8/07

EXT. YOU SCREAM ICE CREAM—TWILIGHT

Arlo is eating a cone as Poppy turns the shop light off and begins to spray down tables.

POPPY

We're closed.

ARLO

But you're still here?

POPPY

I work here.

ARLO

I should probably work here too, then.

POPPY

What about your calling as world's worst barista?

ARLO

My talents are needed elsewhere.

Poppy hands Arlo a spray bottle for him to help her clean up. He does so with gusto.

January 26, 2014
Vera S
Note to my twenty-two-year-old self: This is not how getting a job actually works. There's this thing called an interview.

THE WUNDERKIND by Vera Stein.

CHAPTER TEN

When I got back to Ruby's apartment, the lights were dim, and a low thrum of jazz music curled out from under her bedroom door.

My desire to face-plant on the chaise longue was outweighed by the fear that the soundtrack to my face-planting might very well turn into sensual sounds coming from my grandmother's bedroom.

I scooped up Marlon and one of my swimsuits and decided to give her and whoever she was hosting some privacy.

The sun had dipped below the horizon, and it was still stiflingly hot outside, but I was willing to take my chances on the outdoor pool. If anything, I'd have it to myself.

The pool was incredibly picturesque with a flamingo fountain and matching peach and mint umbrellas and loungers that were perfectly spaced apart. There were even cabanas with fans and a heavy-duty pool chiller. But I could see how during summer even with the heavy-duty pool chiller, that was a lost cause.

I took Marlon with me into the women's changing room, where I slipped on the red swimsuit with white trim that I'd bought for my trip with Brody to Tulum. We were there filming and I only got to use the swimsuit once, but I felt good in it. I guess it didn't hurt that my fondest memory of the trip was of him peeling the suit off me. It had been one of those nights that left me naively hopeful. The moonlight shone in through his balcony and I remembered thinking that in that moment we were so close to being what I'd always dreamed we could be.

But then Brody and I went back home and nothing ever felt quite as special or legitimate as it had that one night in Tulum.

When I walked out of the changing room, the whisper of a moon hung in the sky and I had to admit that back home in LA, I didn't take nearly as much notice of the sky as I did here in the desert. I guess if I had to choose one place to spend the end of my life, I'd want it to be somewhere like this with a sky big enough to make you feel the relief of insignificance.

I set Marlon up on a lounger, nestled in my towel, and then walked onto the diving board, sitting gracelessly on the edge so my toes dragged along the surface.

As I sat there, I tried calling Tess for a much-needed catch-up but got her voicemail.

I weaved my hair into a braid, my curls protesting the whole time, and then decided to swim laps back and forth across the pool. The water was warm, but without the sun, it felt inviting and not nearly as much like I were a tea bag dipping myself in boiling water as I thought it would.

Growing up, I didn't do many organized sports or activities, but I was on the swim team for the local community center for a few summers. Swimming up and down those lanes was the first time I could remember being fast. I loved the sensation of having my head underwater. Especially my ears. Not only were sounds above the surface muffled, but so was the noise in my brain. It was easier to untangle the jumble of thoughts. Which made it especially unfair that my time underwater was limited to how long I could hold my breath.

But my anxiety found me, even under the water. Today had been overwhelming, and it was very clear that I might be out of my depth. Ruby had been right. I didn't like group activities or big social plans. What made me think I could be a professional social butterfly to a surprisingly horny and ruthless group of elderly?

My two options were clear: Go back to Brody. Grovel. Ask for my job back. Make zero demands. Or stay here. Become good at a new, terrifying thing. Avoid Eli. And maybe even rewrite *The Wunderkind* so that I could at least show my face in the same room as Brody again one day and know that when I lied and said the deal had fallen through for my movie, there would actually be a script to speak of.

As I tilted my head for a breath, I heard the distinct hiss of a can opening. I stopped, tripping through the water a little as my momentum broke and blinking rapidly against the sting of chlorine.

The blurry figure solidified into Eli. He sat on a lounger with his legs crossed at the ankles, the collar of his shirt unbuttoned, and a can of beer on the table beside him. His hair stuck up in various directions like it always had in college from him pulling his fingers through it while he was deep in thought. That was a feeling I hadn't forgotten. My hands in his hair.

"Do you want me to toss some diving rings in?" Eli asked, his gaze briefly dropping from my eyes to my bare shoulders and then quickly over the top of my chest. "Play mermaids?"

I dipped down lower under the water and floated to the stairs near him, not wanting him to see my body because it felt like a million beestings to be perceived by him. "There's the asshole I remember."

He didn't argue, but instead raised his brows expectantly. After taking a long sip from his brightly colored can—probably some bitter IPA that he didn't like, because anyone who said they liked IPAs was lying—he said, "What are you out here running from, Vera Stein?"

My hair was beginning to frizz, so I dipped my head back and used the moment to consider my answer. "Who said I was running?"

"I don't know that grown women leave their jobs in Hollywood to jet off to their grandmothers' retirement communities if they're not running from something."

"I wouldn't have called it a Hollywood job," I said.

"Looked like one," he said with a shrug, as though he didn't actually care and was just passing the time, toying with me.

"And what would you know about my job?"

His lip twitched. "How's our old friend Brody, anyway?"

"He's great," I said, my words coming out like a squeak. "We've parted ways, but it was very amicable."

"I'm surprised he let you go."

"He didn't fire me," I shot back.

"I never said he did. I only meant that Brody needed you and he would do whatever it took to keep you around." Eli leaned back against the lounger with his head resting against his hands, his body so full and wide that it practically hung off the sides.

Brody would do whatever it took to keep me around? What did he even mean by that? Because giving me a raise certainly wasn't on that list of things Brody would do.

Before I could figure out how the hell to respond to that, Marlon shot up from a dead sleep and began barking at Eli like he was an intruder. And he was! An emotional intruder! *Good boy, Marlon.*

The elderly pup scrambled down the side of the lounger and began to circle Eli, attempting to nip at him.

"You're an angry little guy, aren't you?" Eli asked.

"He doesn't like men," I said as I stepped out of the pool. I felt incredibly exposed in my wet swimsuit even if it was just a one-piece. It was less clothing than anyone besides Brody and my gynecologist had seen me in for quite some time.

Eli's eyes followed me, his lip nearly curled, as I grabbed my towel, which of course was too small because every fucking towel on the shelf by the entrance was the size of a washcloth. I dried off in a hurry while Marlon continued to bark, exerting more energy than he had in the last three years.

"Except Brody," I said pointedly as I pulled on my cover-up. Marlon quieted at the sound of Brody's name. Mainly because he always fed Marlon table scraps when Brody thought I wasn't looking.

I scooped Marlon up, putting him in what I affectionately referred to as air jail (the best and quickest way to tame my absolutely perfect little asshole dog). I walked out of the pool area without another word as I tossed my micro-towel in the dirty bin.

CHAPTER ELEVEN

Leonard's entryway was overflowing with greenery and the sign on his door said *Stay Awhile (Until You're Asked to Leave)*. That felt pretty on brand from what little interaction I'd had with him.

"Can I get you a cup of coffee?" Leonard asked as he welcomed me in. He wore a fitted yellow coverall and carried a matching cane. It was a very if-Elton-John-were-a-mechanic vibe. I had a feeling there was a cane for every mood hidden away somewhere.

"I'm fine," I told him. "Maybe you could show me what you're trying to sell and we could go from there?"

A chirping sound came from the living room and I peered around the corner to find a bright blue bird with a black-and-white striped head, balancing on a bar inside of an ornate gold cage.

"Oh, that's Patrick," Leonard said. "He thinks every visitor is here to see him."

"Very handsome." I hoped it wasn't the bird he was attempting to sell.

"Just follow me on back to the guest room. It's quite the . . . remarkable piece. But it was a final sale and—well, you'll understand when you see it."

He swung the door open and motioned for me to step inside.

"Oh my god," I said with a gasp, and immediately stumbled backward. "I—uh, that thing is empty, right?"

Leonard laughed so hard he wheezed.

A baby-blue coffin sat displayed on a stand like you'd see at a wake and on the side was a bedazzled dove.

I had yet to breathe. I stood there, unmoving and unable to take my eyes off what I could only describe as the Mary-Kay-by-way-of-Elvis Cadillac of coffins.

Finally, air filled my lungs, and I looked to Leonard, who now appeared to be slightly self-conscious when he saw I wasn't laughing along with him.

As I rushed to regain my composure, I said, "I think I'll take that cup of coffee if you don't mind."

Leonard nodded and led me back to the kitchen, where he directed me to sit down while he let Patrick out of his cage and then began to brew a fresh pot.

He took his time slicing coffee cake and humming to himself while my brain tried to supply reasonable explanations and I also wondered if I was in the presence of the world's most fabulous serial killer.

Patrick landed on my finger, stopping me from drumming them, like the bird was telling me he knew just how bizarre all of this was, but he needed me to calm the fuck down if either of us was going to get out of here alive.

Or maybe he was just annoyed by the tapping sound.

Or maybe he was going to poop on me. Something birds had done to me an unusual amount of times.

Patrick perched on the back of an armchair as Leonard served up the coffee and cake. "Well, what do you think?" he asked.

I took a sip of the coffee, which was in a mug from Marfa, Texas, that said *I Saw the Marfa Lights*. I didn't even bother asking for cream, letting the bitterness force my brain into submission. "I think . . . I think . . . I'm trying to find a way to say this gently, Leonard. But it's a coffin, right? So even if you don't need it now, you will . . . someday."

His brow tilted, like he was ready to use that cutting voice on me again like he had in my office.

"And—and I don't say that because of your age. But if you already have one . . . why not hold on to it? Hell, I'll need a coffin one day. Maybe next week. Maybe in fifty years. I don't know."

"So you would be interested in buying it, then?" He took a bite of his coffee cake and continued to talk with his hand covering his mouth. "That would certainly solve a lot of problems and I'm willing to part with it far below market value, even though it is unused."

Oh god. I would hope it was unused. "That's very generous of you to offer," I said. "But can I ask why you're selling it?"

"It doesn't fit my vision anymore," he said simply.

"For your funeral?"

He smirked. "You're not as dull as they say."

"Who exactly is *they*? Did my grandmother call me dull?"

He zipped his fingers over his lips and then stood up to retrieve a tabbed and perfectly color-coded binder from his hutch.

There was a section for flowers, dress code, menu, musical arrangements, and even guides for how he would like his hair, clothing, and makeup to be styled.

"This was The Plan," he said, flipping through the binder for me to see. "I'm a screenwriter down to my bones. I see the whole picture. So it's important that I have a vision for every major moment in my life."

"I'm a writer too." The moment the words were out of my mouth, I knew they were a lie.

"Are you, now?" Leonard challenged, like he'd heard that line many times before.

Before the conversation turned toward my own doomed writing, I redirected. "So when did your feelings about your funeral change?"

"Well, recently I saw a documentary about environmentally friendly funerals and now I would like to change The Plan."

I skimmed a page about suggested guest attire that called on Leonard's loved ones to upstage him if they dared. "But—but this seems so lovely and well thought out and—"

"We all just end up rotting in the dirt, my dear." His voice went a little high; a little impatient. "So why not get to it sooner without all the waste?"

I couldn't argue with a green funeral, but it didn't really seem to be on brand for someone of his tastes. "Leonard, I wonder if I could ask a sort of touchy question."

He nodded and twirled a hand for me to speed it up.

"How much . . . time do you have left?"

His manicured brows knitted together. "How much time do *you* have left?"

"Well, I—I don't know."

"Neither do I," he said simply. "Why is it always so shocking that someone might plan for the end? We plan weddings and baby showers—none of which I've had, by the way. So why wouldn't I take great care to plan my own farewell?"

"Okay," I said. In some ways, Leonard reminded me of Ruby. This was so far off from my mother's own response to her impending death. She had wishes, of course, but she was more concerned with her last moments on earth and not how we might commemorate her after. She firmly believed that time was for *us* and not her.

But *weddings. Baby showers.* Those words I felt deeply. I didn't have many friends, but among them I was the only one who was childless and single. I'd spent so much energy over the last twenty years going to bachelorette parties or saving up for destination weddings or splurging on baby registry gifts I definitely could not afford.

My friends weren't bad people, but there were never many opportunities for any of them to reciprocate those efforts. There were birthdays, sure, but I was never the type to plan an elaborate celebration for myself. I couldn't think of anything more tedious, honestly.

"So, it would seem that a green funeral would be way more low-key than some of these really impressive plans you already have in place here . . . How long exactly have you been planning for?" I asked.

He leaned back and made a birdcall. Patrick responded by swooping over to sit on his shoulder. "Probably since my fifties. I'm eighty-one now. I've had the coffin for—oh, I don't know. Six years, I suppose. I wouldn't tell a buyer this, but I have taken a nap in it once or twice just to test-drive it. With the lid open, of course."

"Of course," I said, as though leaving the lid open was the most obvious and normal part of that story. "Let me do some research and see what is the best way for us to find a new home for your . . . item."

"Good, good." He nodded. "I've got other things to off-load as well.

Decor. A memorial guest book. Then, of course, there's the headstone, though that might be a sunk cost. But surely there's another Leonard Simmons out there."

"Surely." I drank the rest of my coffee as Leonard proceeded to tell me all about the day he brought Patrick home.

Something about him and this whole situation made me feel like I was in a rapidly filling tank of water with only so much air remaining.

After I left, I locked myself in my office.

This place was supposed to be my escape from Hollywood, but it seemed that my escape plan now required an escape of its own.

The food in the cafeteria at Starlight Palms was so good it had no business calling itself a cafeteria. My meal of choice for my first week was chicken Caesar salad and a side of Parmesan truffle Tater Tots. I also got into the habit of picking up whatever green juice concoction was available because it made me feel like I had my shit together.

Since Morgan or a resident would search me out in the cafeteria, I'd begun taking my lunch back to my office, where I could enjoy it behind the safety of a locked door. Today, though, Hollis beckoned me over before I could make my exit and invited me to sit with her, Ruby, and their table of friends.

"Sort of feels like I'm the new girl at the lunch table," I joked as I sat down between Hollis and Ruby.

Gwen, the woman from the bus with the hearing aid, leaned over and whispered, "We heard you saw the coffin."

I scooted my chair back, the legs scraping against the floor. "Oh no, I'm not here to gossip."

Ruby pulled me by the wrist back into my seat.

"It's not gossip if it's public knowledge," said Gwen.

The man next to her kissed her cheek and let out a little growl. He wore a button-down knit top and white shorts, like he'd chosen a signature style in the sixties and hadn't looked back.

I turned to Hollis. "Do they need a room?"

She rolled her eyes. "Gwen and Harvey have needed their own room since we were all twenty-two and shacking up in one hotel room here because that's all we could afford."

"The four of you have known each other since your twenties? And you used to come here?" I knew Ruby had been a patron of Starlight Palms, but I hadn't imagined that she could have lifelong friends I didn't even know about.

Ruby sipped her smoothie. "Quite a few of us are old lovers of the Palms. And the Palms has always loved us back."

"Except that one time we were kicked out for skinny-dipping during a wedding," Gwen said, her voice light and far off.

Hollis nodded. "That was unfortunate, but none of us had ever tried acid before. How were we to know that we'd end up bathing under the flamingo fountain naked because Ruby said we were baby flamingos, and the flamingo was our mother?"

My brain didn't know which detail to latch on to first.

"I put down my and Gwen's deposit for this place the moment they announced the Starlight Palms was coming back as a retirement community," Harvey said.

"Have you two been together that long?" I asked Harvey.

Gwen turned to him, like she was waiting for him to recite a story they'd argued over many times.

"It was love at first sight," he said.

Gwen pelted him with her napkin. "That's a load of horse shit and you know it." Then she turned to me. "I was head of costumes on the set of *Married to the Devil.*"

"I auditioned for that one, but lost out to Mary Quinn," Ruby said as she slowly drummed her long fingernails on the table. Leonard walked through the door and Ruby's eyes watched him for a moment before flitting away.

Hollis cocked her head to the side. "Was that the same Mary Quinn who joined a cult and killed her husband?"

"Yes!" Gwen told her. "She died a few years ago, but I sent her yearly Christmas cards in prison."

Ruby shook her head. "Leave it to you to befriend a convicted murderer."

"We were friends before the murder," Gwen pointed out. "Besides, she got me out of a real bind that one time in Santa Fe."

Harvey huffed. "Don't say the name of that city out loud. It's bad luck."

The rest of the table nodded knowingly, and before I could ask what the hell happened in Santa Fe, Harvey continued. "Anyway, I was the prop master and the only crew members who feud as intensely as hair and makeup are costumes and props."

Gwen jumped in. "My actor had a bloody letter jacket that kept going missing, and I kept having to replicate the blood splatters, which wasn't easy back then. I was going off of blurry Polaroids."

Harvey slung an arm over Gwen's shoulder. "Well, maybe if you would have realized the jacket was a prop and not a costume, you would have known it was right where it was supposed to be—in the props trailer."

"You know goddamn well that jacket was costume department property," Gwen told him, bristling to the extent that she was wiggling out of his reach.

But Harvey wasn't about to let her go so quickly. Instead, he pulled her in tight and said, "Either way, I wore her down and she eventually agreed to a date after the wrap party."

Gwen rolled her eyes and leaned into him. "Well, first came the hate sex and then came the date—"

"I think Vera gets the picture," Hollis said.

"A very clear picture," I confirmed

Harvey waggled his eyebrows and did something with one of his hands under the table that I thankfully could not see, causing Gwen to shriek.

Once she'd recovered, she focused back on me. "So. What was the coffin like?"

"You know," I said, "if you're all so interested, maybe you should just go befriend Leonard and see for yourself."

"I know better than to cross that line in the sand," Gwen announced.

Ruby rolled her eyes and scoffed.

Harvey leaned in. "Ruby and Lenny haven't been on speaking terms for the last thirty years."

My grandmother was not known to keep things to herself, especially anything salacious. "I didn't realize you two knew each other that well."

Ruby pursed her lips. "There's plenty you don't know, Vera."

I sat up straighter, taken aback by her tone.

Hollis patted her knee. "That's the past," she said softly.

"Back to Lenny and his coffin," Gwen said.

"All right, all right, back off," Hollis piped in, still rubbing comforting circles on Ruby's thigh. "Let the young lady enjoy her lunch without hounding her for information."

I smiled at Hollis, but I had a feeling her intervention wasn't on my behalf at all.

EXT. ABANDONED LIFEGUARD TOWER—MIDNIGHT

They sit side by side in matching uniforms except he is wearing a zip-up hoodie. She's cold. He forgets to offer his sweatshirt.

POPPY (V.O.)

I never expected for him to find me interesting. But every time he looked over at me, I felt like I could be. ~~Like I held secrets unknown to even myself.~~

June 3, 2013
Vera S.
Is the secret that you're constipated, Poppy?

Arlo looks over like he's heard her voice in his head and offers his hoodie.

CHAPTER THIRTEEN

I woke up sad. Maybe it was the research I'd done on the legality of selling a preowned casket on Facebook or maybe it was the half-used bottle of my mom's perfume that had shattered in my toiletry bag when Ruby knocked it onto the floor while she was doing her skin-care regimen last night. Or maybe it was because Brody had stopped calling me and Tess was impossibly busy and even more so impossible to get a hold of. But regardless, this morning I was sad.

And I was irritated at Ruby for humming while she made her toast and having the nerve to be in a good mood. I wished I could blame it on my PMDD, but according to my period app, that was not the culprit. However, living in close quarters with my grandmother . . .

"You look tired," Ruby said as I prepared Marlon's breakfast of prescription wet food and fish oil.

"Because I *am* tired," I said, my voice full of bite. "Your couch isn't exactly ideal for sleeping."

She gave me a look that reminded me I was crashing here for free. Touché. "Which I'm thankful for," I added. "But I'm also sort of stressed about the movie night tonight."

"I can't for the life of me understand why you'd choose *Saving Private Ryan* for your little movie night."

"The internet says World War Two movies are big with your demographic."

Ruby grumbled. "Yes, the one thing missing from the final years of my life is a chance to float in a pool and watch boys stumble around Europe looking for each other."

Okay, well, maybe I wasn't the only one in a shitty mood. "I tried to get all of the glass shards off the floor of the bathroom," I told her. "But be careful if you go in there barefoot. I'll see you tonight?" I asked as I grabbed my tote bag.

"That's what Hollis tells me, though again, I'm not one for wartime features."

I thought the residents would love my idea of a float-in movie night. It had occurred to me after my night swim the other day that the pool was actually lovely at night. But if Ruby was any indication, my film selection might be panned and my first event a bust.

In advance of my Sunset Screening program, I spent an hour decorating the pool area with streamers and a felt red carpet I'd found online. I even wheeled out the popcorn machine and put together a candy cart.

The pool was full of floats that ranged from aesthetic (an inflatable swan) to practical (a raft-like thing that looked way more comfortable than Ruby's couch). Morgan also gave me permission to offer the lifeguards overtime to work the event. With the sun below the horizon, it actually felt good outside.

Despite my shitty mood today, I was settling into the routine of having a real job. Working for Brody was real, especially in terms of LA jobs. But this was a job with a lunch break and coworkers and something about the normality of that was comforting, especially since the last time I hadn't worked for Brody was the Smoothie Hut in college.

The two lifeguards, Mindy and Oscar, were both students at the nearest community college and looked to be bored enough to collect lint from their belly buttons. But at least they'd be paid for their lint picking.

After I went to start the popcorn and grab myself a box of Whoppers,

I checked the time. The event was scheduled to start at eight, but it was already ten minutes after.

The residents of Starlight Palms were still a mystery to me in many ways, but one thing I did know was that they were punctual.

Hollis and Ruby arrived at eight thirty to an empty pool.

"Excuse our tardiness," Hollis said.

Behind her, Ruby wore a botanical-patterned silk caftan and smelled like weed.

"Are you two high?" I asked.

They giggled a little as they eyed my box of half-eaten Whoppers.

Ruby sniffed the air. "Is that popcorn I smell?"

I opened the gate. "Help yourself."

The two of them milled around the snack table before I finally shooed them away and told them there was no use in staying. Besides, the only thing worse than failing was for Ruby to witness it.

"You two might as well go too," I told Mindy and Oscar, who both made googly eyes at each other that led me to believe their plans for the night included more than picking lint from their belly buttons. Was everyone in this place getting laid?

I wasn't wearing a swimsuit, but I decided to risk the raft. I'd set up this whole damn thing for absolutely no one, so I loaded my arms with towels, popcorn, and a few canned Bellinis from the adult beverage cooler.

As I pulled the raft to the steps of the pool, I was incredibly grateful for my idea to attach ropes to each float, should we have a senior go adrift. I tied my rope to the hand railing just as the opening credits began to play for the movie. I should have brought a backup movie that I would have actually wanted to watch.

I wobbled and swayed, nearly wiping out before I plopped down, bringing on a little water and sitting in a puddle, completely resigned to my fate. Whatever. Wet pants were better than being startlingly sober while Ruby ate through our pantry due to a serious case of the munchies.

With one of the towels, I made myself a pillow and used the other as a blanket. The sway of the water was nice. The raft reminded me of the waterbed Ruby had in the nineties. Tomorrow I'd deal with tonight's failure, but for now, I sipped on my Bellini and nommed on popcorn.

I wasn't sure how long I'd lain there when I felt something tugging on my rope, pulling me back to the steps. The movie screen had gone dark and I was curled on my side with the towel tugged up over my shoulders.

With a groan, I yanked the towel over my head and said, "I'm fine, I'm fine, I'm fine."

"If lost at sea is fine, then sure."

I knew that condescending voice. My raft teetered as I sat up, popcorn falling from my lap.

My cheeks were warm, and my vision a little fuzzy at the corners as I shifted, empty cans clattering at my feet.

Welp.

I was drunk and being actively fished out of the pool by Eli Buckley.

As the raft hit the stairs, I swatted the nearby alligator float out of my way and stood up much too fast.

Eli held out a hand to help me up, but I refused and gripped the railing instead. Except, the raft had begun to float back out into the pool, and I was holding on to the railing for dear life, trying to pull the lower half of my body back to safety.

"Help," I squawked.

"Oh, now you want help?" Eli asked as my torso stretched farther across the water.

Instead of letting me slow-motion belly flop into the pool, he pulled the rope back and gripped my biceps, forcibly helping me onto solid ground.

I swayed for a minute, my stomach gurgling.

He caught me by the elbow, his hand warm and firm. "You okay?"

I let out a deep breath and nodded.

Sternness set into the lines of his forehead in a very I'm-not-angry-I'm-disappointed sort of way. "I'm walking you back to Ruby's."

"I think I'd rather sleep here." With that dismayed look of his, it wouldn't matter what he wanted me to do. I would have claimed to have wanted the opposite.

He shook his head. "Not an option. Besides, I don't think Morgan would like that. Or the groundskeepers, honestly. But the residents. Now, that would be some fresh gossip for them."

For the first time, I noticed what he was wearing. Dark blue slacks and a cream knit collared shirt. He looked rich and smart, and it made me feel poor and dull.

"Did you just get back from a very important date or something?" I asked, and he made no effort to correct me. "When did you become so stylish? You know, in college all you wore were khaki shorts and soft T-shirts. The expensive kind that you buy soft. Like, they've been pre-softened for you. Like, it was someone's job to soften the T-shirt."

"You remember my soft T-shirts, then?" he asked. "What else do you remember?"

I remembered plenty. I remembered that even when he shaved, his face and neck were still thick with stubble, like there was no stopping it. I remembered the way he pursed his lips together when he tried not to laugh at something funny. I remembered how he was never late for class and always made time for a full eight hours of sleep before a test. That he smelled like detergent because he actually washed his clothes. And girls panted over him. A soon-to-be doctor who did his own laundry? It didn't get better than that.

"I remember that you barely tolerated me," I told him. "I remember that you started the annulment process before I even got home to LA."

He opened his mouth and then snapped it shut.

I slipped my shoes back on and began to clean up the snack table and the popcorn machine.

"You should get some sleep," he said.

"*You* should get some sleep," I told him.

I opened the glass door of the popcorn machine and the smell hit me so hard I gagged.

"Okay, okay," he said, wrapping an arm around my waist. My back pressed against his chest, his breath warm on my neck. "Let me get you back to Ruby's. I'll take care of the food and the groundskeepers will deal with the screen and inflatables."

I huffed. "But then I'll owe you a favor. I'll be in debt to you. I'll be in the red."

"I might have to send my bookie after you."

"Exactly," I said. "Your favor bookie. But he won't be worse than the guilt I'll feel for owing you a favor."

He led me down the sidewalk with his hand hovering over my lower back, his fingers randomly grazing, sending traitorous chills up my spine each time. If not for fear of puking in front of him, I would have spun right back around and pinched my nose to get through cleaning out the popcorn machine.

"No one came to my event," I said after a few moments of silence. "They all hate me. Especially Ruby. Old people are so mean."

"Your grandmother doesn't hate you." We approached a curb and he said, "Step."

"Thanks," I muttered.

"This place isn't a normal retirement community. You just have to find the right balance and then they'll be eating out of your hand." He sounded as though it wasn't at all hard to imagine. Like I was some sort of charming person.

I couldn't help but think of what Hollis had said in my office as we approached Ruby's front door and I punched the security code into her keypad.

He opened the door and whispered, "No one wants to watch *Saving Private Ryan* for fun. It's not even rated R for the good stuff."

The moment we stepped inside, Marlon started yapping.

"Shhh, shhh," I begged him.

"Hey, little man," Eli said as he scooped him up, startling Marlon into silence. He scratched between his ears, and it was like watching someone hypnotize a shark.

I turned on the faucet and filled a glass of water and chugged it so fast I left the faucet on and immediately refilled my cup.

"Who wouldn't love my programs? I'm a genius. My programs are genius."

Eli nodded. "And geniuses take two ibuprofens before going to bed in addition to drinking a glass of water every time they wake up."

He handed Marlon off to me as I wandered over to the couch that I currently called home. Then he began to open cabinets until he found Ruby's pharmaceuticals stockpile.

With a glass of water and two pills, he crouched down beside me. "Here, take this."

I threw back the pills like a champ and chugged the third glass of water. "I have to sleep. Actually, I think I already am asleep." I scooted back and fluffed my pillow before collapsing, my lower back immediately sinking into the unfortunate space between the cushions.

"Let's get you to bed," he said.

My eyelids began to droop. "This is bed."

"You've been sleeping on a couch for weeks?"

"Technically, it's a chaise longue."

"We've gotta get you off this couch," he said with a barely there laugh.

"Chaise longue. But fuck me. Yes, please," I told him through a yawn that hit so hard, tears began to stream down my cheeks.

He cleared his throat into his fist, his cheeks the slightest bit pink.

Marlon settled on my chest, whining.

"You have to give Marlon a kiss good night. You made him like you and now he demands a kiss. I don't make the rules."

He shook his head. "Small dogs are ridiculous."

"Don't speak ill of my son."

I closed my eyes as he leaned down and gave Marlon a soft kiss between his ears.

A finger—or maybe Marlon's tongue—traced down the center of my forehead and up the slope of my nose.

The next morning, I woke up sore but headache-free and to a note on the coffee table that read:

Two more ibuprofen and a glass of water for the genius.
Doctor's orders.

LOS ANGELES
CALIFORNIA

ELIAS BUCKLEY
SEVENTEEN YEARS AGO
MATURE ADULTS

"I should go," Vera whispered as she and Brody stumbled into our moonlight-soaked room.

One of them tripped over something on the floor, and Vera laughed. Skin slapped skin, and then her voice was muffled, likely by Brody's hand, as she said, "You told me he sleeps like the dead."

"I didn't think you were actually gonna put that to the test, V."

His bedside lamp flickered on. I imagined his fingers on her lips and wondered what it might feel like to run the pad of my thumb along the shape of her mouth.

I lay on my side, facing the wall. In four hours, my alarm would go off for a microbiology test, but I had yet to fall asleep.

Vera and Brody had gone to a *Buffy* pub quiz night. Brody dressed as Angel and Vera as Willow in combat boots, a floor-length silk skirt, and a square-neck top that made her look like a milkmaid. It was an image I couldn't forget if I tried. The only thing that interfered with the boner it could have caused was her fawning all over Brody for getting some kind of callback for a guest spot on a soap opera.

I would have much preferred that time a week before Thanksgiving when she got drunk on Mike's Hard Lemonade and gave a lecture on why some Canadian TV show called *Degrassi* was the most groundbreaking television of our time. I mostly stared at the wall behind her head as she and Brody did a deep dive on an episode with an abortion plotline that was never allowed to air in the US. But admittedly, I did go home, smoke a joint, and binge three episodes while Brody snored from the other side of the room.

"I should just go home," Vera said. "If I knock loud enough, Tess will hear me and let me in. I can't believe I forgot my dorm keycard."

"It's not like this little skanky witch look you've got going on left a lot of room for storage."

"Did you just call me a skanky witch?" Vera asked as she swatted at Brody—from what I could hear.

"Fucking hell," he said. "That stung. And I'm sorry. I meant to say a hot skanky witch. Better?"

She sighed. "Marginally."

"Anyway, just stay here."

My spine stiffened. I could barely sleep as it was. After she'd left earlier that night my whole fucking room smelled like her and that cheap cucumber melon body spray she always wore. Sometimes I'd fake a sneeze and say that I had a sudden headache just hoping that she would get the hint and stop wearing it. I'd ask if anyone smelled the too-sweet aroma. And Vera's cheeks would turn a deep shade of pink, which usually led to a boner on my part.

Vera had become an installment in Brody's life, which was inconvenient, because he lived in my room. After the Halloween party, he'd started inviting her everywhere with us unless he was explicitly told not to. Mostly by me. Like when we met my parents for brunch on my birthday or when we went out for drinks last week and I just needed a break from her laughing at Brody's every word like he was the funniest motherfucker of all time. It was as infuriating as when she'd pick fights with other Sigma Chi brothers about the toxicity of Greek life. All while she wore the most sexless vintage T-shirts that still found a way to cling to her tits. Or how the tips of her ears turned red when she started talking too fast about whatever movie she'd last seen—good or bad, she always had an opinion.

"I gotta take a piss," Brody told her as our door creaked open, "but there are some clean T-shirts on my desk and a couple of gym shorts hanging over the closet door."

Vera sighed as the door shut, and it was suddenly too quiet.

I held my breath as she kicked off her boots and shuffled over to the far side of the room where our desks were.

She mumbled to herself as she flipped through shirts, and then a soft "This will have to do" came out as a sigh.

Clothing rustled as I clutched my fists in front of my chest like for a desperate prayer. She was undressing. In my room. Right behind me.

All I had to do was peer over my shoulder to catch a glimpse, but the only thing worse than her undressing behind me was getting caught as I watched.

The mattress on the other side of the room shifted as she sat down.

"Why are you still wearing that skirt?" Brody asked as the door creaked open, putting an end to any possibility of me catching a glimpse of Vera.

"Your boxer shorts weren't made for my wide birthing hips. You have zero ass."

I swallowed back a laugh, but Brody remained silent for a moment until he finally said, "Then don't wear pants. I don't care. Eli is asleep and he'll be gone before we're even up. It's not like I haven't seen you in a swimsuit, V. And by the way, my ass is very juicy."

"Maybe once I'm under the covers, but wearing a skirt is basically the same as not wearing pants anyway. Do you have an extra pillow and blanket I could use down here?"

"Shut up. You're sleeping in the bed with me." The springs of his double mattress wheezed as he threw himself into bed. A T-shirt flew overhead and landed on the edge of my bed. Brody snorted. If he were actually trying to be a gentleman, he would have just gone down to sleep on the couch and let her have the bed. Not that the half-mast boner under my blankets knew anything about being a gentleman.

She scoffed. "The floor is fine."

"Don't be silly, Vera. We're mature adults. No one's going to get in trouble for sleeping in the same bed. The worst that could happen is that I drool on you or accidentally fart in my sleep."

She sighed. "Okay, but I'm sleeping on top of the blanket with that quilt your mom sent you."

"Be my guest," he said. "You know it's made out of—"

"All the T-shirts from every sports team you were on since T-ball. Yes, I do remember that specific footnote in the history of Brody."

"One day, when I'm famous, I'll let you write my licensed autobiography. You'll be the Brody Turner expert."

"I'm glad you have such big dreams for me," she said as the blankets rustled. "I'm taking off this skirt, but please be warned that my ass is not a hand warmer."

"That was one time!" he said. "And it was my feet. *And* it worked. My toes were very toasty under that ass of yours. It's a ten-out-of-ten ass."

Vera was quiet for a minute until she finally said, "Good night, Brody."

His bedside lamp switched off and I stayed awake listening to the rise and fall of their out-of-sync breaths until they grew longer and shallower.

The only thing worse than Vera implanting herself in our lives over the last few months was watching her fall in love with Brody. The harder she fell, the harder it became to look away. It was painful, and I wasn't willing to figure out why.

CHAPTER FOURTEEN

I found a rhythm. Every morning I stopped by the coffee stand in the lobby on my way to my office. If there were any puddles from the pool in the hallway, I used the mop from the janitor's closet to do a quick spot clean.

After that I'd set up whatever activities were planned for the day. Sometimes it was getting popcorn together for a showing in the movie theater and other times it was rearranging tables for a crafting hour.

I only saw Eli sporadically outside of Tuesday nights, when I helped him set up for his book club. I didn't have to stay, but it was my job to at least put out the sign-up sheet and to make sure that catering was all set up with the snacks we provided.

There was no letting go of the memory of Eli helping me out of the pool weeks ago. He'd mostly ignored me since then. It was college all over again. I spent far too much time feeling the absence of his attention, waiting for him to notice me again—even if his attention felt stifling at best.

I hadn't spent much time off property unless it was to view yet another apartment I couldn't afford, so when Waverly, the sex toy shop owner who had agreed to come out and speak to the residents, asked if I could come by the shop and pick up a few things in advance of her talk, I jumped at the chance. Sex Toy Safety, my first very adult program, had so many RSVPs I'd had to move it to the theater.

I circled the quaint little area where Good Vibes Only was located and found street parking about two blocks away. There were no parking lots, but parking was free for the first hour, which I had to read twice to actually believe.

Getting out of my car, I checked the street signs to remember where I was and took note of the Italian bakery across the street.

I still wasn't used to the desert heat, but the breeze today felt a little less like Satan's asshole farting in your face. It also helped that I'd picked up a few desert-appropriate pieces at a secondhand store I visited with Ruby. Today I wore white linen overalls and a black tank top.

"Be right there," Waverly sang from the back room as I walked into Good Vibes Only. The shop was one hundred percent less skeevy than any sex shop I'd been in back home. The inside was painted lavender with one entire wall quilted in velvet like it was straight out of a boudoir. The neon shop sign hanging above the register felt more trendy than trashy and beneath it was a smaller sign that said *Queer Owned*.

I stood at the counter, feeling a little bit like I was definitely not adult enough to be in a store full of artisanal butt plugs and ethically sourced dildos. But this was for the residents, I reminded myself. I was the facilitator. That was it. And I was an adult, damn it!

"Sorry about that," Waverly said as she stepped past a rack of latex garments. "Oh, you must be Vera from Starlight Palms!"

Waverly was short. The type of short that required a step stool to put away the dishes. Her hair matched the walls of her shop, and her arms rippled with muscles. The bio on the store's website said that she'd spent years working at sexual health clinics and educating the public, but that Good Vibes Only was her dream realized.

"Yes! Thank you so much for coming out to talk to our residents."

"Are you kidding? The Starlight Palms is legendary around here. I've always wanted to get a look for myself, but I don't really meet the age requirement just yet." She circled around the back of the counter and hoisted two huge boxes up onto the counter. "These are the products I pulled for the pop-up shop, but my girlfriend had to make a last-minute trip to San Diego and used my car, so all I have is her Vespa." She motioned to the baby-blue Vespa parked just outside the store.

"No, not a problem at all," I told her. "I've been meaning to check out your shop anyway."

"Oh, yeah?" Waverly was delighted. "Well, is there anything I can help you find? Are we thinking stimulative? Penetrative? Both?"

My cheeks warmed and I felt the heat spreading to my neck. "I, uh, have to get back to the property, but now I know where to find you!" I snapped my mouth shut before I could say something about how the topic of . . . uh . . . self-pleasure always made me feel ridiculously inexperienced and awkward.

"Well, you're not parked far from here, are you?" Waverly asked. "I could run these boxes to your car either way. I would just need you to stay here with the shop for a sec in case I get any customers."

I shook my head. Standing guard at Good Vibes Only felt like a situation that could quickly unravel. "I'm fine."

But I'd spoken too soon. I picked up one box and wondered if these sex toys were filled with lead. Holy hell. "I'll come back for the second," I said with a grunt.

It took a bit to make it back to the car, mainly because the box was blocking my line of sight and also because this thing was as heavy as a medium-size adult.

When I finally got to my RAV4, I loaded the box into the back and trekked back to the store. I was starting to sweat through my linen overalls and suddenly the look felt less vacation and more tourist-who-had-missed-her-group's-bus.

Waverly smiled at me encouragingly when I reentered the shop and offered me a bottle of water, but I declined because I guess I'd rather die of thirst than admit I could have used the help. "I love a good sweat," I blurted for some reason. "You just really feel the toxins leaving your body."

Waverly nodded, like she was really into that.

I took the second box and said goodbye. The moment I turned the corner, my phone began to ring and I immediately set the box on the nearest bench.

Tess's face lit up my screen. We'd been playing phone tag for the last week and I wasn't about to miss my chance for contact with the outside world, so I set my phone on top of the box and answered with the speakerphone. (I firmly believed that talking on speakerphone in public was a criminal offense, but if it meant talking to Tess, I'd gladly do the time.)

"You answered!" she shrieked.

"Yes," I said in a whisper, "and I'm walking on a public street with my hands full, so you're on speaker."

"Vera," she said, scandalized. "You detest speakerphone."

"I know," I whined. "But I miss you."

She sighed. "I fucking miss you too. I think I might have to go into witness protection. I need to hide from my family."

"Did the renovation get delayed again?"

"I don't want to talk about it. I want to talk about you and why are your hands full?"

"Would you believe me if I said my hands were full of dildos?"

She gasped.

"Well, not *just* dildos, I guess, but they're for an event on Thursday."

"*You* are hosting a sex toy party?" Tess asked slowly. "You wouldn't even buy me lingerie at my bachelorette party because it made you feel uncomfortable. You literally fast-forwarded through sex scenes until you were thirty." And then in a whisper, she asked, "Do you even own a sex toy?"

"I . . . have an electric toothbrush," I said, and then felt immediately mortified even though it was just a joke. "I'm kidding by the way . . . and yes, I own a vibrator," I said quietly. Even though it hadn't been used in a hot minute.

"Well, I certainly hope that something in that box of tricks is for you."

"No, but I will consider buying a new one from a discreet website that uses discreet packaging once I have an apartment of my own."

"Oh my god, you're still on Ruby's couch?"

I nodded even though she couldn't see me. "My spine is forever changed."

"I'm guessing the search for an apartment is still bleak."

"Basically, I've looked at every apartment that could possibly be in my budget if I also started driving Ubers on nights and weekends. But I still need a few months to save up enough money for first, last, and a deposit. Some places even want three months up front. And it doesn't help that my boss, who is twenty-six, by the way, emails me every morning to check on my progress. Yesterday she came by my office to inform me that residents were asking questions and hoping that their grandchildren could also visit for extended stays."

"Vera, honey, you know we're happy to help you—"

"I am not borrowing money from my best friend. That is a recipe for disaster. What if I ran away with the cash to another country and changed my name and never paid you back?"

"V, your passport has been expired for a year and a half."

"I'm pretty sure international criminals aren't bothered by using fraudulent passports."

She sighed. "Well, let me know if something turns up. Mama needs a weekend getaway, so helping you move in would be a great excuse. Too bad you can't crash with our old friend Dr. Buckley."

I'd arrived to my car and managed to balance the box on my knee while I opened up the back.

"Yeah, I basically don't exist to him, so not much has changed since college," I said with a grunt as I placed the box inside. I took the phone off speaker and held it to my ear with my shoulder as I sank into the driver's seat.

"I'm pretty sure you can't exactly erase the existence of your ex-wife from your memory. Plenty have tried."

"Well, I can tell you that whatever grudge he had against Brody, he's still holding it." My purse chose that exact moment to spill over from where it had been sitting on the edge of the passenger seat and I groaned as I leaned across the center console to scoop the most random, pointless shit off the floor. Why was I still carrying a two-year-old half-eaten bag of trail mix? And broken sunglasses? Did I actually think I'd find the tiny missing screw to fix them?

Tess kept on talking—something about a themed party we went to in college where everyone had to come dressed as a different version of Adam Sandler.

Eventually, I relinquished all the items I couldn't reach to the black hole under the passenger seat and sat back up so I could get back to—

"Fuck me," I said, and immediately ducked down.

"What's going on?" Tess asked. "You got a case of road rage?"

I slithered down in my seat. "Eli is *here*. He just walked out of the bakery right next to me and he's just standing there like a buffoon staring at his cell phone."

"You should totally troll him," she said. "Roll down your window and ask how much. Or take a picture of him and text it to him."

"He's *smiling*," I said. Eli wore an ironic vintage button-up shirt with blue and orange seashells, and despite the smile, his brow was just as furrowed as it always was. Like he was constantly deep in thought. Or angry. Probably angry. "He is not a smiling person!"

I needed to make a quick escape, so I turned the ignition and the car made a loud thumping noise. Smoke immediately began to puff out of the hood.

Eli's head shot up and I turned the other way like there was something incredibly interesting happening outside of my driver's-side window.

"He. Saw. Me," I whispered through gritted teeth.

God, it was so hot in this car.

"Vera?" Eli asked as he circled around the front of the car.

He stood outside my window, my ear still pressed to the phone.

"What do I do?" I asked Tess, my lips not moving.

Eli knocked on my window with one knuckle, his brows raised and the corners of his lips turned down.

I opened my door because I couldn't roll down the windows without the engine on. "Hi." And then into the phone, I said, "Tess, I better let you go."

"Hi, Eli!" she shouted loud enough for him to hear.

"Hey, Tess," he said in the same resigned voice he always used when speaking to her.

She started saying something, but I was already hanging up.

"Was that your car making that death rattle?" he asked.

"It was definitely more of a boom and less of a rattle. But I'm going to call a tow truck." With the money I shouldn't spend because my next paycheck wouldn't be deposited until Friday.

He motioned to a sleek electric SUV plugged into a charging station on the other side of the street. "I'll take a quick look and then give you a ride back."

"I'll just wait for a tow," I said.

He grumbled, shook his head, and then handed me the bakery box. Without a word, he opened my door a little wider and reached in past my leg to pop the hood.

My spine tensed as his hand brushed my bare ankle.

While he looked at the engine, I poked my head into the box to find a truly ginormous stack of cannolis. My stomach growled. "Did you rob the bakery?"

"Yes," he called back, "and you're slowing down my getaway."

I peered around the hood to see one of his forearms braced against the car, a vein winding up from his wrist and then disappearing into the sleeve of his shirt. I blamed the warmth spreading across my abdomen on the desert sun.

After a few more minutes, he closed the hood and came back around to me, his forehead peppered with perspiration. "It's the belt. I can fix it, but I need to get back for book club first."

I started to protest, but he'd already reached over my lap to take my keys out of the ignition. He was very much in my space and I got an immediate waft of fresh linen and mint.

Totally bewildered, I watched as he took the bakery box from me and then went back to his car to retrieve something. "What are you doing?" I asked as my feet finally caught up to my brain, and I got out of the car.

"Filling up the meter. You got anything you need to bring back with you?"

I didn't think it was possible to feel any warmer than I already did sitting in that car, sweat dripping down my spine. But as I opened the back hatch of the car, my skin could have caught on fire.

"Just some things for an event on Thursday," I said innocently.

He came up beside me, and for a second, his composure was obliterated. His Adam's apple bobbed and his tongue brushed his lower lip before grabbing the first box. And then his expression was completely blank. If I hadn't known Eli before, I would assume it was something they taught med school students. The face of an ER doctor who'd seen it all.

"These all for you?"

"Yes, Eli," I said. "I'm a prepper and you just happened to catch me during my sex toy stockpile."

The pink of his cheeks dipped a slight shade darker as he smirked. "You got room for one more in that doomsday shelter?"

After we loaded up his car, I ran back across the street and scribbled a note on the back of an old receipt from my purse before tucking it under my windshield wiper.

> Please, please don't give me a ticket. My car was being a jerk and wouldn't start. I promise to get it towed ASAP.
>
> Sincerely,
> A Forty-Year-Old Woman with a Meager Savings Account

"Did you just write a note for parking enforcement?" Eli asked as I buckled my seat belt.

"Parking attendants are people too, and I'm hoping whichever one walks down this street is feeling generous, because I can't afford a tow *and* a ticket in the same week."

"I'll light a candle for the patron saint of street parking when I get home."

"I'll take all the help I can get," I said as he pulled out of his spot. "Thanks," I added. "For rescuing me and all my sex toys."

He slid his Ray-Bans on and with genuine sincerity said, "Anything for sex toys in need."

There was a hair tie in the cup holder with two strands of blond hair wrapped around it.

And I could not stop staring.

"Vera?"

I shook my head. "I'm sorry. What did you say?"

"The boxes," Eli said as we pulled out of downtown. "What's up with the boxes?"

"Good Vibes Only. I don't know if you've heard of them, but it's—"

The corner of his lip twitched upward. "I've heard of them."

My mouth was dry and I was still sweating even though his air-conditioning was cool enough to give me goose bumps. "The owner is coming out to do a seminar on sex toy safety and those are for her pop-up shop."

"So you're bringing out someone to sell sex toys to our residents?" he asked skeptically.

"Well, you thinking it's a bad idea is the least surprising thing ever."

"I didn't say it was a bad idea. Did you hear me say the words 'bad idea' even once?"

Reluctantly, I shook my head. "Well, not technically, but I heard it in your tone."

He turned right down the long residential street leading to Starlight Palms. "You think you really know me, don't you?"

"I do, don't I? Or at least I did."

"College was a long time ago, Vera." The security guard named Amanda, who I'd snuck past that first day, waved us through the gates.

"I like the idea," he said as he parked just outside the main entrance in a reserved staff spot. "Definitely not what people expect when they set their parents up at a retirement facility." He took off his Ray-Bans like they were armor and looked at me, his gaze earnest and steady. "That's a good thing."

"Oh. Okay."

He got out of the car and piled the boxes from the shop on top of each other. "You want these in your office?"

"Uh, yeah. That'd be good. I'll grab the stolen cannolis."

A quiet laugh escaped his lips and he shook his head. It reminded me of the few times he would drop the grimacing and let himself be entertained by me and Brody.

There was something deeply satisfying about getting a reaction out of Eli. My smile quickly faded, though, when I remembered the hair tie and the silly grin on his face as he looked at his phone on the sidewalk.

Eli Buckley—my husband—had someone.

And that was totally okay.

So completely fine.

Memoirs and Martinis was held in community room three, which was already full of residents—mostly women—wearing furs and huge sunglasses.

As Eli walked in, a cheer rose through the crowd along with a handful of whistles.

"Was all that for me, the cannolis, or James Gandolfini?" he asked.

"James Gandolfini?" I asked under my breath.

Eli took the box from me and walked it over to the table that was already set with water, coffee, and martinis. "We're a celebrity memoir book club," he explained. "Sometimes autobiographies or biographies, like in the case of James Gandolfini."

I pulled some plates from the cabinet behind the table. "So the mob wife theme is an ode to *The Sopranos,* I'm guessing?"

"Sometimes the ladies really commit," he said with a slight grin. Then he waved to a man in short running shorts and a matching tank top. "Well, it's not just ladies."

"I'm glad to know your fan base is so diverse."

I had so many questions. When I'd heard Eli led a book club here at Starlight Palms, I assumed it was some kind of boring nonfiction book club or a club for spy-thriller books whose characters were constantly calling Langley and slapping hysterical women to calm them down. But this felt completely unserious and like nothing the Eli I knew would actually enjoy. I took a cursory glance at the book club picks listed on the calendar handout.

I must not have hid my reaction very well, because all Eli said with a sly grin was: "Surprised?"

"Yeah, this looks like actual fun," I told him. "I remember how much you loathe fun."

He side-eyed me, his gaze lingering for a moment, and then shook his head as he began to place cannolis on platters.

"Well, I guess I should go. Just put the sign-up sheet in my inbox before you leave for the night."

"Or," he said without looking up. "You could stay."

"I haven't read the book," I said.

"Here are the CliffsNotes: He starred in the greatest TV show ever and then died before his time. Besides, we don't really talk about the book. It's mostly an hour-long name-dropping session."

"Sounds like my entire childhood," I said.

He handed me a cannoli. "Take a seat. It'll be a good way to get to know more of the residents."

Eli ran Memoirs and Martinis like his own personal royal court. Just as he said it would, the conversation rarely stuck to the topic and often strayed into rumor and gossip territory. Eli was seemingly the only person who could redirect the conversation—and had to a handful of times, including when a woman named Melinda gave an eight-minute monologue about auditioning for *The Sopranos,* being offered the role of someone's mother, but ultimately turning it down to narrate a documentary that Maggie Smith had backed out of. That wasn't the part that Eli interrupted, though. It was when Doreen called Melinda a lying tart. According to Doreen, she was at the callback for that same role and Melinda had been cut in round one.

It was truly the most entertaining book club I'd ever been to, except for the time my mom got her nurses to read an opossum-shifter romance with her during an extended hospital stay.

As book club ended, Eli announced, "Next month, we're reading the Leah Remini book, so let's think of what desserts I can bring for that one."

"I was courted by a Scientologist once," Doreen said. "He always ordered key lime pie for dessert."

Eli nodded, his lips in a thin line, his unbiased doctor expression in full effect. "I'll take that under consideration."

There wasn't much to clean up since the residents went feral for the cannolis. I regretted grabbing only one for myself and resolved to return to the bakery when I had a day off. And a working vehicle.

"I'll save you the trip," I told Eli as I took the sign-up sheet from the clipboard and tucked it into my bag.

"Let me drive you over to Ruby's," he offered. "It's late."

I glanced at my phone. "Yeah, the Starlight Palms is notoriously dangerous after eight o'clock."

"You could get stalked by someone with a squeaky walker," he said. "Tennis balls dragging along pavement as they draw closer to their prey."

I shivered. "Chilling."

Once we were in his car again, backing out, he said, "I was thinking. You're still sleeping on the couch and Morgan is—"

"Getting impatient," I finished. "And also being pestered by residents who have the kind of grandkids who live in basements and don't have bank accounts."

"Yeah, Morgan said she planned on talking to you again this week . . . but I told her I'd handle it."

"Oh, *you'd* handle it, would you? I bet you're going to take a great deal of pleasure in evicting me from my own grandmother's couch." I leaned back, preparing myself for the kill. "Well, let me have it, Dr. Elias Buckley. Maybe I'll sleep in my car until more employee housing becomes available."

He shook his head. "What the fuck, Vera? You're not going to sleep in your car. The real estate around here is just as bad as LA, if not worse. And the last time an employee apartment became available, there was a lottery. The insider trading happening made *The Wolf of Wall Street* look like *The Boss Baby*, okay?"

"Thank you for dashing my hopes." Now it made sense why Morgan had laughed when I said a place might become available.

"What I'm getting at is that my apartment has a second bedroom."

"You live here on property?"

He nodded. "Sort of."

"That was more of a yes-or-no question."

He stopped in front of Ruby's building. "I'm trying to offer you my spare room, Vera."

The air rushed out of my lungs, leaving a burning sensation. My heart stuttered in my chest as I waited for him to say he was kidding. But seconds turned into moments, and all that passed between us was silence.

"Like a room in an apartment?" I asked. "Where you currently live?"

He nodded slowly. "That's how spare rooms work."

"An apartment you *sort of* live in?"

"I *do* live there," he said definitively.

"How many bathrooms?" As if I had room to be picky . . . How was I even entertaining this? But god, Ruby and I were one bicker away from accidentally killing each other during a violent sleepwalking episode. On top of that, I couldn't think of anything more humiliating than being formally reprimanded by a boss who I was technically old enough to parent.

"One and a half," he said. "A half bath off the kitchen and the two rooms are linked by a full bathroom."

Sharing a bathroom with Eli? No way. I could barely share a bathroom with my own grandmother. There had to be another solution. Maybe I could rent a spare closet-size room from some college kids.

I opened the car door and got out, but before closing it behind me, I said, "That's really kind of you to offer, but I'm good."

"Think about it." He opened his console and then handed me a small paper bag, his fingers brushing mine. "I may have saved you a cannoli when no one was looking. Tell a soul and I'll deny it until my dying day."

"Thanks." My voice was too soft as I held the bag to my chest and closed the door.

Had Eli Buckley been nice to me today? On multiple occasions? Was I actually in a coma at Cedars-Sinai and this was just my brain pulling together some desperate fantasy of an alternate reality version of Eli?

Real or not, I couldn't bring myself to even consider his offer. The thought of living with him only reminded me of all the times I'd come over to see Brody and Eli would leave the room like my presence had suddenly ruined his mood. But mostly, I didn't think I could handle reliving the disastrous morning after our nuptials every time I saw him with a hint of bedhead or toothpaste on the corner of his lip.

Inside, I had the apartment to myself. Ruby had texted earlier to say she was at a friend's place and wouldn't be in reach of her phone—whatever that meant.

For the first time in weeks, I sat down with the small crate I'd packed full of notebooks and photos and little remnants of the past. The same crate that I had intended to pack my old laptop inside of had I not left it on my car.

There were photos of me and Tess at her first baby shower and Mom at Disneyland and even Ruby, a birthday cake full of sixty very melted candles lighting up her face. There were pages upon pages full of notes on my abandoned script. Most of them were deeply embarrassing and full of half-formed questions and thoughts that I still had no answers to. I didn't know that there was any way I could rebuild what I'd lost. And maybe the best path forward was to just stop. To just give up this half-baked dream of writing. I had a handful of partial drafts, but *The Wunderkind* had been my one sole completed project. My whole identity as a writer was wrapped up in a script I hadn't even managed to properly back up and a degree I had done nothing with. But this was all so much bigger than just a script.

With a sigh, I took my cannoli out of the bag and licked the powdered sugar off my fingers.

Once upon a time, I'd had a life and it was time to get it back.

The first terrifying step was getting off Ruby's couch by whatever means possible.

Fucking fuckity fuck.

THE WUNDERKIND (FIRST DRAFT)
"PILOT" 10/8/07

INT. HER ROOM—EARLY MORNING

She lies in bed. His hoodie is on her chair.

POPPY (V.O.)

He leaves pieces of himself like litter.
And I gladly pick them up.

THE WUNDERKIND by Vera Stein.

I hardly slept the night before. My brain was a constant loop of possible future scenarios. Brushing my teeth alongside Eli. Making dinner. Sorting laundry. Remembering to double-check that I'd locked the bathroom door. Sharing groceries. Staying home while he went off to go on dates with the proud owner of the mystery hair tie.

It took a while, but eventually I fell asleep and the scenarios turned into the most ridiculous fantasies that left me unsatisfied and wholly annoyed with myself.

When I walked out the door for work, Ruby was still asleep and based on the hour I'd heard her stumble back in, that was probably for the best. I was heading out earlier than usual to deal with my car.

Except that the visitor spot where I had been parking wasn't empty. Not only was it not empty, but my RAV4 was there. And I knew for sure it was mine because of the Harry Styles watermelon-scented air freshener that hadn't carried any scent in years hanging from the rearview mirror and the faint crack in my windshield from when an eighteen-wheeler had kicked up some gravel right in front of me a few months ago.

Tucked under the windshield wiper was a Starlight Palms business card with Dr. Eli Buckley's information. On the back in choppy handwriting, it read:

You are once again road safe. Come find me for your keys.
—Eli

First, the offer to crash with him and now he had fixed my car? A small part of me wondered if this was all to get back at Brody, like some incredibly involved long game. Whatever it was, it was too much.

On my way to the main building, I stopped by Leonard's. I'd listed his coffin yesterday and he already had a bite. He asked me if I might be there when the interested party came by, and because I would have to run over myself with a golf cart if some internet stranger killed Leonard and got away with it all because I wasn't there, I said yes.

Patrick chirped in his cage as Leonard let me inside. His potential buyer, a young woman with white-blond extensions so luxurious I could trade them in for a new car, sat perched on his coral leather couch.

"Vera, this is Emery," Leonard said. "Vera assisted me with the online listing."

"Well, it certainly piqued my interest," Emery said as she stood up. Her platformed Doc Martens sandals were paired with lace shorts and a purposefully torn tank top. Maybe it was the Starlight Palms population rubbing off on me, but I almost asked her if the shirt was cheaper with or without the holes.

Leonard led the way to the coffin room and when he opened the door, Emery gasped and let out a squeal that left my ears ringing. Something did not sit well with me about all of this.

"It's perfect!" She circled the room, taking a good look at the glittering dove. "How many other people do you have coming to take a look?"

"Actually—" Leonard started.

"We have two more coming this afternoon," I lied through my teeth, feeling suddenly protective, "and one in the evening. But I have a few other messages I haven't gotten to yet."

Emery nodded seriously. "I'll give you an extra five hundred if you cancel on the others," she said.

Beside me, Leonard was gobsmacked, probably envisioning all the plants he could buy. Maybe even a new birdcage. "That's quite the—"

"What exactly are your plans for the coffin?" I asked, interrupting Leonard again.

Emery spoke nervously with her hands as she said, "Okay, so a little morbid, I know . . ."

"Honey, it's a casket," Leonard said with a chuckle. "It doesn't get more morbid than that."

That seemed to set Emery at ease. "Okay, so I'm a party experience designer-coordinator—"

"So, a party planner?" I asked.

She gave me a brief but withering look. "Right, well, I've booked this joint bachelor-bachelorette weekend with the theme Till Death Do Us Part. The couple is very edgy, and I'm certain this would be perfect as a beverage station. We could tear out the silk lining and put some kind of tarp in it. Fill it with hard seltzers and maybe some premade shots. Voilà!"

Leonard stood there, words coming to him in fits but never fully formed. He was silent for so long that I almost wondered if he needed medical intervention. But most of all, I was a little shocked. Leonard's attitude toward death seemed to lean on the irreverent side, but it became immediately clear that this coffin held more meaning than he was letting on.

Emery looked to me rather than just asking Leonard directly if he was okay.

But physically, Leonard was fine. Emotionally, I wasn't so sure he was handling the coffin cooler idea in stride.

"I don't think this is going to work," I finally said, and the tension in Leonard's shoulders eased. Patrick chirped from the other room. "Yeah, definitely not," I continued. "Maybe you could look into a Halloween store or something."

Emery let out a little pout. "But—"

"Let me help you to the door," I said.

As I walked her out, Emery tried offering an extra two hundred dollars on top of the five hundred and even promised she could have the casket out of here in an hour.

I shook my head as I shuffled her out the door. "Yeah, I think you're going to have to find a different coffin to upcycle."

When I walked back inside, Leonard's bottom lip was trembling, and it hurt to witness. The moment he noticed me staring, he turned to me and said, "Well, I suppose you have more important things to do than sit around here."

I didn't know what I could possibly say. Leonard was an onion and I was nowhere near the center. I could understand why he didn't want to see the casket become a glorified cooler, but I wondered if he even wanted to see the thing go to begin with.

"My writing group meets in the main building bimonthly, by the way," he said as he walked me to the door. "You should come by."

"I just might," I said, lying straight through my teeth.

Eli's office and clinic were on the second floor of the main building. When I walked in, his nurse, Jake, said he was just finishing up with a resident and told me I could wait in his office.

There was no artwork, photographs, or even trinkets in Eli's office. I didn't realize I was looking for hints about his personal life until I didn't find any. What had dear old Eli been up to since college? Did he go into cardiology and then fall from grace? Was he married? He didn't wear a ring, but most of Mom's physicians didn't wear rings during their workday.

"I guess you're here for the car keys."

I started at the deep timber of his voice. "You didn't have to do that," I told him as I turned around.

He sat down and shook his head. There were bags under his eyes and I wondered if he'd stayed up late or got up early to deal with it.

When he set his stethoscope down on his desk, I noticed a grease stain on his otherwise crisp jeans.

"You didn't fix it yourself, did you?" I asked.

"Don't sound so surprised."

"I just never took you for someone who does things you could pay someone else to do."

He grimaced at that. "Ouch. A thank-you would have sufficed."

"You're right. Sorry. I just—" I rubbed my hands up and down my thighs. Eli's mom had a cleaning lady that came out to the frat house every other week and Brody once told me he had a live-in nanny growing up. Not exactly the kind of upbringing that would lend itself to physical labor. But my default setting with him was always so caustic, and I supposed I could try to be more polite.

My palms were sweating now. Last night I'd decided to ask Eli about the room, but being here and actually doing it was much harder than deciding to do it.

"Sorry," I said again. "Do you ever say shitty things when you're nervous?"

He leaned back in his leather office chair, his arms crossed over his chest, that one proud vein wrapping around his forearm. "I make you nervous." It wasn't a question.

"No." I cleared my throat and clenched my fists at my sides where he couldn't see them. "But the possibility of being roommates with the guy I accidentally married once *does* make me nervous."

His pupils widened before that indifferent mask slipped back into place again. I expected him to gloat at the fact that I was doubling back after such an emphatic no, but instead, he simply said, "The room is yours. I'll get you the spare key later today. You can move your stuff in whenever. I'll be home late tonight, so if you'd rather wait, I can help you. And I wouldn't call it an accident. It's not as though we slipped and fell into a marriage contract."

There was a long beat of silence as I found myself wishing I could read his mind and simultaneously thankful that I couldn't.

"The residents can't know," I said suddenly.

"If Ruby knows, everyone knows," he said.

"Are you calling my grandmother a gossip?"

"Are you saying she isn't?" he countered. "Gives 'em something to talk about for a few days. Trust me. Some polycule drama will surface by next week and we will be old news."

Resigned, I stood up and took my car keys. "Marlon can't eat too many table scraps. He has a sensitive stomach."

"Understood."

"And I talk in my sleep sometimes."

"I remember," he said.

"We're splitting everything evenly. The rent, the utilities, everything. Even streaming services."

"Vera, the employee rent is pennies."

"Maybe for you," I spat back.

I could see him chewing the inside of his cheek. "You can start paying next month if you insist, but we're already halfway through the month."

"It's the tenth of September," I said.

He recrossed his arms over his chest, the white fabric of his shirt pulling over his biceps. Those fantasies from last night began to— *No. Bad brain.*

"Deal," I said.

"Deal." His voice was smug, like he'd won a bet I didn't even know we had in place.

"Right." I turned to leave but then spun back around. "Do you know Leonard?"

He inhaled deeply through his nose and nodded.

"What's the deal with the funeral?"

"So he's shown you the binder?"

I nodded. "I'm helping him sell his casket on Facebook Marketplace."

"You're what?" he sputtered, and then held up his hands. "Actually, never mind. I have a patient coming in, but bookmark that story for me, would you, roomie?"

"Sure thing, *roomie.*"

He followed me out of his office and closed the door behind us, but before heading back across the hall to the clinic, he said, "I think he wishes he could be there. Leonard. He would want to be there."

"Huh?"

"At his own funeral." He shrugged. "Can you blame him? Haven't you ever wondered what people might say about you at the end? It's hard not to be a little bit fascinated by it."

I nodded, like I knew just what he was talking about, because it was easier than explaining that I had no interest in hearing my own eulogy. I'd already seen what Brody—someone I'd known for half my life—had to say about me in that email thread.

Here lies Vera Stein. She was a good girl. A good, boring girl.

CHAPTER EIGHTEEN

Waverly's workshop was wildly successful. Even some of the janitorial staff hung around at the back, not even bothering to pretend to clean. Afterward, the Good Vibes Only pop-up shop was busier than the cafeteria on onion ring Tuesday.

Waverly talked about sex toy safety, but also different types of sex (like mutual masturbation) and even came with mobility aids and various forms of lube to demonstrate how sex can be accessible for anyone. I was shocked to find it rather . . . empowering. At least when I didn't find it mortifying.

The success of the event put a bounce in my step as I stacked the extra folding chairs we ended up needing. "We could have filled an overflow room," I told Waverly. "You've got to come back some time."

"I'd love that," she said, "and your residents certainly cleared out my stock. I had planned on leaving you a toy or two for yourself."

My hands flailed as I waved her off. "Oh, I couldn't let you do that."

"The lady doth protest too much," she said with a chuckle.

I choked on a laugh and blurted, "I-promise-I've-had-an-orgasm-before." Because I had. I just . . . didn't want to have public discourse about it. But fucking hell, did I really just say that?

There was a knock on the doorframe. Eli stood at the threshold, one brow arched curiously.

Yeah, he'd heard that. His expression was too smug and he took up too much of the doorway. Who gave him permission to be so broad? He scratched his chin thoughtfully. And the scruff! The scruff made him look suddenly laid-back, but he wasn't fooling me. I remembered his tightly trimmed hair and clean shave and obsession over every class and every grade. And how anything that didn't serve his purpose was just taking up space.

"Waverly, I'm Eli Buckley," he said, "the physician on staff here. I just wanted to say that was one of our most well-received programs ever. And truly very much needed." He turned to me. "Good work, Vera."

"Thanks," I said on a breath, my chest feeling tight. Was I really about to move my shit and my dog into his apartment later today?

He set off down the hallway and I drifted over to the comment box near the door, definitely not watching him go.

"Something going on between you two?" Waverly asked. She was intuitive like Tess, which was a great trait when you didn't know what you needed or how to ask for it, but it was total shit when you just wanted to avoid reality like a big girl.

"Oh, no. Not at all. Eli is—he and I—we're just coworkers."

She grinned. "Well, whatever you two are, you've got a serious case of sex flush."

I touched the back of my hand to my cheek and shook my head. "Just warm from moving all those chairs." Opening the comment box, I dared a peek inside to find it completely empty. "They never tell you when you're doing a good job, do they?" I said.

Waverly smiled. "Hot Doc certainly thought you did a very good job."

CHAPTER NINETEEN

Ruby was thrilled to see me go. Not just because she would have her privacy back, but because she was gobbling up Eli's invitation to be roommates like it was the latest plotline to unfold on her favorite TV show.

"I have to text Gwen," she said.

I shook my head as I folded up the bedding I'd stolen from Brody's pool house—which would come in handy. "Why would Gwen care that I'm moving out?"

"Oh," she said with a snort. "I think she'd be more interested to hear who you're moving in with."

I narrowed my gaze at her as she pecked at the screen of her phone. "Ruby, you didn't tell people about me and Eli, did you? You know us getting married was just a silly dare from college. The ink hadn't even dried on that marriage license by the time it was annulled."

She swallowed and looked up with such convincing innocence that I almost bought it. "I don't recall you categorizing that information as private."

"Ruby, are you serious? Was I supposed to have you sign an NDA or something?"

She sat back at the kitchen table and took a sip of her iced tea. "Couldn't hurt."

"My life is not your entertainment," I said, trying to keep my voice even.

THE WUNDERKIND (FIRST DRAFT)
"PILOT" 10/8/07

EXT. FARMERS MARKET—SATURDAY

He steals a strawberry from a table.

She swats his hand and then pays.

ARLO

You're my moral compass with great calves.

February 14, 2020
Vera S.
Two glasses of wine in, but this line still does it for me.

THE WUNDERKIND by Vera Stein.

She shrugged. "Well, I've never really considered your life to be entertaining, so this is new territory for me, I suppose."

I took a deep breath and walked into the kitchen to gather up Marlon's food. "When you spend the first half of your adult life taking care of two grown women, then you can talk to me about living a more entertaining life."

She was taken aback, the dramatized hurt clear.

Ruby and I had gone toe-to-toe plenty of times, and the outcome was always the same. She would stand up and give a monologue about how ungrateful I was for her and how I could never understand all the sacrifices she'd made for Mom and therefore me. She'd dramatically storm out and I'd be left wondering if this was all real or just a truly compelling performance. I'd apologize, because it was easier than ever expecting things to change.

"I'm sorry," I blurted before she could tell me all the ways that I was wrong. I couldn't hear it right now. "I'm glad I was there for Mom . . . and that you were too." Even if she hadn't been. Not in the same way I had. Even if the moment I was old enough to wear a bra, she clocked out of adulthood and suddenly, I was the one organizing bills and reminding Mom about her prescriptions in between school and homework.

"It's fine," she said curtly.

It wasn't, but I'd settle for fine.

"I'm going to start packing up the car."

She nodded.

"Marlon's going to miss you," I said, trying to soften her just a bit. "But I'm sure he'd love to visit. We'll be just at the edge of the property."

"Yes, I fear he's been spoiled by my velvet settee." Then she spoke to Marlon. "You'll just have to grow accustomed to used IKEA furniture, my darling."

I glanced at him over my shoulder. Paws crossed, he looked like a little prince sitting on a silk pillow. He really was meant for designer purses and private jets. "He'll weather the storm."

Packing up my car took longer than it should have, because even though I'd hardly accrued new things since crashing with Ruby, my belongings seemed to have somehow expanded and nothing fit back in its bags or boxes.

The employee housing sat at the edge of the property in apartments that looked like they'd been added on in the eighties and had seen a few sparing cosmetic updates. The architecture didn't quite match the mid-century aesthetic of the rest of Starlight Palms, but each mint-colored door was painted with the silhouette of a pink flamingo, which served to unify the building with the rest of the complex.

Eli had put my key on an elongated diamond-shaped Starlight Palms key ring that was included in the resident welcome packs and was a replica of the original property keys. Regardless of how long this living situation lasted, I decided that the key ring would be mine to keep because I'd coveted one since seeing Ruby's.

With Marlon tucked under my arm, I let myself in and found the lights had been left on. The door led right into the living room, where there was a modern but plush-looking sectional sofa and one of those TVs that looked like it could be a painting.

I snorted when I noticed the selected artwork was *The Treachery of Images* by René Magritte. On a cream background was a painted pipe with the French translation of "This is not a pipe" in cursive below.

The only class I ever shared with Eli was art history, and though he was always so hot and cold during that time, he did choose to sit next to me during lectures. Our professor was obsessed with this painting and I once scribbled a note on the edge of a paper for Eli to see about how our professor probably wanked to fantasies of this painting. Because I can't have nice things, I accidentally dropped the paper on the way out of class only for the professor to pick it up, read my note, and then return it to me, all while holding the most awkwardly intense eye contact.

I snatched the paper back and Eli and I stumbled out into the hall, barely holding it together before laughing our asses off. The painting was probably our only inside joke that didn't include Brody.

The kitchen counters of Eli's apartment were bare save for an espresso machine that was worth more than my car. On the breakfast bar was a note in his familiar slanted handwriting.

Your room is the first one off the hallway. I'll be home late. —E

Home. I was in Eli's home. And for a short while, it was mine too. A sharp chill ran up my spine at the thought.

After I got Marlon settled with his bed and a chew toy full of frozen peanut butter, I brought the first load inside, including my bedding.

When I let myself into the guest room, I didn't expect to find a mattress on the floor bachelor pad–style, but I also hadn't expected a room that looked like it came straight out of an Anthropologie catalog. There was a sage-green arched cabinet in the far corner just waiting to be filled with books and knickknacks. The queen bed was made with a fluffy cream duvet and pillows that looked like they could absorb every neurotic thought I'd ever thought until my brain was blissfully empty. The headboard was a mauve tufted velvet arch to complement the cabinet and the closet was full of unused hangers—the fancy slim velvet kind. It was more like a hotel room than a guest room.

With the bed already made, I stored Brody's pool house bedding on the top shelf of the closet like a forgotten trophy. I'd never been the kind of woman to have the luxury of multiple types of bedding, but maybe this was indicative of a new era. An era where I owned white shirts that weren't stained and I remembered to send my dry-clean-only clothing to the actual cleaners.

I spent the evening getting settled in and ordered myself a poke bowl for dinner. When I got to my toiletries, I ventured into the shared bathroom. Were it not for the half-burned cucumber melon candle and electric toothbrush charging on the counter, I would have no idea which side was Eli's.

Just about every bathroom I'd ever had looked like a drugstore had thrown up on the counter, but since Eli had set such a tidy tone, I found a home for each thing in the cabinet under the sink.

I opened the drawer in the middle of the vanity, hoping I might be able to store my toothpaste there, but instead I found an unopened box of condoms and a few small bottles of lube.

Slamming the drawer shut as though I were in danger of getting caught, I decided to leave the toothpaste on the counter. Eli could handle toothpaste on the counter. It was better than toothpaste in the lube replenishment drawer, which would immediately indicate to Eli that I knew he had a lube drawer. It threatened the kind of embarrassment I'd felt the one time I attempted to shop for lingerie to wear for Brody and then immediately ran into my high school geometry teacher and his wife while she shopped for new bras post–breast reduction. I was holding a thong. A crotchless thong. (Granted, if you asked me, all thongs might as well be considered crotchless, because my vagina has been known to swallow thongs. Surely I wasn't the only person whose vagina was wider than that appalling excuse for a gusset.) The continued embarrassment of that interaction still kept me awake some nights.

By the time midnight rolled around, I was still wide awake. Or maybe it just felt too weird to fall asleep knowing that Eli could walk in the door at any moment. So I decided to take out my notebooks and see what notes I could piece together on *The Wunderkind*.

The problem was the couch was fucking cozy. I could say a lot of things about Eli, but the man knew how to buy a couch. As I settled in, I found myself slipping into a reclining position until I was just fully horizontal with my head on the armrest and my notebook on my chest.

The Wunderkind was about a young female piano prodigy who was older now and less remarkable with age. She fell for a charismatic boy at college who always seemed to stumble into good luck. In so many ways, it was a story about me and Brody. Except for the part where I was once a prodigy.

I got only a few pages in before my vision began to blur. It didn't help that Marlon was already fast asleep between my legs.

I should have been a big girl and taken myself to bed. It wasn't like I needed to stay up and wait for Eli. He didn't have a curfew. It didn't matter where he was or who he was out with. I wasn't his keeper. I was his roommate.

Briefly, I wondered if he would bring someone back here at some point. I mean, he could. It was his right, of course. But surely with these old, thin walls, I'd hear everything.

And something about that thought made my chest tighten and my abdomen burn. It was a very confusing combination of sad and horny.

My eyes were so, so heavy. Heavier than anything I'd moved today. Heavier than the boxes of sex toys I'd carted down the street in the stifling heat.

"Vera," someone whispered a few seconds later. Or maybe it had been a few hours. "Let's get you to bed, Vera."

"It's so comfortable," I whined, my words coming out mushy and my tongue feeling too big for my mouth.

"It is a great couch," the voice confirmed. Arms were pulling me up into a sitting position and then helping me to my feet. "Up, up, up."

My vision was just two little slits, but it was enough to see Eli, his hair a little wild, almost windblown or like someone had run their fingers through it. How was he so handsome? The insides of a person should match their outsides. Not that Eli hadn't been perfectly nice lately. He was letting me stay with him, but the *memory* of Eli . . . that was not nice.

"I want to sleep here," I said, falling back down to the couch, but he yanked me up before I could reach my destination.

"You've spent enough time sleeping on couches lately."

I growled at him and began to stomp off down the hallway.

He pulled at my elbow. "Wrong door. Back this way."

Inside my room, I stumbled to the bed and he threw back the duvet before I could face-plant directly on top of it.

"Good night, Vera," he said as I yanked the covers up over my shoulder until I was perfectly cocooned.

And for the second time in recent memory, Elias Buckley put me to sleep.

This time, it was in a bed. A real bed.

MOJAVE DESERT
NEVADA

ELIAS BUCKLEY
SEVENTEEN YEARS AGO
SOMETHING THAT SCARES ME

"Are we there yet?" Brody asked from the passenger seat of his 1998 Nissan Altima.

He'd bought the car off Craigslist after he booked his first daytime TV job on *The Hands of Time* three weeks ago. It had been an open casting call. I'd dropped him off for the audition, and when he bounded out of the building with the news that they were calling him back, he called me a "fucking fuck" for looking so shocked. Then I treated him to thirty bucks worth of Taco Bell to make up for it.

"No, but we're still close enough to turn around," I said from the back seat as I watched the desert pass by in a blur.

I hated Vegas. It was like a theme park that was trying to sell you on the *feeling* of traveling the world without the actual experience. Vera said that was because my family could afford to actually travel and, honestly, did so lavishly. Maybe she was right. She usually was.

She glanced at me in the rearview mirror, and her gaze settled on mine before flickering back to the road. Every moment of eye contact we shared had started to feel like we were challenging the other to look away. I didn't know when it started, but it was turning into my favorite game.

Her eyes found mine again after a moment. Those thick brows of hers wrinkled and her wide brown eyes studied me. Like I was an unsolvable equation. But *I* was the open book. *She* was the one full of secrets.

Brody had asked Vera to drive once we crossed the state line because of his unpaid tickets in Nevada. At first, he'd lobbied for us to take the cheapest flights we could find, but I didn't need Vera to see what heights did to me, especially when I didn't have a Xanax on hand.

Brody shook his head, his knees bouncing impatiently. "I can't believe you got into Stanford Med and you expect us not to celebrate. Can you believe this guy, Vera?"

She looked to him and smiled. Really fucking smiled. "Yes, actually, I can."

I gritted my teeth but tried not to sound like a complete asshole as I told him, "When you said 'celebrate,' I thought you meant a round of beers at Caves. Not crossing state lines. We could have at least taken my car." Which had a moon roof and temperature-controlled seats.

Brody's shoulders slumped slightly. I was an asshole. He was proud of the fact that he bought this car on his own. But still, temperature-controlled seats.

"I like this car," Vera said pointedly.

In response, Brody bopped his head like a golden retriever and then rolled his window down, holding his arm out to let it surf over the wind. "Me too," he howled.

I was happy for Brody and his shitty car. Despite what Vera likely assumed I thought, driving around in the Altima wasn't beneath me, but I also didn't want it to break down on its maiden road trip to celebrate my med school acceptance. Which wasn't even anything to celebrate. I had the grades, sure, but with the Buckley name, I probably would have still gotten in if I used the MCAT test booklet as a paint-by-numbers demonstration.

Idly, I scrolled through my phone, hovering over a text I'd received from my mom but hadn't replied to yet.

Mom:
You did that, baby! You got in. You deserve it. I'm so proud of you. We both are.

Of course my mom was tasked with letting me know that my dad was proud of me. Nathaniel Buckley didn't expect anything less, and if I simply met expectations, then what was there even to congratulate me on? Would it be med school graduation? Would that be enough? Securing a residency at his top pick? Starting my own practice? At what point would my father consider anything I'd done an achievement worth acknowledging?

Eli:

Thanks, Mom. Going to celebrate with Vera and Brody.

It made her feel better to know I had friends. Especially since her diagnosis. She needed to know I had a life outside of the family and the path to med school. Although, I may have slightly exaggerated my friendships.

Well, Brody was a friend. Technically, Vera was . . . Brody's friend. They were attached at the hip. However, I didn't need Vera at my hip, because for the last year she'd wiggled her way into a vulnerable spot right between the ribs. And that's why she couldn't be my friend. I held her at a distance, because I liked her too much. I liked how much she infuriated me and how she would talk at anyone about the things she cared about until they cared too. I liked the way her curly hair expanded as the day went on and how on the nights she would crash with Brody, I'd get up to find that there was no telling which way her head was facing in that jumble of hair. I liked that sometimes she laughed in her sleep. I liked that she talked about her mom like they were best friends. I liked that even baggy clothes found a way to mold to her ass and tits. I liked that she was kind to people that no one else had patience for.

I liked Vera and she loved Brody.

And I hated that. I hated that she was more concerned with him passing his classes than she was with anything she wanted for herself. I hated that she was constantly a supportive wingwoman and would beam and laugh alongside him no matter how much it pained her. I hated how she melted into a corner when she felt intimidated, most often by other fawning girls. I hated that the handful of times she and I started to have a conversation, her eyes would wander past me the moment Brody came into her field of vision. I hated how enamored I was with her and how so many other men—men like my father and most of my Sigma Chi brothers—looked at her and only saw her as unremarkable.

Brody rolled his window up and the smell of Vera's cucumber melon body spray filled the enclosed space. A single curl hung loose from the knot on top of her head, and my mind became lost imagining what it might feel like to touch that curl and let my finger ghost across the back of her neck. Would it give her goose bumps? Would the most minor of touches excite her as much as it would me? My cock twitched against the fly of my jeans, and thankfully a response from my mom lit up the screen of my phone, killing any bit of arousal.

Mom:
I expect you to run your father's credit card so many times it melts. Do something that scares you. But please don't get arrested. And if you do, call me and not your father.

I sent a heart in response and pocketed my phone. I would never understand how someone full of so much whimsical hope had decided a person like my father was worth spending her life with.

Vera rolled down her window again as we began to fly down a slight hill and farther into the desert. The wind blew a few more curls loose and gave me a couple seconds of relief from the smell of her. A scent I couldn't forget if I tried.

Mom wanted me to do something that scared me. Vera Stein scared me plenty.

CHAPTER TWENTY

Marlon woke me up in the morning, ready for breakfast and a bathroom break. I had to pee and brush my teeth and do normal human things, but first: dog duty.

I stumbled out of my room and past the kitchen and the living room. The refrigerator door was open and I could hear Eli on the phone, laughing. Nothing in the world could possibly be funny to me before I'd had a chance to brush my teeth.

Marlon spun in circles outside, searching for the perfect spot to do his business, and when he was done, I opened the front door quietly and attempted to sneak past Eli. But he was off the phone and waiting for me, leaning against the counter with a cup of espresso.

And he wasn't wearing a shirt. The planes of his chest were tanned and the dusting of hair visible.

"Good morning," he said, his voice low and still a little sleepy.

"Thanks for steering me to my bedroom last night," I said. "You have a very good couch, though."

"You would know," he said. "You are a connoisseur of couches. Espresso? I have a coffee maker too."

I nodded. "Regular coffee would be good."

I sat down at the little breakfast table in the kitchen as he pulled out a fresh filter. "I've got a churro-flavored creamer in the fridge."

"Mr. Fancy Espresso Machine has flavored creamer?"

"I have nothing against creamer, but for the record, it's not mine."

It was like he was *begging* me to ask. He wanted me to know he was with someone. And now he was just rubbing it in, but I didn't plan on giving him the satisfaction of my curiosity.

He threw back the rest of his espresso and sat down at the table across from me as we waited for the coffee.

I might not have been interested in asking him about the mystery person in his life, but there was one question that had been gnawing at me.

"Eli," I said, "how did you end up here?"

"I'm guessing you don't mean here in this kitchen."

"You were going to be an interventional cardiologist, right? This feels way less high stakes than that."

He nodded, tracing a small circle on the table and concentrating carefully on it. "I changed course after the first year of medical school."

"Your whole family is full of cardiologists, I thought."

"Except for my cousin, Stacy. She's a podiatrist. A real rebel."

I snorted softly. "And then came you."

"Yeah, my dad wasn't really thrilled by the thought of geriatric and palliative care."

It was so far off from what I knew about him all those years ago. It struck me as the type of medicine that required patience, something I never considered Eli to have in abundance.

The drip on the coffeepot stopped and Eli stood to pour me a cup. I accepted the creamer, because regardless of who it belonged to, it did sound good.

The mug he set down in front of me had a spaceship shooting around it and in bold letters it read *Crawford Basin Astronomy Camp*. I topped the coffee off with creamer, his brow rising as I continued to pour. It was infinitely unfair how much he could communicate with just a single eyebrow.

Holding the cup up to my lips, I couldn't resist a smile. "So what was the inciting incident? With med school."

"The inciting incident? Is my life some kind of script treatment in need of workshopping?" He smirked before dropping his chin to his chest. "Someone I loved very much got sick. The medical community cares very deeply about lifesaving efforts. That's where the money is. But death? We're not very good about helping people die. We're all so scared of the end, but it's the one thing we can't prevent. Only delay. And only for so long."

I blinked, not realizing that my eyes were welling with tears. "I'm sorry," I said. "That was just . . . My mom was dying for a very long time before she finally went."

He nodded, running a hand up the back of his neck. "So you're part of the Dead Moms Club too? I'm so sorry, Vera."

"It's okay," I told him. "But your mom . . . Is that— Was she—"

He nodded. "Parkinson's. What about your mom?"

"Colon cancer."

"That's a fucking miserable way to watch someone die."

It was. It really fucking was. Amid all the condolences and encouragements, this exact moment was the first time someone had acknowledged the pain of watching her deteriorate. Mom endured the truest misery, of course, but watching it unfold had turned into an immovable part of me. Not only her death, but the process of watching it happen was a canon event in the story of my life.

"Parkinson's couldn't have been easy," I said.

"It made me furious. It made me want to punch walls." His eyes, green with a lighter ring around the pupil, shifted down to where Marlon was curled up like a croissant at our feet. "Sometimes I did."

"I liked your mom," I said. His parents were big donors, so it wasn't unusual to see them on campus. We'd met only two or three times, but she actually made eye contact with me. And she remembered my name and my major and one time during parents' weekend at Sigma Chi, she said I had a contagious laugh.

"She liked you too," he said.

"You're just saying that to be nice."

"You should know by now that I don't say anything just to be nice."

My stomach clenched. It was true.

"I didn't have a lot of friends growing up," he went on. "I mean, I was always surrounded with people. Like my Sigma Chi brothers or the lacrosse team in high school, but she liked knowing that I hung out with

Brody. And you. Plus I told her about the time you got drunk and called me an entitled sycophant. She was an English major. She liked big words."

I laughed. "*Sycophant* maybe wasn't the right word."

"But *entitled* was," he said quietly.

I swallowed, running my tongue over my bottom lip. "Maybe. But you obviously had things going on. Like with your dad. He sounded like a ray of fucking sunshine." I'd only heard about Eli's dad from Brody, but from what I knew, he was the kind of man whose approval and affection was a moving target, which was what I'd always thought of Eli, to be honest.

"I told her," he said, his chin in his hand. "About our short-lived marriage."

"Oh my god." I wanted to melt into my coffee cup and then be poured down the drain. "She must have been horrified."

He shook his head. "It surprised her. I don't do that to people often and she liked surprises." He went silent for a moment, and then looked back to me all serious and earnest. "For the record, surprises are awful."

"Well, you've been surprising me since I showed up here," I admitted.

He leaned back, with his arms folded and his feet crossed at the ankles. My fingers itched to run through the hair on his bare chest. "Nah. I haven't changed, really. I think I was always there deep down."

I gave him a pointed look.

He bit back a smile and shook his head. "Okay, maybe I have changed a little. But not too much."

"Well, considering you could barely stand to have me in your room back in college, and now you've asked me to live with you, I'd say you've changed quite a bit."

His forehead creased with concern. "Is that what you thought?"

"What else was I supposed to think?"

He thought for a moment and then opened his mouth to speak before simply saying, "I'm sorry. I . . ." He shook his head, whatever he was about to say dying before it could reach his tongue.

"What did you think of me back then?" I asked because I was too nervous to urge him to complete that last sentence.

Sucking in a deep breath, he took my empty coffee cup and rinsed it out in the sink. "You . . . made me feel like a bad person."

"What! What does that even mean? I never once said you were a bad person."

"No." He shook his head, like he was trying to shake his thoughts loose. "You didn't make me feel like that because of anything you said. But I was a jerk, Vera, and being around you made that easier to see."

I didn't know what to do with that. What did he want me to say? That he wasn't a jerk? He was moody and gruff. I rarely felt welcome in his company. If it weren't for that night in Vegas, I would have thought he despised me entirely. Hell, even after that night, I figured he might.

"What are you doing today?" he asked suddenly.

"Um . . ." The truth was I had planned on rotting in bed all day, but that didn't sound so great when you said it out loud. "I don't know. I've got some work to do for upcoming programs. I need to find a tarot reader . . . but I was thinking of checking out drag bingo to see if we could set one up for the residents."

"I'll drive," he said.

CHAPTER TWENTY-ONE

Hanky Panky was a few blocks from Good Vibes Only. Based on my internet sleuthing, it was definitely not the trendiest of the local drag haunts on offer for drag brunch, but I was immediately charmed by the drag queen working the sidewalk to bring in street traffic. She wore a shimmering teal bodysuit that matched her glitter-caked beard.

"Come on in," she said in a sweet Southern accent. "You two might get lucky." Then she looked to Eli. "Though it looks like you already have."

It was just a line, but my cheeks still warmed as Eli held the door open for me.

We were seated and handed menus with bingo cards on the back and blotters stamped in the shape of eggplants. Very subtle.

The half-circle booth we sat in was small and cozy, positioning us close enough so that our thighs touched and we occasionally grazed elbows.

Without any explanation, Eli swapped my menu–bingo card for his.

"What'd you do that for?"

He shrugged. "Just making things interesting."

The brunch was a set menu of chicken and waffles and it came with a bottomless pitcher of mimosas. The place was a bachelorette party fly-trap, and I had no complaints.

"Good morning! Good afternoon! Good evening—depending on whether or not you made it to bed last night," said the drag queen we'd seen outside.

Eli took a swig of his drink and draped his arm over the back of the booth behind me, the heat of his body pulling me toward him. As nonchalantly as possible, I leaned back and pretended not to notice how close he was and how it made my heart feel like it was skipping rocks.

The queen strutted through the crowd, purposefully running into people with very generously padded hips. "I'm your bingo hostess for today's brunch. My name is Him Kardashian. You may have heard of my slightly more well-known sister, Kim."

Eli's breath danced across my neck as he chuckled, sending little sparks of electricity down my abdomen.

"I don't see the resemblance!" the bartender shouted.

"Fuck you gently, Ryan," Him Kardashian responded without missing a beat. "Now, the rules of bingo are simple. First player to get five in a row vertically, horizontally, or diagonally wins bingo. You can pick a prize from our prize dumpster." She pointed to a box that had a printed picture of the dumpster fire meme taped to it. "And if you manage to get me vertical, horizontal, or diagonal, you've already won. Lastly, if you cheat, we'll give you a bad spray tan and send you on your way."

"You ready to lose, Vera?" Eli pulled his arm back and leaned over his bingo card.

"Look alive, Buckley." I uncapped my blotter and stamped the top of his hand with bright orange ink as Him Kardashian began calling numbers.

Eli made a move to retaliate, but Him Kardashian was too fast for him to look away from his card.

Between numbers and forkfuls of food, we warred back and forth with our blotters until both of our arms were covered in eggplants. Eli admitted defeat when I managed to partially blot his cheek.

"Am I going to have to separate you two?" Him Kardashian purred as she sauntered past us.

"Miss Kardashian," Eli pleaded, "she's manhandling me."

The drag queen winked at me. "I'd say he looks like a willing participant."

The moment she turned her back, Eli blotted me right on the tip of my nose.

Unfortunately for me, it quickly became clear that Eli had the superior bingo sheet. By the time we finished our pitcher of mimosas, Eli was just one square away from a vertical win and two away from horizontal and diagonal wins.

My bingo card, however, was stamped randomly so that only one square connected.

"That was *my* bingo card," I told Eli. "You sabotaged me."

"These were randomly handed out, Stein," he shot back as he blotted another square.

"And then you blatantly changed the randomization by swapping our cards!"

"Twenty-two!" Him Kardashian said into the microphone.

When Eli looked up for a second, I reached over and grabbed my rightfully owned bingo card.

Eli scoffed, but he couldn't hide his delight at my willingness to play dirty.

"Just making things interesting," I told him as I stamped the winning square. "Bingo!" I yelled, and then chugged back the rest of my drink.

"Hallelujah!" Him Kardashian sang. She reached into the box and tossed me a rolled-up T-shirt, but Eli caught it before I could.

"You can have it," I said. "But only if you wear it right now."

"Deal," he said, unrolling the light pink T-shirt for us both to see.

There was a huge lifelike crayfish on it and then below that, it read: *Craw Daddy*.

He glanced over to me, and I dipped my chin toward him.

"Well, go on." I twirled my finger instructively. "Fashion show."

Begrudgingly, he pulled the shirt on over his vintage Hawaiian button-up. With his arms raised, I noticed the sliver of abdomen peeking out from the bottom of his shirt and I was just buzzed enough from the mimosas to admit that I wouldn't have protested to him removing his shirt again for a reprise of this morning's show.

Him Kardashian whistled. "I'm no waitress, but I'll take your tip!"

The hungover bachelorette party in front of us catcalled Eli to the point of blushing.

He stood and took a bow before reaching for his wallet and throwing down a couple twenties. "Let's leave your business card at the bar. I think Him Kardashian would be a hit among the residents."

"Is Eli Buckley a sore loser?" I asked. "And I don't have a business card."

He took one from his wallet and used the pen we'd written our names on our bingo cards with to cross out *Dr. Eli Buckley* and jot down *Vera Stein*.

He wrote it so quickly, and I got this strange sense of pleasure at seeing my name in his handwriting. It looked so right that it made even my own signature seem wrong to me.

Then after my name, he added *Bingo Grifter* and *Activities Coordinator*.

"Thanks for that," I said.

"Just had to let them know who they're getting into bed with."

"You would know from experience." Oh shit. I did not mean to say that out loud.

His pupils widened and then his lips curved into a devious smile. "Yes," he said, "I would, actually. You never forget your first wedding night."

I shook my head and swatted at his chest. "Let's go, ex-husband."

He held his arm out for me to take and we walked out onto the sidewalk. "Could I tempt you with a few boring errands?" Eli asked. "Grocery store, dry cleaning, et cetera."

"You don't have any prior commitments?" I asked. "Any dates to go on? As your ex-wife, I would hate to cockblock you."

He snorted. "No dates today."

I made a sad attempt at smiling. "And you're okay to drive?"

"Yes. You monopolized the pitcher of mimosas."

"For which I will not apologize!" As he closed the passenger door behind me, I asked, "So, there are other days when you do have dates?"

The time it took for him to walk around the front of the car felt like years. And then when he finally slid in behind the wheel, he buckled his seat belt in silence before saying, "I don't really do casual dating."

I didn't find that surprising. Eli was the furthest thing from casual.

"I don't really do dating," I blurted.

He pulled out into the street, and after a beat, his voice dropped as he asked, "Because you were with Brody?"

I barked out a stiff laugh. "Oh my god, no."

His lips pressed into a thin line. I was surprised to hear him bring up Brody to begin with. They had a fraught past, and I always felt like I was missing a few details.

"Why would it even matter?" I asked.

He turned his head to look out the window so that I couldn't see the expression on his face when he said, "Because he never deserved you."

Now it was my turn to look the other way, because what he'd just said brewed a war of emotions inside of me. Anger, validation, frustration. "I was his secret." The words slipped out before I could catch them. "For years." I didn't know what Eli knew about us. If maybe he'd heard rumors from other acquaintances, but I doubted it. Brody was very good at keeping us a secret.

From the corner of my vision, I noticed the whites of his knuckles as he gripped the steering wheel.

"That's not why I quit," I said. "It was just—he was going to replace me with two younger part-time assistants. A cost-saving measure."

"Good," Eli said with a grunt.

"What?" Did he really just say that? "What the hell, Eli? I take it back. You haven't changed at all. In fact, you're still a colossal asshole."

"Oh, call off your troops," he said. "You never would have left him on your own and you know it. Vera, you've gotta know that you can do much better than being Brody's assistant."

I wanted to tell him about Brody's plan for a production company and how I was constantly troubleshooting scripts with him and helping him strategize career moves and how I was so much more than an assistant. But it didn't make a difference. None of those things amounted to career experience or opportunities.

"Yeah, because planning group activities for a ton of horny seniors is such an upgrade."

"It is," he said firmly. "Now at least your whole world won't revolve around Brody's every whim and need. More time for—writing. You're a writer, aren't you?"

I shook my head instinctively. People who wanted to be writers were often insufferable, but people who *talked* about being writers without ever actually doing it? The actual worst. Straight to jail. And me? I didn't want to be a talker. Especially when I was already failing so hard.

Eli glanced over at me for a moment and then said, "You're incredibly gifted at creating things for other people, Vera. But not everything you do has to be in service of other people."

I didn't say anything after that. He wasn't wrong, but he had no idea how easy it was for him to say the right thing versus how incredibly difficult it was for me to do it.

THE WUNDERKIND (FIRST DRAFT)
"PILOT" 10/8/07

EXT. BEACH TOWN STREET—EARLY EVENING

He's walking backward, talking too much. They are both in work uniforms. She's on her way from one job to another and is trying not to smile at Arlo.

ARLO

You're very good at pretending not to like me. It's almost convincing.

POPPY

I'm not pretending.

He laughs, because she is.

August 9, 2018
Vera S.
What does Poppy WANT?
Why is Arlo's attention so special?

THE WUNDERKIND by Vera Stein.

CHAPTER TWENTY-TWO

I stood on the edge of my bed, trying to reach the chain for the ceiling fan. When it came to my ideal sleeping conditions, I had always been a ceiling fan princess. The circulation was nice, but the sound was what really lulled me to sleep, and I'd had withdrawals while crashing with Ruby.

"Damn it," I muttered. I was about three inches too short to reach the chain. I stepped onto the edge of the footboard, testing my weight. I leaned out and up in an effort to make up those three inches, but my socks foiled the plan, and I began to slip, letting out the scream of a woman who was falling to her death.

"Vera!" Eli rushed into the room as I landed on the floor in a heap.

"Ow," I groaned, both body and ego bruised.

"Let me help you up," he said.

I rolled over and sat up against the foot of the bed. "I think I'll just stay down here for a minute."

"I'll join you," he said, and sat down beside me.

I held up my palms to examine and saw that I'd broken the skin against the hardwood floor.

Eli gently took one of my hands and examined the heel of my palm. "Any other scrapes?"

"I can feel a bruise forming on my hip, but other than that, it's just the sting of embarrassment."

He stood up and went into our shared bathroom before coming back with a first aid kit. "Let's get you cleaned up."

I rolled my eyes. "There's nothing to clean."

"So says the woman with an open wound on her hand. What kind of doctor would I be if I left you unattended?"

With a sigh, I presented my hand to him.

He went in with an alcohol swab, swiping gently against the skin.

I sucked in a sharp breath at the slight sting and instinctively pulled my hand back. But he didn't let me go, and instead brought my hand close to his mouth and blew on the scrape. His breath was cool as his bottom lip brushed my wrist, and a terrifying thrill raced up my spine.

I watched as he made no effort to pull away at the touch and, instead, concentrated on my hand for a while longer, before peering back to me. "Better?"

With a nod, I licked my lips. One of us needed to say something. To just talk. About anything.

"What were you up to today?" I asked.

He set my hand down on his thigh and searched through the extremely well-organized first aid kit. The faint orange mark from my bingo blotter still lingered on the top of his hand.

The first three buttons of his white collared shirt were undone and his black shorts showed the thick muscle of his thighs. I tried not to stare, but they were exceptional thighs.

"I had dinner and saw a movie. Something about a woman who goes on one date with every ex she's ever had. I don't know. I wasn't really paying close enough attention. Did some shopping beforehand."

"Oh. Nice." That sounded like the kind of day you would spend with a significant other. Maybe he didn't pick up on the plot of the movie because he and his mystery lady were making out like horny teenagers. *Good for them.* I forced the thought into my brain over and over again in the hopes that I would believe it.

Eli pulled out a butterfly bandage and carefully stuck it to my palm, his fingers smoothing over the edges.

His touches were so much lighter than they had been that night in Vegas. Neither of us had handled the other with care, and I liked it that way. It felt reckless and like we were saying things with our bodies that our mouths would never be capable of. But now he was so soft and careful, and it turned out I liked that just as much.

He gave my hand back to me, and I let it fall between us, my pinkie finger brushing the side of his thigh as he shifted.

I expected him to get up and leave, but instead he leaned back and tilted his head up. "The fan has a remote."

"Are you serious?"

He closed his eyes and smiled. "I forgot to show you where it was. Top drawer of your nightstand."

"Well, that's handy."

"How were your first two nights?" he asked. "You and Marlon sleeping okay?"

"Yes. Marlon, especially."

We both eyed the dog, sleeping on the floor with his limbs spread out like Superman.

"Thank you," I told him. "I can't remember if I said it or not, but thank you. I don't know if I would have made the same offer had the roles been reversed."

"I find that hard to believe. You were the one always dragging me along with you and Brody so I wouldn't sit in that room by myself. Even when I was a moody asshole."

"We really needed a moody asshole to even out the group dynamics."

"I still can't believe you're here." He set his hand on my thick thigh, his fingers managing to span the width of it.

I studied the vein that lined his forearm and then forked around his knuckles. Eli was touching me. For no reason at all. My ex-husband was touching me. And less than an hour ago, he was out with another woman.

I shook my head and reminded myself to breathe. "I didn't exactly have this scenario on my midlife vision board."

He shook his head. "Of all places? Starlight Palms. That day I saw you in Ruby's apartment, I thought I was having a stroke. You know, I used to think of you and wonder if you still looked the same way you did in my memories. And then, there you were in the flesh. And you looked exactly the same."

Eli *thought* of me. "Plus a few gray hairs and some forehead wrinkles," I said to deflect, because I didn't want these feelings. The last thing I needed was to want a person I couldn't have. And not just any person. Eli—a person who had left me before.

He sat with one elbow perched on his knee as the other hand left my thigh to push a curl out of my face. "I would do a lot of things differently."

"You look like you did pretty well for yourself in the end."

"I should never have left you in Vegas like that."

I nodded. "Yeah, me and Brody kept thinking you would come back and that you just needed space."

"Not Brody," he said. "I shouldn't have left *you*."

"It's getting late." I didn't know where this conversation was heading and with the chaos of my first few weeks here, I hadn't emotionally rehearsed how I wanted to talk about that night. How I wanted to talk about us. I knew how I felt about it, but those feelings weren't anything I could say out loud. Those feelings weren't anything I could trust Eli with.

With a sigh, he nodded and leaned toward me.

My heart stilled.

His lips pressed against my cheek, and I felt his words take shape against my skin. "Good night, Vera."

After he left, I turned off my lights and lay there staring at my now spinning ceiling fan. The bathroom light turned on, the amber glow seeping under the door to my bedroom.

The shower door creaked, and the water began to rain down. I listened to the sounds of his feet on the tile and drawers opening. The scent of cucumber melon unfurled into my room. He must have lit his candle. The shower door creaked again and then shut.

It felt suddenly humid as I was enveloped in the smell of sandalwood mixed with the cool scent of the candle. I knew that what he'd said yesterday about me deserving more than being Brody's assistant had more to do with his beef with Brody than it did with me, but it had been enough to spur me on to tinkering with my *Wunderkind* notes for a bit today. For the first time in a very long time, I felt excited about what I might create.

And now, another kind of excitement fluttered in my lower abdomen as I wondered what it might feel like to touch that doorknob and step inside that bathroom. The two of us standing under the warm spray of the showerhead until my skin had absorbed the smell of him. His fingers connecting the dots of my freckles. His lips following close behind.

My fingers dragged down the length of my stomach until they slipped under the waistband of my sleep shorts. Most of my memories of him were sour, but the few hours I spent as Eli Buckley's wife would forever be seared into my memory so permanently that it might as well have happened yesterday.

My fingers slipped through my soft, wet center, and I thought of Eli. I thought of the shortest honeymoon of all time. I thought of him in the shower and how maybe he was stroking himself right now. Just on the other side of the door. So close and still impossibly far.

My chest heaved as the shower turned off. The light from under the door flickered as he seemed to pause there for a moment before walking away.

Come in, I nearly begged. *Please come in.*

A moment later, the light from the bathroom shut off and I closed my eyes. The moment was gone.

I slipped my hand out of my shorts. I'd almost gotten off to the thought of Elias Buckley and that terrified me.

Monday felt like going back to school after a long break. Like I'd been gone for enough time to become a different person.

When I got to my office, the door was already unlocked and I immediately recognized the sequined head wrap and silk muumuu–clad person waiting behind my desk.

"You know," I told Ruby, "this office does indeed have a lock and I'm pretty sure it was in use."

She crossed her legs with her arms draped on the armrests of my chair like she was the president. "Gavin in maintenance is a big fan of *Prom Queen from the Swamp*. I've signed his entire DVD collection of my oeuvre and gifted him a few signed headshots. He was kind enough to let me into my own granddaughter's office."

I dropped my tote bag on my desk and sat in the chair across from her, bracing myself both physically and emotionally. "You know that just because I work at your senior living facility doesn't mean you can go into my locked office, right?" This felt pretty on par with working at your kid's school.

Ruby gave me a sharp, feline-like smirk. "Well, one weekend out from under my roof and you really do have a sudden sense of boundaries, don't you?"

"Sorry, sorry," I conceded. "I just want to make sure people take me seriously, and that's hard to do with you tromping into my office like you own it. Of course I don't care that you're in here, but it also feels a little like Take Your Grandmother to Work Day every day. And I know how much you hate identifying as a grandmother."

Her lip curled with offense. "Do I look like I would ever agree to work in an office without natural light?"

I held one hand up and then walked two fingers through the air. "This is you." I moved my fingers faster. "And this is you speed-walking past the point."

"How were the first few days living with Dr. Buckley?" she asked so loudly I swore I heard a group of giggling women in the hallway fall silent. "I'm curious to know: Does the good doctor prefer boxers or briefs? How does he take his morning coffee? With or without a shirt?"

I hopped up and closed the door, my cheeks flaming red. "Could you please be a little more discreet?" Though that was asking a lot of Ruby. Discretion was not something she came by easily.

"Shacking up with your ex-husband is hardly discreet. But leave it to you to steal my fun." She rolled her eyes and then cleared her throat dramatically. "Anyway, I have big news."

I held my hand to my chest and fanned myself. "I think I'm having a stress response to the thought of you and big news. Did you sell my car? Donate Marlon to a science research facility? Am I the secret love child of a politician who believes we didn't land on the moon?"

"It's a wonder you never went into acting. You're more dramatic than Susan Lucci."

"Susan Lucci was dramatic for good reason. They should do anthropology studies on what the Emmys did to that woman. So, what's the big news?"

"I've been invited to Global Horror Con in New Orleans as a guest of honor." To the untrained eye, Ruby looked cool and indifferent, but I could sense the nervous excitement thrumming there, beneath the surface.

"That's great, Rubes," I said. Ruby had done a couple handfuls of conventions over the last few decades, but the requests had certainly dwindled recently. Global Horror Con was a biggie, though.

"That's not the news," she said, clearly annoyed that I hadn't given her sufficient time for the big reveal. "They've giving me a lifetime achievement award. And it's about goddamn time that someone did! I'm not getting any younger."

"That's—that's amazing!" I leaned over the desk to hug her. Neither of us had ever been physically affectionate with each other, but this was the kind of occasion where Mom would have made a cake or at least ordered baklava from Ruby's favorite bakery down the street. It fell to me now that it was just the two of us, and the reminder sent my stomach plummeting. With Mom sick for so long, people would tell me all the time that she was out of her misery and that it was okay to be relieved and that caretaking wasn't easy. But I'd do it all again for tonight and for her to be here so that Ruby and I could fall into our usual roles—the ones we've been rehearsing for years. But instead, we are this indecipherable jumble of mother, daughter, and granddaughter.

She pulled back and primly smoothed out her muumuu. "Well, the especially good news for you is that I'm allowed to bring a guest. Isn't that lucky?"

"Me?" I asked. "You want *me* to be your guest?" The thought of Ruby and me trying to navigate the security line and boarding process at an airport was nightmare-inducing, but the fact that she wanted me to be her guest felt—

"Well, technically Hollis is going as my guest, and I've listed you as my personal assistant."

I snorted. "Well, my travel is still covered, right?"

She nodded. "Exactly! And that's what counts. They'll hold a special gala and I'll be on panels and—goddamn it, I need to go shopping." She looked me up and down, a determined spark lighting her eyes. "As do you, my dear. Badly."

"That's fair," I said, my jeans and oversize blue-and-white-striped button-down from Old Navy not really feeling very guest-of-the-lifetime-achievement-recipient-y.

"You'll really go, then?" Ruby asked, and in a rare moment, she seemed almost timid. It made me want to be there for her even more so. For her to ask point-blank like this meant that she needed me, even if she couldn't bring herself to say it.

"Of course," I told her. "I wouldn't miss it, Rubes. Plus, a free trip is definitely in my budget."

She laughed, almost surprised that I was clever enough to say something funny, and then hopped up from my chair, muumuu fluttering behind her as she left.

WELCOME
TO Fabulous
LAS VEGAS
NEVADA
LAS VEGAS
NEVADA

ELIAS BUCKLEY

SEVENTEEN YEARS AGO

TRUTH OR DARE

We'd only been in Vegas for five hours and Brody had already lost six hundred dollars of my dad's money at the roulette table while Vera and I sat at two nearby Dolly Parton slot machines, pulling the levers over and over again.

Now we were in the bowels of one of the casinos, eating New York–style slices from some Guy Fieri–branded pizza parlor while Brody chugged his beer, then finished Vera's and eventually mine.

"Let's play a game," Brody said.

"We've been playing games all night," Vera told him. "I think I'm on the verge of crashing. That drive wiped me out. I did the opening shift this morning and I barely slept last night. I got to that point in the night where it was just easier to stay awake than it would be to try to get up at four thirty."

"No one needs smoothies that early," I said.

Vera looked at me, a little taken aback that we were both in agreement or maybe that I even knew where she worked. But of course I knew. I regularly drove past Smoothie Hut just to see if she was there in the glow of the drive-through window.

She sighed. "I never see anyone before eight a.m. anyway."

"You are not fucking crashing," Brody said, his words tripping one over the other as he slung an arm around her shoulder.

I almost told him to fuck off, but then Vera giggled and dropped her head against his chest.

I'd gotten used to it. The bitter burn I felt every time they touched. Every time her body arched toward him like he was the sun on a chilly day. I wanted to know what it felt like to be her fucking sunshine, but I doubted I'd ever been anyone's light a day in my life.

He came home from one of their study sessions at the library the

Wednesday before spring break. They'd rented a private room and he said he'd kissed her. A kiss turned into making out and ended with her going down on him. I wanted to hate him for it. But when he told me, it wasn't some sort of trophy or locker room story. He was delightfully surprised and not even a little worried about what it might do to their friendship. There was no mention of him reciprocating the favor, but maybe she didn't want that. It wasn't my business, anyway.

That didn't stop me from imagining myself barging in on the two of them. But the scenario always ended there. I never knew what came next. Did I sweep her off her feet? Did I try to beat the shit out of him? What right did I even have to imagine the possibilities?

"What's the game?" I asked.

"Truth or dare on steroids," Brody said. "If you refuse your truth, you have to do whatever you're dared to do next. No exceptions. Same goes for dares."

"I've never actually played truth or dare," Vera admitted.

"Seriously?" I asked.

Brody practically jumped out of his seat. "Oh shit! We're about to conquer some virgin territory!"

Vera's cheeks warmed with a soft pink. "Truth or dare, then," she said to Brody without missing a beat.

He shrugged indifferently. "Truth."

"Tell us about the most devastatingly embarrassing thing that's ever happened to you." She grinned devilishly. "Or don't and I'll give you a dare that will set a new benchmark."

He pursed his lips and thought for a moment. "Christmas break. Last year. I was on my way back to LA and I fell asleep. Middle seat. Back of the plane. I dreamed that . . . I shit my pants. And for whatever dumb psychological reason, my body decided that dreaming about shitting my pants wasn't enough—"

"Oh no," Vera said through a gasp.

He nodded. "It was so bad they had to make an emergency landing in Salt Lake City and wait for a new plane."

"You said that was because of some kind of mechanical issue," I said, feeling slightly jealous at how easy it had been for him to fess up to something like this. He wasn't even that embarrassed! I grew up in a medical family where bodily fluids were regular topics of dinner discussion and even I was mortified on his behalf.

"Yeah, did you think I was pumped to tell everyone it was because I shit my pants?"

Vera watched him and then slowly began to nod before dissolving into a fit of giggles. "Well, Brody. You set a high bar. I guess I'm next."

He turned to her, his legs spread so that her knees were tucked nicely between his thighs as he braced his hands on the tops of her legs, one thumb stroking back and forth along the worn, thin denim of her favorite jeans that I'd seen her in so, so many times. The ones with the small bleach spot near the hem from when she'd helped us tie-dye matching jumpsuits for the Sigma Phi track-and-field day last month.

"Truth or dare?" he asked.

She inhaled deeply, a wild look in her eyes. "Dare."

"Get us kicked out of this casino."

I looked from Brody to Vera, who was such a diligent rule follower that she once waited the required fifteen minutes before class could be officially canceled for a professor who had already emailed the class to say she'd gone into labor.

She bit down on her lip and nodded repeatedly, like she was psyching herself up. "Okay, okay, okay."

"Just do a truth," I told her. "I really don't want to bail you out of jail."

But she didn't hear me. She was already standing up and storming out of the pizza place.

"Fucking yes!" Brody grabbed his half-eaten slice of pizza and pumped a fist into the air as he jogged after her.

I dropped a few bucks into the tip jar at the counter and then followed them both.

I was not nearly drunk enough for this.

CHAPTER TWENTY-FOUR

The next morning, I exited the shuttle bus with about sixteen residents in swimsuits and cover-ups. We were returning from a bikini car wash, which had been a highly requested activity. The money would be donated to some local foster care funds since there wasn't actually anything the residents needed to fundraise for. There was just a small but die-hard group determined to participate in a bikini car wash. Admittedly, our shuttle driver did most of the washing and many of the cars still had a film of desert dust when they drove away, but we didn't get any complaints.

With an hour to go before lunch, I was on my way to set up a flower-arranging class a local florist had agreed to teach when I ran right into Morgan as she turned the corner from the front offices.

"Vera," she said. "I need you on morning duty."

"Like tomorrow morning? Or this morning? And duty for what?"

She shook her head as she checked a text on her watch. "No, *mourning.* As in sad. I need you to go to a funeral."

"Um . . . do I know the deceased?"

She sighed and I could see she was getting a little impatient. "When a resident passes away, Dr. Buckley and I try to go to the funeral or wake if we can, but I'm double-booked, so Dr. B is flying solo."

"And he needs a chaperone?"

"Yes. A hundred percent yes. He says weird shit sometimes. One time, he tried to comfort a resident's granddaughter and ended up telling her about some kind of sound you make when you're dying called a death rattle. It was very much the opposite of comforting."

I nodded. We hadn't seen each other since the other night. Not that anything should be awkward. Nothing even happened. Well, except for the part where I tried to get off to the thought of Eli in the shower.

"Okay, yeah, I can go. I'll share our condolences and make sure Eli leaves his morbid chitchat at the door. When is it?"

"I need you there in thirty minutes."

"Uh, can you get my flower-arranging seminar going in the demo kitchen? I just need to grab my car keys."

"Dr. B prefers to drive. Besides, when I've driven us, he gasps like a little bitch every time I hit the brakes."

"Got it."

"Don't forget to wear your name tag, so they don't think you're some random funeral crasher."

She was gone before I could even ask why the hell someone would crash a funeral.

As Eli and I stepped inside the front door of the Trinity Grove Funeral Home, I nudged him with my elbow. "Does this count as a Dead Moms Club field trip?"

He glanced down at me from the corner of his eye with a slight smirk, before an elderly woman hobbled over to him. "Dr. Buckley, what on earth are you doing here?"

His lips spread into a warm, rehearsed smile. Not that it felt fake. Just prepared. "Clara, please accept my deepest condolences." He held a hand out to me. "From myself and everyone at Starlight Palms. This is my colleague Vera."

Clara's white hair had a slight curl and was cropped close. She pursed her trembling lips together in a closed-mouth smile. "We can't thank you enough for all you did for our Russ."

"Well, he'll be terribly missed," Eli said, and then in a conspiratorial voice, he added, "But just between the three of us, I think I'll miss having a reason to see you most of all."

Clara shook her head with a sly smile and reached up to pinch Eli's cheek before giving him a gentle slap. Then she turned to me. "This one is a damn flirt."

Her gaze drifted beyond us to the group that had just come in, and then she waved us farther inside before ducking away.

"Very smooth," I told him. "Morgan told me you needed a babysitter to contain the morbid word vomit."

"It's early yet," he said. "And Russ was a bit of a bastard. In the final hours, he kept calling his wife by his former mistress's name. He was also one of the twitchier bodies we've had. Scared the new orderly to death while we waited for the funeral home to pick him up."

"Did it feel good to get that out of your system?"

He exhaled. "God, yes."

I scanned the foyer to find a large portrait of Russ, a man who I vaguely recognized as a grandfather on a long-running network sitcom that was always on in the waiting room of the ER I usually took Mom to. "What do we do now?" I whispered to Eli.

"Well, we sit in one of the back rows for a little while and look like we're contemplating the beauty and tragedy of life and death, then we lay eyes on the deceased before we make our escape. Respectfully."

We sat in the second-to-last row of pews, thighs pressed together. I tensed, but Eli was wholly unbothered by our proximity, so I let myself relax into the warmth of his like it was the most normal thing. Like when you brush up against someone you know so well that you don't even think about it. And I wanted to punish myself for the way my pulse quickened at the slightest touch.

From where we sat, the profile of Russ's face was visible. His casket was open from the waist up. All around him were elaborate floral arrangements and stills from his time on *Family Unit*. It was one of those shows that had been on the air since before I was born and well into my college years.

Something about all of these photos of Russ felt wrong, because none of them were *him*. Nearly every photo was of a man he'd played on TV, but where was Russ? Were there wedding photos? Did he have grandkids? An obscure hobby? Had his life started and ended with a silly network TV show? Was his former mistress here? Did Clara know about her?

I had a hard time imagining what photos might surround my resting body, but the idea that a life could be captured by a few snapshots made a knot form in my chest. It was too much pressure. To be summed up in a two-hundred-word obituary and a few snapshots.

"Go time," Eli whispered as he stood.

I stepped out into the center aisle and his hand grazed my lower back as he guided me toward the front.

We approached the casket and stood there above the body. He wore a golf polo, matching pants, and one of those hats with a pom-pom on top. At least the clothing his family had chosen reflected an apparent love for golf.

"Yep," Eli whispered. "Still super dead."

I coughed back a snorting laugh. "You are wildly inappropriate."

"I see a lot of nearly dead people every day. Gotta find the jokes where you can."

We stood there in silence for a moment. After what felt like a respectful amount of time, I felt his gaze slide over me. "Ready?"

I nodded and we ducked out of the room to the foyer. We moved along the outskirts of the guests toward the exit, but just as we were about to leave, a woman in a navy blue skirt suit stepped out in front of us. "Hi there," she said. "I couldn't help but notice your name tags."

I glanced down to the Starlight Palms tag on my chest. "Oh. Right."

"I hope this is okay, but I'd love to send you back to the facility with some literature for your residents."

Eli eyed her suspiciously.

"I'm new here," she quickly explained. "I'm looking for ways to capture new clients, but, um, there's no real way to go about that without feeling like a leech." She shrugged. "But hey, everyone dies, right? And planning in advance really is the kindest thing you—"

"We'd love to take some pamphlets back with us," I said.

Eli made a grumbling noise as she stepped into the front office to retrieve a handful. "Maybe she wouldn't feel like a leech if funeral homes weren't in the business of draining the life savings from grieving families. What's the point of an upgraded casket if it's just going in the ground?"

"Is that more trauma I smell?" I asked.

"Not trauma," he said. "Annoyance."

As we walked past the guest book, I noticed Hollis bent over as she signed her name. She wore dark green slacks and a black silk blouse.

"I'll be right out," I told Eli, and he nodded.

"I hear we're going to New Orleans together," I said to Hollis.

She stood up and turned to me, her expression moving from briefly uneasy to her usual nonchalance. "Vera, so good to see you. How did you know Russ?"

"Oh," I said, "I didn't. I'm here as a Starlight Palms ambassador."

She stepped aside so the next guest could sign the book. "Right."

"And you?" I asked.

"Old rivals, you could say. We never liked each other, but we always shared a sort of respect. Despite playing a handsy grandpa, he actually looked out for the women in this business behind the camera. Even if his ego was more inflated than half the breast implants in Hollywood."

My lips parted into a slight smile. That was the kind of thing I wanted to hear about someone at their funeral. It was the sort of honest truth I hoped people would say about me one day.

Hollis cleared her throat. "Vera, you should know that I won't be going to New Orleans with you and Ruby."

I shook my head, trying to understand what she meant. "Something more important on your dance card?"

She moved half a step closer to me. "We decided to take a little break."

"Oh. I . . . I'm sorry." Ruby was definitely the kind of person you might need a break from, but she and Hollis had seemed more closely sewn since I'd arrived at Starlight Palms.

She nodded. "Would you do me a favor and check on Ruby?"

"Of course," I said. Although, I'd only seen Ruby wounded a handful of times. She tended to be a little vicious during moments like these. You approached at your own risk.

In the car, I thumbed through one of the pamphlets from the funeral home.

The outside read *End of Life Planning* and then in a smaller font: *The earlier you plan, the more control you have.* The inside broke down every possible option in broad strokes. Burial, cremation, a memory grove for natural burials, and even a burial at sea.

On the back, the last heading read: *Living Funeral.*

Say goodbye on your own terms. A living funeral is sometimes referred to as a pre-funeral or a living wake and is held while a person is still alive. It is a chance for the predeceased and their loved ones to celebrate life and ease anxiety surrounding death.

"Have you heard of this?" I pointed to the section in the pamphlet. "Living funerals?"

Eli nodded. "My mom had one, sort of. It was really just a dinner party with her favorite people and favorite food. I was dreading it, honestly. I almost didn't even go. But the memory of it outweighs the pain, I think." He shook his head like he was trying to push it back into a safer corner of his brain. "Besides, all these people get together to say nice things about you at your funeral and you don't even get to hear it. I guess it's a good option if you're not a shitty person."

"Or if there's anything to say about you at all."

"Don't worry," he said. "I have plenty to say about Vera Stein."

~~**EXT. YOU SCREAM ICE CREAM ROOFTOP-NIGHT**~~

~~*They climb up just to watch the lights.*~~

~~**POPPY**~~
~~What are we even doing?~~

~~**ARLO**~~
~~Saying hello to the moon. What if it's lonely?~~

~~**POPPY**~~
~~We have to get back to work.~~

~~**ARLO**~~
~~Not until you say hi to the moon.~~

~~**POPPY**~~
~~*(sighs and screams)*~~
~~HELLO, MOON!~~

CHAPTER TWENTY-FIVE

Eli's phone rang just as we were about to pull out of the parking lot. His navigation screen read *Brigid.* ♥

"Sorry, I better get this real fast."

He grabbed his phone from where it sat in the cupholder and bypassed the car's Bluetooth as he answered.

"Hey there," he said softly, and then after a moment, "You're okay, though?"

He nodded and then quietly sighed. "Of course. No, I get it." He paused. "Okay, I'll be there as soon as I can."

With a quick glance, he gave me a small, apologetic smile. "Yeah, I love you too."

My stomach sunk so very slowly as he hung up. I knew he had someone. But I supposed a silly, senseless part of me was holding out hope for . . . I don't even know what.

"Hey, I'm going to drop you off real fast and then I've got to take care of something," he said as he began to reverse.

"I can catch a ride back with Hollis or get an Uber back," I offered. Him dropping me off made me feel like an annoying little sister.

"No, no." He shook his head. "It's fine."

Obviously whatever he had to do, he didn't want my company, but in an effort to save time, I said, "I could just go with you if that's easier."

He bit down on his lower lip as we idled at the exit of the parking lot. "I don't want to keep you from your work."

"I'm not a brain surgeon," I told him. "Lives aren't at stake here."

He nodded. "I'll be quick."

We drove across town in the opposite direction of Starlight Palms past all the picturesque parts of Palm Springs until we arrived in an area that could only be described as normal. There was a Target with ample parking and a Chili's and a big chain movie theater with twelve screens.

Eli pulled into a Walgreens. Without a word, he ran in and quickly returned with a small bag.

I didn't know where we were headed, but I did not expect to find us parking in the third visitor spot at Los Santos High School.

"Is your girlfriend a teacher?" I blurted. It was hard to imagine Eli dating a teacher. A lawyer maybe or even another doctor. But a teacher felt . . . sweet. And if she was sweet, I'd have a hard time justifying my distaste. Which was for no valid reason already.

He turned the car off and got out. "Not a teacher," he said. "A student. My daughter, actually."

My eyes widened and my stupid mouth fell open. "Your— How do you— You have a daughter?"

"You coming in?" he asked, leaning through the still-open door.

I scrambled to open my door and followed him in through the entrance, where we were buzzed into the front office.

"Are you here for an early pickup?" asked the woman behind the counter. Her hair was jet black with white roots coming in.

"No, actually." Eli cleared his throat. "My daughter started her period and asked me to bring this to her."

He held up the bag from Walgreens and took out a small box with a menstrual cup inside.

"We have pads and tampons in the nurse's office," the woman said.

"She's a cup kind of girl," Eli said with a shrug. "It's Brigid Buckley."

As the secretary got on her phone, Eli turned to me. "As of last summer, Brigid is very eco-conscious and refuses to use disposable menstrual products."

Behind the counter, the woman covered the receiver with her hand. "The nurse said she's been free bleeding in her office for the last hour."

"Does she need a change of clothes?" he asked.

"Does she need a change of clothes?" the secretary repeated into the phone. She listened for a second, hung up, and looked to me. "Your daughter is on her way up."

"Oh, she's not my—" I began.

"Thank you," Eli said.

We waited for a moment before a girl with wild pale blond hair stormed in through the door leading to the office.

"Hey, pumpkin," Eli said like she wasn't a day over five.

Brigid was stunning, which probably meant her mom was too. She was at least five foot nine and her heart-shaped face wore full lips and wide eyes. Back when I was in school, she would have been the kind of girl who could wear pajama pants and a messy bun every day while still being everyone's number-one crush.

She hugged her dad for a millisecond as he asked, "Do you need a change of clothes?"

"No, I wasn't even free bleeding, I stuffed some toilet paper up there. And I don't get why the nurse was freaking out. It's just a little bit of blood. She whispered every time she said the word *period*, like I'm supposed to be embarrassed or something." Brigid threw her arms up and said loudly enough for everyone in the office to hear: "I'm bleeding from my vagina. My uterus is shedding its lining. Just a little PSA for anyone wondering." She took the bag from Eli. "Is this a cup?"

He nodded. "I think I got the right one."

Brigid's gaze cut over to me. "Who are you?" she asked bluntly.

"We're coworkers," I said just as Eli said, "An old friend."

She shrugged, already bored. "Well, which is it?"

"Both," Eli said.

With a nod, she looked me up and down. "I don't use disposable menstrual products. They're bad for the environment. And totally toxic."

"That's commendable," I said.

"Try telling the school nurse that. She wanted to give me a pad that was the size of a fucking raft."

The secretary gave her a pointed look. "Language."

Brigid waggled her eyebrows as Eli shook his head. "Anyway, I gotta go."

Eli gave a little laugh and leaned forward to give her a kiss on the forehead. "Tell your mother I said hi."

"She broke the pool filter," Brigid said. "She told me not to tell you."

Grinning, he ruffled her silky hair. "I'll send the pool guy out to take a look."

Brigid skipped out of the office, swinging her bag at her side.

Eli and I headed back out to the car, and I didn't know where to start. Eli had a daughter. And maybe an ex-wife. Well, *another* ex-wife. Or they could just be separated, I supposed. It sounded like she was still living at their house. Wherever that was. I guessed that helped make sense of why he chose to live in staff housing on a doctor's salary.

"You have questions," Eli said.

"A few." He didn't owe me answers, but we *were* living together. However temporarily that might be. And if he was technically married, I didn't want to complicate anything.

Eli had always been like this. He never felt the need to fill in the gaps or explain the context of his life. It was the difference between people who couldn't handle awkward silence and those who were entirely unbothered by it. It was as though he didn't need or want anyone to understand.

Brody was always the one to give me the CliffsNotes of Eli's life. Explaining his tense relationship with his father and how they had a summer house with a live-in chef and how he went to the kind of high school that had a rowing team and a library with stained-glass windows.

The fact that Eli appeared to be willing to answer my questions now felt like a trap.

"How old is Brigid?" I asked, not ready for the answers to the big questions.

"Fifteen going on twenty-eight."

"She's fiery."

He nodded, the corners of his lips lifting. "God, don't I know. We gave her my mom's middle name. Brigid, the goddess of poetry and midwives, which was fitting. Her mom is a labor and delivery nurse."

We drove through the gates of Starlight Palms as I pushed onward. "So are you two separated or . . . ?"

He shook his head. "No, no. Nothing like that. Selene and I were a one-night stand during residency. We tried to make it work once we found out she was pregnant, but—" He shook his head and left it at that.

"And she's staying at your house?"

"She's going through a messy divorce, so I gave her and Brigid the house until things settle. I'd had the apartment at Starlight Palms for when I need to be on call or if something came up in the middle of the night." With a chuckle, he added, "I didn't want to put Brigid through the trauma of watching Selene and I try to cohabitate. We've figured out the parenting game. We're good at that. But not under the same roof. The only thing we agree on is Brigid's well-being."

"Wow. I, um . . . This whole time I thought you had a girlfriend, honestly. I mean, I guess you still could, but I just figured all the late nights and—and the hair ties."

"The hair ties?" he asked.

I pointed to a couple hair ties in the cupholder with a few blond strands of hair wrapped around them.

"Brigid leaves things everywhere she goes. Like breadcrumbs."

I smiled. "We should go inside."

He looked over at me, his Adam's apple bobbing as he swallowed. "We should . . . but Vera?"

"Yeah?"

"I don't have a girlfriend."

My chest swelled, burning with stupid, stupid possibility. "Good to know."

I was buzzing from a good day at work, and I wasn't even high. Though at least half my residents were.

I had hosted a high tea with infused beverages and cakes from a local dispensary with a café. The residents turned out in their Sunday best. Huge, flamboyant hats. Seersucker suits. It was genuinely delightful. Though it wasn't until after I checked over the sign-in sheet that I realized Ruby had skipped the event despite RSVPing in the affirmative.

That night, I went back to the apartment to pick up Marlon for a walk. Well, technically, a walk and carry since he always protested after the first hundred yards or so and demanded to be held.

I headed over to Ruby's because I'd told Hollis I would check in on her, and I was also a little bit curious to find out what exactly had happened.

On my way, I stopped at Leonard's building and left one of the pamphlets from the funeral home in his mailbox with a note to check out the section on living funerals.

When I reached Ruby's, I knocked on the door and waited for her to answer.

"The Winner Takes It All" by ABBA played at full volume from inside.

That was not a good sign.

I pounded on the door more aggressively this time. "Ruby!"

After a moment, she flung the door open and then walked away without saying a word. She wore a pink-and-orange-paisley apron and pink rubber gloves and held a Windex bottle poised like a weapon.

Oh fuck, she was in a frenzy. Ruby hated cleaning. *Loathed* it. But when she was backed into a corner and her brain was too full of her own thoughts, she would do anything to distract herself, including recklessly cleaning the house. I say recklessly because not only did Ruby hate cleaning, but she was also appallingly bad at it.

Behind her, I noticed her vacuum abandoned in the living room, clearly clogged, and the oven smoking, likely from a self-cleaning cycle gone wrong.

"Vera, dear, I'm a bit busy."

"Oh, I can see that," I said, stepping past her as I released Marlon onto the floor and into the chaos.

She huffed. "Well, since you insist on interrupting, I suppose you could at least take a look at my vacuum. I probably ought to buy a new one."

I walked over and opened the canister of her brand-new Dyson to find it full of lint, dust, and probably Marlon's hair. "You can't just buy a new vacuum every time you have to empty yours."

She turned her nose up and abandoned her Windex to spray the inside of the sink with far too much foam cleaner.

First, I would help her get this disaster under control, and then I would pry.

Humming along to the best of ABBA, I dealt with the stove and then finished the rest of the carpet and even vacuumed the sofas before emptying the canister again so it would be cleaned out for her next manic cleaning spree.

As the apartment began to return to its usual state, I lowered the volume on Ruby's record player. "So I ran into Hollis today."

Ruby turned her back to me and wiped the same stretch of countertop over and over again.

"She said you two were taking a break."

Ruby paused, and then shook her head. "You can't take a break from something that never existed."

Ouch. I sat down on the couch and pulled Marlon up into my lap. "Do you want to talk about it?"

"What's there to say?" she asked as she finally turned around and removed her gloves and apron. "We spent sixty years crossing paths at the worst possible times. We made debris of each other's lives every chance we got." She shook her head and leaned against the counter with her arms crossed. "I'm a fool for spending my life loving her—mostly from afar, and now . . . finally we're here. In the place we always promised each other we would be at the end. I finally told the woman I loved her and she backpedaled out of that door faster than Ginger Rogers in heels."

It took a great deal of force not to react to the declaration of love baked into that last statement. Having meaningful, heartfelt discussions with Ruby was as rare as finding parking at a Trader Joe's. The moment it was time for vulnerability, she morphed into a moody cat who would receive affection only on its own terms.

"Why did you two spend all those years playing tag?" I asked. "You know me and Mom wouldn't have cared."

Ruby sat down on her chaise longue with her feet up and her back to me as though it was easier to say the words if she didn't have to make eye contact at the same time. "I was twenty-three and she was twenty-one the first time we kissed. She was delusional enough to think that we could work. That people wouldn't blacklist us. But I knew better. I knew no one would put me on camera again if I let it go on. She never would have made it as far as she did with me by her side."

"Rubes," I said, "you can't know that for sure."

"Well, it doesn't matter now, does it?" she snapped back. She took a moment, and then inhaled deeply. "What's done is done. I can't sit around living in a moment that's passed me by. I tried to make it right. To give her the future she'd always wanted us to have, but it's too late."

I wanted to tell her it wasn't too late and that there was still time, but I was half Ruby's age, and even I felt like it was already too late. But maybe Ruby was right. Maybe she couldn't have at eighty-two the life she'd missed out on when she was twenty-three. Even if all the puzzle pieces were there, they'd never fit back together in the same way.

"I was foolish for wanting more," she said so softly that I didn't think I was meant to hear her.

"I'm sorry," I said simply, because what else could I say? How could I possibly express how much it sucked that she'd never been with the love of her life even though she'd been standing right in front of her all along? It was the kind of heartbreak that could fill a book's worth of pages. "Let's order some takeout," I said. "And we can watch whatever you want."

"*Cats*," she said with a sniff. "I'd like to watch the 2019 feature film *Cats*."

"I thought you said that movie was an atrocity and an insult to artists everywhere."

She nodded, blowing a sigh through her nose. "Yes, but I'd like to watch someone else's train wreck right now. I find the thought deeply comforting. Besides, a hostess once gave my reservation away to Dame Judi Dench and I'll never forgive the dame or the hostess."

I smiled at that as I began to scroll through delivery options. Beneath the heartbreak, Ruby was still there.

CHAPTER TWENTY-SEVEN

Last night, I walked Marlon home and then returned to Ruby's, where we went through two and a half bottles of wine, and by the time I stumbled back to Eli's, the apartment was dark and quiet.

"Marlon," I whispered, searching for my favorite old man.

I checked under the bed and even in my closet, but I couldn't find him. A heavy dread settled in my chest as I continued to look. It was the same feeling I got any time I couldn't find him and my brain began turning to worst-case dead-dog scenarios because he is old and fragile.

"Marlon," I whispered again, but this time it came out more desperate.

Eli's door was cracked open. Slowly, I tiptoed down the hallway until I stood just at the edge of the doorframe.

It took my eyes a second to adjust, but there, curled on his side, with his bare back to me, was Eli, a sheet shucked around his waist, and nestled right behind his knees was a shameless Marlon.

I let out a shaky breath. My aging Pomeranian would live to see another day!

Marlon lifted his head, looking very smug about being alive, and I silently begged him not to bark. I really did not need Eli to wake up to find me lurking in his doorway like some kind of specter. Thankfully, Marlon plopped his head back down and his eyes immediately began to drift shut.

A very foolish part of me wondered what it might feel like to slip under the covers. Would the other side of the bed be cool? Or was Eli the type to travel across the mattress throughout the night? Would his body heat linger on the sheets as I curled beneath them?

Between Marlon and me, only one of us would ever know.

That night I slept with my door cracked just in case Marlon came to my room, but by the time I woke up, my bed was still dog-free.

It was early yet, but soon he would be barking to go outside, and I definitely did not expect Eli to take on dog dad duties. I was perfectly capable of being a strong single dog mother, thank you very much.

Walking light-footed through the apartment, I searched for Marlon in the kitchen and living room. I noticed Eli's coffee cup in the sink and his keys were gone from the usual place where he kept them on the breakfast bar. It must have been an early morning.

With no sign of Marlon, I circled back to my room, where I found the little perv tearing through my dirty laundry, likely searching out the stinkiest garment in the pile.

"Marlon!" I said. "No!"

He emerged from the heap with my oldest, granniest underwear, complete with ripped elastic.

"Drop it," I threatened through gritted teeth as I marched over to yank it out of his mouth.

But with the spryness of a puppy—or at the very least a thirteen-year-old food-motivated dog—he dodged past me and down the hallway into Eli's room, squirming through the cracked door.

"Are you fucking serious?"

Without too much forethought, I followed him down the hall and burst through the door to Eli's room. "Marlon, you gross motherfu—"

I choked on that last syllable, begging my body to backpedal. But I couldn't. My feet were stuck. I was rooted to the floor, unable to move.

Eli lay in bed, the duvet slung low on his hips as he pumped his fist. His eyes were shut, like he was trying to revisit a trapped memory, and I couldn't pull my gaze from the head of his thickened penis, the only visible part of his anatomy. My filthy imagination didn't require much else. Before I had a second to be embarrassed, my thighs clenched against the slow throb building in my lower abdomen.

Eli froze, his eyes now wide.

And then the panic hit. My body suddenly remembered how to move and I stumbled backward. "Oh my god, oh my god. I'm so sorry. I am— I'm so— I shouldn't have just barged in like that and—" I spun around so I couldn't see him and then I shook my head. "I'm—"

Behind me the sheets rustled. "Maybe knock next time." There was a slight laugh in his voice.

"Well, that's helpful. The door was open, by the way," I told him. "It was technically cracked. And your keys weren't in their normal—" Why were we having this conversation right now? Why was I arguing the technicalities of his door and car key placement? Why was I still in the same room as his erect *member*? His manhood. His velvet rod. His shaft of steel.

Fuck, fuck, fuck, fuck.

Did this make me a peeping Tom? A peeping Tammy?

"Vera." His voice was even, and if he was uncomfortable, he was doing an excellent job at hiding it.

"I'm sorry," I squeaked again, and then rushed toward the hall.

Fuck. My underwear.

I spun back around with my eyes shielded and tugged the underwear free from the vicious clutches of a very disgruntled Marlon.

"Okay, I'm going now." I rushed back to my room and slammed the door shut.

Immediately, I jumped into bed and pulled the covers over my head as if Eli and his dick were some kind of monster I could hide from. Like I was the terrified woman in one of Ruby's creature features.

Maybe if I closed my eyes and fell asleep, I would wake up in a different dimension or just die in my sleep.

EXT. CLIFF OVERLOOK—MORNING

Sitting on the hood of his car, they eat cereal out of the box.

POPPY (V.O.)

I knew he couldn't possibly be mine.
But he kept showing up like he could be.

May 23, 2021
Vera S.
For posterity's sake: Every time I decide this whole thing is shit, I read this line and think I could write a novel about it.

CHAPTER TWENTY-EIGHT

After a few moments, Marlon began to scratch at the door and whimper.
"Sorry, buddy," I said mostly to myself. "It's every mammal for themselves right now."

And then there was a knock.

Maybe I could ignore it.

"Vera?" Eli called.

Marlon continued to scratch and whimper.

"Can Marlon and I come in?"

"No," I yelled back from under the blankets. "Go away, go away, go away," I muttered.

"That was a good example of how coming in and out of each other's rooms should work, so good job setting a boundary. But seriously. You don't have to make this weird. We should talk."

"I'm not *making* this weird," I said. "This *is* weird."

"Come on, Vera."

Yes, this was weirder than weird, but I also didn't have any other immediate housing prospects. Eli and I couldn't avoid each other forever, though I could certainly try if Morgan would let me conduct my job from the safety of my own bed with the covers pulled over my head.

With a huff, I threw my blankets back and stalked over to the door.

Marlon trotted in as I opened it just a crack and then darted back under the covers. It was better under here, where I could be mortified in peace.

The mattress sunk beside me as Eli sat down. "You gonna stay under there?"

"I'd rather not make eye contact right now."

My headboard creaked as he leaned against it. A thrilling warmth unfurled from my belly button and radiated outward. The last thing I needed was to be mortified and turned on at the same time, but here we were.

"That wasn't anything you haven't seen," Eli said.

"Not in twenty years," I reminded him.

"Nineteen," he corrected. "Vera, come on. We're two grown adults sharing eight hundred square feet. Something like this is bound to happen."

"No." I shook my head beneath the covers. "It is not."

He was quiet for a moment too long and the curiosity was enough for me to lower the blankets so I could peer up at him.

As I emerged, he slid down beside me on his side and propped his head in his hand. His breath smelled like coffee, and I couldn't look at his hands without picturing his wrist disappearing under the sheets and that look of desperate arousal he'd worn on his face.

"Vera, I hate to break it to you, but I think it's safe to say that at some point in time one of us is going to be masturbating while the other person is home. We just need—"

"Speak for yourself." I bit down on my lower lip in an effort to shut myself up.

The muscle in his jaw jumped as he looked down at me from under those unfairly long brown lashes. "Vera." He said my name like he was scolding me, and holy hell, the way my body responded to *that* was absolutely godless. "If you're saying you only treat yourself to a little self-care when I'm not home, that is severely limiting your—"

I yanked the blankets back over my head to hide my violently red cheeks. "We are *so* not talking about this."

"Maybe we should, though. We could at least establish a schedule. I'd hate to barge in on your morning activities."

"I'm not— I don't—" My words erupted into a frustrated groan.

Slowly, he peeled the blankets back, so that he could see me again. I instantly regretted not getting dressed before going in search of Marlon. Whether it was from exposure to the air or the fact that my brain was currently a pornographic wasteland, my nipples had pebbled beneath my cropped black tank top. My breasts spilled out the armholes so that the curve of my chest was exposed on either side.

I lost myself in his lips as he sucked in a shallow breath. His gaze left a trail of heat from my throat and over my chest as he assessed my current clothing situation. "Vera Stein, are you saying you don't masturbate?"

"Yes," I said. "Wait. No." I shook my head, giving up on words altogether.

"Have you— You've had an orgasm, right?" His voice was even and judgment-free and so much like the calm, certain tone he used at work when talking to residents.

Despite the smooth quality of his voice, I found myself resenting him for using his patient voice on me. "If you recall, you were there for one of them." My throat felt warm and tight, the memory of us in that hotel room still so fresh and yet frustratingly distant. I sat up a little, holding my arms over my chest in a feeble attempt at modesty.

"People fake it sometimes. I was young and not nearly as adept as I am now. I guess if you'd been faking it, though, you did put on a good show."

I forgot my embarrassment for a moment, letting out a sharp guffaw. "Adept, you say?"

He leaned toward me with a dastardly smirk. "Quite."

The shape his lips took as he spoke was mesmerizing, and I felt like an absolute pervert thinking about the things I would like to do to those lips or see them do to me.

"My eyes are up here, Vera."

I threw myself back against my pillows. "I didn't fake it with you, Eli. There. Are you happy?"

"Elated," he crooned. "Smug, even."

Everything was too hot. My skin felt like it was two sizes smaller than my body and even the soles of my feet ached. "Can you just leave so we can pretend this never happened?"

"That depends," he said. "Is it going to be awkward now?"

"Well, if you won't shut up, then I'll have no other choice than for it to be awkward."

"It doesn't have to be. I don't want it to be."

"Good," I said, willing myself to believe him because I certainly didn't believe in my own ability to be at ease. "Fine."

"Fine," he echoed. "I better get ready for work."

Fuck.

Work.

I had literally forgotten that time outside of this room even existed.

"I'll be quick," he said as he got up and strode out of the room. "Then the bathroom is all yours."

"Thanks," I told him, and finally pulled the blankets back over me as he stood up and began to walk away.

"My pleasure."

I waited until he had crossed the threshold of my doorway before I decided to torture him with a fraction of what he'd just put me through.

"Eli?"

He paused, his hand gripping the top of the doorframe. "Yes, love."

Oh god, the core temperature of my body could not currently handle a pet name, but somehow, I found it in me to push past the horny desperation raging inside of me. "I'm more of an evening girl. Helps me fall asleep."

He froze for a moment, eyes wide and unsated, and then a placid doctor persona smoothed over his features. "I'll take that under consideration."

I listened as he walked down the hall and his door clicked shut. The moment he was out of earshot, I threw the blankets over my head again and let out a muffled scream into my pillow.

WELCOME
TO Fabulous
LAS VEGAS
NEVADA
LAS VEGAS
NEVADA

ELIAS BUCKLEY
SEVENTEEN YEARS AGO
PUBLIC DISTURBANCE

Vera marched with purpose into the casino. She wove through slot machines and poker tables, like she knew just what she was looking for.

Brody skipped behind her looking like some sort of disturbed sidekick.

Then she stopped abruptly and took a few deep breaths before turning back to us. "Be ready to run."

"Oh shit!" Brody bounced forward as he followed her again.

I stayed close behind, suddenly thankful that I'd remained sober.

She walked directly into the sports bar, where crowds of viewers teetered on the edge of their seats, most of them likely to have big money riding on their chosen sporting event. Vera stopped short behind a huge, hulking beefcake with a shiny bald head. He wore a fitted white button-up and black slacks that clung to his muscular thighs. A gold chain sat snug around his veiny neck. The man was a walking warning label for steroid abuse.

"I don't like where this is going," I said, but Brody wasn't listening.

In an act of unhinged bravery, Vera tapped on the man's shoulder.

He turned around, obviously annoyed that someone had the nerve to touch him.

It took a second for him to look down, and it was obvious that he did not expect to find Vera Stein there in her jeans, vintage Pepperdine T-shirt, red cardigan, and Converse.

"What's her name?" Vera yelled. "What's her name, Bobby?"

"Who the hell is Bobby?" the man asked, his friends all leaning in for the show.

Vera pointed to the men and handful of women behind him, all dressed for a night of clubbing. "Oh, so you're not just lying to me? You're lying to all of them too?"

"Tyler, what's this about?" asked a woman a few feet behind him.

The man quickly went from panic to rage. "Lady, I don't know who you are or what you're on, but—"

"You don't know the mother of your own children?" Vera screeched.

I turned to Brody, his eyes full of glee and jaw practically on the floor, and that's when I saw the security guards starting to fill in. "Uh, it might be go time," I said.

Brody looked around with a childish giggle and then nodded before we both stepped closer to Vera. But then she grabbed a beer from the nearest table and splashed it right into the guy's face.

"You fucking bitch!" the man roared and surged forward without any sort of compunction about going after a girl.

Okay, this was about to get bad. Don't get me wrong. I was impressed. But I didn't think I could fight off this guy if it came down to it. The best Brody could do was a convincing stage punch and I came from a family full of insured hands.

I grabbed Vera's arm and she spun around, her eyes full of adrenaline and a hint of fear. "Come on," I told her, tilting my chin back to the security guards.

With barely a thought for Brody, I pulled her behind me as we snaked through the crowd. Hopefully we would get lost in the swarms of people. I knew these places were covered in cameras, but maybe a bookish-looking girl in a cardigan causing a scene with some guy who looked like a walking mug shot would be low on the priority list.

I glanced over my shoulder to see Brody splitting off toward the exit and a group of security guards on his heels.

"This way," I told Vera.

Her cheeks were flushed and she held a hand to her chest, constantly checking behind us. "Oh my god, oh my god, oh my god. I thought about punching him, but that felt way more like assault and then I couldn't remember if your thumb is supposed to be inside or outside of your fist."

"Outside of the fist," I told her as we ducked into a small souvenir shop off the lobby.

"Where's Brody?" she whispered as I pulled her behind a rack of silk jackets with the *Welcome to Las Vegas* sign embroidered on the back.

"He made a run for the exit, but he had a few guards on him, so we'll have to meet him out there in a few."

"Whatever happened to leave no man behind?" Vera asked frantically as she peeked her head over the rack.

"I don't think we agreed to that in advance. Besides, you're the one who assaulted a guy. For all they know, Brody was just an interested bystander."

"It was a splash of beer!" she quipped back.

"Can I help you two?" the clerk asked with her arms crossed. Her white-blond perm formed a nest on the top of her head and her tattooed eyebrows had faded from black into a dark bluish green.

"No, we're fine," I said. "Just playing hide-and-seek with some fr— Fuck!" I dropped down to the ground and took Vera with me.

"What the hell?" she asked.

"Your baby daddy is out there looking for us."

She rose up on her knees to sneak a glance, but I yanked her back down again.

"I don't tolerate shenanigans," the clerk said as she tapped her long red fingernails on the glass countertop. Then she turned to a new customer. "Hello there, young man."

That's him, Vera mouthed.

"Can I help you find something? Or someone?" the woman asked, her tone nothing short of devious.

The man made some kind of grunting noises in response.

I scrambled for my wallet and took out my credit card. The same card my mother told me to melt tonight. I was about to light it on fire.

I held up the card until I caught the clerk's attention.

She looked to me, her eyes bored and lazy.

With a finger pressed to my lips, I pointed to the glass case full of overpriced shitty-ass crystal souvenirs. "Get rid of him," I barely whispered. "And I'll buy it all."

In front of me, Vera's eyes went wide and she tried swatting my card-carrying hand down.

I took the finger from my lips and pressed it to hers. Her breath was warm on my fingertip and I had to force myself not to let my finger trace her lips.

"Well, if you don't need anything," the woman said, "I'm closing up for the night."

After a torturously long moment, the man huffed a thank-you and left.

The woman raised an eyebrow as she walked over to us with her hand held out. "Time to pay up, handsome. I get a commission on everything that's in a locked case."

I relinquished my card and decided that if we didn't get our asses beat or arrested, this was worth every penny.

"Would you like me to Bubble Wrap everything?" she asked.

"Oh, I'm not keeping it. Give it away for all I care."

She gave me a slightly confused look and then nodded. I had to assume that working in Vegas, this was one of the least weird things she'd ever seen.

I gave the keychain display next to the counter a quick spin and grabbed a plastic poker chip with *Viva Las Vegas* stamped onto one side.

"Don't want to forget the time I went toe-to-toe with a Goliath-shaped human?" asked Vera as she hovered behind me.

"Oh, please trust that the last thirty minutes have been burned into my brain for the rest of my life."

When the clerk read the total, Vera balked. "You can't spend that kind of money on—" She turned to the clerk. "No offense—this crap."

The woman was unbothered. "Wouldn't be the first time someone blew their money in this place."

Before we left, Vera asked if she could keep one of the crystals and chose a small die with *Las Vegas* engraved on the side.

There were still some security guards milling around the perimeter, but by the time we stepped outside of the store, the crowds had calmed and thinned.

"Take off your cardigan," I told Vera. "Just in case."

She did so without arguing and followed me as we walked at a normal pace toward the exit.

When we walked past a security guard, she took my hand and tucked her head against my chest so he didn't see her. It was fake. It was make-believe, but holding her this close felt all too real. When we were in the clear, I didn't let go.

The moment we stepped outside onto the strip, she broke away from me and searched for Brody. We didn't have to go far.

The back seat window of an old white limo slowly rolled down to reveal Brody with a glass of champagne in one hand. "Your chariot," he said.

Vera laughed as the driver got out and opened the door.

"Eli, pay the man!" Brody called.

My nostrils flared as I reached for my wallet again. This time in search of cash.

"A hundred bucks for a thirty-minute joyride up and down the strip," the driver told me. "Your friend already agreed to it."

I fished a few twenties out of my wallet and handed them over. "Of course he did."

Brody wasted no time pouring us each a glass of champagne before turning to Vera. "Technically, Vera, my dear, you failed because you didn't get kicked out."

She sputtered and nearly threw her champagne in his face, but then Brody began to pet her shoulder. "But that was the ballsiest thing I've ever seen, so you get a pass. However, since you didn't technically complete your dare, I retain the right to serve up the next truth or dare."

Vera rolled her eyes and threw her head back against the seat before downing her champagne in one go.

"Eli." Brody said my name like it was a challenge. "Truth or dare."

I weighed my options for a moment and decided they were both equally bad. "Truth."

He nodded dutifully. "Good sir, what was the last thing you yanked your wank to?"

Vera's eyes widened and the apples of her cheeks turned pink as she opened the second bottle of cheap screw-top champagne.

I had to stop looking at her.

Okay. My options were minimal. I could lie. I could just fucking lie, and say that I hadn't gotten off this morning to the image of Vera's bra strap sliding down her shoulder and what it might feel like to hook my finger through the light pink strap. I was coming in my hand in a matter of moments. Over a bra strap. I was pathetic.

I definitely could not say that out loud. But Brody had told the truth and Vera had nearly started a riot. So I couldn't bring myself to lie as much as I wanted to.

"What the hell kind of question is that? Dare."

Brody shrugged and swirled the champagne in his glass simply because I was pretty sure he'd seen someone on TV do that with a glass of wine before. "Hmmm . . ." His eyes roamed, searching for inspiration. After a second, his whole face lit up and he snapped his fingers. "I dare you to marry Vera."

"No," I said. "Fuck you. No." What was he playing at? He was the one who had made out with her and more. What kind of mind game was this? Or was he just that wasted?

Beside me, Vera choked on her bubbles.

"I don't know what to tell you, man. You had your chance to answer your truth and you chose dare. This is the dare."

"This isn't a dare. This is a legally binding contract."

Vera hiccupped and quietly chimed in. "I did almost get arrested."

"Exactly!" Brody said. "Vera dumped a beer on that guy. And you can't walk down an aisle so some dude dressed as Elvis can pronounce you man and wife?"

I turned to Vera. She had to see how messed up this was. "This isn't Vera's dare," I said. "It's mine. I hardly think it's fair to drag her into this. I'm not going to ruin her first wedding just for your stupid game."

"You act like I believe in the sanctity of marriage or something," Vera murmured.

I shook my head and threw my hands up. "How am I the only sane person here?"

I could not marry Vera Stein. That only ended in disaster. I already wanted to strangle Brody when the three of us were together, despite the fact that I didn't actually hate him. I just hated him for her. And if she and I got married tonight—even if it was just a dare—and then she went back to him afterward, I would fucking snap.

"It's only a silly dare," she said. "Can't we just immediately file for divorce or something?"

"It's called an annulment," I told her.

Brody bobbed his head to the music as he drained the rest of the second bottle. He seemed to think my fate was determined and now it was simply a matter of time.

"Unless you think it's going to be some kind of scandal for you," Vera said softly, worrying on her lower lip. I wondered if anyone had ever nipped at those lips before. "I'm definitely not the kind of girl that people like your parents approve of." Her words ran together, the champagne doing its work. "Wouldn't want to piss off Daddy."

Was that really what she thought? That the only holdup here was the fear of shame? I leaned forward across the back of the limo to knock on the divider and the driver slid the glass open. "Take us to the nearest wedding chapel."

"My babies are getting married!" Brody howled as he rolled down the window. "I'm a proud mama!"

CHAPTER TWENTY-NINE

After the coldest shower I could handle, taking Marlon for a short walk, and downing two cups of coffee, I set off to the main building, where Leonard was already waiting outside of one of the meeting rooms to host his bimonthly writing workshop.

He sat perched on the little stool that popped out of this particular cane he sometimes used. "I thought you forgot about me."

"I could never," I said as I speed-walked past him to open the door. "I'm going to grab the coffee and pastries," I added as he ambled inside.

When I returned with the cart from the cafeteria, I parked it in the corner of the room and helped him place at every seat character questionnaires that he'd asked me to print.

"Did you see the pamphlet I left in your mailbox?" I asked as we sat down, waiting for residents to trickle in—hopefully. When I'd gone through all the activity attendance records for the last year, I'd noticed that attendance had dwindled over the last few months, which was technically fine since this was a resident-led activity and not planned by me. But I felt bad for Leonard.

"I did," he said thoughtfully. "Seems like a lot of trouble to go to just to have your ego stroked."

"I think a living funeral could be great, actually." Even if it sounded a little bit like my own personal nightmare. "You've already done all the planning," I said as I tore at the edge of my pain au chocolat. "You could have the best of both worlds. The funeral you've spent so much time planning and then, when the time really comes, your green burial."

Leonard held his hand to his ear like he was on the phone. "I'm so sorry," he said. "My service is awful."

Just then an orderly wheeled in a woman from one of the assisted-care floors. Her eyes were far away and glassy.

"This is Wendy," the orderly said loudly, but the woman didn't flinch. "Her grandson said she worked in the writers' room on *Star Trek* and I thought she might like to sit in on this. I'll be back in an hour. Ring the patient care station on floor four if you need any help with her."

"Sure," I said with a nod. "Hi, Wendy. Thanks for joining us today."

Her vacant gaze held steady, and her hands lay in her lap like she was a doll that had been posed.

"Long time no see, Wendy," Leonard said, and I could hear a hint of sadness in his voice.

"You two know each other?"

"Small town, right, Wendy?" He winked at her.

The woman's lips twitched.

I liked having the assisted-care residents come down for activities, but I hoped someone else would show up, because I couldn't leave Leonard here to lead a workshop for a nonverbal woman who might require additional help.

I checked the time on my phone. The program started six minutes ago and it was still only the three of us.

I'd managed to avoid Leonard's writing workshops up until now, but it seemed that my streak ended here. Maybe this would give me a reprieve from the next few meetings, and, besides, my brain needed a distraction, because currently it was a horny wasteland.

With a sigh, I rolled my chair up to the table. "Well, what's on the docket today, Leonard?"

His eyes brightened a little as he realized that after his many invitations, I was finally sitting in on his workshop.

He cleared his throat. "Well, today, we're diving into character. For some writers, the story starts with the pitch or the plot and then for some, it starts with the character. Whichever approach you take, both elements are necessary. Take a go at this character survey to start cooking with grease. I wrote it myself and used it for nearly forty years."

I stared down at the page of questions. Many of them were basic, like name, age, location, and hobbies. But some asked you to dig a little deeper. *What's hiding under your character's bed? If they could have dinner with any dead person, who would they choose?*

Wendy watched the window but seemed to be happy enough where she was, so without any remaining excuses, I focused on the page in front of me.

I'd filled out tons of things like this in college and had extensive character sketches for the cast of *The Wunderkind*, so it felt silly to rehash a character I already knew.

"Something on your mind?" Leonard asked.

I looked up from my paper. "I just . . . There's this project I've been working on for—god, almost twenty years . . . and I need to go back to it, but I don't know where to start."

"It's only an exercise, Vera. Not every creative penny must be spent on the big, serious work. You can just have a bit of fun." He laughed to himself. "I won't tell."

After a moment of thought, I pressed my pencil to the paper and decided to make something up. Just for fun.

First name: Josephine (Joey for short)
Last name: Lynn
Job: mail carrier
Hobbies: calligraphy, online poker
Currently residing: Savannah, Georgia
Originally from:
Under their bed is: a box of unsent letters
Age: fifty-two
Body type:
Hair color/type:
Eyes: Brown
Height:

Dinner with any dead person: Princess Diana or her first husband
Scent:
Tattoos or piercings: the white tree of Gondor from Lord of the Rings on the top of her foot
Astrological sign: Cancer
Special features: birthmark shaped like a paw
Goals:

"Okay, time's up," Leonard said.

I looked up, blinking with my pencil still hovering over one of the many lines I'd left blank. According to my phone, I'd been noodling over the character survey for almost twenty minutes.

"Come up with anything good?" asked Leonard.

I thought for a moment before answering. "The potential for good? Sure. Actually good? Unlikely."

We spent the rest of the hour going over our character sheets and imagining all sorts of possibilities. *Is Josephine an empath? Did she kill her ex-husband? What if he was haunting her? Are ghosts real in this world? Who are the letters for?*

We talked for so long that we didn't even make it to Leonard's character survey, but he didn't seem to care even a little bit.

When Wendy's orderly came back, she took a cinnamon roll with her and I helped Leonard pick up the rest of his sheets and pens.

"You coming back next time?" he asked.

"I think this might have been a onetime thing for me."

"You said you had a script, right?"

"Yeah. I lost the file and it probably wasn't working anyway." I almost threw my survey away, but I hesitated as I hovered over the trash can before folding the paper and putting it in my back pocket.

"You know, your work is more than a file. Years ago, when we were on typewriters, you were fucked if you lost a page or even a whole stack. But you might find that losing it and starting over again is a blessing. A clean slate. Or hell, you could just write something new."

"Maybe one day."

"You'd think working at a place like this would teach you not to put so much faith in 'one day.'" He huffed, his frustration growing.

"All right, all right," I said, trying to lighten the mood. "You've inspired me, okay? Are you happy?"

His bushy brows rose with delight as he stood up with the help of his cane.

"So are we throwing a funeral?" I asked.

"That depends. Are you gonna write me something I can read?"

I shook my head. "I didn't say this was a negotiation."

"Do you really think I should do this living funeral thing?" he asked.

"I do."

"Well, I think you can't be a writer if you don't write."

Ouch. "I never said I was a writer."

"No, but you wanted to be once. Didn't you?"

That sunk in for a moment. The thought of Ruby the other night was fresh on my mind. All the things she wished she would have said or done. My own grandmother, who I was certain would never in her lifetime own up to regretting anything. "I'll book the community room for you," I finally said. "You choose the date and time. And I'll . . . I'll see about the writing."

"Chop, chop," he said as he put his papers back into his Louis Vuitton folio.

At lunch, I thought about searching for Eli. Surely we should talk about what happened.

But maybe we didn't have to. Maybe he was right and it didn't have to be awkward. I wasn't foolish enough to think that it could have been the beginning of something bigger, but the thought was nice. Going to him now, though . . . that would just be desperate. I didn't want to scare him away or make this into something it wasn't.

I opened a blank document on my work computer. I didn't even have the proper software to write a screenplay. But I guess if Leonard could rough it on a typewriter all those years, I could live without my snazzy formatting software.

The cursor flashed on beat with my pulse.

Everyone had to start with a blank page, right? I'd gotten that far. That was something.

Forty-five minutes later, the only thing I had to show for it was the design I'd traced in my hummus with a pita chip, my own personal Zen garden.

I had just a few minutes before I had to go set up for the knickknack swap meet I had scheduled for this afternoon, so I began to type.

Dear Leonard,

You asked me to write something.
So, SOMETHING.
To be continued . . .

Sincerely,
Vera

~~**EXT. HER HOUSE-MORNING**~~

She finds a note on her car. It says: "I talked to the moon last night. The big disco ball in the sky. She said hi."

November 8, 2021

Vera S.

I would join a cult dedicated to the big disco ball in the sky.

CHAPTER THIRTY

"What kind of dog name is Marlon?" Brigid asked as she lay on her stomach eye to eye with Marlon, who was stretched out on the area rug.

"That was his name when I rescued him."

I'd spent the last few hours on the couch watching and rewatching iconic scenes from some of my favorite movies, searching for something that excited me. Or even something to flat-out steal. *The Wunderkind* had lived so permanently in my head that I was having a hard time finding inspiration beyond it or even imagining myself reaching the finish line on another project.

It had been two weeks since the incident with Eli, and he seemed to be doing everything in his power to not make it awkward—including being too nice, which then actually felt a little awkward. The only signs of discomfort were when we touched. The other day, I accidentally backed up into him while I was emptying the dishwasher, and the man *flinched.*

I spent two hours in bed that night replaying the moment over and over. And then out of frustration, I took myself to bone town and fell asleep with my hand still between my legs. Despite my hard-fought orgasm, I woke up just as unsatisfied.

It was Friday night and Leonard's living funeral was scheduled for two weeks from Thursday. Once he reserved the community room, he sent me a mildly threatening note on some very lovely personalized stationery saying that he would no-show to his own funeral if I didn't give him something to read by the night before.

I'd already watched *Gone in 60 Seconds*, *Notting Hill*, and *The Family Stone*. Now, I was on to *My Best Friend's Wedding*, which was way more sad than I remembered.

"I don't get it," Brigid said. "Julia Roberts is obviously superior. The blond is such a pick-me girl."

"Cameron Diaz," I said. "And I don't know what a pick-me girl is."

She rolled over to her back. "You just know it when you see it."

Marlon pawed at her hair and pounced. This was the most spry I'd seen him since he ran off with my dirty underwear two weeks ago.

Brigid lazily scrolled through her phone and without looking up asked, "So how long have you been hooking up with my dad?"

I choked on a swig of sparkling water and fumbled to recover. "Uh, since never."

"You're the same Vera he married in Vegas, right?"

I closed the notebook that I'd been taking notes in . . . most of which were just doodles of flowers and stick figures holding knives because that's how the prospect of writing made me feel. I paused the TV, leaving Rupert Everett mid-song during the iconic "I Say a Little Prayer for You" scene.

"That was a long time ago," I told her. It was hard to imagine Eli telling anyone about our short-lived marriage. It felt like the kind of thing that was meant to be kept secret. Surely, he was embarrassed by it all. I mentioned it once in front of Brody and he turned into a brick wall, only saying what a stupid idea it had been. Tess knew, but that was it. If Eli had told his mom and now his daughter too, who else knew? What was there even to talk about? I supposed it was a good story for a party or two truths and a lie.

"I found a photo of you two at his house when I was in middle school, so yeah, I pestered him until he told me the story. It's not a big deal or whatever. Marriage is a sham and, like, a total societal construct. I guess it's pretty cool that you guys made a joke of it."

"Yeah," I said as I hit play again on Rupert Everett. "A real joke."

"Have you heard from my dad?" she asked.

I checked my phone, but no messages from Eli. He was supposed to take Brigid driving tonight since she'd just gotten her learner's permit, but one of our residents had a big fall today. When they got to the hospital, they were having some cognitive issues, so he went up there to check in on them. It was supposed to be a quick in-and-out trip, but Brigid had been here for long enough that I went ahead and made us artichoke and goat cheese pasta.

"Nothing yet," I told her. "But I'm sure he'll be back soon."

She tossed her phone under the coffee table, the boredom seeping off her. "It's fiiiine. Cars are ruining our environment and communities anyway."

"So if your dad buys you a car for your sixteenth birthday, you're going to say no thanks?"

She smirked. "Well, if he'd already bought it, I wouldn't say no. That would just be wasteful."

"Totally," I said. "Strong logic."

We finished *My Best Friend's Wedding* as we shared the last of a pint of ice cream, and by the time we were done, Brigid was yawning and practically using Marlon as a pillow.

"Is your mom coming to get you?" I asked.

She shook her head. "She doesn't get home from work for a few more hours."

"You want to wait for your dad? You can always sleep here."

"Or maybe you could give me a ride home and I could use this as a chance to guilt him into a pair of Golden Gooses?"

"I don't know what those words mean, but yeah, sure. Let me grab my keys."

"Can I drive?" she asked. "Legally, I'm allowed to with an adult in the car."

"This feels like a trick," I said as we made our way out to the parking lot. "Besides, unlike your dad's electric car, mine takes regular old gasoline. I wouldn't want to sully your eco reputation."

She rolled her eyes and held a hand out for my keys. This was probably not a good idea. Eli might be mad. And I didn't even know her mother. But for reasons I was not willing to confront, I really, really wanted Brigid to like me.

I dangled the keys in front of her. "Which side is the gas?"

"The right," she said. "Brake is on the left. I'll stop and look both ways at every stop sign and I'll only take residential streets home."

"Oh good," I said. "More pedestrians for us to murder."

She squinted, her brow furrowed just like I'd seen Eli do so many times when he got the joke but didn't think it was especially clever. He made you earn every laugh, and it seemed that Brigid did too. "Are you just eternally worried? Is that exhausting?"

I dropped the keys into her open palm. "Terribly."

We got in the car, and Brigid adjusted the seat to her liking, then buckled her seat belt and flipped through the radio until she found the local top one hundred station that was currently playing "all your favorite TikTok hits."

As we set off down some back roads that seemed to take the long way around downtown, Brigid rolled the windows down and consistently went five miles under the speed limit. I wasn't going to complain. The streets were relatively quiet, so I rolled my window down too, and okay, fine, I sort of felt like the cool girl I never was.

Eli's house was only a short ten-minute drive away and was at the center of a neighborhood full of mid-century modern gems. Brigid pulled into a driveway in front of a sprawling ranch with a pitched A-frame. Warm lights lit the breeze-block wall surrounding the entryway.

"You're sure you're going to be okay here by yourself?" I asked as she pulled up the parking brake like a pro.

With a death stare, she said, "Thanks for letting me drive your car." She opened the door and stood, slinging her backpack over her shoulder. "Just don't tell my mom, okayyy?"

"Brigid! Seriously?"

She turned around with another eye roll, but this time she wasn't annoyed. "I'm kidding, I'm kidding! But maybe don't say anything just in case. See you around, Vera! Oh, and by the way, you have my approval to hook up with my dad."

"Oh . . . um, thanks?"

"You're welcome!" she sang.

When I got back to the property, I pulled up to the security gates, but Victor, who worked most nights, didn't automatically let me in. He leaned out the window of his little hut and pointed to a black Ferrari SUV that I immediately recognized.

Brody stood leaning against the hood with his arms crossed. He wore black jeans and a white T-shirt that stretched across his biceps. I didn't feel the usual fluttery feelings, though. Instead, I felt a distinct sense of dread.

When he noticed me, he gave me a little wave.

"Fuck."

"That guy says he's here for you, but I can't let him in without your permission." Victor eyed me carefully. "If you don't want him around, I'm happy to be the bad guy."

I shook my head. "It's fine. Let him in."

Victor gave me a salute as he opened the gates and then waved Brody in.

I pulled up enough for him to file in behind me. As he got in his car and drove forward, I gave myself exactly thirty seconds to hold my hands over my face and silently scream with my mouth closed. How did he even know I was here? Surely he knew by now that I'd lied about the screenplay. What if he was here to get his bedding back? That would at least be simple, if humiliating.

He parked beside me in what was technically Eli's spot. I almost asked him to move, but I didn't plan on letting him stay long.

"You don't answer your phone anymore?" Brody asked the minute he got out of his car, like he'd been holding in that sentence for the entire drive.

I walked up to the apartment door and shook my head. "Can we please not do this outside?"

With his fists clenched at his sides, he followed me inside. Marlon blinked a few times before charging at his ankles. Brody scooped him up and tucked his squirming body against his chest like a football. "We didn't even get to say goodbye," he said to Marlon.

"I am sorry about that," I conceded.

I tossed my keys onto the coffee table and gathered up the decimated bowls of ice cream I'd left out when I took Brigid home. "What are you doing here, Brody?"

Gently, he set Marlon down on the couch. "What are *you* doing here, Vera? Everything was *fine*." His voice dropped as he added, "*We* were fine. And then I left for Scotland and you disappeared. What the fuck? We've known each other for twenty years and you just *ghosted* me."

I chewed at the cuticle around my thumbnail. "How did you find out where I was?"

"Don't get mad—"

"Brody, nothing good ever starts with the phrase *don't get mad*."

He rolled his eyes. "It was Tess. It wasn't her fault. She was toasted at the after-party for *Revenge Is a Girl's Best Friend*. She never goes to those things and she was really letting loose. I figured if anyone knew where you were, it would be her. She told me you were out here with Ruby and that the sale of the script fell through."

"That fucker." I leaned against the breakfast bar, my cheeks flaring with anger at my best friend for selling me out. At least she had the good sense to lie about my screenplay.

"But that can't be the only reason you left, right?" He stepped toward me, drawing me closer with a hand on my waist.

My breath caught. This felt . . . comfortable. Easy.

But not intoxicating. Normally when Brody touched me, I was lost to the moment. Whether it was time or distance, for the first time ever,

I was able to slide a slim partition between my feelings for him and this moment. I wondered if even unbeknownst to him, Brody was just playing another part when it came to me. The part that would satisfy me and lull me into acquiescence so that I could play my own part as the Vera he needed.

His other hand framed my face, a manicured thumb caressing my cheek. Oh, but I *did* like that. My head tilted into his touch and my chest bloomed with warmth as every logical thought left my brain.

"Come back, Vera. Everything is a mess without you."

The cloudy haze cleared, and ah, there it was. "But are *you* a mess?" I asked softly. "Or is your professional life a mess? Why would you want me to come back when getting rid of me was part of the business plan anyway?"

His forehead creased for just a moment before realization hit him. He cleared his throat. "You have to know that I was never going to follow—"

"Did you notice someone parked in my spot?" Eli asked as the front door swung open.

I could practically see the inner workings of Brody's brain right there in his brow line as he placed that familiar voice. With his hand still on my waist and his other hand cradling my cheek, he glanced over his shoulder to see Eli, who looked dead tired. But not so tired that he didn't have the energy to grit his teeth and shake his head.

"No," Eli ground out. "Get out."

I pushed Brody back and stepped out of his reach. "Brody was just leaving."

"Uh, like fucking hell I am," Brody shot back. "I'm here to see Vera," he said to Eli. "Definitely not you." He turned back to me. "What the fuck is he even doing here?"

"Vera can see you if she wants to. But not in my apartment."

Well, that was convenient. It's our apartment until I invite Brody in and then the place is Eli's again.

"What's going on?" Brody asked, turning to me in disbelief. "Wait. Do you two live together? Are you two a thing? My god, Vera. You can't be serious. This asshole?"

"He's not an asshole," I said.

"I sort of am," muttered Eli.

"Not helping," I told him. "Brody, let's talk outside."

He threw his arms up like I'd seen him do so many times when he needed me to come and fix something. A publicist he didn't want to fire himself. A costume that he didn't like. A company that stopped making his favorite undershirts. (Yes, really.) "You just told me to come inside!" he said.

"And now I'm telling you to go *outside*." My voice was firm and unyielding. It was a tone I'd used plenty of times on behalf of Brody, but never directed at him.

Eli stood with his arms crossed just in front of the door, so that Brody would have to squeeze past him, which was very childish. But then in an equally childish move, Brody let his shoulder ram into Eli's as he walked by.

A vein in Eli's neck twitched, but he didn't move.

"I'll be right back," I told him.

"I can make him leave," Eli said quietly. "Just say the word."

I shook my head. "I'll be right back," I said again. "Can you please take a breather? This whole macho energy is not helping."

"Sorry for not being more chill about seeing that fucking piece of shit inside my house with his hands—" He inhaled deeply, his nostrils flaring. "Never mind."

I had to fight every urge to ask him to continue and lean into every animalistic tendency and describe in detail what it felt like for him to see me with Brody.

But then he sunk down onto the couch and closed his eyes. "Just go."

CHAPTER THIRTY-TWO

"Let's get out of here, Vera," Brody said as he opened the driver's-side door and then motioned to me expectantly. "Get your shit. Get Marlon. Let's go home. I'll even have someone come out and drive your car back. We can talk things out on the way back to LA."

"What?" I stood on the sidewalk, my feet so heavy they felt like they might sink into the concrete at any moment.

He slammed the car door shut and walked back over to me. "I know you lied about the script, okay? And I don't care. I can explain about the restructure in the car if you'll just give me the chance, but first come back with me. Let's get you out of this place. What are you even doing here with all these old people? It's depressing as hell, honestly."

Was this really it? The moment I'd always dreamed of when Brody wanted me. The moment when he would pick me and sweep me off my feet. And I could only describe it as . . . disappointing.

"What do you want, Brody?" My voice broke. "Which Vera is it that you're trying to get back? Your assistant who saves your ass? The one who you planned on firing to trim the fat from your payroll? Or is it the friend who keeps your secrets and never lets you feel alone? How about the girl you've slept with for years but have never taken on a date? Take your pick."

I balled my fists to stop my fingers from trembling. Somewhere deep inside of me, I thought I'd always have Brody. I might never have him in the way I'd wanted him for all those years, but I could always be his

Vera who saved the day and remembered he was allergic to pineapple and that he liked to stock up on old iPhones from eBay because he missed the home button.

His face twisted with confusion, and that angered me even more. "I don't know what you want me to say, Vera. You want a raise? You want me to help circulate your script? We can talk about all those things and . . . and all the other stuff too. I know this feels complicated. But it doesn't have to be." He pointed back and forth from me to him. "We work, Vera. And yes, I didn't appreciate you like I should have. I shouldn't have even entertained letting you go. We can talk about—"

"You need to go," I said too softly. There was no more use in fighting.

"What?"

"You need to go," I repeated again with assurance. Whatever we had become wasn't worth fighting for. "You need to go back to LA, Brody."

He pointed to the door of Eli's apartment. "Whoever you think he is, you're wrong. He's always looked down on you, Vera. On both of us. You have to know that."

"This isn't about you or him," I told Brody. Especially when neither of them was even capable of being what I wanted. "It's about me."

He paused for a long moment, then nodded to himself. "Please answer next time I call. This conversation isn't over. It can't be." My heart pulsed erratically in my chest as he got into his stupid expensive car and I watched him drive away.

I hardly registered my body walking back inside until I saw Eli pacing in front of the couch.

"You're leaving, aren't you?" His voice was quiet. Wounded. Resigned. "Just tell me and get it over with." His hair was a mess, like he'd taken out all of his stress on it. "I shouldn't be surprised. I knew it was a matter of time and that you'd eventually go back." He continued to pace, and I think this was the closest thing to panic I'd ever seen Eli get.

I stepped into his path and wrapped my fingers around his forearms. "I'm here," I said. "I told him to leave. I'm still here."

He heaved in a breath, his hand lifting to me briefly before he turned back and sat down on the edge of the couch with his head in his hands.

"Hey." I went to sit beside him.

He let out a stuttering sigh, his spine arching with every breath.

"Hey." I nudged his arm. "What's going on?" This couldn't just be about Brody.

"Edmundo," he said. "The resident that went into the hospital tonight. He had an aneurysm." He shook his head. "I couldn't get a hold of his family in time. They were too late." He squeezed his eyes shut and a few tears fell down his cheek. "I don't know why this one hit me so hard. I think—I just didn't expect it. I thought he was fine. I *told* him he was fine. Fuck. Sorry."

I pressed the palm of my hand to his back and rubbed circles just like my mom would when my head was too full of what-ifs or when Ruby had done something particularly infuriating.

"And then I got home to see Brody Turner standing in my living room and I just wanted to eviscerate him."

"Eviscerating sounds very messy." He didn't laugh, so I went for what I really wanted to say. "Can you please tell me what happened between the two of you?"

He shook his head. "He's a user, Vera."

"What did he do to you?" I asked. "Was it something to do with your family? Some kind of connection he took advantage of? I don't get it."

His green eyes searched mine. "What did he want from you?"

"He wanted me to come back."

"As his employee?" His voice was low enough to graze the floor.

"What else would I be to him?"

He swallowed slowly as his gaze lingered on my lips. "You loved him."

I couldn't find the words to say he was wrong.

"You always did, Vera. You loved him. He needed you. And maybe you loved to be needed by him. Whether you were helping him study or coaching him through family drama or giving him a pep talk before an audition. He would always do whatever it took to keep you around. Whatever it took."

My chest flushed with shame. "Whatever it took? What's that supposed to mean?"

"Tell me you didn't love him. Through all those years. Tell me and I'll shut the hell up right now."

"Why would that be any of your business, Eli?"

"It's not. It stopped being my business the moment the annulment was finalized. Trust me. I know that. But let's just say you did love him. What were you to him? Were you ever more than an employee and a friendly fuck?"

I couldn't open my mouth without telling him the truth. A friendly fuck. It sounded so vulgar. So insignificant. It sounded nothing like how I felt for Brody and everything like how he treated me.

He went on, his tone softer. "Did it ever occur to you that he gave you just enough of what you desired to keep you around? That he'd been stringing you along for twenty years with no plans for the future?"

I shot up from the couch, my balance unsure as the pain of what he said rocked through me. Eli could play the nice guy all he wanted, but he always found a way to make what he thought of me crystal clear. My head was full of angry static. "Is that how you see me? Just a pity fuck?"

"No," he said firmly as he stood to meet me. His eyes were wild and begging me to understand. "God, no, Vera. I see a boy—because that's what Brody is. A boy. A boy who got used to needing you and knew that he could keep you around if he gave you a small taste of what you wanted in return."

"And is it so incredibly impossible that someone like Brody could just want me? No strings attached. Is my presence—my body, my homely personality—such a nuisance? Am I that grotesque?"

He lunged forward then, his warm, trembling fingers curled firmly around my upper arms. "Don't you ever—*ever*—refer to yourself that way again. For fuck's sake, Vera. Don't you get it? Brody's been keeping you like a fucking houseplant. Giving you just enough light to stay alive, but not enough to grow."

A few slow tears began to brim at the corners of my eyes as he pulled me in closer so that we were nearly pressed together. The angry heat I'd felt just moments ago took root in my gut and turned into something hungrier. It was the first time we'd intentionally touched since that morning in my room. Not that he'd even really touched me then, and yet it still felt impossibly intimate and vulnerable.

"Vera Stein, you deserve all the light."

I sucked in a breath as he traced a finger across my forehead and then pushed my overgrown bangs behind my ear.

He curled an arm around my waist, breath hot as his lips found mine. It was tentative at first. Exploratory. A soft, dragging touch.

Every time his mouth left mine—however briefly—I went in search of him so that whatever he did, my lips were there waiting to be found. "Please," I said on a whisper.

He nodded against my neck as his lips danced across my jawline and nipped at the lobe of my ear. His hands began to move frantically, like he was trying to memorize me by touch. And then his mouth found mine again.

My nails scraped up the back of his neck and into his hair as his tongue moved against mine, and our kiss grew deeper and wider.

My brain didn't even have a moment to metabolize what my body would feel like to him and the rolls at my hips that so many others politely referred to as curves and the way some of my stretch marks were purple and angry instead of faint and translucent.

Blistering need spread through my chest and into my abdomen as I sighed into his greedy mouth. I shouldn't want this. I shouldn't, I shouldn't.

The feel of him made Brody's touch just moments ago feel clinical. Eli left no room for questions as he directed us to the couch. The backs of my calves hit the sofa and I fell back into the cushions.

He sunk to his knees in front of me so that we were eye to eye and then with his hands wrapped around the backs of my thighs, he pulled me to the edge of my seat. My center pressed against the fly of his jeans, where he was already hard. For a moment, he pulled back and my lips followed him as though we were tethered. Like he was baiting me.

A devious grin spread across his lips. Fingers danced across my collarbone and then around my neck and then to the back of my head as he pulled me to him and left a trail of kisses along the blade of my shoulder. His other hand roamed up from my waist and cupped my breast. "I've been dreaming of this since you walked in on me. Fuck, even before then.

I don't think you understand how impossible it's been to exist under the same roof as you and not touch you. How unfair it was for you to wander back into my life and for me to not immediately kiss you?"

My eyes rolled back as he snapped his hips against me. He was aroused by *me.* There was no mistaking the hard bulge in his pants.

Eli pulled back again for a moment, his breath indecipherable from mine. "I'm sorry . . ." He glanced down at his erection. "I've wanted to do this for so long."

This time it was me who kissed him, my tongue lacing with his. I kissed along the scruff of his cheekbone and to his earlobe, where I sucked and nibbled.

He groaned into my ear and the sound of him broke any remaining resolve I might have had.

The hand cupping my breast moved down past the waistband of my linen shorts. I let myself glance down for a moment as I watched his hand disappear into the leg of my shorts, my body rocking forward to meet him. To beg him to move faster.

"Do you know how hard I am every night thinking about you in the bedroom next door? Ever since that morning in your bed, I've held my breath, hoping that I would hear you moan. Do you know what kind of torture it is to have you as a roomate?"

Roommate. That word yanked me back to reality just as his fingers traced the scalloped trim of my underwear.

I pushed myself against the back of the couch in an effort to put space between us. Maybe space would give us both a shred of sense.

His hands dropped to his sides when he finally realized that I wasn't pulling him with me.

I shook my head. "We . . . we live together. And we work together. And . . . you just told me I love Brody and now you have your hands down my shorts."

His lips parted and his gaze fell, confusion and disappointment heavy in the soft lines of his forehead. "I should have asked," he said, pushing himself to his feet.

"I am more than willing. It's not that. Trust me. But that doesn't mean this is a good idea." It sounded like lines from a script. The kind of thing you said when you knew someone had to be the adult and ruin the fun. "I need this job, Eli. Desperately. I can't even begin to explain to you how desperately I need this job. And I can't risk things getting weird. Especially while I'm living in your apartment."

"Nothing has to get weird," he countered.

I gave him a pointed look.

"Okay, well, maybe it's been a little weird."

"The fact that you're my ex-husband isn't really helping things either."

"We were kids," he said firmly, and then groaned. "Forget it ever happened. Okay? I was angry and sad and acted out. That's all this was."

I nodded, because that was something I could believe. "That's all it was," I said, my voice hollow and unconvincing.

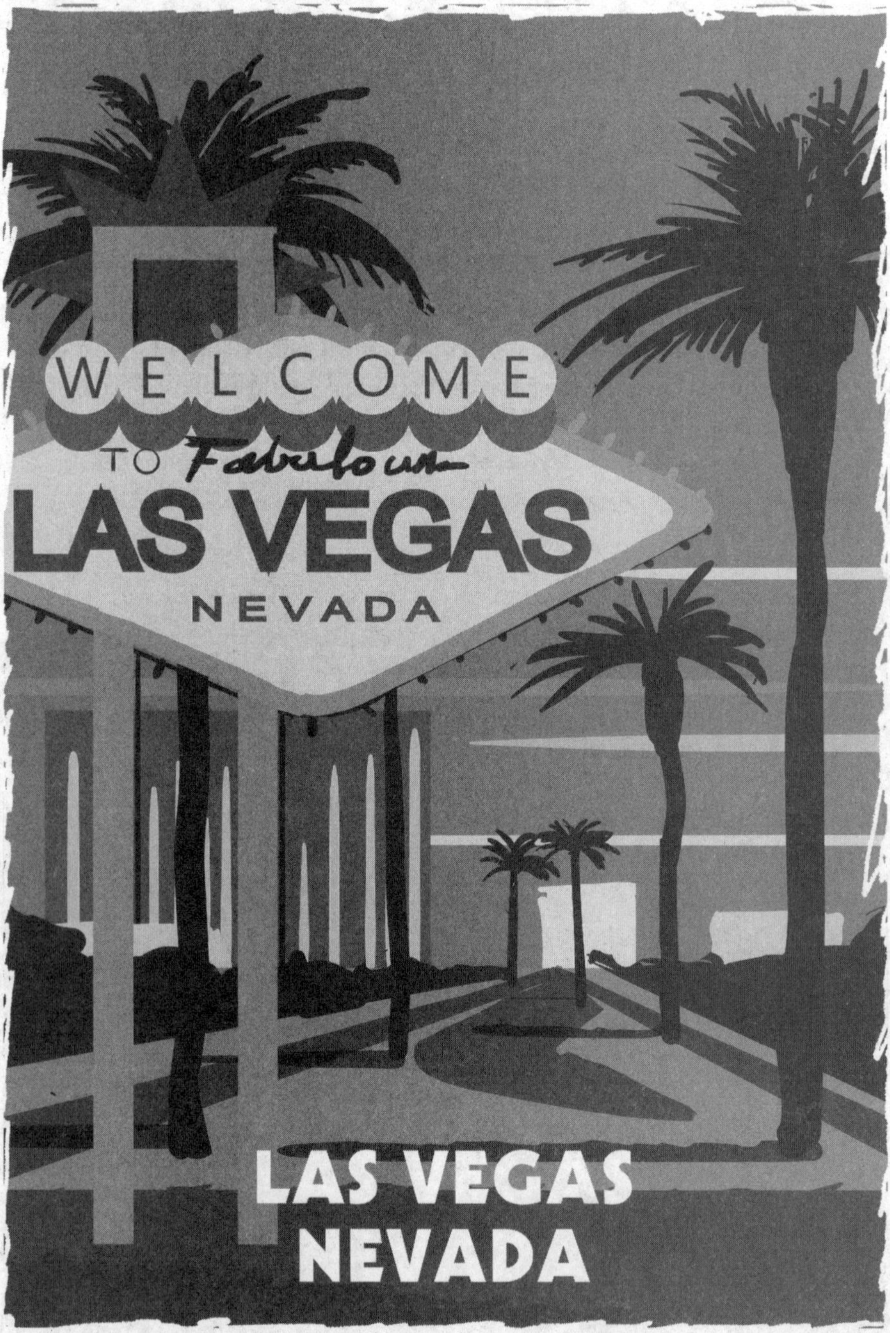

LAS VEGAS
NEVADA

ELIAS BUCKLEY
SEVENTEEN YEARS AGO
WITH THIS RING

It turned out that we actually needed to go to the Clark County Marriage Bureau first. Regretfully, the office was open until midnight and our limo pulled up at exactly 11:23 p.m.

It was too simple. We each presented a form of ID and I footed the bill for the license.

I held my breath as Vera signed and when it was my turn, she placed a tentative hand on my forearm. "You can't say this won't make for a good story."

"I never took you for a daredevil," I told her.

She shrugged. "It's Brody. He's reckless. It's contagious. He makes life a little more . . . unexpected. Besides, there aren't really any guys lining up to marry me, so my dance card is free."

I hated the way she talked about herself. I hated how uncomfortable it made me and how I couldn't put my finger on why.

"I'm lining up," I told her.

Her lips quirked and she studied a loose button on her cardigan. "On a dare."

I signed my name on the application beneath hers. The man behind the counter took our paperwork and began rapidly checking each page.

Then I turned to her and said the truest thing that had ever come out of my mouth. "Vera, don't think for a moment that I couldn't have said no. You think I'm scared of Brody? You think I give a shit about him getting riled up over me skipping out on a dare? No."

She nodded, a deep, steadying breath moving across her lips. "Okay. Let's get married."

Our next stop was a twenty-four-hour tux and bridal gown rental store off Freeman. Neither Vera nor myself cared too much about what we were wearing, but Brody insisted and we were fully committed at this point. So I went in and came out with a light blue tuxedo complete with a vintage ruffled shirt that smelled like a cigar. For his official duties as both best man and maid of honor, Brody opted for an orange tux to fulfill his *Dumb and Dumber* fantasy. The salespeople in the shop were truly entertained and leaned into the bit, presenting us with canes and matching top hats. I had to admit that I was sort of having . . . fun.

We waited outside next to the limo, which I'd hired on for an additional two and a half hours for an extra two hundred bucks.

Before we'd walked into the store and veered off in separate directions, Vera nervously picked at the skin around her thumbnail and wondered aloud if they'd have plus sizes available.

"If this place doesn't have anything, we'll just go on to the next," I promised her, because even though this was a sham of a wedding, I'd be damned if she didn't get exactly what she wanted. I had no right, of course, but the moment we signed that marriage license, something in me claimed her as my responsibility. This wasn't a new feeling, but I felt the freedom—if only for one night—to act on it.

Brody sipped a foot-long margarita he'd bought off a street vendor.

"You need to start hydrating," I told him.

He held his drink up. "I am hydrating."

A few moments later, the door to the store opened, spilling fluorescent light out onto the dark sidewalk.

Upon seeing Vera, Brody let out a wolf whistle, which was loud enough to cover my throaty gasp.

She wore a short ivory dress that just brushed the tips of her fingers. The top of the dress was corseted and molded perfectly to her breasts. Billowing sheer sleeves gathered at her wrists and the hem of the dress looked like it had been dipped in light pink, which matched her floor-length veil. It was the most I'd seen of her legs ever and if I didn't look away, I was in danger of tenting my tux trousers. She wore ankle boots covered in rhinestones and white heart-shaped sunglasses.

She looked like she'd stepped out of a movie.

"Shit, Vera," Brody said, sounding the most sober I'd heard him all night.

Something deeply territorial and probably a little misogynistic spurred me to step forward and take her hand before Brody could say another word to my future wife.

"You look beautiful," I told her. It was too simple of a word to properly describe her. She exuded a flirty confidence that made me want to follow her around like a puppy dog.

"I wanted it to be pretty, but . . . of the moment," she said, her self-assurance wavering slightly. "It's not too much?"

I pointed to myself and then to Brody. "Is that a serious question?"

She snorted softly as she took my proffered arm so I could escort her to the car. "Fair."

"To the wedding chapel!" Brody called out to the driver.

There was only one package available that evening, which was a surprise to us. It turned out that most people had booked their ceremonies in advance and walk-ins were left with whatever was available. So when the guy at the front desk informed us that the only time slot open included a pink Cadillac and a Gene Simmons impersonator, I put my credit card down on the counter.

The Gene Simmons officiant was very committed to his role. His platform boots made him nearly seven feet tall. We were assigned a wedding planner, who informed us that our ceremony would take twenty minutes and that we would get married in front of the pink Cadillac in the parking lot with the city's neon lights as the backdrop.

I expected to have a minute with Vera before it all began, but the wedding chapel moved us along like cattle and suddenly I was standing in front of the pink Cadillac with Brody beside me and a clearance rack Gene Simmons at my back.

"You're a lucky man," Fake Gene Simmons said, and I was pretty sure it was a line he gave to every groom, but it still felt like something that uniquely applied to me.

Vera stepped out of the front doors of the chapel with our driver, whose name turned out to be Alvin, escorting her down the aisle, which was a white shag carpet that led straight to me.

Vera held a bouquet of fake peonies wrapped in tulle in one hand and kept her eyes on the ground in front of her, only looking up to glance at me a few times. As if she was expecting to find that I was no longer there.

Beside me, Brody reeked of booze, and I was pretty sure he'd thrown up in the bathroom while I was paying for the ceremony.

But that didn't matter. Because for the first time, Vera wasn't walking to him. She was walking to me.

Once she made it to the end of the aisle, Alvin peeled off to smoke a cigarette and Brody took her bouquet after Fake Gene Simmons nudged him to do so.

"Let's rock and roll," Fake Gene shrieked before sticking his tongue out, which was unimpressively short—couldn't fake genetics—and a moment that the photographer capturing the ceremony was very used to anticipating.

I took Vera's hands, both of our palms slick with sweat, which I found comforting.

She looked up to me, her warm brown eyes bright and open, despite being laced with hesitation. My heart was doing things that would concern any medical professional.

I gave her hands a squeeze and her pursed lips eased with relief.

The next few minutes were a blur and only came into focus when it was time for me to say my vows. I repeated after Fake Gene Simmons, concentrating on each syllable and the shape of Vera's mouth.

"I, Eli Buckley, take you, Vera Stein, to be my wedded wife."

She looked up into my eyes, tugging her lower lip between her teeth.

"To have and to hold from this day forward, for better, for worse, for richer, for poorer . . ."

We were two people playing make-believe. Just pretending to be something we were not.

"In sickness and in health, in times of rock, and in times of roll, to love and to cherish, till death do us part."

But this didn't feel like pretending. Not to me.

Vera repeated the vows back to me and then Fake Gene Simmons asked, "Are you two exchanging rings?"

"No," Vera said just as I said, "Yes."

He shrugged, which seemed very un-KISS-like of him. "Which is it?"

"I don't have a ring for you," Vera told me.

"It's okay. Not like we really planned this."

"But you have one for me?"

"I might have perused the jewelry counter at the rental shop." I pulled the simple gold band from my pocket. It was genuine gold and the inside was engraved with a ring of vines. It was shockingly overpriced for what it was, but I didn't care. If I was going to marry Vera Stein—even just for a day—I was going to do it right. "It's not a rental," I quickly explained. "This is for you to keep. A souvenir."

Her lips slipped into a perfect *O*, her shoulders slumping in disappointment. "I'm sorry I don't have anything for you."

"Kids, I don't mean to ruin the moment, but my next couple is teed up to go in just a few minutes," said Fake Gene Simmons as he swallowed a burp.

"Oh, right," Vera said to him. "Sorry."

I held the ring up and she offered me her left hand. "With this ring," I said, my voice so low that I wondered if she could even hear me, "I thee wed."

"Hell yeah," Fake Gene Simmons said, throwing his hands up in the rock-and-roll gesture. "I now pronounce you dude and babe."

We both turned to him, our brows furrowed.

"Husband and wife," he clarified. "You may now suck face."

Oh fuck. Kissing. We hadn't discussed this.

"Kiss, kiss, kiss, kiss!" Brody chanted behind me.

Vera's smile faltered for a moment at the sound of his voice.

I wanted to grab her by the shoulders and make her understand that he didn't see how special she was.

I couldn't tell her that. But maybe I could show her.

I stepped forward slowly to give her the chance to back away. "May I?"

She nodded slightly and tilted her face up toward me. The purples and pinks and oranges of the neon signs reflected off her cheeks and white dress. She looked like a sunset, and I knew I needed to close my eyes to kiss her, but was it so wrong that I wanted to watch her too?

I lifted the front of her veil and smoothed it back as best I could before wrapping an arm around her waist. "Hold on," I whispered.

Vera's eyes went round and I silenced her startled shriek with my lips pressed against hers. I wanted so badly to deepen the kiss, but I had to leave that to her.

Instead, I braced her body against mine, and with each of her inhalations I exhaled. Then I did the single smoothest thing I have ever done in my life and I dipped Vera Stein in front of a pink Cadillac and a Fake Gene Simmons.

As I righted her back on her feet and began to pull away, her lips chased mine, parting just enough for her tongue to swipe against mine, and the softest, most erotic moan slipping from her mouth to mine.

Blood rushed straight to my dick.

She pulled back first and I held on to her until I was sure she was steady on her feet.

In front of us a camera flashed, and Brody gagged into his fist before puking onto the pavement.

"Joey," Fake Gene Simmons called, "I need someone out here to hose down this spot before my next ceremony."

"How romantic," Vera murmured, her lips curling into a smirk.

CHAPTER THIRTY-THREE

"You're a rat," I said plainly. "My best friend is a rat."

Tess groaned and dragged her hands down her face, her phone in its holder as we shared a video call while she sat in traffic. "I'm sorrrrrrry. I wanted to get drunk, okay? I never get to drink and I just wanted to be irresponsible for one night and then I saw Brody and you know I can't be trusted after two drinks."

"You do have a two-drink limit," I confirmed.

I stood in my room, folding my laundry, as she chattered.

"But he showed up to win you back," she said suggestively. "That's pretty hot."

"He wants me to work for him again. There was no mention of rekindling whatever dumpster-fire situationship we had." I shuffled through my pile of T-shirts as I set aside clothes to pack for New Orleans. My favorite sleep shirt that I had admittedly stolen from Brody years ago was missing and I was about to burn down my whole closet to find it.

"Whatever. Brody is jealous. I guarantee when he realized you were living with Eli, he turned into a fucking primate."

I shook my head and continued to fold. "So why did you want to get drunk? It's not like you to get sloppy at a work event."

"Well, the renovation was delayed again and Max asked if he could take weekday evenings off from dad duty, because he's getting a little stir-crazy with the limited space and the kids getting antsy. And I get it.

He's the full-time parent. He needs time to himself too." Her words were a little frayed at the edges like she was frazzled. "But the loophole is work events. So I wanted to blow off some steam and I had an invite to this premiere. I believe this is what they call two birds, one stone."

"Yeah, what's the phrase for when your best friend betrays your top-secret location?"

She jabbed her finger at me through the screen of the phone with her eyes on the road as her car began to roll forward. "You never explicitly said it was a secret."

"Fair, fair, fair."

We talked for a while longer until she got to her meeting. My brain circled around the heavy petting session I'd shared with Eli. But I didn't know how to make Tess understand that it was just a onetime thing and that we were both acting out for different reasons. I guess it was a two-time thing if you included Masturbation 101. (Another thing I hadn't figured out how to explain to Tess.) Either way, I kept it all to myself for now.

As we hung up, there was a knock on my bedroom door.

"Come in," I called.

"Hey."

I glanced over my shoulder to see Eli hovering at the threshold. He wore gray sweatpants and a T-shirt from a local elementary school that I supposed Brigid once attended. It had been almost a week since the day Brody showed up and Eli had gone to great lengths to be nonchalant about it all. We were constantly apologizing to each other for the smallest, most inconsequential things. Maybe some time away and distance would help us both settle.

It didn't help that I went to bed every night thinking of him and woke up horny and pissed off.

"I think I might have lost some stuff in the laundry," I said. "Let me know if you see anything?"

"Of course." He eyed the open suitcase on the floor, his voice guarded. "You going somewhere?"

"Um, yeah. Not for another two weeks. I'm just a nervous packer. Don't worry, though. I'm boarding Marlon."

He gripped the top of the doorframe, like he might do a pull-up. The edge of his T-shirt drifted up, showing a sliver of skin. "I could have watched him."

"No, no. I'm not dumping my high-maintenance dog on my roommate so I can jet off to New Orleans."

"New Orleans should be a good time. Are you going alone?"

He wanted to know if I was traveling with someone else, and I tried my best to suffocate the thrill that gave me. It wasn't his business, except I liked being his business even though I knew that I shouldn't. The amount of conflict warring inside of me was worthy of daytime television.

"I'm going with Ruby to a convention she was invited to. Pray for me and whatever TSA employees might cross our path."

He barked out a laugh. "Well, hey, I was supposed to take Brigid to a movie tonight, but she canceled on me to go watch some boy play video games in his basement."

"Brigid!" I said. "She's better than that."

He grinned. "So, you in?"

I hesitated for a moment before shaking my head. "No. Actually, I have some, um, writing to get done, so I'm going to run up to the office for some quiet time."

"You can have the apartment. I promise it will be quiet."

I shook my head. "Nah, I'm going to use my computer in the office, and this way if I get nothing done, I'm the only one to blame."

He nodded and then tapped the top of the doorframe once before turning down the hallway toward his room. "I'm glad to see you writing," he called.

"Don't get ahead of yourself. I haven't actually written anything yet," I called back.

EXT. BOARDWALK—DUSK

They walk close but don't hold hands.

POPPY (V.O.)

If he kissed me, it would break the spell. And I really liked being under his spell.

March 12, 2011
Vera S.
Is it still a love story if he doesn't love her back?

CHAPTER THIRTY-FOUR

I buzzed myself into the building and noticed that a new lobby display entitled "Starlight Palms Throughout the Decades" had been set up.

A wall of frames displayed various photos of former guests from when the place was still a resort. Some were even very famous, like Robert Redford and Doris Day.

In the glass case were memorabilia like coasters, swimming caps, beach towels, cocktail glasses, and valet keychains.

As I perused the photos, I found a small picture of Ruby. My fingers traced over the glass as I studied the image. She was lounging in a cabana with four other friends. One of them, a woman, sat behind her at a table with a cigarette dangling between her fingers. Over her modest one-piece swimsuit, she wore a flowy linen shirt. Her gaze was solely on Ruby while two men and another woman laughed hysterically with each other, cigarettes dangling from their fingers.

The other woman was Hollis. It had to be. It felt so odd to see the two of them like this in a glass case, like they were just another relic of the past. And yet, their story was still very much alive.

I walked back to my office and settled at my computer with an inappropriate amount of beverages. Ice water, raspberry tea, and a coffee I had no business drinking after six o'clock at night. As I waited for the computer to run an update, my thoughts wandered back to the display case and how, at a certain point, our lives become memories. Inactive chunks of time. Things that had been or could have been, but would never change. For so long, Eli had felt like a memory. But then he reappeared in my life, opening our book. Unsettling the dust.

I knew that life was supposed to be a journey and not a destination. I'd seen those words on hundreds of inspirational posters and embroidered pot holders. But that felt so easy to say when your journey was worthy of a destination.

I knew all the countless reasons why Eli and I were a bad idea. I knew all the things it could ruin. My job. My living situation.

The computer screen lit up and I opened the document I'd been tinkering with.

My job. My living situation. Those things were not worth risking by giving in to hormones and lust.

Because that's all this was.

My time off for the next few days was spent running errands with Ruby. Having her gown for the awards ceremony tailored. Hair and nail appointments. Last-minute shopping. It was the kind of busywork that kept me out of the apartment. In between all of that, Ruby would type text messages to Hollis or sometimes even attempt to write them out like a script. Some versions were as simple as a hello while many were paragraphs long. (I knew this because the text size on her phone had to be at least twenty points.) Every text was deleted before it could be sent and every piece of paper torn.

Eli was hardly around. He came back late just about every night, and I told myself it was easier this way.

I'd come home from New Orleans and I'd get serious about finding a place of my own. Then Eli and I would once again be a memory. A piece of time so far removed from the present that there was no point in untangling it.

The morning of Leonard's living funeral, I left my little homework assignment under his doormat.

To my surprise, I didn't hate what I'd written. After several failed attempts at resurrecting *The Wunderkind*, I used the character survey from the writing workshop instead and ended up with a few aimless pages about a postal worker who delivers letters from the afterlife. It was actually sort of . . . clever.

The invitation Leonard sent out specified that the dress code was Disco Western. When he came by my office to ensure I had something appropriate to wear, I told him I was hoping to swing by the costume aisle at a party store beforehand. His upper lip curled in disgust and he told me he'd have options for me in the morning that were not made of flammable textiles.

And options there were! The contents of the bag he'd left in my office this morning looked like Elton John and Dolly Parton had a baby and then donated their wardrobe to a less fortunate middle-aged woman.

I pulled out a multicolor fringe cape and then slid on pink leather gloves. It was what my childhood self probably imagined fancy dress to be.

"Very funeral appropriate." Eli hovered in the doorway, wearing snug black jeans and a pearl-snap shirt with a cactus embroidered on each chest pocket. His hair was longer than he usually kept it, and I wondered if he was busy or just not paying close enough attention to himself.

"You really dropped the ball on the disco part," I told him.

"I'll be the Western to your disco." He gave me a once-over. "You're really pulling your weight."

"Leonard was concerned about my wardrobe options, so you can thank him for this."

He fisted his hands into his pockets as we stood there in silence for a moment. "We let it get weird, didn't we?"

I sighed. It at least felt good to acknowledge it out loud. "It's probably for the best."

He shook his head, his expression turning serious. Almost annoyed. "Yeah. Sure. Whatever you want, Vera."

He walked away and I stood there for a moment, watching my reflection in the framed print of the original Starlight Palms hanging in my office.

I needed things between us to be okay. I told myself it was because of work and the apartment. That was the tidy reason. But he was back in my life all of a sudden and it was hard to believe that it wasn't for a reason. Even if that reason was to resolve the abrupt way things ended almost two decades ago.

"Eli," I called after him, peeking my head out my office door.

He was already halfway down the hallway with his fists clenched at his sides. For a second he paused and just stood there before turning around.

"I want . . ."

His mouth fell open, but he held his words at bay.

"I want us to be friends," I finished, and felt embarrassingly proud of myself.

He was quiet for a moment before he rolled his lips together and shook his head. "I don't think we want the same things."

A heavy dread settled in my chest as I felt punished for what felt like bravery to me. I glanced back to make sure we had the hallway to ourselves before I walked down toward him.

He took a step closer but then paused, letting me establish the space between us.

I wanted to touch him. His shoulders. His forearm. Just to let his warmth seep into my skin. I didn't trust myself, though, so I stood just out of reach for both our sakes. "I need this job," I told him.

His face was blank as he nodded.

"And I *really* need the apartment."

Then his measured features morphed into disappointment and anger. "What? You think I'd kick you out because you don't want to dry hump on the couch like a couple of teenagers?" He scoffed. "Ya know, I was a little shit back in college. I know that. But it was so, so easy when you always expected the worst of me."

"What the *hell* is that supposed to mean?" I said in a low, urgent voice.

"Just because I expected you to act like an asshole, that gave you the right to *be* an asshole? You hated me in college. What else was I to expect from you besides the worst? And I'm sorry for being worried that getting physical with you could fuck up my very fragile living and working situation."

"I would *never* kick you out, Vera. Hell, I'd go find a place of my own before I did that to you. Just say the word if that's what you want."

I shook my head. "No, I'm not asking you to leave your own apartment. I want you there. I just . . ." The supply chain between my brain and my mouth came to a grinding halt, because I didn't actually know what the hell I wanted.

He watched me carefully and when he realized I had nothing else to say, he gave me a curt nod. "I'll see you at Leonard's thing."

"Okay." The moment he turned away, all the words I might have said fell into place and I pushed them aside along with any remaining hope that things might return to normal between us. Whatever the fuck that looked like.

As he walked in the opposite direction, I stood there in my cape and gloves, reminded distinctly of a time nineteen years ago when I stood in an empty hotel room with a sheet wrapped around my chest and a veil discarded on the floor.

The community room had been transformed. The far wall of floor-to-ceiling windows overlooked the iconic pool and was framed with red, pink, and teal tapestries. What Leonard had managed to arrange in only a few weeks was astounding. The ceiling was draped with more of the same tapestries and a disco ball hung from the center. It felt like the inside of a jewelry box. Rows of rented chairs faced his prized casket and along the back wall was an open bar. Waiters in black pants, white shirts, and hot pink vests circulated with hors d'oeuvres.

According to Morgan, the room had been rented for anniversaries, birthday parties, and even a few weddings, but this was the first she'd heard of a living funeral. Thankfully, the room was full enough—even if many attendees were there to assuage their curiosities—that any concerns I'd had over attendance quickly evaporated.

I was shocked to see Ruby sitting near the back with Gwen and Harvey.

"You look like a piñata," she said as I sat down beside her after signing the guest book.

Gwen leaned forward. "I think you look nice."

"Thank you, *Gwen*," I said as I flung my cape back hard enough to hit Ruby on the shoulder.

Beside Gwen, Harvey bounced his foot aggressively. She placed a hand on his knee and then turned to me. "He's not big on funerals."

Ruby rolled her eyes. "Leonard isn't even dead. And my granddaughter calls *me* dramatic."

"I think it's a nice idea, actually," I told her. "And it was nice of you to come," I whispered.

"Good exposure therapy for me," Harvey said with his eyes trained on the ceiling.

"I'm here for the show." Ruby glanced around with a mask of indifference.

"I haven't seen her walk in yet," Gwen whispered, and I inferred that *her* meant Hollis.

Someone tapped my shoulder, and I turned to find Morgan standing in the empty row behind us. "We have a runaway bride."

"What?"

"Well, not quite runaway, but on the verge of running away."

I shook my head, still not understanding her.

"Leonard has cold feet," Ruby deadpanned.

"Well, I don't know what to say to him," I said.

"You're the one who recommended he do this in the first place," Morgan said with a huff.

I looked over to Ruby, the palms of my hands suddenly slick with sweat. Had this been a mistake? Did I push Leonard to do something he didn't actually want to do?

"That old queen spent way too much money on all of this to miss his own party." Ruby groaned. "Come on. I'll go with you."

I didn't argue or point out that Ruby was probably the last person Leonard wanted to see as we followed Morgan to the office across the hallway that I'd never actually been inside of before.

We walked in to find a very beige space with ivory sofas, calming music, and lavender air fresheners.

"What is this place?" I asked.

"It's the we're-sorry-your-grandpa-died room," Ruby said.

Morgan shrugged. "Well, today it's Leonard's dressing room, but on most days it's the room we send mourning families to when a loved one has passed away. So yeah, it's the dead-grandpa room."

Leonard sat in an accent chair with his fingers digging into the armrests.

"I'm going to update the minister," Morgan said as she slipped out of the room.

I sat down on the sofa to the left of Leonard and Ruby gingerly sat on the coffee table in front of him with her legs crossed so that Leonard couldn't even look up without seeing her.

"What's going on?" I asked Leonard. "The place looks great. And there are lots of people here too."

"This was a bad idea." He wore a lavender suit and a matching cowboy hat—both of which of course matched his cane.

"Okay, well, seeing as this was *my* idea, I'm going to have to disagree with you," I told him.

Ruby sighed. "I should never have quit smoking."

"I agree," Leonard sneered. "You might not still be haunting this mortal plane if you hadn't, and wouldn't that be ideal at the moment." He turned to me. "What is she doing here anyway?"

Well, shit.

"I'm here to tell you to stop being such a pussy and get out there," Ruby told him.

I shot her a look.

She shrugged. *What?* she mouthed.

"Wow," Leonard said. "I'm so inspired. You may leave now."

I opened my mouth, but Ruby leaned forward and spoke first. "What are you so scared of, anyway? You've been obsessing over your goddamn funeral for the last three decades and suddenly it's here and thanks to my genius granddaughter, you get to witness it yourself."

My eyebrows shot up at the word *genius*, but Ruby didn't skip a beat. "You're all dressed up. Now, you just have to walk out there and sit through your own funeral. It's your greatest dream realized. Congratulations."

Leonard leaned back and looked to Ruby and then to me. "I don't dream of dying. Obsessing over the details of my funeral is very different from attending it myself."

"Just spit it out," Ruby said. "What's got your panties in a twist?"

"Ruby," I said, quietly chastising her. I shouldn't have let her come with me.

Leonard closed his eyes. I knew he was no young thing, but in this moment especially I noticed the near translucence of his skin and the way his breath softly rattled as he inhaled. "All these people are here. Shockingly. But what if they have nothing to say? What if the minister does her little song and dance and I read the eulogy I wrote for myself and then people are invited to speak and then . . . ?"

"Don't pretend like you're not friends with rejection," Ruby told him. "How many scripts of yours went into production?"

"Including the shows I worked on? At least a hundred."

"And how many did you write that never made the cut or were started and never finished?"

He frowned, very clearly understanding where she was going and obviously annoyed by her sensible logic. "Too many to count."

Ruby held her hand out for me to help her up from the coffee table.

I stood and gently pulled her up with me.

"I've said what I needed to say," Ruby told him. "We'll see you out there."

I looked down to Leonard expectantly. "Will we?"

He nodded, his lip curled.

I reached for his hand and squeezed it. "I followed through with my end of the bargain. Now it's your turn."

In the hallway, Ruby looped her arm through mine and patted my forearm.

"You *hate* Leonard," I said. "Why would you do that?"

"I'd never miss an opportunity to give Leonard a verbal kick in the ass."

"At least it was for a good cause this time. Are you ever going to tell me what happened between you two?"

"Not likely."

We sat back down and ten minutes later, Leonard walked in behind the minister as ABBA's "Fernando" played.

Leonard sat down in the front row with who I guessed were a few of his nieces and nephews and some of their children. For the most part, they all seemed unsure of how to navigate this situation or what their mood should be. A little girl who couldn't have been older than three wore pink cowboy boots and a sparkly dress. She hopped up from her seat at the end of the row and wiggled in close to Leonard, and the tension slowly escaped his shoulders.

The minister was young and wore a rainbow stole over her clergy robes. All the while, Eli lurked at the back of the room, stepping in and out occasionally. The sermon was brief without any mentions of religion. Instead, the discussion was about accepting that your mistakes are just as much a part of you as your successes. I didn't know if Leonard had a hand in picking the topic, but it felt like a personal attack on me.

When the time came for Leonard to give his own eulogy, he made the short trek to the podium and cleared his throat. "Leonard Eugene Marvis came into this world on February 14, 1944. Despite being born on the universally acknowledged day of love, he never married. However, Leonard did father hundreds of scripts and was lucky enough to see many of them grow up to become TV shows and movies."

The crowd chuckled at that.

"A workaholic through and through, Leonard did truly consider his work to be his baby and his coworkers to be his family. As the last living of his siblings, he was well loved by his nieces and nephews and their families. He is survived by his bird, Patrick, and an unwieldy collection of houseplants."

There was a sniffle from the front row, and I felt my own throat tightening as the silence held for a minute to signify that the eulogy was over. But before anyone could clap, Leonard folded his paper and looked up at the crowd. "I think as a writer, there's the expectation that I should come up here and give you all some nugget of wisdom—some indelible truth—that you can carry with you from this day on. But the more words I write, the more I realize that words are at a surplus. We talk so much. We say so much. There comes a time when we trick ourselves into believing that saying is doing. But that's not true, is it? So, I suppose my nugget of wisdom is this: Do. Fail. And then do again. Words to live by are just that: words. They mean nothing if you're not waking up every morning and living. I don't say this because I mastered the art of living. I say this because I didn't. And hey"—he winked—"maybe after I'm gone from this earth, you will come a few steps closer than I ever did." He took a deep breath. "Oh! Always ask for a producer credit, never trust a plastic surgeon whose practice is in a strip mall, and sleep naked at least once a week."

The applause was immediate and beside me Gwen murmured, "He's not wrong about those last three."

"Thank you, Leonard, for putting my sermon to shame," the minister said.

"With pleasure!" Leonard barked back as he took his seat.

With a grin and a shake of her head, the minister continued. "At this time, I would like to open the podium up to those who might like to say a few words about Leonard."

Leonard's spine was rigid, his gaze trained straight ahead on his coffin.

A quiet moment passed, and I almost forced myself out of my seat. I had no idea what I would say, but someone had to say something.

Then, to my surprise, Ruby braced herself on my knee and stood up. It took her a moment to wriggle past the other residents, who were slow to move out of her way. "Allow me," she said as she finally stepped into the aisle.

Leonard turned back, his face full of trepidation and just a pinch of relief.

The minister smiled at Ruby as she stepped behind the podium and readjusted the microphone to her liking.

She took in her audience, and I watched as she became that heightened version of herself. It was Ruby, but bigger. More confident. More sultry. It was the Ruby you would meet at an audition or in an interview, and it was the Ruby I hadn't seen in quite some time.

"Let me be the first to say that Leonard is the second biggest asshole I've ever met."

You could feel the oxygen being sucked out of the room. The minister froze.

Ruby leaned into the microphone, holding her pause for the perfect amount of time. "Second only to me."

Then Leonard choked out a laugh and everyone else followed.

Ruby smiled. "Leonard and I have been in each other's orbit for over fifty years. The first thirty or so years were great." She turned to Leonard. "They really were."

He nodded in agreement.

"And then there was a man. There's always a goddamn man, isn't there?"

Someone in the audience hooted.

"I won't share the specifics, because I like being the center of gossip and if you all knew the truth, there wouldn't be anything mysterious left to gossip about, but trust me when I say that the details are salacious."

"Can't let one of these fools sell the rights to our life story before we can," Leonard called.

"Now, that's the Leonard I have known and loved," Ruby said. She looked down at the podium for a minute before tilting her chin back up, her expression more serious now. "Leonard and I put down our Starlight Palms deposits at the same time with big plans to be next-door neighbors. When I moved in and found that our long-forgotten request had been honored, I was prepared to hitchhike back to LA. I'd like to tell you this story has a happy ending, but it doesn't. Not yet, at least. Because since the moment I moved in, we have bickered and feuded for no other reason than to wreak havoc on each other's lives. At this point Leonard could water his plants and I would find a way for that son of a bitch to annoy me."

There were a few soft chuckles in the crowd.

"But the truth is that my friendship with Leonard was one of the longest-standing relationships in my life and I have spent many years wondering what would have happened if one of us had just let go of our astounding egos for long enough to mend the bridge." Ruby shook her head. "But we can't change what's done. And that has to be okay. I can't undo the past. None of us can. But the future is yet to come."

My throat was dry and my chest tight as the weight of time hit me like a boulder.

"Despite my and Leonard's schism, I can say without a doubt that no one has ever been more willing to help a friend in need. Leonard would help you hide a body just as quickly as he would offer to make some calls around town to find you a gig. And honestly, I don't know which of those is more of a hassle."

That got another knowing laugh from many of the residents.

Ruby held up her champagne glass. "To my dear friend Lenny and to not letting the past write the future."

Leonard nodded and held his cocktail up. Glasses clinked and there were rumbles of agreement as Ruby moved toward the aisle. Leonard held out a hand to her and she stopped for a moment before coming to sit down beside me.

I glanced back to see Hollis clapping, her brow furrowed and her lips parted, like there were endless words on the tip of her tongue. At the back of the room, Eli nodded to himself and walked back out into the hallway.

As another person stepped up to the podium, I leaned over to Ruby. "That was good of you."

She sighed. "It's a start, and at our age, that's the best we can hope for."

CHAPTER THIRTY-SIX

"And this is free?" I asked the flight attendant as he set down two mimosas between Ruby and me.

He nodded and smiled. "Complimentary."

Once he had stepped back to the front of the plane while boarding continued, I leaned over to Ruby. "And we're not supposed to tip?"

She rolled her eyes. "It's as though you've never flown business class."

"Um, that's because I haven't." Because Brody never upgraded me.

"Well, you could stand to at least pretend like you belong here." She glanced down at my pants. "I still can't believe you wore *athletic pants*."

"I like to be comfy on a flight. Plus, I expected to be smooshed into a middle seat in coach. And those seats are not meant for my hips, especially in pants that have zippers and buttons."

She sighed.

"We are nearing the end of our boarding process," said a voice over the loudspeaker. "If you are unable to find overhead space, please alert a flight attendant so that we can facilitate gate-checking your bag."

I took a sip of my mimosa and began to settle in. I dug out my headphones and e-reader. There had never been a time when I was actually looking forward to a four-hour flight, but I was more excited for the next few hours in business class than I was for New Orleans itself. It had been a chaotic morning dropping Marlon off at the pet hotel and then trying to get Ruby out the door. We had to turn back twice. Once for the shoes she planned on wearing to the awards banquet and then a second time for her wallet, which actually turned out to be packed in her checked baggage instead of her purse.

But we were on the plane. We'd made it. I was going to sleep in a bed I didn't have to make myself in the morning and apparently I was also going to sip *complimentary* mimosas for the next four hours.

"You're my last passenger," the flight attendant said to the incoming person walking down the jet bridge.

I looked up just in time to see Eli turn the corner and search the boarding pass on his phone before his gaze landed on the open seat across from Ruby and then on me.

My jaw dropped, and I had to ignore my instinct to slither down into my seat and disappear.

"Dr. Buckley! I'm so glad you could make it." Ruby unbuckled her seat belt and took her time standing up. "Here, here. You and Vera sit together."

I gripped my grandmother's wrist and, through gritted teeth, asked, "What's going on?"

She shrugged. "I had a third ticket and a second hotel room. I ran into Dr. Buckley—"

"Eli," he insisted as he put his bag into the compartment above us.

Her lips spread into a grin and she winked at him. "I told him all about our trip. When he told me he'd done his residency in New Orleans, I insisted on him joining us as our own personal tour guide."

Ruby stepped into the aisle and swapped places with Eli.

"I have a very hard time saying no to beautiful women," he explained as he buckled his seat belt.

That warranted an eye roll.

Ruby chuckled and swatted his chest before taking her new seat across the aisle. "Dr. Buckley, you flatter me."

I let out a long breath and then chugged the rest of my mimosa.

Maybe I could just pretend to sleep.

For the whole trip.

The flight attendant offered Eli a mimosa.

"She'll take another as well," he said.

I made to protest, but Eli already had two flutes in hand. He shot back the first drink in two gulps as I reached for mine.

"Uh-uh," he said, batting me away, then chugged the other one.

"I thought you grew up rich," I said. "Surely free booze in first class is not a novelty for you."

"Where do I start? Technically, this is domestic business class and not first class. Rich people love free shit. And the only way my feet go higher than ten feet off the ground is if I am just sloshed enough to fall asleep."

"Well, don't let me stop you."

Eli held up our empty glasses for the flight attendant, who seemed eager to fawn over him. "Any chance you could sneak me one more before takeoff?" he asked with a wink.

She giggled and whispered, "I'll see what I can do."

"You smarmy motherfucker."

He sucked in a deep breath, his hands gripping the armrests. "I didn't have time to get a refill on my Xanax, and I'd rather be smarmy than think too much about the fact that we're about to fly through the air in a glorified tuna can."

I didn't realize he had a fear of heights. It was hard to imagine him being scared of anything at all. "So does you crashing my trip with Ruby mean we can be friends?"

He turned to me, his head resting against the plush leather seat and a charming, almost mischievous smile curling at his lips. "You think I'm rawdogging this flight on two watered-down mimosas so that you and I can be just friends?" His fixed gaze relented only long enough to linger on my mouth as his teeth dragged across his lower lip. "I think not, Vera Stein."

Well, shit.

INT. ART MUSEUM—NIGHT

He made a short film. It's bad. She claps first anyway.

POPPY

It was brave.

ARLO

It was garbage.

POPPY

Brave garbage.

LAS VEGAS
NEVADA

ELIAS BUCKLEY

SEVENTEEN YEARS AGO

THE HONEYMOON PHASE

"I didn't even know hotel rooms with two bathrooms existed," Vera said as she kicked off her boots and threw her small overnight bag onto the coffee table of our suite at the Bellagio. "This had to be so expensive, Eli."

"My dad probably has enough points here to buy out his own floor."

Brody hurled into the toilet bowl loud enough for us to hear from the other side of the door.

Vera grimaced as we continued to explore the corner suite.

"Oh," she said, taking in the sight of the single king-size bed. "We could probably all fit, actually."

"I am not sharing a bed with Brody in his condition and neither are you."

She nodded. "That's probably for the best."

"There's a couch in that front room and, honestly, he's been known to sleep in a tub when he's coming down from a night of drinking," I said. The gentlemanly thing to do would have been to offer to sleep in the other room too and let Vera have the bedroom, but I wasn't feeling very gentlemanly.

She flopped down on the edge of the bed, her skirt poofing out around her. "Do you have the photos from tonight? I didn't get to see them."

I nodded and opened the small plastic bag the wedding chapel had given us with our marriage license, honeymoon pamphlets, a list of businesses that gave discounts to newlyweds, business cards for family attorneys who specialized in divorce, and some of our photos tucked inside a mini souvenir album along with a flash drive containing the rest.

I sat down next to Vera and she scooted in, closing what little gap I'd left between us. With a sigh, she rested her head on my shoulder and I had to clench my fist so hard that my nails dug into my palm as a reminder that just because I wanted to touch her didn't mean I could.

She traced a finger over the pictures as we both studied them. The first photo was her walking down the aisle with Alvin. There was us holding hands. Me slipping the ring on her finger. The kiss. Both our eyes closed and my grip so tight on her waist that I could see my fingers digging into her dress.

I cleared my throat into my fist and tried to push down how exposed it felt to see my own intensity reflected back to me. Could she see my desperation in the way I held her? The last photo was of the two of us, a sallow-looking Brody, and Fake Gene Simmons.

The doorbell buzzed and Vera jolted upright. "What was that?"

I stood and walked to the door. "The doorbell."

"Hotel rooms have *doorbells*?" she asked.

"Ones that are this big," I called back to her.

I opened the door and was greeted by a hotel employee holding a silver tray and two sets of silverware. "For the newlyweds," he said with a wink.

I fought the urge to correct him and tell him it was all just a dare, but I was a sick fool who liked the idea of people thinking this was real.

"Who is it?" Vera asked behind me.

I thanked the man and dug a few bills out of my pocket before shutting the door. "The hotel sent something up for us," I said.

She clapped her hands together and gave a little twirl. It was so adorable that it almost distracted me from Brody's guttural moaning.

Vera took the tray from me and practically skipped back into the bedroom, where she set the tray on the bed. "This is the closest thing I've ever had to room service," she said excitedly.

"Do the honors," I told her.

Gleefully, she gasped as she plucked the lid off the tray. On the platter was a mini heart-shaped cake with soft pink flowers and flourishes. Cherries lined the top and in a delicate cursive: *Just Married*.

"A wedding cake," Vera said with a swoon. "Oh my god, I'm starving."

She ripped the blankets back and slid into bed, wiggling her toes. She placed the cake in her lap and patted the space next to her. "Come on. I can't eat our wedding cake alone."

We unwrapped the silverware and shared the cake in a contented silence, the pictures still open on the foot of the bed.

She pointed to the photo of us kissing. "You really went for it."

"You only get married for the first time once."

She snorted back a laugh and took another bite. After a moment, she said, "It didn't surprise me that you didn't back down from the dare. But the kiss . . . that did surprise me."

"Isn't that what two people do when they get married?" I didn't want to get too into the weeds with this line of questioning. I needed to keep it casual, because she was in love with Brody. The image of her disappointed expression when Brody chanted for us to kiss swam in my memory. Nothing I could do would ever change that.

"I know you didn't really have many other options for a last-minute spouse tonight, but I always thought you hated me."

My fork clattered onto the tray. "What?"

"Oh, Eli, come on. You can't even be in the same room with me without making a face. I get that I'm not your favorite person, but you've never even pretended to like me."

I took the decimated cake from her lap and set it on the bedside table before crossing my legs and turning to face her.

She shifted a little so that she was doing the same, our knees touching. I knew I couldn't have her. I knew that. But I couldn't let her wake up in the morning with this thought in her head.

"I don't *hate* you, Vera. You piss me off sometimes because you can't let an argument die. And you don't see how smart you are. In big groups, you say smart things under your breath instead of out loud. Sometimes your hair gets so frizzy that I wonder if it's a cry for help. I also wish you'd put yourself first." I nearly added *over Brody*, but that wasn't going to help anything.

"Sounds like you have a growing list there." She twirled her finger around a loose curl. Her veil sat discarded next to the TV, but she still wore the ring. "I don't hate you either."

"Well, that's good, because we're legally bound together."

Her finger danced along the blanket and then across my kneecap, tracing circles there. I didn't know a knee could have so many nerve endings, but I felt her touch coursing up my leg like a rapidly spreading burn.

I cleared my throat. "Um, I just wanted to say that I can call my family attorney tomorrow and I'll cover the cost of the annulment. You don't need to worry about that."

She nodded and then looked up at me, her brown eyes heavy with something that felt like curiosity. "Let's not worry about that tonight, okay?"

"Okay."

Her touch expanded from one finger to her whole hand as her palm slid up my thigh.

I watched the path she made and inhaled sharply.

"It *is* our wedding night," she said, and then glanced behind me to the closed door of the bedroom.

I agreed with a nod, because if I spoke, my voice just might crack like that of a boy in the throes of puberty.

The truth was some days I didn't like Vera. Some days I was so angry with her for making me feel this uncertain and uncontrollable. My whole life had fit into tidy boxes before her. My feelings took up just enough space without becoming tyrannical. My dreams were given to me the moment I was born, and I didn't feel the need to consider much beyond that.

And then Vera appeared in my life on Halloween and she was everything I wasn't supposed to be interested in. She was aimless and unrefined and I thought I was jealous of her. But that wasn't the case at all. I wasn't jealous of Vera. I was jealous of everyone who knew her better than I did. Who held more pieces of the puzzle that made her.

Her other hand, the one with my ring—the ring that promised she was mine, if only for a night—slid up my thigh until both hands were at the critical juncture of my hips. Just inches from the fly of my baby-blue trousers.

"Some people say a marriage isn't legitimate until it's consummated."

"I think the whole point of the annulment is to prove—"

She pressed a finger to my lips like I'd done to her earlier tonight in the souvenir shop. The moment felt like a decade ago. Like we'd lived a hundred lives since I'd bought that display case of crystal trinkets.

"Vera, I need you to know that I'm not a good person and if you are implying what I think you're implying, you shouldn't expect me to be a gentleman. I won't say no."

She rocked forward onto her knees and braced herself on my shoulders so that I was at eye level with her breasts. I nearly leaned forward and ghosted my lips over the fabric covering her nipples, but I needed to know first if she was certain.

I tilted my head back, looking for a response.

"Good," she said. "I'm not saying no either."

With that last bit of encouragement, I reached up and snaked my arms around her, and pulled her into my lap. I pressed my face into the crevice of her cleavage and breathed her scent in. Cucumber melon and the slightest bit of sweat.

Her back arched forward as she surrendered to me.

I lay back and pulled her on top of me so that she straddled my hips.

"I don't want to put too much weight on you," she whispered.

I held her glorious, full hips in my hands and looked into her eyes with the utmost sincerity. "I cannot stress this enough, Vera. I want to feel you everywhere. I want you to let go."

Her brow creased as she considered the possibility.

I nodded slowly, encouraging her.

"Okay," she whispered as her body eased against me, and I groaned as the full weight of her pushed against my cock.

"You're so good," I told her, and watched her cheeks flush in response.

Our lips found each other, and she tasted like sugar, the frosting still fresh on her lips. My fingers traveled up her spine until I found her zipper.

She froze and reached over me to switch off the lamp.

"Leave it," I told her.

She shook her head. "I don't want the light on."

I took her wrist, but she pulled out of my grasp.

"That's nonnegotiable, Eli. I only fuck with the lights off."

I hated that. I wanted to ask her why so that I could poke holes in her theories, but I was too scared of ruining this moment.

She flicked the light off and I was at least thankful for the Las Vegas glow that illuminated the dips and curves of her body. After that, she let me resume unzipping her dress, and she slid off the sleeves so that the dress bunched around her waist.

Her beautiful porcelain breasts hung right above my mouth and I greedily licked and sucked.

"No bra," I managed to say.

"It was built into the dress," she said breathlessly as her head rolled back.

"You'll find no complaints from me."

With trembling fingers she unbuttoned my shirt and tossed my already untied bow tie to the floor. Her hands ran a course up my chest before she leaned back down again to nip and lick the space below my ear.

"Fucking hell," I said on the tail end of a moan. I was fully hard now and based on the way her hips circled over my erection, I wasn't alone in how badly I wanted this. "I need to get this dress off you."

Together, we pulled the filmy fabric over her head until she sat astride my lap in only a pair of white cotton panties with a lace band around the waist.

"I know it's nothing special," she started, "but—"

"Stop," I said firmly. "I literally want to tear these off with my teeth. They're plenty special."

She gasped quietly and in a sliver of light, I watched as she took a gulp of air and worried at her lip.

Vera needed someone to turn off her brain. I was willing and able.

I held her to me as I sat up and then rolled her onto her back. Leaning back on my knees, I watched as a passing light swept over her body, and I saw exactly what I was so scared of missing out on. Her brown curls radiated from her head, her full breasts rose and fell to the rhythm of her breaths, and her nipples were so hard that I was tempted to see how she would react to me simply blowing on them.

I wanted to make this good for her, but I was in serious danger of coming in my pants. It had been a few months, and the last time was with my high school ex-girlfriend, who my father was convinced would make the perfect partner. She'd said something about how she knew we would come back to each other, and I had to stop things right there. Because I didn't need her to confuse that hookup as me going back to her. I was simply an asshole looking for a lonely fuck while I was visiting my parents. It wasn't fair to her or to me, especially since when I closed my eyes, I saw Vera there on the backs of my eyelids like a flickering movie screen. So even that last time hadn't ended in satisfaction.

Vera began to writhe under me as we explored each other with open, panting mouths. I pressed my thigh against the warmth of her core and she let out a low moan.

"Do you like that?" I asked. It had been moments since I'd heard her voice and I already missed it. The girl normally couldn't shut up and the moment I needed to hear her voice the most, she was all too quiet.

"Yes."

I ground my thigh against her again. "Talk to me, Vera."

"About what?" she asked. "I can't even—what are words?"

"Tell me the plot of your favorite Christmas movie."

"*Love, Actually,*" she said as I peppered kisses up her sternum before moving on to her clavicle and then her neck. "It's about . . . it's about people."

She reached between us and began to tug on my belt buckle.

My hand slithered down her stomach to cup her still-clothed cunt. I pressed hard, hoping the fabric created a torturous kind of friction.

"You need to take your pants off. This isn't fair." Her head lolled to the side and she let out a high-pitched whine.

I almost told her to be quiet, but Brody was either draped over the toilet bowl or passed out so hard he was bordering on the edge of a coma.

"I don't have my pants on," she said.

"You never had pants on," I corrected her, then treated her to another tight grip that mellowed into a circular motion.

"You should fuck off on med school and become a lawyer. You argue too much."

"Only with you."

She laughed and something in my throat burned at the sound.

I leaned back for a moment to unzip my pants and kick them off. I'd barely undressed before Vera was sliding her warm hand past the waistband of my boxer briefs and over my stiff cock. The tip was already wet with precum.

"What else about *Love, Actually*?" I managed to ask through a throaty groan.

"I changed my mind," she said. "I hate Christmas movies."

My fingers slipped past the lace waistband of her panties, but she gripped my wrist, stopping me.

"I want you inside of me. We can do more . . . some other time. But right now I need you inside of me."

Some other time. Was that a promise? Could this be more than a onetime thing? Or did she just mean later tonight after both of us had recovered? Surely not. It was nearly three in the morning.

She rubbed a finger over the tip of my penis and I was quick to oblige.

My boxer briefs were gone moments later and I took pleasure in rolling her panties down her thighs, my mind wandering to fantasies of my tongue sinking past her pretty slit.

"I want you on top," I told her.

She nodded. "You're sure—"

"Fucking hell, Vera. Sit on my dick right now. I'm sure."

We rotated back around so that she was straddling me again. She sat up on her knees, creating enough space for my cock to run along her seam.

I gripped the base of myself and pressed against her there. Her head fell back with a breathy sigh.

She reached down between us, her fingers wrapped around mine so that we could both guide myself inside of her dripping opening.

"Wait," I said. "Let me grab a condom."

I reached back to the nightstand where my wallet was and she ground herself against my cock. I gasped as it slid in just slightly.

"Just let me feel you," she said. "Just for a second. And then we can be good and responsible people."

I shuddered as she sank down farther. There was more to consider than pregnancy, but logic was the furthest thing from my brain right now. "Vera, you need to know how much fortitude it's going to take for me to slide my dick out of you and wrap it up."

She nodded. "I know, I know, I know." For a moment, she just sat there, warming my cock and only occasionally circling her hips in search of friction.

"Okay," she finally said, and sat up, letting me slip out of her. "Fuck," she hissed.

My body was practically offended at the loss of her warmth. I scrambled quickly to free the condom from my wallet and then tore at the wrapper with my teeth. Vera's fingers wrapped around my base as I rolled the condom down.

"Ready?" she asked.

"Painfully so," I said back to her in the darkness of our room.

Carefully, I lined myself up against her wet entrance and then I thrust up with one quick go. She crumpled against my chest and just breathed against my neck.

Then, after a moment of adjusting, she began to rut against me a little. At this angle, my shaft dragged along that sensitive bud at her center. She stayed there. Using me. And fuck, I could not imagine a more worthy purpose in life than to be used by Vera Stein.

I needed to know if she was just horny or if this felt as wildly personal and sensual to her as it did to me. For the first time in my life, sex felt like I was cracking my ribs in half and letting someone see inside of me. I could never have enough of her. I was starved for her and my appetite was bottomless.

Her breath fluttered against my neck and my eyes burned with unshed tears and, fuck, I could not be the guy who cried during sex.

But it felt that good. It wasn't the same with the condom on, but being this near to her was the closest to my truest self I'd ever been.

My hands found hers and I sunk my teeth into her shoulder as I pushed her arms behind her back and held her wrists with one hand.

"I'm going to fuck you now, Vera. Is this hurting you?"

She shook her head. "No."

I bucked upward once, forcing her to bounce on top of me.

God, I wanted to drown in her. Put it on my death certificate. Cause of death: willfully drowned in his desire for Vera Stein.

"Do you like it when your husband pins your arms back and takes you?"

"Yes." She whimpered. "Please keep going."

And so I did. I fucked her from below and the sounds of our bodies meeting was vulgar. My balls slapped against her perfectly round ass and her tits swayed above. I let myself give into temptation over and over again as I licked and scraped my teeth across the curve of her breasts.

"I'm going to let go of your hands now, Vera, but I want you to keep them there for me. Can my little wife follow instructions?"

"I'll try," she whined.

"That's my girl."

I found her clit with my thumb and drew circles around it. My movements were erratic and sometimes painfully slow or relentlessly fast.

In a moment of heated desperation, Vera sat back and braced her hands on my thighs so that she could regain some control and move against my thumb more freely.

I almost teased her about ignoring my instructions, but the view of her like this, stretched back, lost in pleasure, was too perfect. I slid my free hand up her waist and cupped one of her breasts.

"I'm close, Vera." She was so soft and warm and I was wholly undeserving.

She sighed.

"But I think you're closer."

The tips of my fingers dug into her waist as I held her steady and thrust into her channel over and over again. My thumb rubbed her lovely center with new purpose now.

Above me, she cried out as pulses of pleasure coursed through her body and had her quivering in my hands. The walls of her tightened around me, and I held her waist steady as I chased my orgasm. A painful groan ripped through my chest as my warm release spilled into the condom.

She held me inside of her as we both came down, her warm cheek nestled against my chest. I wanted to freeze time and live within this moment indefinitely. I didn't want to open the door of this room or for the sun to rise. I just wanted to be here with her forever.

It took her shivering and yawning twice before I untangled our bodies to dispose of the condom and to clean up a little.

Vera stepped into the bathroom behind me and turned on the shower. Steam filled the marble bathroom and I decided that if watching her fall for Brody over the last few months meant that I got her in the end—that it was my body she curled around at night and my pillow where she rested her head—then it was all worth it.

But that happy ending was wishful thinking. Daylight would come and with it, the consequences of our actions.

CHAPTER THIRTY-SEVEN

The Le Pavillon hotel was located just outside the French Quarter. The convention itself was at the Marriott on Canal Street, but the guests of the convention were put in a separate hotel to minimize fan pandemonium. Though, I was pretty sure Ruby was pro-pandemonium.

Our car dropped us off under the carport, which looked more like a coliseum entrance than a hotel. The ground of the driveway was marble along with the hulking statues and stretching pillars.

Eli and I hovered behind Ruby like two children waiting for their mother to pay as she checked in.

"Miss Stein," the front desk clerk with a German accent said, "we have you for two nights in two king rooms."

"That's correct," Ruby said as she fanned herself with the small rechargeable fan I'd bought her online.

"And how many keys will you need?"

"Just one for mine, and then two for theirs."

"Um, excuse me," I said. "We will need two keys for her room and he will need just one for his."

Eli laughed quietly.

"Is this funny to you?" I shot at him over my shoulder.

He arched a brow, irises sparkling with mirth. "I find many things about this current situation humorous."

The clerk looked to Ruby, who rolled her eyes and then nodded her approval.

I took my key from the clerk and immediately headed for the elevators. Ruby followed me, and Eli took up the rear with both his and Ruby's bags.

One silent ride on an archaic elevator later, we stepped out onto the eighth floor. Eli's room was three doors beyond ours, so he helped Ruby with her bags first.

After he put Ruby's suitcase on the luggage stand, he walked out into the hallway and I let the door shut behind both of us.

His mouth gave a satisfied twitch.

"Okay, now that you're not double fisting mimosas, do you mind explaining what you're doing here?" I asked.

"The categorical truth? Ruby invited me. I have an ungodly amount of vacation time stored up and I like this city. The actual truth? I want to be everywhere you are and I'm not apologizing for that."

My mouth opened and closed and my arms flapped helplessly.

"Do you want me to leave?" he asked.

"Would you even if I wanted you to?"

"The only way to find out is to ask." This was nothing short of verbal chess. Something Brody and I never did, and I hated how thrilling I found it to be.

"I'll see you at six," I said, as though it were a threat.

The vein running along the side of his neck pulsed as he briefly smiled before letting himself into his room.

The Global Horror Con Awards banquet was a much bigger ordeal than I anticipated. Truthfully, I thought a convention for and planned by horror fans would have mom's-basement energy. But when we arrived, we were greeted by Alton, a young kid who introduced himself as the co-chair of the awards committee. He wore a tux with tails and a top hat.

On his jacket was an Edgar Allan Poe lapel pin alongside a button that read *Jennifer's Body Is a Masterpiece.*

"Well, isn't this a dashing look," Ruby told him.

Poor Alton nearly fainted as he fanned himself. "I'm not worthy!"

"She doesn't say anything she doesn't mean," I said.

"And this must be your granddaughter!" Alton said, and then pointed at Eli. "And this husband-shaped person must be a grandson-in-law."

Eli grinned but said nothing and as I started to object, Alton led us toward a back hallway for employees only and turned the conversation to business. "Okay, we've got a little step and repeat for you to do as you walk in. You'll find your table right up at the front, but I'll escort you there, of course."

We followed him onto a freight elevator, and I couldn't help but enjoy how much Ruby was eating up this kind of VIP treatment.

"The speech you sent over is on the teleprompter," he continued, "but feel free to go off script. Anything you say will be iconic. Tomorrow we have you scheduled for a panel in the afternoon and then a charity dinner in your honor tomorrow night. More casual than this. Sort of a mingling situation. And that's really it. The fans are ecstatic to even be in your presence. You're truly a living legend, Ruby." He let out a giddy shriek. "I can't believe you're here. Would it be weird to ask you to kiss a napkin for me so I can get a tattoo of your lip print?"

Eli and I looked at each other with wide eyes, but Ruby was undisturbed. "Just as long as you let me apply a fresh coat, honey."

Alton sighed. "My boyfriend is going to be so jealous."

We stepped off the elevator and immediately into a bustling hallway just outside of the banquet hall.

"Maybe I should quit my job and sell off Ruby's belongings online," I whispered.

Eli snickered, and then I remembered I was irritated with him.

As we walked toward the step and repeat, Ruby stood a little straighter and fluffed up her hair before turning to me. Only because I knew her so well did I recognize the slight panic gathering in her worry lines.

"You look amazing," I assured her.

She wore a deep green gown that hugged her curves in a way that would've made me question gravity and the laws of time if it weren't for the thirty minutes I had spent helping her maneuver into her undergarments. Shiny sequins shimmered from head to toe and the V-cut bodice was topped off by long, billowing chiffon sleeves that joined in a cape at the back with a train. It was completely emblematic of the swamp creature movies that made Ruby a staple of the genre.

"But do I look *sexy*?" Her smile sparkled, and it was the same flirty grin I'd seen in photos of her since she was a little girl. There was something comforting about carrying the same smile all your life despite the weight of time. Sometimes I looked at Ruby and had difficulty remembering the buxom scream queen she once was, but she was there. She'd never gone away. She was always there.

"I don't really think of my own grandmother as sexy, but if I did, you would be the epitome."

"You look stunning," Eli added.

Ruby blushed slightly. "Thank you, Dr. Buckley."

I nodded to him, a silent thank-you for his encouragement.

"You know what the great thing is about a lifetime achievement award? You've got nothing left to prove. You already did the damn thing." I gave her hand a squeeze.

"I wish Hollis were here," she said softly. "And my Annie."

My heart collapsed a bit. Hearing her mention Mom was such a welcome reminder that I wasn't alone in my grief, but it stung all the same. "I wish Mom could be here too. And Hollis."

"Miss Stein, we're ready for you," called a woman from just off the carpet, which was black with red blood spatters. These people knew how to lean into a theme.

I watched as Ruby stepped out onto the carpet, and while it was nothing like the chaos of an actual Hollywood premiere, her eyes lit up the moment the first photographer called her name.

She fell into poses, saucy grins, and haughty pouts like she hadn't been warming the bench for the last few decades.

In fact, I was so enamored by her that I hardly registered when the woman directing carpet traffic shuffled Eli and me in front of the cameras.

"No, no," I said, "we're here to supp—"

"Vera Stein, Ruby's granddaughter, and her husband—" She motioned to Eli for him to fill in his name.

"Eli Buckley," he supplied.

"Not my husband," I called helplessly.

"Her *ex*-husband," Eli corrected, despite not a single person registering what either of us had said. "We should smile."

"But how will people know that you're accompanying me against my will?"

"I offered to go home. All you had to do was ask."

A camera flashed, and Eli's arm wrapped smoothly around my waist, pulling me to his side.

"You look delicious," he whispered.

And I smiled, because I couldn't physically stop myself. Not to mention that I'd actually put in a great deal of effort tonight. I'd worn a strapless bra for the first time in at least ten years. My gown was a deep magenta silk with a sweetheart bodice that crossed in the front. The cap sleeves draped off my shoulders and the floor-length skirt split up the front to my midthigh. It was the flashiest thing I'd ever worn and something I only had the courage to buy because I'd reasoned that no one I knew would actually see me.

Stepping out in the hallway to meet Eli earlier tonight, I was riddled with nerves. He'd looked me up and down, with an appreciative hum, and swiped his thumb along his lower lip in a way that made my knees tremble.

We posed for two more photos before meeting Ruby on the other side of the carpet.

Inside the room, we were seated at the front like Alton had said. Most of the awards committee sat at our table and they were all enamored by Ruby, who was on the receiving end of constant compliments and questions.

Eli and I sat there, doing our best to read lips from across the table to follow the conversation, but eventually I gave in and turned to my ex-husband. "So you just had a tuxedo lying around, waiting for a tux-appropriate invitation?"

"My mother always said that every gentleman needs one good tux at the ready."

I nodded. "For formal emergencies."

"Precisely."

"That sounds like rich-kid propaganda."

He grinned and took a sip of his wine. "Oh, most definitely. This dress is unfairly distracting, by the way. Hazardous, honestly." His voice was soft and full of awe.

A warm confidence settled across my shoulders, and I found myself sitting up taller, my neck straight and proud. It was a fleeting moment, but one where I didn't feel self-conscious or unsure about the bright color of my dress or how much skin I was revealing.

Eli peered over my shoulder. "And it appears I'm not the only person noticing you tonight."

I chanced a peek and quickly glanced back to see a man with dark brown cropped hair, a tailored suit, and thick-rimmed black glasses. He was definitely a film nerd hipster, the kind of guy I would probably drool over until he proved himself to be insufferable. But when he saw me turn to him, he didn't look away. The corner of his mouth lifted, sending a thrill down my spine.

I smiled back before saying to Eli, "Are you gonna be my wingman tonight?"

His face became serious and he looked to the man behind me, a challenge in his narrowed gaze. "No, Vera. I don't think I have the stomach for that."

I waited for him to make some other quip or give a hint that this was just banter, but he only took a sip of the whiskey he'd ordered from the bar and then swirled what was left in his glass for a long, silent moment.

We sat through dinner, popping in and out of conversations on either side of us and sometimes joining in on each other's chatter. When the time came for the awards, there was lots of polite laughter, measured clapping, and highly specific jokes that played well with this crowd.

Ruby's award was the second to last to be presented and when her name was called, Eli stood up and walked her to the stage. My chest ached as he guided her through the tables and up the steps. I'd spent so much of my life taking care of Mom and Ruby, and it had never occurred to me what a lonely job that had been.

Eli sat back down beside me as the applause drowned out.

"Thank you," I whispered.

He nodded with his eyes on the stage.

Ruby's speech was exactly right. Not too long and full of clever innuendo. The single moment she stumbled was when she nearly mentioned Hollis, and I only noticed because I'd proofread the speech for her early on. But she cleared her throat and quickly recovered.

As her speech came to a close, she looked away from the teleprompter and focused directly on the audience. Standing up there, she reminded me so much of Leonard, and I wondered if she'd had the same thought too. Like this was the beginning of her farewell tour.

"If I can leave you with one final piece of advice from someone who's nearly outstayed her welcome on this earth." She did the public speaking thing where you make meaningful but brief eye contact across your audience, but then her gaze homed in on me and stayed there as she said, "I would tell you that as a woman in the film industry, I quickly learned that no one will take you seriously until you take yourself seriously. Why be a dreamer when you can be a doer?" She dipped her head in thanks, and the audience enveloped her in applause.

It was smart and inspirational. It was a call to action. It was the kind of thing self-identified girl bosses would put on their vision boards. And it was pointed right at me.

CHAPTER THIRTY-EIGHT

I sat on the edge of my bed, waiting for Ruby to finish in the bathroom. When she finally emerged, she wore one of her satin nightgowns and matching robes with her hair in a silk bonnet and her face slathered in moisturizer.

My makeup was still done and my curls swept up into a messy bun. I'd discarded my dress the moment we returned for a linen jumpsuit.

I had a question, and I'd held on to it until now because I didn't want to upset our balance before she gave her speech. "Ruby, why did you invite Eli?"

"I happen to like the doctor's company," she said. "And if I'm not getting a happily ever after, I might as well orchestrate one for you."

Of course. *Marry a doctor, Vera. That will fix everything.* "Well, if you'd even checked with me first, you would know that I needed this time away from him. I needed space."

With an air of dismissiveness, she folded back the covers on the bed and began to set up her nightstand with her pillbox and other bedtime essentials. "You've had space for nineteen years, Vera."

"I don't think that's really something for you to judge." My jaw tensed as I tried to keep my voice easy and neutral.

She propped up her pillows and got into bed with the thriller novel she'd picked up at the airport. "Your mother loved you so much, you know that? But Annie's love was soft, and it made you soft. She was always so gentle with you. Too much so. Never pushing you. Never encouraging you to get uncomfortable."

Okay, maybe I couldn't do neutral tonight. "I don't think you're really someone who should be giving opinions on a mother's love."

She took a deep breath and opened her book, ready for this discussion to be over. "You asked why I invited Dr. Buckley and I told you. Is there anything else?"

I should have let her end the conversation there, but rage had already sunk its hooks into me and I wasn't going to let this go. "Did it ever occur to you that maybe Mom loved me how she did in a response to how she wished you had loved her?" Harsh, but I meant every word. I would never understand Ruby's inability to love people how they *needed* to be loved versus how she thought they *should* be loved.

She paused, shut her book, and set it in her lap before looking at me, her eyes wide with indignation. "*Maybe* once you've had a daughter of your own, you can come talk to me about how to love a child. Until then, I think you should go wash that makeup off your face and go to bed before you say something else you'll regret. Don't forget to moisturize. You've carried your age in your forehead since you were a little girl."

I felt chastised and I was blistering with anger. "The kid thing? Really?" I wasn't even going to touch the comment about my apparently ancient forehead. Children had been one of Ruby's talking points on her Vera Agenda for a few years, but she dropped it when Mom got sicker. Maybe because she knew that working full-time, being a caretaker, and mothering a child would be next to impossible and some sort of responsibility might tragically fall to her. "You don't even *like* kids. You wouldn't even let me call you Grandma. How fucked is that, by the way?"

"Well, it's not as though you had some fulfilling career, Vera. At least if you had a child, your endless martyrdom would be put to good use."

My chest was heaving now, tears burning at the corners of my eyes. I'd never wanted kids. It was one thing I actually did know about myself. But the idea that I didn't have dreams? That I didn't have hopes? That I wasn't disappointed for myself? That broke me.

"Why do you care so much?" My voice was tinged with defeat. "You hardly even like me. Is it because you need someone to remember you when you're gone? Another generation of Steins to carry the Ruby torch? I may not be special or memorable, but at least I didn't sacrifice so much only to be so incredibly forgettable." There it was. I'd said an awful thing and now I couldn't help myself. "Did you just love tonight? All those little horror nerds kissing your ass? For doing what? What groundbreaking thing did you do with your life, Ruby? You screamed into a camera and showed your tits from time to time? Someone call a goddamn historian."

I was a bad person. I was a bad feminist. I was a bad granddaughter. And I didn't care.

With gritted teeth and eyes wild with fury, she flung her hand toward the door. "Get. Out. Get the fuck out."

I grabbed my purse and room key and slid my shoes on.

She crossed her arms over her chest and looked out the window as I marched to the door and slammed it behind me. (Well, as hard as you can slam a soft-close door.)

"Fuck," I cried out quietly.

I needed to get down the elevator and out the door and onto the street. Then I could just sob. It was dark and loud outside. The streets were crawling with drunks and bachelorette parties. One more crying woman in a sea of chaos would be nothing to look at.

The elevator doors opened to the lobby and I walked straight through the bar to the side exit on Baronne Street.

"Vera?"

No, no, no.

If I didn't look back, I could claim I hadn't heard him or that I was distracted.

I opened the door, and a firm hand gripped my elbow.

"Vera," Eli breathed. "Are you just going to ignore—"

I turned around just as the torrent of tears began to fall. *Shit.* I did not want to be perceived at this moment and especially not by Eli.

His taunting expression quickly shifted to deep concern, a muscle in his jaw clenching.

"Vera," he said tenderly. "What's wrong? Are you okay?"

My lips parted and I shook my head because I couldn't let the words come out without a chorus of hiccups and sobs.

And then he pulled me into his arms, turning me away from the entrance. He smoothed a hand over my hair while his other hand rubbed broad circles on my back.

I gasped at the relief of being touched. Being held. Brody and I had gotten to a point where we rarely touched outside of sex. But being held by Eli, his body shielding me from the very full lobby and bar . . . I felt briefly soothed.

"I'm getting your shirt all wet," I said. "And I'm wearing all this stupid makeup." I pressed a palm to his chest and tried to push back from him, but his arms only tightened around me.

He rested his chin atop my head. "Don't push me away right now." His voice verged on desperate, like he needed this as much as I did.

We stayed like that for a while and if anyone noticed or cared, I couldn't see them.

I focused on the sandalwood scent of his cologne and the fresh linen detergent he kept stocked in the apartment. At least he'd changed out of his tux and into a black T-shirt, so my mascara stains would be hidden.

"Do you want to go for a walk?" he asked.

I nodded into his chest.

"Wait here," he whispered into my hair. "I'm going to close out my tab."

While he ran back up to the bar, I turned to the window to see a distorted version of my reflection. I rubbed under my eyes as best I could to wipe the makeup away. There was nothing to be done about my puffy face and the swelling under my eyes.

Eli returned and without hesitating took my hand, pulling me out to the street and through the throngs of people. Once we had made our way past the crowds, his thumb ran back and forth across the top of my hand before he let go.

I fought the hollow feeling at the loss of his touch. There was no excuse to hold hands. I hadn't even wanted him to in the first place.

We walked in silence up to Canal Street, and I felt Eli's eyes on me, concern radiating from him.

"I'm okay," I finally said.

"It's okay if you're not."

We paused at the crosswalk, waiting for the signal.

He rocked back on his heels with his arms folded over his chest. "Do you want to tell me what had you so upset back there? Did someone say something to you?"

I sniffed. "You gonna beat them up?"

"Maybe. I'm not a surgeon, after all. These hands aren't too precious."

"Well, unless you plan on going a few rounds with Ruby, then down, boy."

"Ahhh."

We crossed the street into the Quarter and he didn't press for information, but I wanted to talk to him. I wanted him to know.

"I asked her why she invited you."

"Did you, now?"

"She thinks she knows what I need, but she never asks what I want."

He inhaled through his nose and nodded slowly. That was the closest I'd gotten to asking him to leave.

"It's not that I don't want you here—"

He shook his head. "Don't worry, Vera. I know this isn't about me. What else did she say?"

I didn't know how to explain to him that I wanted him here so badly for plenty of reasons, but none of them were good for me. "She's just disappointed in me. I'm not married. I don't have kids. No real career. I'm not adventurous or outgoing. I'm not any of the things she wants me to be."

He steered us around a corner, down a quieter street full of darkened art galleries and restaurants that were closing up for the night. "But are you any of the things *you* want to be?"

I sucked in a deep breath, the thick, humid air coating my lungs with condensation. "No. Yes. Maybe. Sometimes. I don't know how to tell her that I'm disappointed in myself too without feeling like she's somehow won. It's like . . . I can talk shit about myself, but when she does, it's different."

"No, you can't."

"What?"

"Talk shit about yourself," he said. "I'm not okay with you bullying yourself like this, Vera. And respectfully, fuck Ruby."

I laughed. I couldn't help it.

But he wasn't laughing with me. "How the hell do you not see what I see, Vera?"

I shook my head. "Tell me, then. What do you see?"

He stopped and turned to me. We stood in the darkness just outside a circle of light emanating from a courtyard.

"I see the girl who did extra credit in classes she already had an A in. And the woman who cared for her dying mother through an illness that hurts nearly as much to witness as it does to experience. The open and kind person who let Brody in and treated him like family even though he's a human wrecking ball."

"I liked to think of him more like the Kool-Aid Man," I said quietly.

He shook his head. "Sure. The Kool-Aid Man. You encouraged Leonard to finally go through with the funeral he spent years planning. And you're one of the funniest motherfuckers I know. You're smart and curious and thoughtful. You put me in my place."

I looked up at him then. His green eyes were silver puddles in the moonlight. "You make that part easy."

He threw his head back with a knowing grin. "You need a drink," he finally said. "Let me buy you a drink."

THE WUNDERKIND (FIRST DRAFT)
"PILOT" 10/8/07

INT. RECORD STORE–DAY

Arlo scours the crates. Vinyl in one hand.

ARLO

You can tell everything about a person by the songs they skip.

POPPY

I don't believe in skipping. It feels like cheating.
~~Each song is there for a reason. Even the quiet ones.~~

THE WUNDERKIND by Vera Stein.

CHAPTER FORTY

We walked a little farther down until we stumbled upon a bright building with a canopy that read *Hotel Monteleone.*

The lobby was brimming with people in various stages of their night. Wedding rehearsal parties saying good night before the big day. Freshly minted twenty-one-year-olds who went too hard too soon. Hip travelers on their way out of the Quarter to find more authentic local experiences.

We turned the corner into the bar, and then I stopped. The view was absolute brain candy, but the most surprising thing of all was— "Is that bar moving?"

Eli doubled back, realizing he'd left me a few steps behind. "Welcome to the Hotel Monteleone's Carousel Bar. It rotates every fifteen minutes or so."

In a cheeky nod, the back of each bar seat was embroidered with an exotic animal you might find on a carousel ride.

Long fingers threaded through my own. "Come on. That couple over there is about to get up."

While I always felt like I had to yield the right of way in a busy place because I was a bigger person, Eli used his broad shoulders and height to part the crowd.

He gave a nod to the man who was helping the woman beside him up from her seat. "They're all yours," the man said.

Eli stepped up and took a card out of his wallet for the bartender.

"I can get—"

"No protesting," Eli said. "You don't cry on my shoulder and then buy your own drink. It's a universal law."

The bartender, an older man who looked like he could play a very convincing Santa Claus at a rich-people mall, took Eli's card. "What can I get you two?"

"I'll have a Sazerac," Eli told him.

"A mint julep, please," I said.

The bartender nodded and then held up Eli's card. "Leave it open or closed?"

"Leave it open for now." Eli rested his elbows on the bar top, his hands clasped.

I stared at the vein traveling up his forearm for a moment too long before I realized he was talking to me.

"I'm sorry. What was that?"

"I was just saying that I can take Ruby around to all her events tomorrow. You should stay back and enjoy the hotel."

"We'll see. This isn't really new territory for us." I hadn't even considered tomorrow. Or even the next few hours. I'd have to go back to the room eventually and see her, but that was a Future Vera problem. "This place is . . . great . . . " I said over the swelling music.

"Except?"

"Please don't judge me."

"Judgment-free zone," he said, although I could barely hear him.

"I hate live music. And I don't get people who like it."

He snorted. "I'm sorry to tell you this, but you're in the wrong city."

"I don't know what to tell you! If I want to hear music, I'll go to a concert. But I don't want to stumble upon it when I'm just trying to have a conversation with someone."

"So *unexpected* live music?"

"Yes. Red flag."

"What are your other red flags?"

I leaned in closer to him as the music started up again so he could hear me. "Um . . . grapefruits."

He studied me with bemused confusion.

"But just *actual* grapefruits. Not grapefruit-flavored things."

"That hardly seems fair to grapefruits."

"Do you work for Big Grapefruit? I'm pretty sure grapefruits are doing fine without my support. And the aftertaste is . . . blech!" Just the thought made me gag. "What are your red flags?"

"The Rainbow Bridge."

"The Rainbow Bridge? As in when a pet dies, they cross the Rainbow Bridge?"

"Yes!" he said with conviction. "My cat of twelve years died last year—"

"I never took you for a pet person."

"I'm not a barbarian, Vera."

"I guess I just thought you would have an exotic fish tank in your fancy cardiology practice and that would be enough animal companionship for you. But I'm sorry. I derailed you. Your cat . . ."

"Right. So Bear—"

"Your cat was named Bear?" That was aggressively cute.

His brows arched in mock annoyance.

"No more interruptions!" I promised.

"Okay, so when Bear died, the vet's office made this huge deal of him crossing this supposed Rainbow Bridge and then they even had a Rainbow Bridge out front that crossed over the saddest pond I'd ever seen. When you pick up your pet's ashes, you're supposed to walk over the bridge with them."

"Well, that's cheesy, but it could be sort of comforting for some people, right?"

"It was patronizing."

I nodded along. "I am outraged on your behalf."

"Losing Bear wasn't easy, okay? I'd gotten him for Brigid, but then it turned out that her mom developed a late-in-life allergy to cats, so Bear came to live with me and . . . Don't laugh . . ."

"I will do my best."

"My house was henceforth called the 'catchelor pad.'"

My eyes burned at how goddamn sweet that was. "That is the single greatest thing I've ever heard." I held up my drink. "To Bear!"

Eli clinked his glass against mine and took a long sip.

"So how did Bear get his name?"

"Well, would you believe me if I said it was a family name?"

I laughed and motioned for him to continue.

"My first pet was a hamster. I was four. I named her Bear. I don't know why. But I was distraught when she ran away, and then we got a goldfish."

I held up a hand. "Your hamster ran away?"

"She was in her little hamster ball and I guess my dad left the garage door open one day. We never saw her again."

"That's . . . traumatic."

"Exactly. My peanut-size brain thought that maybe I wouldn't miss Bear the hamster so much if I named the new fish Bear as well. And then it stuck. Bear the corgi, Bear the gecko, Bear the betta fish."

"So the child who was devastated by loss decided to go into a profession that forced him to regularly confront it? That feels masochistic."

He waved me off. "That's human loss. Much different. Now, if I were a veterinarian, *that* would be masochism."

We finished our drinks and Eli closed out his tab to rescue me from the live music that only seemed to be growing in volume.

"So that's it?" I asked as we stepped back outside. It had cooled down a little, but the damp humidity still clung to our skin. "Anything besides the Rainbow Bridge?"

"Oh, I've got plenty." He held out his hand and began to count out his red flags on his fingers. "Finance bros, people who say *Die Hard* isn't a Christmas movie, and my uncle Barry. It's a long saying but trust me. The guy is such a sketchy doctor that someone made a podcast about him."

I nodded with conviction. "Uncle Barry can go fuck himself."

"Never let anyone say you aren't loyal, Vera."

As we crossed the street to continue deeper into the Quarter, stumbling partygoers spilled out from Bourbon Street.

We walked down to St. Louis Cathedral and Eli led me to Royal Street.

He walked behind me with his hands on my shoulders as he turned me to face the shadow of the Jesus statue with outstretched arms projected onto the church.

"You can't go to New Orleans without seeing Touchdown Jesus," he said solemnly.

After a stroll around Jackson Square, we got a bag of beignets to go and took them back to the square, where we settled onto a bench, tucked away under a giant tree covered in Spanish moss.

We dug into the beignets and were covered in powdered sugar in a matter of seconds.

A guttural moan came out of my body as I took my first bite.

Eli's eyes briefly widened at the sound before he cleared his throat and looked away.

"Okay," I said, trying to recover from my absolutely pornographic response to powdered sugar–covered deep-fried balls of dough. "I would sit through *hours* of unexpected live music for these."

He made a pleased noise. "That good?"

"So good."

We ate the rest in silence and watched people and snippets of their lives pass us by.

As I finished the last of my beignet, a joint bachelor-bachelorette party meandered through the square with the bride and groom taking up the rear as they engaged in a drunken shouting match loud enough for everyone in a two-block radius to hear. It was hard to follow their inebriated argument, but it seemed that the groom didn't think the bride was ready and she was very upset about something that had happened on a swamp tour earlier that day.

"Do you ever wonder," Eli said softly, "what would have happened if we'd woken up in Vegas and just . . . stayed married?"

I looked at him, but it was too dark to fully read his expression and gauge how he might answer that question himself. Not that Eli was ever an easy read.

"Sometimes," I whispered. I did think about it, especially that first year or two after he'd disappeared.

"I think about it," he said. "A lot."

I wanted him to give me more. To say the vulnerable things first.

"Do you still have the ring?" he asked.

I nodded. "I do." I'd always liked the ring. "I'd wear it for months at a time, take it off, and then see it sitting in my little jewelry dish. I don't wear much jewelry, ya know, but I would spin it around my finger and fidget with it. In waiting rooms. During phone calls. God, even when I waited with my mom's body for the paramedics to come. It was comforting."

He paused for a moment so long that I thought maybe he hadn't heard me. "I'm glad the ring was there for you even if I never was. I haven't seen you wear it, so I wasn't sure."

"I didn't want you to think I'd been holding on to it in the name of something that never really was."

"What if I was holding on?"

My breath caught. "What if?" I asked, because I couldn't bring myself to answer his questions before he did. I couldn't let myself be the one who put themselves out there only to be rejected or, even worse, shoved into the dark corners of his life like I had been with Brody.

The wedding party disappeared into a souvenir shop and I groaned, holding my hand up. "I hate having sticky fingers."

Without a word, Eli took my hand, his thumb rubbing a circle into my palm. Then he pressed each of my fingers to his lips, sucking them clean one by one. My heart practically crashed into the ladder of my ribs. His warm tongue sent tendrils of heat through my arm and up to my neck.

"That's one way to clean them," I said quietly, my voice trembling.

Eli leaned his head down to me, his pointer finger hooked under my chin as he tilted my head up to meet him.

And then I yawned.

I ruined the fucking moment with a tear-inducing yawn.

With a sigh that turned into a chuckle, he stood up and held a hand out for me. "Let's get a cab before you turn into a pumpkin."

I yawned again as he pulled me to my feet. I could kick myself. But I really was exhausted, and we had definitely been heading toward dangerous territory.

Eli wrapped an arm around my shoulder and tossed our trash in a wastebasket as we walked down to the street.

I didn't know exactly what it was he had been planning on doing after his finger grazed my chin, but I couldn't help but feel like I was falling asleep just as the movie was getting good.

CHAPTER FORTY-ONE

We took the elevator up, and by the time the doors opened to our floor, I was swaying on my feet.

Eli walked beside me with his hand pressed lightly against my lower back. We stopped in front of my and Ruby's room and I dug through my purse, searching for my room key.

"Shit," I muttered once it became very clear that the key was missing.

I patted Eli on the shoulder, feeling a little punch-drunk from the lack of sleep. "I'm going to head down and get another key. I'll see you in the morning."

His mouth opened and closed before I spun around back toward the elevators, but then he caught my hand and pulled me back. "Stay. With me."

My heart fluttered up into my throat. I shook my head, unable to voice a reason because I didn't want there to be one.

"You're basically asleep on your feet. And it's almost morning, anyway. Come on. You and Ruby could both use some space."

My resolve was rapidly crumbling.

"I'll be a gentleman," he promised.

Another yawn answered for me and I followed him to his room.

Eli's hotel room was spotless. The only sign of life was the slight indentation on the end of the bed from where he must have briefly sat down before going out for the evening.

"Did you unpack your suitcase for a two-day trip?" I peered into his bathroom to see his toothbrush perfectly situated beside his toothpaste, face wash, and cologne. The closet was cracked just enough for me to see his clothes hanging up in a neat row. "Red flag."

He laughed. "I can sleep on the floor."

"No, no," I said. "The bed is huge." I was already slipping under the covers, my shoes kicked off behind me. "Is this okay?" I asked. "Do you have a particular side?"

"This is okay," he said softly, clicking off the bedside lamp as my head sank into the pillow. "I'm going to get a shower. Do you want to use the bathroom for anything? You could borrow a T-shirt if you want."

I nodded. "That's nice." But my eyes were already closing.

A sliver of light passing across the room woke me as Eli walked out of the bathroom. This felt familiar. The clean, humid feeling of him showering in the other room. It was a good memory. One that I was currently inside of.

"Vera," he whispered.

A soft noise of recognition pushed against my lips.

"I left you the T-shirt I was going to sleep in on the bathroom counter if you want it, love," Eli whispered as he petted my back in circles.

I stretched into his touch, and managed to open my eyes, lashes blurring my vision for a moment. "Th-thank you," I said as I felt the underwire of my bra rudely cutting into my side. I didn't know that I could bring myself to go braless, but it would be nice to get out of these clothes at least.

The bed sank slightly as Eli sat down on the opposite edge.

I glanced over my shoulder to see him in cotton sleep pants and no shirt. The muscles in his back strained as he rolled his neck from side to side.

"There's an extra toothbrush in there too. I left mine at home and the one I picked up at the airport was a two-pack."

"Thanks." I slid out of bed and tiptoed into the bathroom.

It felt so good to brush my teeth and splash water on my face. I eyed the shirt on the counter. Eli was a broad guy, so I knew his shirt would fit, but it wouldn't be big enough to be appropriate to wear on its own. However, I was wearing a jumpsuit, so leaving my bottoms on wasn't really an option.

I could just go back to bed in my clothes. That was what I should have done.

But I wanted to wear something of his. It was that painfully simple.

Pushing aside reason, I stripped out of my jumpsuit and tugged his T-shirt over my head. It was huge in the shoulders and even the chest, but snug on my hips. I gave myself a little twirl in the mirror and found that it barely covered my ass. I unhooked the black strapless bra and slid it off. The matching—though somewhat cheeky—underwear I wore had been bought at the behest of Ruby because they had some sort of bullshit smoothing panels that didn't actually do anything.

I set my toothbrush in the cup near the sink and flicked the lights off before stepping back into the bedroom.

I'd expected to find Eli with his back to the bathroom door, already asleep, but instead he sat on the edge of the bed with his hands clasped in his lap.

He looked up at me and let out a strangled sound. "Vera," he whispered.

"It's a little short," I said. "I'm sorry. I can put my clothes back—"

"No," he snapped. "No. Does the fact that I like seeing you in my clothes make me a Neanderthal?"

I shook my head, taking a few steps closer.

"Especially after watching you walk around the house in Brody's old T-shirts."

A fluttering warmth spread across my chest. I knew it was sinking to the lowest common denominator to feel turned on by him being possessive. But I was. Very much so. "It's just the one that I sleep in sometimes," I told him. "And I can't even find it, anyway."

"I know," he said. "I may have been the reason it was lost in the laundry."

"What?" I'd been looking for that shirt for weeks.

"I threw it in with some donations."

I gawked. "That's some psycho shit."

He shrugged. "Were you expecting me to apologize?"

I shook my head because I didn't want him to. "Did you mean what you said about being a gentleman?" My voice didn't even sound like my own. Low and breathy.

He slid his hands under his thighs, like that might help him resist temptation. "Unfortunately." He groaned. "But maybe you could indulge me."

"Maybe," I conceded.

"Vera, will you turn around for me? I just—I need to remember this. I know it's fucked up to even say that out loud, but—"

I stepped between his legs, pushing them a little farther apart. He leaned back, taking in the view, his stare heavy.

Slowly, I turned around. The T-shirt had ridden up my ass a little so that my cheeks were peeking out the bottom. It was a part of my body that I genuinely liked.

I took a glance over my shoulder to watch him.

Pupils blown and hungry, his eyes traveled up my thighs and backside. His hands gripped the mattress now, knuckles white.

"Elias." His name felt like a sin. The sex we'd had in Vegas—our bodies younger and less experienced but eager all the same—had been hurried and almost antagonistic. This felt different. "What if I don't want you to be a gentleman?"

He sucked in a breath and tilted his head back, his Adam's apple bobbing. "Fuck," he whispered. "We should go to bed. You had a long night and—"

"No." I turned around, and pulled his hands, guiding them under my T-shirt.

He watched me with reverence as the tips of his fingers dug into the soft curve of my hips.

My lips parted on a gasp as his hands roamed my body, his nose dragging along the side of my neck, his breath hot and impatient.

"I need to know that this isn't the end." His teeth nipped at my ear, and it was so distracting that I hardly registered what he said.

His touch ran up my thighs and slid inward until he was parting my legs, forcing me to straddle one of his thighs. Unanswered pleasure rolled up my spine as I arched my back, letting my body curl against his.

"I need to know, Vera," he demanded. "I need to know that this isn't going to be something you're getting out of your system. I need to know that you're not going to feed me some bullshit line about the apartment or your job, because no matter what happens to us, I will never put your well-being in jeopardy. I need you to trust in that."

"But—but—"

He pressed his thigh upward, creating a painfully frustrating pressure.

"This isn't f-fair," I stuttered. "I can't even think right now."

One hand slid up my shirt, exposing my belly. Outside, the sun was beginning to rise, and the sudden lightness in the room had me gripping his wrist and trying to push him away. I hadn't thought this through. Not at all. I wasn't ready for this. I wanted the pleasure of feeling him, but not in the vulnerable morning light. In Vegas, the lights had stayed off.

His thigh thrust up again, my middle pulsing. He was hard against my leg and suddenly his thigh wasn't nearly enough. Instead of letting me push him away, he circled his fingers around my wrists and held my hands on my thighs.

"If we do this," he said, "you're not ignoring me when we wake up, Vera. Do you understand?"

With my hands braced on my thighs, I attempted to grind against him, but he forced me to still.

"Vera. Please." The desperation in his voice momentarily broke through my veil of lust.

"Goddamn it," I said. "When did you turn into such an open communicator?"

He laughed, teeth dragging along the crook of my neck.

"Yes. Okay. Yes. I won't ignore you."

He tilted his head into the back of my neck, lost in my tangle of curls. His hand spread across my stomach as he stood up and turned me around. With such care, he wrapped his arms around me, his arms cradling me as he laid me back against the mattress.

"Let me taste you," he said.

I shook my head, pushing up from beneath him on my elbows. "No, no, that's— I don't need you to do that."

"*You* might not need it, but I do," he said.

My breath hitched and my brain would not shut the fuck up. I hadn't shaved in a few weeks. Brody had gone down on me a handful of times, but he never seemed to enjoy it and any time he did, my mind populated with reasons why he should stop, like some sort of toxic search engine results. What if I tasted off? What if I smelled? What if he didn't like that I wasn't fully shaven? (Not that his pubic hair ever stopped him from receiving oral.) How could I possibly shut off my brain long enough to enjoy something that intimate?

Eli inhaled deeply as he dragged his nose down my chest, pushing the hem of my shirt up. He groaned at the sight of my breasts.

I did that to him. I was the reason for that desperate noise. I said it over and over again in my head. A mantra. I wanted him to touch me. I didn't have to be the person who only had sex in the dark or hid under the cover of blankets.

His gaze scraped over my body. "Please let me eat your cunt."

I sat up partly, and the sight of him standing there, panting for me, that filthy word fresh on his lips . . . it was vulgar and exciting. Exciting enough to edge the uncertainty out of my brain. "Okay."

Then he was crowding over me, his thigh heavy between my legs. His fingers mapped a course along the line of my jaw, his thumb tracing my lips. "I'm going to kiss you now," he said. "And I won't be a gentleman about it."

I lifted my head, unable to wait any longer. My lips nearly brushed his, but he pulled back with a taunting grin. That was all it took for me to reach up and pull him to me. Our lips collided with enough impact to bruise. We were teeth and tongues and swallowed moans.

He pulled back for a moment and held my neck as he panted in my ear. "It's been a while," he admitted. "And god, you're so fucking sexy. I don't know how long I'm going to last."

A streak of bravery chased through me and I reached down between us to rub my hand over his erection.

His forehead lolled into the dip of my shoulder with a grunt. "If you don't stop that I'm going to come in my pants like a teenage boy."

I laughed softly as I gripped him tightly. "That long, huh?"

"It doesn't help that I've dreamed of having you again for the last nineteen years." He ground his thigh between my legs and surely he could feel how wet I was.

I whimpered in response. My body was on fire as the sun began to stretch across the room in earnest now, turning us into shadows. I pulled my shirt off over my head and his hungry lips dragged across every bit of newly exposed skin.

There was no darkness left to hide in and I was a woman driven by need. That was the only excuse for how ready and willing I was for him to see me—fully see me.

But then my brain caught up to my body and my hands froze. Something in my expression must have given me away, because Eli tucked a stray hair behind my ear and asked, "What's wrong?"

"I—I've never been a small person. I know that."

His eyes hardened, as though he was prepared to rebuke whatever it was that I might say.

"But my body is—it's a forty-year-old body, Eli. My tits aren't perky and my rolls used to be soft and—cute. Like a Botticelli." I shook my head. "Of course I didn't think that then. But now I have the kind of stretch marks you can't hide and I'm lumpy and—"

He pressed a finger to my lips and drove his erection against me. "I don't want the girl you used to be, Vera. I want the woman you are. There is no polite way for me to tell you that your body is so arousing I had to take three cold showers the day after you moved in." His hand left my mouth as he lay beside me, our legs still twisted together. "I'm not going to tell you that you have to love yourself before anyone else can, because that's bullshit. If that were true we'd all be waiting around for the rest of our lives. But I need you to believe me when I tell you that I am deeply attracted to you *and* your body."

My options were to give in to this doubt or move on. That was it. There were only two paths forward.

"Okay," I whispered.

Each of Eli's hands cupped one of my breasts, rolling my nipples between his fingers. "Perfect." His finger followed the line of a dark stretch mark that spanned from under my arm to my breast. "Goddamn perfect."

He dipped his head down and licked along my chest, careful not to touch my nipples as his beard brushed against my skin.

I threw my head back at the cool drag of his tongue. "More," I whispered.

His mouth covered my nipple then as he looked up from beneath hooded eyes and sucked.

After doing the same to the other breast, he danced his fingers along the waistband of my underwear for a moment before I lifted my hips for him to pull them off.

His intent green eyes held mine as he ran one finger up my slit before pressing in, his finger brushing against my clitoris. "That's it," he said.

He sunk down to his knees, his free hand sweeping over my body and then to my inner thigh. "I'm going to make this feel so good for you, Vera. I'm going to ruin all other men for you."

"That's some big talk," I said as he pulled one of my legs over his shoulder and then dragged me down the bed by my hips.

"I'm done talking." And then his mouth was on me, spreading me apart with the flat of his greedy tongue and his facial hair scraping against my inner thighs.

"Oh—*oh* my god," I rasped as I instinctively squirmed up the bed, trying to escape the torturous, teetering pleasure.

Eli pressed a hand to my pubic bone, keeping me right where he wanted me. In the past, Brody had been exploratory and timid, but Eli was purposeful and relentless. His tongue stiffened against my clit before sucking down on the collection of nerves.

He lifted his head for a moment, his chin glistening with my arousal. "If this were my last meal, I could die happy."

A smile tipped my lips and I laughed. This was . . . fun. The doubt and the worries had seeped to the edges of my brain.

I tugged his hair, pulling him back down to me.

"Yes, ma'am," he said, each syllable tickling my inner thighs.

He eagerly tended to me again, licking and sucking. A moan broke from my chest as he slid two fingers past my entrance, curling them against my inner walls. The sensation stretched every muscle in my body taut like a canvas. Tension curled in my belly.

"Eli," I panted. "Eli. I'm—"

"Come for me, love." He maintained his rhythm as I shamelessly sought out my orgasm. A satisfied warmth spiraled from my core to the tips of my toes.

He stayed there for a moment kissing up and down my thighs as I unwound, every muscle in my body turning limp.

"Goddamn it," he said as he stood, kicking off his pants and stroking his cock and licking his lips, eyes dark and a little amused. He'd made good on his promise to ruin me. "I want to fuck you so bad, but I'm going to come, Vera. It's been a while and it's . . . you. When I fuck you, I plan on taking my time."

I wanted to give him what he gave me. It was the only thought I had as I slid off the edge of the bed and onto my knees. Tilting my head back against the bed, I wrapped my hands around the backs of his thighs and pulled him to me, his swollen dick bobbing inches from my lips.

"You don't even have to—I'm going to—"

But I didn't give him a moment to finish. Instead I gripped his cock and began to polish the head of his penis with my tongue, teasing him gently.

His hand went to the back of my head, fisting my hair as he let out a painful noise. I opened my lips fully then, letting him sink all the way in to the back of my throat.

"Vera, fuck, baby . . . I'm going to come . . ." He tried to pull out, but I didn't let him.

I wanted to share this deeply intimate moment with him even if I didn't know what would happen when we inevitably woke up in a few hours. Even though I'd told him that I wouldn't pretend it all away. I wanted this one moment even if, in the end, we were too complicated and impossible to untangle.

His fingers tightened in my hair as his warmth emptied down my throat.

He let out a painful grunt as he tilted my head back and watched me with awe, my lips wrapped around him. His eyes rolled to the back of his head as he shuddered one last time before pulling out and crumpling to the floor in front of me.

Without any hesitation, he pulled me to him, his lips caressing mine.

I hated that most of my other sexual experiences were with Brody and so I kept comparing the two. But Brody would never kiss me after what I'd just done. I always rushed to the bathroom and brushed my teeth and, already half asleep, he would call me a good girl. But it made me feel anything but good. It made me feel dirty, the same way I did when he attempted to go down on me just frequently enough to make himself feel like oral sex was a two-way street.

Eli sat back on the carpet and pulled me between his legs. His kisses were soft as he stroked my cheek and rubbed up and down my spine.

When he pulled away, my lips moved silently, searching for a way to tell him I wasn't ready for him to let go. But I was immediately sated as he tucked my head against his chest and placed a collection of kisses against my hair.

"No disappearing," he muttered. "If we go to sleep, I can't wake up to find that you've disappeared."

I nodded, because even if it was messy and scary, I didn't want to disappear either.

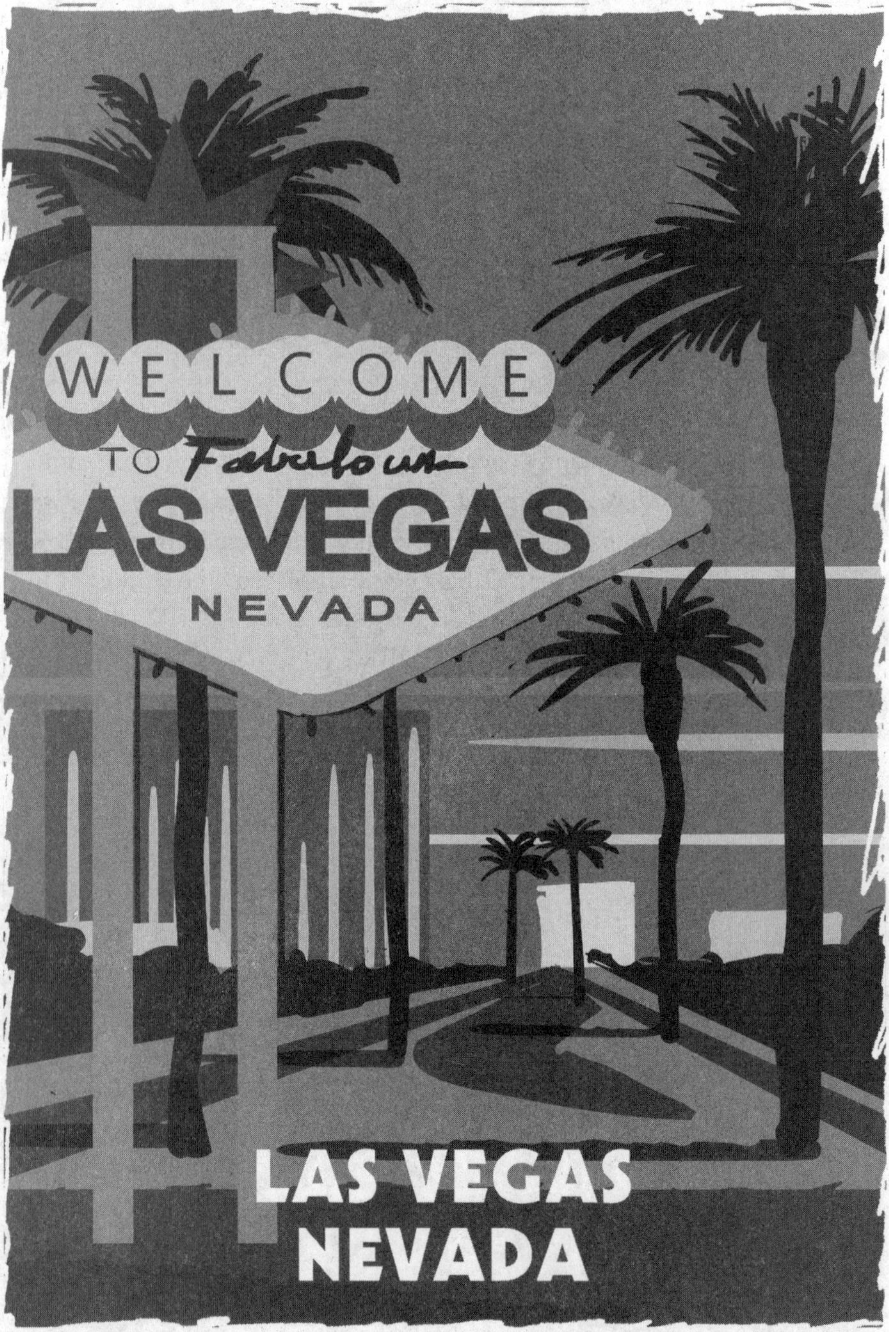

LAS VEGAS
NEVADA

ELIAS BUCKLEY
NINETEEN YEARS AGO
THE MORNING AFTER

I was normally a fitful sleeper. My exes rarely stayed the night because I'd never been a good bed partner.

But that night with Vera, my limbs were heavy from the adrenaline crash and something that felt like serenity. At one point in the early hours of the morning, my body jerked awake as I tried to recall where I was.

It took a moment to realize the warmth radiating beside me was a nearly naked Vera tangled in the sheets, her body curled against my side. I was hard again, but she looked too peaceful for me to wake. Wisps of hair curled around her ear and after a moment of memorizing this feeling, I settled down with her back pressed against my chest and fell asleep.

"Fuck, fuck, fuck!" a voice said in a hushed shout. "Wake up. Eli! Wake. Up."

My response was delayed, but eventually I sat up and rubbed my eyes. I glanced down to find the blankets had been ripped from the bed and Vera was pacing the length of the room, wrapped in hotel bedding.

Our rented wedding clothes littered the floor and the newlyweds' cake sat on the side table where we left it, stuck with two forks and most of the cherries missing.

Oh god. Panic gripped me. What if Vera . . . what if she was more drunk last night than I thought? What if she woke up and didn't realize what had happened?

"Are you okay?" I asked, pulling a pillow into my lap. "Do you want to talk—"

She turned to me, eyes welling with tears. "Brody's awake. He just yelled out that he was going for coffee."

"So glad he didn't die of alcohol poisoning," I said, relaxing slightly against the headboard.

She shook her head. "He can't know. He can never know. Eli, I need this—" Frantically, she waved her hands between us. "To never get to him."

I slid to the edge of the bed and then asked a question best left unspoken. "Why? He quite literally dared us to get married last night."

She spun around and wound her hand in circles, like that might make the words come easier. "Because—because he's our friend and I don't want this to hurt him."

Tugging my boxer briefs up, I stood and walked around the bed to her. Anger twisted in my chest like a ratchet, growing tighter and tighter. "You don't want to hurt him or your *chances* with him?"

"What's that supposed to mean?" She wore her surprise well, but I noticed the way her lips trembled, and I knew I'd hit on something.

"Oh, come the fuck on. Seriously? You're in love with him, Vera. Admit it."

She was practically panting with anxiety but said nothing.

I wanted this to hurt her as much as it did me. "Answer me this: What man dares another guy to marry the girl he's in love with?"

She pulled the sheets tighter against her chest, and her nostrils flared as her breaths came quicker. "You wouldn't understand."

Her admission—or rather lack of denial—felt like a serrated knife to the gut. "What is there to understand? Your world revolves around a guy who views you as a convenience. Need help with an assignment? Call Vera. Need an ego boost? Call Vera. Need a quick suck? Call Vera."

Her jaw dropped then and she was frozen for a moment before she roared right back. "What are you saying, Eli? Because what it sounds like you're saying is that Brody, or anyone else for that matter, could never love someone like me. And don't pretend like you're incapable of using people. Don't pretend like you're above it. You don't even like me, but you sure didn't mind fucking me just a few hours ago."

"And you let me do it." The words were out before I could stop them. My whole body was on the verge of seizing. What was I doing? How had this devolved so quickly?

"I might be in love with someone who doesn't return those feelings," she said in a quiet but fierce tone. "But at least I'm not out here living some color-by-numbers life. Do you even *want* to go to med school, Eli? Who the fuck are you? Do you even know? Maybe I don't know what I want or who I am, but at least I'm brave enough to ask. To hope."

"How noble of you," I said. "How brave of you to have no direction or ambition."

She looked pleased, like I'd just proven her right.

"You know what, Eli? You're a mean fucking son of a bitch. You're miserable, and the only thing that makes you remotely happy is bringing everyone else down with you."

Her words hit me in rapid succession, each one landing like a bullet. And it hurt, because it was true. I *was* miserable. I did hate seeing her and Brody happy. Even if their affections were unevenly matched. Even if it was complicated. There was still joy. I was hurt, and just like she'd said, I would only feel a glimmer of anything if I could bring her down with me.

"He'll never love you," I said, hoping my words haunted her for the rest of her life. "He'll drain you, Vera. And you'll let him. You'll let him soak up all that love you have for him just for a fraction of affection in return. If you can't see that—if you can't want more for yourself—then maybe that's what you deserve."

"Go," she said sternly.

"I'm gone," I told her as I pulled my pants on and grabbed my shoes. My heart felt like it had been put through a meat grinder and I needed to get as far away from her as I possibly could. The closer she was, the more this hurt. The more irreparable the damage would become. "You'll get the annulment papers in the mail. Sign them and you'll never have to see me again."

I allowed myself one last look at her. Wild curls and pillow lines still pressed into her cheek. Eyes wide and wet as tears began to spill. "Go," she screamed again, and threw my shirt at me.

"Gone." I quickly grabbed the rest of my clothes, my shoes, and my wallet before walking out of the bedroom and slamming the door shut behind me.

The living room of the suite was a mess. Brody had created a pallet on the floor with the couch cushions. He had a bathroom trash can and an ice bucket staged as puke receptacles.

I could fucking kill him. I didn't care about the mess. I cared that he had to go and ruin everything. I cared that because of his idiotic dare, I could no longer just exist in Vera's world. I could no longer enjoy the painful pleasure of hovering in the backdrop of her life. Even if we hadn't just fought, there was no going back. I'd had her last night, and it was an experience I could never unlearn. There was no way I could go back to how things had been. And it was his fault.

I grabbed the backpack I'd brought with me for the trip and yanked a T-shirt on over my head.

For a moment, I stood there at the door, waiting to see if maybe she might come after me. Even if it was only to yell at me again. I already missed her. But the only thing I found was more silence.

I forced myself to turn the doorknob and walk out into the hallway. I'd purposefully left my room key on the counter so I couldn't let myself back in. The temptation would be too strong.

As I walked the endless corridor to the elevator bank, I let my anger grow until it was immovable. Uncompromising. I turned the corner and there was Brody with a coffee and a huge water bottle.

"Hey, man," he said. "Vera up yet? I don't know if you guys heard me say I was going down for coffee."

I walked right at him, shedding my bag and the rental shoes dangling from my fingers, and shoved him against the wall.

He dropped the water bottle and the coffee, which had to be one of the least offensive things to happen to this carpet in its lifetime.

"What the fuck?" He shook his head. "I'm way too hungover for this shit."

I crowded in, not letting him move off the wall, and gathered the collar of his shirt in my fists. "Fuck you, Brody."

"I'm obviously missing something here. Let's go back to the—"

"You ruined everything last night with that stupid dare. You know she fucking loves you, right?"

That last sentence didn't even faze him, and that pissed me off even more. His mouth lifted into a smirk, and he rolled his eyes. "What happened with you guys last night, anyway? I barely remember anything after the wedding."

"She loves you and you dared me to marry her. Are you hearing me right now, you thick motherfucker? Do you know how fucked up that is? People aren't just puppets for your entertainment."

"Vera doesn't love me like that." But even he sounded barely convinced.

"You *know* that's not true. Not only that, but you are constantly taking advantage of that love. And now—"

"Oh my god," he said.

I wanted to punch the damn smile off his face.

"You *like* her." He shook his head. "No, you *love* her. No fucking way! You're such a moody shit bag when she's around."

I'd wasted the last year. Not only did Vera think I hated her, but so did Brody, the least intuitive person I knew. "My feelings for her don't matter. There's no room for them." I stepped back and finally let go of his shirt.

He slumped against the wall, smoothing out his collar. But he was silent, which meant he knew I was right. I didn't even realize it was possible to weaponize incompetence until I'd met Brody. It encouraged Vera to either do everything for him or hold his hand like he was a child.

"You need to tell her," he said. It was the last thing I expected to hear from him. But there was no fixing what I'd just done.

I shook my head and grabbed my stuff from the floor. Telling her would never make a difference.

"One day," I said, "you're going to wake up and realize she's given you everything. Every part of herself. And she'll hate you for it, because you just take and take and take." I closed my eyes, my throat dry and aching from talking too much so soon after waking up. "Let her go," I begged him. "Let her go before she has nothing left to give."

Brody propped his elbows up on his knees and turned his head away from me, refusing to answer.

I went straight to the airport and took the first flight back to LA. I was moved out of my and Brody's room before he could even make the drive back.

Then I called my mom. She helped me convince the family lawyer to handle this as quietly as possible without involving my father and to bill her directly. The only evidence was the album I'd stuffed into my backpack and couldn't bring myself to throw away.

It was as if it never happened. A brief memory that walked the line between reality and fantasy. My marriage to Vera Stein.

CHAPTER FORTY-TWO

When I woke a few hours later, the decadent New Orleans hotel room was dark save for a sliver of sunlight peeking through the blackout curtains.

Featherlight touches twisted and curved over my shoulder and once my eyes adjusted to the darkness, I looked up to find Eli sitting up against the headboard, wearing wire-rimmed glasses and holding an e-reader in his free hand. I had curled into him with my head in his lap and my arm slung around his waist.

At my stirring, Eli set his tablet down and let his hand drift down my naked back. "You're awake," he said.

"You wear glasses."

"Only under duress."

"Did you get any sleep?" I asked though a yawn as I pulled the sheet up to my chin, suddenly remembering just how naked I was without my blinding lust as a distraction.

"I did," he said. "But not as well as you did."

"What's that supposed to mean?"

"Just that you were obviously clocking some deep REM." With a grin, he brushed the tip of my nose. "I never knew how much you talk in your sleep."

"I do not!" I said. "Besides, how would I even know if I'm asleep?"

"I can't be the first one to tell you that you talk in your sleep."

I frowned. "Did I at least say anything good?"

"You kept mumbling about *La La Land* and frowning."

"I hate that movie."

"So does your subconscious." He snorted lightly. "I regret to inform you that you are distressingly adorable in the morning."

With a huff, I plopped my head back down in his lap. "Do I want to know what time it is?"

He slid down in the bed and pulled me tight against him, his excitement very obviously growing. "Twenty after one in the afternoon," he said as he feathered kisses up my throat.

"I really like what you're doing here," I told him. "No notes, but I do have to go check on Ruby. She has a panel in a few hours and then a dinner tonight." His teeth grazed the soft spot behind my ear. It was dizzying, and it took an extraordinary amount of self-control to push my hand against his chest. "To be continued, I promise."

With a sigh, he planted a kiss on my forehead and let his hold on me loosen.

I leaned over the edge of the bed to find my underwear, which I quickly slipped into before he could convince me to change my mind.

After a quick trip to the bathroom to brush my teeth and put on my bra and jumpsuit, I ducked out of the room with a promise to update him on my plans for the day.

He stood in the doorway, his pants slung low on his hips, and watched me go until I stepped into the elevator to get a new key from the front desk.

I waited in line downstairs, caught in a sudden surge of hotel guests who were either checking out late or checking in early. As I scrolled through my nearly dead phone, I opened my text thread with Tess to find a new message.

Tess:

You know the guys who played the strings on the *Titanic*?

I grinned and typed back.

Vera:
You mean the ones who kept playing while the ship went down?

Tess:
Yes, that is me and my renovation right now. 🎻

"Vera?"

I froze mid-response and spun around, looking for the source.

Hollis leaned out of the line two guests behind me.

"Hollis," I said, squeezing past the other guests to stand with her. "What are you doing?"

She wore a sleek Prada belt bag across her chest and had a small carry-on suitcase at her side. For the first time since I'd met her, Hollis appeared uncertain. "I would have been here last night if it weren't for some broken latch on a lavatory door. They had to delay my flight until this morning."

"Does Ruby know you're here?" This could be bad.

She bit down on her lower lip and shook her head as the line shifted forward. "I came to make things right. We're too old for this shit. I'm done playing tag with the girl of my dreams."

"But—and I'm sorry if it's not my place—you told her that you wanted to keep seeing other people, I thought."

Hollis wrung her hands together. "The thing you have to understand about me and Ruby is that we're decades in the making and our timing is worse than my niece's community theater production of *Who's on First?*"

"That's very specific."

"It was a *terrible* show."

The person in front of us approached the front desk and we were next.

"I think I told Ruby I couldn't commit to her because . . ." She sighed. "The woman had fed me that line so many times, and I suppose a part of me wanted her to know how badly it hurt."

"Oh." It was wrong, but it made sense. I'd wondered plenty of times about what it might be like to inflict the pain on Brody that he had inflicted on me.

"Next," the clerk called.

I turned back to Hollis with a shallow nod before approaching the desk and explaining that I'd lost my room key.

After checking my ID, the woman got to work creating a new key.

"Actually," I said as she slid the key into a small holder. "Could I get a second one?

When I had both keys in hand, I pulled Hollis along with me. "Room six thirty-seven. Go get your girl."

She gave me a soft kiss on the cheek as she held the key to her chest and stepped away toward the elevators.

I was still very upset with Ruby, but I knew what Hollis had said was true. They'd been at this for decades, and even if Ruby thought she knew how I should live my life, at least I knew how she wanted to live hers. With Hollis.

THE WUNDERKIND (FIRST DRAFT)
"PILOT" 10/8/07

INT. POPPY'S BEDROOM—NIGHT

She's lying on the floor. Wearing his sweatshirt like armor.

POPPY (V.O.)

He told me I was pretty enough to be a muse. It was a lie, but a sweet one.

December 31, 2014
Vera S.
Poppy, I want more for us, girl.

THE WUNDERKIND by Vera Stein.

CHAPTER FORTY-THREE

"That's pretty romantic," Eli said as he pulled out a barstool at Herbsaint for me as I explained how I stumbled upon Hollis in the lobby. The restaurant was packed and we'd gotten lucky to snag two seats at the bar for lunch.

After retrieving my room key, I'd returned to Eli's room, where he pulled me back into the shadows and kissed me against the wall until one of our stomachs growled.

He led me by the hand for the five-minute walk. I kept waiting for him to let go and for things to return to how they'd been, but he didn't. And it was nice to not be the person constantly fighting for something.

Eli ordered several dishes for us to share and swore the spaghetti would change my life.

While we waited for our food, the sky outside opened with rain. Each drop practically steamed as it hit the pavement. I asked about Eli's dad. He was retiring soon and a cousin would take over the practice. He discussed it so bitterly that I had to assume his cousin was more in line with the version of Eli his father had hoped for.

"I see my father every other year," he explained. "Brigid or I will go for Christmas or Thanksgiving. He remarried to a woman a few years younger than me, and"—he shook his head—"after my mother died, we didn't really have a reason to maintain the appearance that we liked each other."

I talked about my mom and how she'd wanted to go back to school for social work but never did. After we got our food, I sent Ruby a brief question to see if she needed me for her events today. My wish was that she and Hollis had mended things and hopefully Hollis would attend to her. The only response I received was an ominous I'm fine . . .

I held out my phone for Eli to see as he placed a napkin in his lap.

"Does your dad do this shit with the ellipsis?" I asked.

He grunted. "Yes, and he writes texts like they're letters. He even signs off with his name."

I shook my head and dropped my phone back into my bag. "Red flag."

"Huge red flag," he confirmed.

We talked about Hollis and Ruby and missed connections. It was hard not to wonder if we were also talking about ourselves.

Just as Eli started to prod me about my writing, a drenched young couple sat down beside us.

"It's okay," the girl with long black braids said to the other girl, who had cropped blond hair. "Rain on your wedding day is supposed to be good luck."

Eli and I shared a sympathetic look as I twirled some (obscenely delicious) spaghetti around my fork.

"It doesn't *feel* lucky," the blond said, plopping her head against the other girl's shoulder. "We should have just gotten married in Vegas when you proposed."

"That's where we got married," I blurted.

Eli's eyes widened. Whether it was because I was making small talk with strangers or because I'd mentioned our wedding, I couldn't tell. Probably both.

But it only took a moment for him to recover and take my hand in his. "Twenty years next spring," he told the couple.

"Wow," the girl with braids said. "That seems like forever."

"Sometimes it feels like it," I muttered as I began to feel a little uncomfortable with the direction this was heading.

Eli chuckled. "I'm Eli and this is Vera."

The blond leaned over her fiancée. "I'm Lilly and this is Tori."

"Congratulations," I offered. "How did you two meet?"

Lilly and Tori shared a knowing glance and then Lilly rolled her eyes. "We met on an app. Sometimes we lie to make it more interesting, but the truth is, we were both looking for a hookup and ended up with—"

"More," Tori finished for her.

"How did you guys meet?"

"In college," I said just as Eli said, "She was obsessed with my roommate."

Tori waggled her eyebrows. "This sounds juicy."

"And so tortured," Lilly said. "How did you two actually start dating?"

Eli squeezed my hand gently. "That's the funny thing. We never did."

Okay, I could play along for the sake of entertaining two nervous brides. "We were on a trip to Vegas just before Eli graduated, right, honey?"

He nodded. "Indeed, we were. A few drinks turned into truth or dare and then my roommate dared me to marry Vera at one of those twenty-four-hour wedding chapels."

Tori's jaw dropped. "Seriously?"

"Did you two even like each other before then?" Lilly asked.

Eli let go of my hand and slung his arm around my shoulder, nestling me in closer to him. "At the time, I had convinced myself she was annoying, but looking back, I was just annoyed by how much I liked her."

My head swiveled back to him. "You liked me?" I asked softly.

"Don't pretend you didn't know," he said conspiratorially.

But I didn't know. Truly.

Without turning back to Lilly and Tori, holding a steady gaze on Eli, I said, "And I was always curious about him."

It was his turn to be surprised now. "You were?"

I nodded sincerely.

After a moment, Tori let out a fluttery swoon. "You two are so dreamy. What a story."

"And you've been together ever since?" Lilly asked.

A wave of emotions passed over him. Hope, regret, and then something soft and vulnerable. "There have been a lot of ups and downs," he told them without looking away from me. "But we're here now."

A soft smile formed on my lips and I nodded once before we both turned back to our companions.

"They're so cute," Lilly said to Tori, and then in unison, they both said, "They should come to the wedding."

My body physically retreated from the two girls. A little fib over lunch was one thing, but dragging this out into one of the most important events of their lives felt flat-out unethical.

"Please say you will," Tori said to us both.

Lilly nodded vigorously. "With a story like that, you two have got to be some kind of good-luck charm."

I turned to Eli and gave a subtle shake of my head, but his mouth was already moving. "We'd love to."

The Eliza Jane hotel was on the north end of the Quarter, and while we could have walked there, the rain had been on and off all day and we decided it was best not to arrive to the wedding of two strangers looking like wet rats with humidity-induced swamp ass.

Eli watched me while we sat in the back seat of our cab. "Two dresses in one weekend," he said wistfully.

My cheeks warmed. I still wasn't used to Eli being so vocal, especially when it came to me.

Since he'd walked down to my and Ruby's room to pick me up—as though we were on a real date—he'd kept at least one hand on me. I tried to fight him on going to the wedding, but he simply said it would be rude to back out now and I supposed he wasn't wrong.

Over the course of the day, he'd slipped into what felt like a familiar role. Like, there was never a time when we didn't hold hands, and it was normal for him to look for me first in every room. I'd become so used to being Brody's secret that I didn't even think to take Eli's hand in public until he took mine.

I didn't hear from Hollis or Ruby, but Hollis's suitcase was open on a luggage rack when I went to Ruby's room to get ready and there was a third toothbrush in the bathroom. I took that as a sign of at least one good thing. Before we left, Eli moved my suitcase over to his room so I could give Hollis and Ruby privacy and hopefully avoid the inevitably uncomfortable reunion with my grandmother for a little while longer.

Thankfully, I'd packed another dress. Red A-line with a form-fitting boned bodice, a scoop neck, and thick straps. It was simple, but when I tried it on, it had felt like the kind of dress I'd want to wear for years to come. I opened the small silk pouch where I kept my limited collection of jewelry and dumped it out on the bed to find the yellow gold wedding band I'd held on to for all these years and slipped it on my right ring finger.

Once we got out of the cab, Eli and I stood on the sidewalk, each waiting for the other to go inside first.

"We could just go to dinner," I said.

"We'll eat dinner at the reception," he said as he took my hand and led me behind a slew of other guests. "Come on, Vera. Play pretend with me. For one night."

We were directed out to the courtyard, where chairs were set up under a canopy of botanicals and palm trees.

The ceremony was short and had a few Jewish wedding traditions to honor Lilly's side of the family. Otherwise, the event was deeply nontraditional and casual. Not in an irreverent way, but in the sense that even though we'd spent only thirty minutes with the brides this afternoon, I felt as though we knew them.

While Tori said her vows to a tearful Lilly, Eli mindlessly took my right hand. His fingers brushed over my ring and the recognition on his face was immediate when he looked down.

He pursed his lips for a minute before sliding the ring off my right hand. My lips parted as I looked up to him, the sounds of the ceremony dulling as the moment seemed to become only us. Then he took my left hand and slid the band onto my left ring finger.

"We've got to play the part," he explained quietly.

Before I could respond, the officiant reintroduced the brides to their loved ones and we were standing and clapping. My eyes were full of tears I didn't know I'd begun to shed.

As the couple swept down the aisle hand in hand, Lilly pointed to us and waved, Tori following suit. "Our good-luck charms!" one of them said as they passed us by.

The clouds cleared in time for the reception, which was held on the other side of the courtyard under strings of lights and bled into a dining room with rows of open French doors and gauzy curtains billowing in the breeze.

When we made it to the front of the guest book line, Eli wrote our names as Eli and Vera Buckley-Stein. He handed the pen to me and motioned to the request that everyone jot down their marriage advice. "You're the writer."

I thought for a moment, grateful that no one else was waiting behind us. I was the least qualified person on earth to give marriage advice to two newlyweds, but as I glanced at the ring on my left hand, I decided that I could at least play the part of someone who knew what the hell they were talking about.

Eli watched over my shoulder as I began to write.

It's okay to make it up as you go along. And at the very least: do it for the plot.

"I like that," Eli said as he pressed a kiss to the top of my head.

"I thought it was better than 'Get a bunch of secret credit cards you don't tell each other about.'"

"Yeah, that doesn't have the same ring to it."

We found our table at the back of the room with a random hodgepodge of older guests, which meant we were right at home. Eli dove right into small talk and soon we were fabricating a whole life for ourselves. We stuck to the Vegas story, but I was a screenwriter-turned-picture-book-author with a passion for roller derby.

"And what about you?" an older man with a walrus mustache asked Eli.

"I'm a physician," he said honestly.

I nearly smacked his leg. No way was he going to play it safe after we'd concocted an elaborate cover story for me.

"But his true hobby is cake decorating," I chimed in. "He's auditioned for seventy-three reality TV baking competitions."

Eli sighed. "And never got a one."

"But I have a feeling seventy-four is the lucky number," I said, resting my head on his shoulder.

"Oh, I just love those shows," said a woman across the table. "Might you have any pictures of your work on your phone?"

Eli began to shake his head, but I leaned forward and said, "Oh, honey, I have plenty of photos."

Eli eyed me suspiciously but kept the act up while I googled for the worst possible cake decorating fails I could find and rapidly saved them to my phone.

"Here's his latest," I said, holding up a photo of two breasts that looked more like sad pancakes with an uneven cursive across the top that read: *Hasta la vista to Bethany's titties!*

Eli cleared his throat into his fist and jabbed my foot with his. "Uh, our friend was having a breast reduction. It was a . . . uh, special request."

Our tablemates nodded politely with wide eyes as they leaned back a little from Eli, reconsidering him.

"Oh, don't be shy, darling." I turned to the other guests. "He really excels in anatomically correct cakes."

Eli sputtered as he saw the giant penis cake complete with sprinkle pubes on my phone just seconds before I was about to whip it out for the rest of the class. He yanked the phone from my hand and shoved it into his pocket before pulling me to my feet. "If you'll excuse us for a moment, I owe my beautiful wife a dance."

I followed him and gave a little wave over my shoulder to our still-gawking table.

"You are diabolical," he said as he wound his arm around my waist.

"I didn't know you liked to dance so much."

"I would rather eat glass, but I wasn't about to let you scandalize that whole table with a dick cake."

"It wasn't just a dick," I said innocently. "There were balls and pubes too. I really think it showed range."

With a reluctant smile, he pulled me to the edge of the dance floor. A slow folkish song started up. The kind that was romantically sorrowful with just enough hope to hurt.

Eli heaved a sigh as he wrapped his arm around me and held my hand over his chest, his cheek resting atop my head. We swayed in silence for a moment before he said, "I've enjoyed tonight. Despite the character assassination."

"That's a touch dramatic, don't you think?"

He pulled back so I could plainly see his outrage. "I gave you a great roller derby name and you gave me perv cakes."

"Vera Vengeance does have a nice ring to it." I shrugged and let myself nestle back into him. "It's been nice," I said, "to play a little bit of pretend."

His chest hummed as the song changed to something a little more upbeat. His broad palm splayed across my back and drifted down, landing on the curve of my ass as he held me even closer.

"I like this dress on you," he told me. "I think I would like to see what it looks like off you as well. For science."

"For science," I echoed. "Sure."

Just then a rush of what seemed to be younger male cousins from Lilly's side charged the dance floor. One jumped up to the DJ's booth and yelled into the mic, "Lil, you know we couldn't let you leave here a married woman without dancing the hora!"

Several of the men ran toward the brides with two chairs hoisted above their heads and within seconds they had Lilly and Tori riding over the crowd.

The opening notes to "Hava Nagila" began to play as Eli and I slowly backed away from the dance floor.

"Oh no you don't," said an older woman in a teasing voice as she took my hand and the man who I assumed to be her husband looped an arm through Eli's.

A circle began to form and Eli and I were suddenly separated by a handful of people.

I don't know if he registered my panic, but he shrugged and mouthed, *Play the part.*

The circle began to rotate from left to right in slow, steady movements as Lilly and Tori bounced overhead, joy vibrating from them as they held on to the edges of their chairs.

As the song sped up, so did the dance. I was tripping over my feet despite the wedding guests on either side doing their best to instruct me, but no one seemed bothered by my clumsiness.

The courtyard turned into a blur as we spun. I could only just make out Eli as he sang along with the older woman beside him.

My chest burned from laughing and I could hardly catch my breath. When the song finally ended, I stumbled off the dance floor, flushed and breathless, as the crowd cheered.

Everything was wobbly and loud and overstimulating and I needed a moment of quiet. So without looking back, I slipped away into a quiet hallway just inside the hotel. Down at the end, a young couple sat curled into each other, enjoying the quiet refuge.

I kicked off my heels and studied the arched brick ceiling above. A few feet beyond was a cozy library with vivid red shelves and plush armchairs that called to me.

As I circled the shelves, Eli walked into the library, nearly passing right by me before doubling back.

"There you are," he said, stalking toward me.

I stepped farther back into the small alcove, and he sank against me, his lips grazing my neck and then his tongue washing over the path.

"We have company down at the end of the hallway," I whispered.

Eli stepped back wordlessly and scooped up my shoes before leading me farther into the venue. He led me to a cracked-open door and we stumbled inside.

It was mostly dark except for some fairy lights and the early evening moonlight. A soft forest green velvet sofa sat in the middle of the room atop an elaborate oriental rug. Against the wall were multiple vanities covered in makeup, curling irons, hair products, and an open box of tampons.

"This must be the bridal suite," I said, motioning to the duffel bags and suitcases left behind as well as several bottles of champagne now sitting in buckets of fully melted ice.

Eli flipped the lock on the door. "Well, I guess it's a good thing that the brides are currently indisposed."

He dropped my shoes and loosened his tie before spinning me around and pressing me into the door, his fingers digging into my waist.

"Is it time for science?" I asked, referring to his need to see me out of my dress. "Maybe we should head back to the hotel. Someone might need to get in here or something."

He shook his head as he bent down and began laying kisses atop my cheeks and forehead, like it was bad luck to leave a single surface of skin untouched.

"We're going to need a robust sample size," he said simply.

His lips swept across mine and he kissed me slowly. Torturously so.

I parted my lips to coax him in deeper, but he took his time, letting his tongue trace mine as his hand cradled my neck.

A frustrated groan pushed against my lips. There would be time later to explore and tease, but right now, I needed him in the most basic of ways.

"You were magnetic out there," he whispered. "I almost trampled the woman beside me because I couldn't take my eyes off you."

"I nearly brought the whole dance floor down with my inability to put one foot in front of the other." I bowed my forehead into his chest. "I have an IUD. And I'm clean."

"I am too." Eli sat down, his arms spread over the back of the sofa.

Hiking my dress up, I straddled his lap. He was solid and warm beneath me, and we both let out choked noises as I settled against the erection pushing against the fly of his trousers.

He kissed and sucked along my neck while I reached between us and frantically unbuckled his belt before taking care of the zipper. "I can still wear a condom, Vera. Whatever you want."

"I want to feel you."

He hissed as I unzipped his pants and pulled him out of his boxer briefs, so that he was still fully clothed except for his weeping cock.

"Completely," I added.

"Okay, okay," he said. For a moment, he slowed down as he leaned back and pushed the skirt of my dress aside so that he could watch as he pulled my simple black panties to the side. With unadulterated wonder and adoration, he looked up at me and dragged a finger through my channel. "You're so—"

I stole the words right out of his mouth as I covered it with mine, his breath filling me. My hand worked between us to position him at my entrance.

He took the base of his cock, stroking it twice before rubbing the head against my swollen clit.

My head dropped back, and a broken moan cracked my ribs in half.

Seconds slowed to milliseconds as he held my waist with one hand and began carefully guiding me down. "How long have you been this wet?" he asked.

"Since the ceremony," I confessed. "When you put that ring on my finger."

He grunted a little as he brought my left hand to his mouth and kissed each one of my fingerprints before sucking my ring finger into his mouth. Once it slid out with a pop, he looked up to me, eyes weighty with lust.

The only thing that could distract me from that heady gaze was the will to watch him disappear into me.

The stretch was a steady, welcome burn. Once I was fully seated, my head dropped down against his shoulder as I held him inside of me.

Thoughts of Eli had occupied every corner of my brain for the last few months, but to have him filling me now brought back so many memories of that night in Vegas. Except this time, it wasn't the shouting or the slamming doors I remembered. It was the moments before as we panted into each other's necks and chased that building pleasure.

He thrust up into me and in return, I moved my hips in tight circles. His head rolled back against the sofa, throat working in a swallow as he closed his eyes for a moment, feelings rapidly washing across his features.

I curled one arm around his neck as I raked my fingers through his hair until he opened his eyes to watch me, dark and hungry.

We kept a constant pace as he lifted his head again, his teeth dragging along the tops of my breasts, leaving what were certainly the beginnings of marks. Just some sort of evidence to remember what we had here in this sultry, humid town. Because tomorrow we would leave and all the promises in the world couldn't guarantee what came next.

Behind the sofa, the doorknob rattled, and for a brief moment we both froze.

I moved to stand up even if my body begged me not to.

But Eli held me in place, fingertips digging into my waist. He shook his head as he began to slowly fuck me again. I made a sad attempt at pushing him away, but I was far too greedy to actually stop and he knew it.

"Someone must have accidentally locked the door," a woman's voice said.

"Let me see if I can find an employee," another replied.

"We have to go," I whispered, the last syllable turning into a quiet moan.

Eli's lips curled into a devious smirk as he held his hand up over my mouth and all I could do was pant against his fingers.

With his free hand, he pulled me flush against him and began thrusting mercilessly from below. From this slight change in position, my anguished cry fell against his hand as his length slid against the most sensitive part of me.

The blacks of Eli's eyes grew as his hand fell to the point where our bodies joined. His fingers worked unforgiving circles.

"That's it, that's it, that's it," he chanted in my ear as a warm tension began to build in my belly. "Good girl."

The phrase didn't feel like an insult in the same way it had when Brody had told his business adviser that I was a good girl and that I would understand why he had to fire me. I wasn't good in a self-sacrificing way or because I picked up the slack for everyone around me. I was good because I was chasing my own pleasure. My own want. And Eli praised me for it.

Footsteps sounded down the hallway, but I couldn't stop myself long enough to concentrate on them.

And then I fell apart, my teeth biting down on his palm as he continued to thrust, our bodies dovetailing together like the answer to a riddle or when the chorus meets the bridge.

"That's it," he whispered again. Then, with a grunt that broke into a silent moan, his throat a flash of red and veins pressing against skin, Eli rode out his release. Warmth filled me, leaking out and onto my inner thighs, coating the point at which we were joined.

Lazily, he thrust in once and then twice more before hugging my limp body to his.

The footsteps in the hallway continued in the opposite direction and I sighed into his neck.

We stayed like that for longer than we should have, his cock still inside of me as his taut muscles began to ease.

One wide, careful palm smoothed over my hair while the other held my left hand to his lips, kissing my palms and fingertips and the gold band on my ring finger before pressing both our hands over his heart.

My forehead rested against his, satisfaction thrumming through my veins. "We should go."

"Only so I can get you back to that hotel room," he said.

"I might need some room service fries first," I said, my postcoital appetite growing.

"I will buy you every fry in this fucking city."

After another moment, he let me stand up, and I made the game-time decision to remove my underwear. They were soaked with both of our releases. Tess had always said she liked going to important meetings commando in a skirt because it was an adrenaline rush. I wasn't sure I needed that sort of rush, but I was willing to chance the experience for the length of a cab ride.

After a quick visit to the attached bathroom, I found Eli stuffing my underwear into the pocket of his suit jacket draped over his arm.

"I hope you know you're not getting these back," he said with a devilish grin as he held his arm out for me to make our escape.

"You're a sick fuck," I told him.

"Yes, love, I know. Have you seen my anatomically correct cakes?"

THE WUNDERKIND (FIRST DRAFT)
"PILOT" 10/8/07

INT. COMMUNITY THEATER—NIGHT

She watches him in a show his friend is directing. He forgets his line and looks to her. She mouths it.

THE WUNDERKIND by Vera Stein.

CHAPTER FORTY-SIX

The next morning, the only acknowledgment I received from Ruby was a barely audible hello.

Right before we boarded, Hollis patted my shoulder and said, "Give her time. She's got a short fuse, but that means she burns out just as fast as she catches."

Eli and I weren't as forthright with our affections in front of Ruby and Hollis, but it was hard not to chalk that up to the thick tension between me and my grandmother.

When we landed, Ruby and Hollis took a cab back to Starlight Palms while Eli and I drove home in his car, which he'd parked at the airport. The moment the doors sealed us shut inside, I flung myself against the passenger seat and sighed.

Eli squeezed my thigh before reversing out of the parking space. "You survived being in a flying can in the sky with Ruby. Congratulations."

"I deserve a reward," I said with a pout.

"How about a slumber party?" he asked.

"Can we do face masks?"

"Only if we can get into a sexy pillow fight first."

"Deal," I said.

As we drove home, Eli kept his hand on my upper thigh, straying only when he needed two hands on the wheel.

The higher his fingers inched, the more restless I became. The moment he parked the car in front of our apartment, I nearly threw my body over the console at him until he said, "Is someone at our door?"

I leaned forward, squinting at the tall, slim figure with a blunt shoulder-length bob. "Oh my god . . ."

Eli was saying something, but I was already out of the car and running for the door. "Tess! What are you doing here?"

My best friend spun around, her eyes puffy and her cheeks red. The moment she saw me, she started sobbing for what was definitely not the first time today.

Before I asked a single question, including *Who the fuck made you cry?* I enveloped her in a hug. The one and only time I'd ever seen Tess cry was when we saw *The Notebook* in theaters after chugging a bottle of Yellow Tail in the parking lot, so this felt monumental.

Speaking of intoxication . . . "Tess, you smell like a bottle of scotch. Did you drive all the way out here before or after the scotch?"

She sniffled and shook her head. "I took an Uber. It was four hundred dollars." She half hiccupped, half sobbed. "Before tip. He let me drink in the back seat and he stopped at In-N-Out."

"I hope you gave him a great rating."

She nodded. "He even let me listen to"—she sniffed—"the Fleetwood Mac 'Silver Springs' live recording from nineteen ninety-seveeeeeeeeen on repeat."

I cupped her face in my hands. "Okay, okay, you're all right. Let's get you inside."

Behind me, Eli cleared his throat. "Hey, Tess."

She frowned at him. "Ugh. You're even hotter than you used to be." And then she turned to me, stabbing a finger at Eli. "That's not fair."

Eli blushed a little, running a hand up the back of his neck.

"I know," I said, and then gave him a meaningful look that I hoped he understood to mean: *Please don't get handsy in front of my distraught best friend before I have the chance to tell her that we sort of hooked up . . . several times in the last forty-eight hours.*

Eli nodded once and then stepped around us to unlock the door.

Tess stumbled inside and announced, "I need to pee."

I pointed her to the bathroom and then took my bag from Eli.

"I guess our slumber party is going to be postponed," he said, his hand ghosting down my backside.

"Consider it a rain delay."

Once Tess returned from the bathroom, I sat her on the couch with a huge glass of water while Eli got to work on making her an egg and cheese sandwich, which was about the current sum of the refrigerator's contents.

"Okay, now tell me what happened."

Tess laid her head in my lap and guided my hand to play with her hair. "The shower fixtures I picked out are on back order."

Eli either coughed or quietly snorted but had the good sense not to say anything.

"Okay . . . maybe I could help you pick out new fixtures?"

She shook her head and then turned on her side, so her body was curled into the back of the couch and she could properly cry into my shirt. "No, it's not the fixtures. That was just the tipping point. It's working seventy hours a week and eating a cup of microwaveable mac and cheese even though Max always leaves me a plate of homemade food in the refrigerator."

"But Max is a great cook."

"I just . . . got married when I was twenty-four and I woke up one day and realized that I am living the life that twenty-four-year-old me chose and is that fair to me now? And I hate that when I get home at night, I have to eat dinner alone. It makes me sad when I see the artwork the kids bring home but they aren't awake to tell me about it and then . . ." She paused for a moment. "Oh god, does that make me sentimental?"

I shook my head as I gathered part of her hair in a loose braid. "No, just human, I think."

"And then we're still down to one shower and there's only one working outlet in our bedroom right now, so I'm always showing up to work with a dead phone. And I forgot Violet's science fair last week and when I said I was sorry, she said, 'I'm not mad. I'm just disappointed.' Vera! I'm the mom. That's my line!"

Eli set the plate with the sandwich down on the coffee table with a quiet "Oof."

Tess rolled over onto her other side, her pants twisting around her ankles. "But I'll tell you what! Twenty-four-year-old Tess didn't know she was signing up to be a bad mom." She gestured to Eli. "Even he thinks I'm a bad parent."

Eli shook his head. "Not judging. Just relating, I swear. When Brigid was in preschool, I was doing a rainy day pickup where they load your kid in the car for you. It took me two blocks before I realized they'd accidentally given me Javier, one of Brigid's classmates."

Tess sniffed. "Okay, that *is* pretty awful."

"Thank you?" Eli questioned.

I mouthed a silent *thanks* before resuming my best friend duties. "Last year, I left Marlon at the dog park," I admitted in a rush of shame. "I took his leash and just walked right out. I made it all the way home and poured his dry food in his bowl before it dawned on me."

Tess flopped back over and looked up at me. "Was he traumatized forever?"

I shook my head. "When I showed up, he was rolling in the grass, nipping at another dog's back paws. But I did buy him those little doggy ice-cream cones to assuage my guilt."

"Where is that little shit?" she asked.

"At the boarders'. We just got back into town."

My best friend narrowed her eyes at me. "*We?*"

"Ruby was receiving a lifetime achievement award at a horror convention in New Orleans."

"Well, that explains why you were there, but what's his deal?" She hiked a thumb over at Eli, who was leaning up against the TV cabinet now with his arms and ankles crossed.

"I went as Ruby's physician," Eli said evenly.

Tess looked from me to Eli and then back again before sitting up and reaching for her sandwich suspiciously. She pulled the plate to her chest and sat in the corner of the couch as she continued to eye us, looking more like Gollum and his precious than a ferocious entertainment lawyer who was more trusted by her clients than their favorite plastic surgeons.

"Right," Eli said. "I'll be in my room if either of you need me."

His door wasn't even shut before Tess pointed at me, her mouth stuffed with the egg and cheese sandwich. "You're fucking the good doctor!"

I waved her off but couldn't hide the searing blush on my cheeks. I supposed if there was anyone who I could tell the messy, complicated truth to, it was Tess. "I guess you wouldn't believe me if I told you Ruby has Eli on call like she's Elvis or something."

"How was it?" she asked dreamily. "Our walls are too thin to have the kind of sex I need to have right now. I just want someone to pull my hair. Did he pull your hair?"

I frowned at her and then stuffed a pillow in my face. "It was . . . really hot," I said into the fabric. "But it's so new too. Casual. No hair pulling yet, but he is very adept at locating the clitoris."

"He *is* a doctor. Please do explain how hooking up with your ex-husband is casual."

"He was my husband for less than twenty-four hours."

Her empty plate clattered as she placed it on the coffee table and then slumped down into the sofa with her eyes closed and her arms flung in the air. "Time doesn't matter in the eyes of God, Vera!"

"You're a reformed Catholic who doesn't believe in God," I reminded her.

She waved me off. "Old habits and et cetera."

After divulging a few more tipping points from the last few weeks, Tess dozed for the rest of the afternoon. I knew things at home were tense for her, but her life had always seemed so . . . full to me. Success, a solid marriage, good kids. On paper, she had it all. And yet, she still felt trapped by decisions made when we were barely adults.

I let Tess epic cry and sleep off the scotch while I unpacked and did laundry. Eli did the same, leaving kisses on my shoulders or brushing fingers along my hips every time he walked past me. It was decidedly . . . domestic.

When he left to see Brigid and pick up some groceries, Tess woke up groaning and in need of a shower.

She dug into the giant Birkin her boss bought her for Christmas a few years ago and sighed with relief when she came up with a tan stitch of fabric.

"Spare underwear. I have never regretted having spare underwear," she said. "Purse underwear will never let you down."

I got her set up in the shower and then I settled onto the couch with the notes and pages I'd compiled on the project that might someday be a screenplay, and gave them a thorough read. Maybe it was the high of my trip to New Orleans, but what I had here on the page didn't feel so . . . bleak.

When Eli returned with his arms full of groceries, he laid a kiss on my forehead before heading into the kitchen.

"You writing?" he asked casually.

"Something like that," I said as I took an inventory of the random scraps and thoughts I'd jotted down. A few lines of dialogue. Scenic descriptions.

"Good, good, good," he said, his lips curling into the ghost of a smile before he fell into the silent rhythm of rinsing vegetables and organizing the refrigerator.

"Eli," Tess called as she walked back into the living room, scrunching her curls with one of the old T-shirts I'd loaned her. "I like your choice of candle in the bathroom."

He glanced over his shoulder like he'd been caught, but the look vanished a second later.

"Doesn't it smell familiar, Vera?" she asked.

I only vaguely recalled the candle in the bathroom, so I shook my head.

"Cucumber melon?" she asked, her arms crossed over her chest. "That Bath & Body Works body spray you wore for four years straight in college?"

Eli was blushing now.

"Oh, yeah." I bit down on the inside of my lip. That couldn't be true, though. He wouldn't buy a candle because of some random lackluster scent I'd been obsessed with in college.

"Huh," Eli said. "What a coincidence."

Tess's gaze narrowed on him. "Yeah, especially since the scent was discontinued *years* ago."

"When did you become a Bath & Body Works scholar?" I asked Tess.

She turned to me with a whose-side-are-you-on sort of look. "You mean to tell me you don't go into a Bath & Body Works once a year and panic buy thirty-seven candles just so you can feel alive?"

I shook my head. "You know that's too rich for my blood."

"They brought it back," Eli murmured. "For some anniversary thing."

We both looked at him, jaws slack.

"What?" He shrugged and then turned back to the groceries.

Tess looked at me with a silent but frantic *Oh my fucking god* and kicked my foot *hard* before sitting down beside me.

"What's this?" She tilted her head to get a better look at what I was working on.

"Nothing," I said. "Nothing in the most nothing form."

She pulled some pages out from under me. "Are you writing *by hand*?"

"Not by choice," I told her. "But I guess it's kind of nice. I can't really go back and fidget without a backspace button, ya know? And it's just a baby idea, anyway. Just a little brain detour. A distraction."

"I promise not to stage mom you and tell you how proud you've made Mommy so that you don't panic and never touch this thing again."

"And I appreciate that, Mommy." I gave her a grateful smile and patted the seat beside me for her to sit down.

She reached for the remote and flipped through streaming services until landing on *Never Been Kissed*, a staple of ours in college.

And that was the start of a very perfect night.

Eli made gnocchi while we watched movie after movie. Tess and I cuddled into each other while I tucked my toes under Eli's butt and only wiggled them a few times, which elicited some sort of shrill noise.

As we all started to fade and get ready for bed, Tess pushed me toward Eli's bedroom.

I shook my head. "I'm not missing a chance to have a slumber party with my best friend."

Eli squeezed my shoulder before Tess and I broke off toward my bedroom.

"Good night, ladies," he said as he shut the door behind us.

Tess took a good fifteen minutes to find the perfect configuration of pillows and then she tossed for a few minutes before deciding she wanted to be big spoon. "Sorry," she said. "I'm too used to sharing a bed with Max."

"It's okay," I told her, as she nestled into my shoulder. "It's nice to know you're still a big spoon."

She sighed. "That candle, huh? V, that's some lore shit. He's got it bad. Hell, he's *had* it bad."

"I don't know," I said, trying not to let myself read too much into it. "Maybe the candle is just a dumb nostalgia thing. Or more likely a coincidence."

"I miss a lot about those days. But your body spray is *not* one of them."

It was an inoffensive enough scent that conjured memories of cinnamon pretzels from the mall and ironic T-shirts from Spencer's. But definitely not something I would actively choose for myself now. But during college, those little bottles of body spray were my most beloved splurge purchase. The thought of Eli buying that candle because it reminded him of me made my chest swell to the point of stinging.

"It was really sweet of Max to let you get away for the day," I said.

"Ummm." She unhooked her arm from around my waist and plopped back against the pillows.

I turned over to face her and sat up with my arm propped behind me. "Um, what, Tess?"

She gritted her teeth but said nothing.

"Um, *what,* Tess?"

She squeezed her eyes shut. "I might not have told him where I was going. Or that I was leaving at all."

I sat up fully now and shook her shoulders. "Are you telling me I'm harboring a fugitive?"

"I didn't break a law, Vera! I'm more of a . . . missing person."

I shook my head and crawled over her body to dig her phone out of her purse on the floor.

When I finally came back with it, I found that it was dead. "It's off?" I asked. "The last time you were without a phone was when you accidentally ran over your BlackBerry freshman year. *You*, the same woman who thought airplane mode was a conspiracy theory until five years ago!"

She shrugged. "I kind of still think it is."

"Did he do something to you?" I asked, reining myself back in. "Is there something you're not telling me?"

She shook her head aggressively. "No, no. Of course not. God, no. I just needed . . . quiet. Have you ever needed quiet so badly that you wanted to throw your phone off an overpass?"

"I'm not exactly that popular, but I get what you're saying." I held the phone out to her. "You have to let Max know you're okay, though. He's probably crawling the walls *Exorcism*-style. I bet the man has the coast guard on the line."

She sighed and reluctantly pressed the power button on the side of her phone. Alerts sounded almost immediately. Nonstop. A symphony of chimes and beeps.

Tess cringed and I took the phone from her, immediately silencing all notifications. "Do you want me to message him or would you rather?" I asked.

"I will." She huffed. "This probably warrants a phone call."

She slithered out of bed and into the living room, holding her phone like it was a live grenade.

There wasn't much I'd been thankful for in the last few months, but running away . . . starting over . . . It had been *hard*. It was hard in the same way that it is hard to take a deep breath when you're sick. Painful, but necessary. Tess didn't have the luxury of running away, though. The job, the house, the kids . . . Max. It was all so firm and immovable. For as aimless as I felt, she was just as hemmed in.

I heard her muffled voice from the other room as the light in the bathroom flicked on and Eli started the shower. I lay there in the dark, enjoying the sounds of the water hitting the tile and waiting for Tess to return.

And there, after a moment, was the faint smell of cucumber melon.

I called in late to work the next morning and grabbed breakfast with Tess while we waited for Max to make the drive out to pick her up after doing morning drop-off with the kids.

She was jumpy and nervous all morning, which was so unlike her. The woman set the tone of every room she walked into. In college, professors were intimidated by *her*.

I prodded a bit and she swore she was fine. But I could see her trying to calculate how badly she'd fucked up and what her liability was.

On our way back to Starlight Palms, we picked up Marlon. Max arrived less than thirty minutes later, and he and Tess shared a long, intense embrace in my living room while Marlon circled their feet.

I scooped him up and stepped into my room to give them a little privacy. Through the wall, I heard hushed whispers, quiet soothing, and fierce promises.

Tess called for me and I said goodbye, holding her for a long moment while Max scooped up her purse and gave Marlon a pat on the head.

When I opened the door for them both, Max, who looked like he hadn't slept in thirty-six hours, gripped my forearm before pulling me in for a solid hug. "Thanks, V," he said softly.

I watched as he opened her door for her and they fell back into their respective complementary roles with ease.

Once they'd left, I headed into the main building, where I found a full inbox and a small potted cactus with a thank-you card from Leonard.

This cactus will likely outlive me, but only one of us had a truly fabulous funeral and lived to tell the tale. Thanks for the push. —L

I spent the rest of the morning in my office hashing out the calendar for the rest of the year, including speed dating, the weekly movie nights, and early voting shuttles. Above all, I tried my very best not to be distracted by the man one floor above me.

Before lunch, I heard Ruby's voice in the hallway, and I sat there for far too long, waiting for her to walk past my office and at least acknowledge me in some sort of way. But her voice faded, and I was left waiting.

That afternoon I prepped the theater for the weekly documentary club. I rolled the popcorn machine in and laid out snacks and beverages for a free all-you-can-eat concessions stand.

As I lined up the boxes of Dots in a row, the door at the back of the theater swung open and shut, followed by the click of a lock.

"I'm pretty sure most of that food is not denture-friendly," Eli said.

A little burst of excitement sparked in me at the sound of his voice. "Anything is denture safe if you just believe in yourself," I called over my shoulder.

He let out a short laugh and the heat of his body closed in at my back. I turned to face him, and he was near enough for our chests to brush on each exhale.

We hadn't seen each other yet this morning, so now was my first chance to appreciate his dark green chinos, white button-up shirt with the sleeves rolled up to his elbows, and a pair of camel oxfords. His hair was pushed back except for a rebel strand that curled over his forehead.

"I missed you," he said.

"We saw each other last night," I reminded him, even though I'd missed him too.

The scruff on his chin tickled my neck as he leaned in closer, placing his hands on the table, bracketing in my hips. "You think I could cash in that rain check tonight?"

"I'll have to check the terms and conditions and confirm that tonight isn't a blackout date."

He chuckled and took my hand, pulling me toward the row of seats directly in the middle of the room. The Starlight Palms movie room rivaled most local theaters except that it was smaller and completely handicap accessible. To the delight of many residents, the decor honored the midcentury modern aesthetic carried through the rest of the property in the teal theater seats and deep orange drapes along the walls. The curtains framing the screen were magenta with gold tassels and starbursts embroidered into the fabric. It was probably one of my favorite places on the whole property.

Eli led me to the center of the row and immediately pulled up the armrest between us. The Universal opening logo glowed from the screen, where I'd paused the movie until the residents arrived.

"I've never actually made out with someone in a movie theater before," I told him as I closed the distance between us and let my fingers trace up his biceps.

"I would really love to help you check that off your list, but can we talk first?"

My head dropped back against the headrest. "Am I in trouble?"

"No." He laughed. "Why would you think that?"

I shrugged. "I don't know. Hearing someone needs to talk to you is like getting sent to the principal's office, even when it's not for a bad thing. Or when someone texts and asks if you have time to talk, but then they disappear on you for hours."

He traced a finger over the planes of my face. "You are not in trouble, Vera Stein."

I swallowed, my mouth dry despite his assurances.

"I stopped by my house yesterday to check on Brigid."

"Is she okay?" I asked.

"Oh, she's fine. I think she's in love with both her best friend *and* her best friend's boyfriend, but that's a story for another day."

I nodded slowly. "That sounds like a great bedtime story."

His finger brushed over the tip of my nose. "Noted."

"Okay, so your house. Brigid."

"Right, well, Selene found a new place, which means I'll be getting my house back . . . soon."

My stomach did a little flip-flop. "That's great." But it came out a little half-hearted. "You must be really excited to get your place back."

He nodded as he studied our joined hands, his thumb running over my knuckles and then his fingers spinning the gold band. I'd moved it back to my right hand after the wedding, but I'd noticed him glancing at it a few times since we'd been home, like he found its presence amusing or reassuring, even.

"You can have the apartment, of course," he said. "I don't want you to worry about that. There's a waitlist for apartments, but I'll keep it in my name so you don't have to deal with any of that."

"Oh. Okay." A sudden and deep disappointment began to burrow in my chest, but I didn't know what else I expected from him. In fact, he was going above and beyond by securing a place for me to live. Whatever this was between us hadn't even taken shape into something that could be properly labeled. "That's really thoughtful of you. I'll obviously pay the rent in full."

His eyes found mine, and I was struck by how beautiful he was in the bluish wash from the movie screen: his dark blond hair, manicured beard, the green of his eyes reflecting in the light.

This felt like the beginning of the end somehow. The end of something very short-lived. I hadn't yet found a reason to regret anything that had happened other than the thought of it being over simply making me sad.

"Or," he continued, breaking my circuitous thoughts of doom, "you could make the move with me."

It took a moment for his words to formulate into meaning. But when it finally did hit me, my heart sped up as I searched for the proper reaction.

His mouth was moving before I could formulate a response. "Y-you could still have your own room. Nothing has to be much different than it is now. This invitation is not dependent on us being romantically involved." His head bobbed to the side, so that I had no choice but to look him in the eyes. "I need you to know that."

I nodded. "Okay." I didn't have any other words to say just then. He'd taken me by such surprise.

"But if it did turn into more . . . over time, maybe that could be okay too. I just like spending time with you, Vera. I like knowing you'll be home. At my home. I like watching movies with you even though you have to read multiple detailed reviews before you'll commit to something you haven't seen."

"It's due diligence," I mumbled.

The corner of his mouth lifted as he brushed his knuckles across the swell of my cheek. "And even though you whisper the subtitles to yourself."

I shrunk down a little, my shoulders level with my ears. I forgot that I did that, honestly. "It helps me follow along."

I noticed the contrast in our hands. My fingers were short with chipped nail polish from my pre–New Orleans manicure with Ruby. His palms were broad with long, delicate yet strong fingers. I liked the way my hand disappeared inside of his.

"It's something to consider. That's all. Take as much time as you need." He used the same calm, almost clinical voice I'd heard him use with residents when they stopped him in the hall to ask about a rash or an unusual dream they'd had. It wasn't a patronizing tone. No, it was a tone I took comfort in now. A tone that said someone had answers and, for once, it didn't have to be me. It was the same feeling I got when I took my mom to the ER toward the end. For so long I had hated that place, but at the end, they would take her back and for a little while I could at least find comfort in the fact that she was looked after and I could just take a moment to breathe.

I nodded and tilted my head up.

He swiped a thumb across my jaw and dipped his tongue out to wet his lower lip.

I felt the pull between us, my body so ready to lose itself in him. To make out in this room on our lunch hour like a couple of teenagers.

Just as I was about to give in to his touch, I remembered the thing that had been on the tip of my tongue since last night.

"The candle," I finally said.

He pulled away slightly, blush coloring his cheeks. "That."

"Tess seems to think there's a story there."

"Tess shouldn't start rumors," he said. "Especially ones that are true."

My mouth spread into a slow grin. "Okay, now you have to tell me."

"Back in college, I may have observed that you were a fan of cucumber melon body spray." He laughed softly. "It reminded me of the mall, honestly."

"Well, that *is* where I bought it."

"Fair." He nodded. "But after a while, the smell reminded me of you. The mall reminded me of you. Brody would come home from hanging out with you and the faintest trace of it would linger on his T-shirts."

My finger traced the shell of his ear as his gaze drifted between me and a faraway past.

"Mind you, this was at a time when I couldn't decide if I was fascinated by you or wanted to put my head through a wall every time you spoke. So it was a little frustrating to be . . . assaulted by this scent at random."

"'Assaulted,' you say? What a strong word."

He rolled his eyes. "Is this my story or not?"

I nudged his shoulder with the side of my head. "Go on, go on."

"Well, you know everything that happened between us, so by the time I started med school, the scent was cursed. It took a few years, but eventually I noticed that I didn't smell it as often as I used to. Either because of changing trends or time. I don't know. Then two years ago, I was in Bath & Body Works with Brigid on Christmas Eve getting her mom something for Christmas." His eyes dropped down to his lap. "And I recognized that smell."

"Two years?" I asked. "That candle's lasted you a good long while."

"Well, I bought the candle. Telling myself it was just a curious nostalgia. But then I burned through it and went online and ordered a little supply of them."

"Oh." Now it was my turn to blush.

"And if you're wondering why I've kept it in my bathroom . . . the reason is as depraved as you think."

I gasped softly, feeling inappropriately turned on in the middle of the work day. "That is . . . incredibly hot."

"You mean incredibly stalkerish?" he asked.

I weighed that thought, my head tilting back and forth. "Stalker lite," I confirmed. "But in a hot-Lifetime-movie sort of way. Like stalker role-play."

He tucked a curl behind my ear, his forehead tilting down to rest against mine. "Now, about making out in movie theaters . . ."

Eli didn't bring up the move for the next two weeks and we fell into a comfortable rhythm. I'd text him a recipe in the morning. He'd pick up the ingredients. We'd make dinner together. Usually, at least. Sometimes I'd get a little lost in the writing I was dabbling with.

Okay, well, I was more than dabbling. But for the sake of my sanity, I called it dabbling.

On those nights, Eli would silently take over dinner duties and I would hardly notice until there was a warm plate of food set in front of me. Sometimes we would talk through dinner and other times he would read while I continued to work.

He made noises about letting me borrow his laptop, but I liked the routine of working on paper and then transcribing in the morning when I got to my office.

Then we would go to bed, both brushing our teeth at the same time. Every night I went through the motions of intending to go to my own bedroom, but he always waited in his doorway for me and dragged me by the waist to his bed.

(Marlon caught on rather quickly and had taken to automatically nesting at the foot of Eli's bed after the first two nights.)

Some days Brody texted me, asking me to talk. I was surprisingly delighted by how simple it was to just delete those messages and move on. It felt good. I felt more whole than I had in a long time.

Every morning I woke up wrapped in firm arms, and now I didn't want to wake up any other way.

Eli Buckley was absolutely ruining me, and I started to think that I might be okay if he would just continue to ruin me forever.

THE WUNDERKIND (FIRST DRAFT)
"PILOT" 10/8/07

INT. PHOTO BOOTH—DAY

She kisses him on the third flash. He blinks and pulls away.

POPPY

(gasps)

I'm sorry!

She runs out of the photo booth, leaving him alone for the last picture.

POPPY (V.O.)

The danger of Arlo was that I would always love him more than he could ever love me.

THE WUNDERKIND by Vera Stein.

It had been just over two weeks since Leonard had left me the cactus, and I hadn't had a chance to go by and say thank you. After setting up for his writing workshop last week, I had to skip for a staff meeting and only had a chance for a quick hello, so I was long overdue for a visit to Leonard and Patrick.

I walked past Ruby's door, tempted to let myself in, but decided that probably wasn't the most productive way to start my day or to mend that fence.

As I stood in front of Leonard's door and knocked, I noted that his *Stay Awhile (Until You're Asked to Leave)* doormat had been rolled up and was leaning against the doorframe.

My phone rang from the depths of my tote bag. I checked to see who was calling as I waited for Leonard.

Brody.

Immediately, I sent the call to voicemail, pushing away every possible reason why he could be trying to reach me.

I knocked again, more impatiently this time, and only after a moment did I hear footsteps approaching.

"You here for the donations?" a deep voice asked as the door swung open.

Standing there in Leonard's partially emptied apartment was one of our managing custodians in his tan uniform.

"Vera, right?" the man asked. "Was there something you needed? I'm just finishing up this removal cleanup."

Something in my chest cracked and the next words came out on a choke. "Removal cleanup?"

The man nodded as he stepped back into the apartment, leaving the door open for me to enter if I so chose. "The next of kin already came through yesterday and took what they wanted."

Logically, I knew what all of this meant, but I refused to allow myself to even think the word before I had confirmation.

I peered inside, frantically searching for Patrick's birdcage. "Stop." I'd never heard my own voice boom with such force.

The man turned around slowly; confusion furrowed his brow.

"Just stop. Don't move anything else. Not yet." I didn't know why that was my first inclination. I refused to name what I knew to be true, and something about keeping Leonard's belongings in place allowed me to believe that this was reversible. That this wasn't . . .

He waited for a moment for further explanation, but then he must have recognized something in my expression. Grief. Shock. Anger. It was all there. "Yes, ma'am," he said.

I practically ran to the main building, leaving my bags right where I'd dropped them on Leonard's doorstep, completely unaware.

I found myself breathlessly barging into Morgan's office without knocking.

Before she even acknowledged me, the man sitting in the chair opposite her desk turned then immediately stood up and moved toward me.

Eli.

My resolve crumpled.

"Leonard," I said on a sob. "No one told me." I was nearly yelling now. "Neither of you told me!"

"I only just now found out," Eli said, pulling me into his chest.

Over his shoulder, Morgan's gaze met mine before wandering, like she was embarrassed to witness such an unguarded moment. The fact that she was even capable of embarrassment came as a shock.

And then I remembered that Eli had been off yesterday. He was on call, but they wouldn't have called him for a resident's death. There was nothing left that a doctor could do once they were gone.

A death.

Leonard's death.

Leonard was dead.

"He went in his sleep," Morgan said softly.

I stepped back from Eli, suddenly very aware of Morgan. I hated when people said that, like dying in your sleep was some sort of consolation prize. And maybe it was. But not for the living. "And his nephew already came by to collect his belongings?"

"Well, some of them," Morgan answered.

Eli guided me to the other chair in front of Morgan's desk and then sat down beside me.

With her hands folded on her desk, Morgan continued. "We contact next of kin with instructions based on the wishes of the deceased."

"His name was Leonard," I said. "You don't have to call him *the deceased*. We all knew him. He's not just some protocol."

"Right. Sorry." She nodded and took a breath. "Sometimes it can take a few days to clear out someone's apartment or room, but Leonard had said that his next of kin could take a pass through his belongings and then we should donate or dispose of the rest. What will likely happen in his case is that his belongings will be put in a storage unit while his lawyers settle the rest of his estate."

"What about Patrick?" I asked. "His bird."

"His nephew took him for now."

Morgan went on, sharing more details, but it was all white noise. Finally, there was a long-enough lull that I took as my cue to stand up.

My body guided me out the door and down the hall. I faintly heard my name being called and it wasn't until I heard the fall of footsteps behind me and then felt a warm, cautious hand on my shoulder that I stopped.

"Where are you going?" Eli asked.

I shook my head even though it wasn't a yes-or-no question.

"You don't need to be alone right now," he said.

And then I looked up to him and it felt like I was seeing him from underwater, the surface above me creating waves and distortions.

"I think I do, actually," I found myself saying.

The worry etched in his brow sank past the waterline, filling me with guilt. "Just for a little while," I added.

"Where are you going? Leonard's?"

I hadn't decided until that exact moment, but of course that's where I needed to be.

Without a moment to even make sure we were alone, Eli leaned down and pressed a kiss to the top of my head. "Keep your phone on you, so I can check on you."

"Okay," my lips said. "Okay."

CHAPTER FIFTY

Leonard's unit was too quiet. The place where Patrick's cage had been felt like some sort of wormhole. Patrick being gone was the surest evidence that something was truly wrong and that Leonard wasn't just out at his writing workshop or the cafeteria.

The plants lining his space seemed to droop even though it had only been one day without his attention. I wished I had a place for them all, despite the fact that I'd murdered enough plants to be a serial killer.

Most items in the apartment were tagged with blue stickers, which indicated they should be packed and stored. Similar-looking red tags said *Destroy and discard.*

I found myself gravitating to red-tagged items. It was mostly perishables and junk mail and magazines and a few broken items like a chipped vase.

As I pressed deeper into the apartment, I found that Leonard's casket had been returned back to his spare room. Since it wore a blue tag, I assumed that meant Leonard had made arrangements for the green funeral he'd pivoted to in the last few months. I'd never met someone in my life so prepared for death, and yet I couldn't make sense of the devastating shock I felt now that he'd actually died.

Regret stung most of all. I'd been home for two whole weeks and because I was so caught up with Eli and doing everything in my power to avoid Ruby, I had barely seen Leonard. I didn't even get a chance to find out how he felt about his living funeral, and I'd never be able to share the cryptic notes I'd made on my story.

It struck me then how deeply unfair it was that Leonard still probably had so many movies and television shows that he was looking forward to watching and would now never experience.

I hiccupped a laugh at the thought, which then turned into a fresh round of sobs. Leonard was dead and somehow the thing that wrecked me the most was that he'd never get to see the next seasons of *The Real Housewives of Salt Lake City* and *Sister Wives*.

My phone—all but forgotten—vibrated in my pocket. When I scrolled through the notifications, I found that I'd missed another call and received six texts—all from Brody.

Whatever he needed from me wasn't relevant in this moment. There was a time when I couldn't even let his calls ring more than twice before rushing to answer, but right now, he was so far beyond my concern.

I plopped down on the office chair in the corner of the room, letting the weight of grief hold me in its gravitational pull. Under the desk was a metal filing cabinet with folders all labeled with red stickers. *Discard, discard, discard, discard*.

Normally, I wouldn't just start digging through someone else's paperwork, but Leonard was a meddlesome bastard, so surely he would understand. Encourage me, in fact.

I unhooked the first folder from the metal lining of the drawer and opened it on the desk.

It was a script.

`My Mother's Father` Draft 4

I took out the next folder.

`Paid Vacation` Pilot Episode Draft 6

`Something in the Water` Draft 2

Working Title: `Depressed Cheerleaders` Draft 6.5

`Happy Hour` Pilot Episode Draft 11

I continued through the drawer to find that folder after folder was full of what appeared to be unsold scripts. Some half complete. Some marked up so heavily with red that the pages looked like a crime scene. And all of it had been marked as trash. There were a handful of floppy disks too, but most of the scripts were hard copies from a typewriter.

Going through my mother's belongings had been a Herculean task. And similar to Leonard, Mom had prepared to die. Yet there was still so much to sort. I knew the danger of being overly sentimental and keeping things that would only one day become my own trash. But these pages . . . The thought of seeing them tossed and then never seen again made my stomach turn. What would I even do with them? They couldn't be sold—at least not by me—but to see them just forgotten left me hollow and aching.

Maybe I could digitize them. I could at least read them. That felt like something.

In the kitchen, as I searched for an empty box, I found the Marfa, Texas, mug he'd served me a cup of coffee in that first day I came to his apartment. Even though it was in a box with a blue tag, I decided no one would miss this one memento if I took it with me. At least I'd have something of Leonard's after I undoubtedly killed his cactus.

After consolidating the packed kitchen appliances to free up a box, I filled it with the contents of the filing cabinet and decided to head home.

It was well past lunchtime, and I needed to drop this box off before I could get back to my office and set up for the Marijuana as Medicine presentation tonight.

As I closed the door, a familiar voice drawled, "Knocked down in his prime, wasn't he?"

I shook my head, hiking the box up with my knee before looking over to see Ruby sitting on the bench between her and Leonard's places.

"I'm so glad you can see the humor in Leonard's death," I said, every syllable falling flat.

"This is familiar territory for us," she said. "I'm so very sorry for not responding to Leonard's death with one of the three Vera-approved reactions."

"I'm not doing this with you right now."

"We could just wait until I die," she said. "With Leonard gone, I suspect I won't be far behind. He and I always did have similar timing."

She was hurting. I could see that. But I'd spent so much time after Mom's death catering to Ruby and her grief. I couldn't do it again.

"Sure, Ruby," I said. "Sounds great."

And then I took my stolen coffee mug and the scripts I couldn't bring myself to let go of and I left.

Mom had made Ruby and me promise to take care of each other after she was gone, but maybe the best way for us to care for ourselves now was without each other.

CHAPTER FIFTY-ONE

When I returned to our apartment, I decided to sleep through my lunch break. I'd spent most of the days immediately after my mother's death asleep. There was something so tempting about snoozing through the day as much as I could, like I was bypassing my sorrow by sleeping. Of course, grief sometimes found me in my dreams, but it always felt a little more distant. A little more manageable.

I lay down in my room for a few minutes with Marlon curled at the foot of the bed. Despite being emotionally exhausted, I was restless. Which was how I found myself traveling down the hall to Eli's room with Marlon tucked against my chest.

I slid beneath his comforter and was enveloped in his scent—sandalwood and fresh linen. Scooting closer to the center of the bed, I nestled into his pillow, and my mind finally began to slow enough for me to drift into the quiet of sleep.

A shift on the mattress woke me gently. I blinked lazily, my vision blurring at the edges until I realized how far the sunlight had moved across the room.

My eyes fluttered shut again as a broad palm smoothed my hair off my sweaty forehead.

Eli.

The actual smell of him was so much better than the lingering scent on his bedsheets.

He slid under the covers behind me, his arm wrapping around my waist and pulling me snug against his chest.

"What time is it?" I dared to ask.

"Nearly six," he whispered into the nape of my neck.

"Fuck." I shot up—or attempted to, but Eli pulled me back down before I could get too far. "I lost a whole day," I said. "I had an event to set up—"

"Morgan and I took care of it," he murmured.

"What if I get fired?" I moaned.

"No one's firing you."

I rolled over and curled into his chest. "I played hooky."

He curled a finger under my chin and tilted my face upward. "Your friend died. That warrants hooky. I can't imagine Leonard wanting anything more than for you to use his death as a reason to skip out on work."

"He was my friend," I whispered. It was the first time I'd referred to Leonard as anything beyond a resident and I hoped that he knew it too. Hearing Eli say it only made it more true.

Somewhere behind me, my phone began to ring and I blindly fumbled around for it until I'd silenced the ringer.

"You need to answer that?" Eli asked.

I shook my head.

He held me like that for a while longer and when I woke up again, the sun had dipped below the horizon.

I watched him inhale and exhale slowly, appreciating his angular jaw and the pout of his lower lip.

His shirt was untucked and the first few buttons undone. I couldn't resist the temptation of pressing a kiss against his throat and then his sternum.

His hand flexed against the small of my back as he pulled me closer to him and placed a sleepy kiss atop my head. My hands roamed across his shoulders and down his arms and chest.

"I want to be close to you," I whispered. "I need to." It was more than that, though. I wanted to burrow inside of him and be consumed by his constant warmth and protection. I wanted the comfort that could only be found in two people moving in synchronicity.

He didn't ask any questions as he rolled us over and settled between my legs. Our kisses were soft and unhurried. Clothing peeled away like falling leaves. Eli touched every inch of me, taking a careful inventory, and every point of contact was a reminder that I was here and I was alive. *I am here. I am alive. So is Eli.*

Every insecurity I had felt so small and insignificant. I couldn't bring myself to hide my body in the shadows. I let the light from the hallway leak in for Eli to see me. Each time instinct told me to cover myself, Eli gently pushed my hands away and addressed that part of my body with his mouth. His lips absorbed every discomfort and hesitation.

"You deserve to be seen," he whispered as he slid into me, slowly stretching me. "Let me see you."

I nodded, tears brimming, and hooked my arms under his. My nails scraped across his back as he thrust deeply and I let out a soft cry in response.

He took his time, not letting me disassociate from this moment. His gaze held mine as he swept my hair back and traced a map of my face, his eyes following every line. The pad of his thumb dragged down the center of my lips, opening my mouth as a prelude to a stream of velvety, languid kisses.

When the torture of going slowly became too much, he guided me onto my stomach and pulled my hips up to meet his. He slipped a hand between my legs, his fingers stirring against me. My orgasm curled like a fist in my belly, tensing every muscle in my body before a violent release sent a tingling numbness down to the tips of my toes.

"That's it," he said, his body blanketing mine now so that his breath was hot on my neck. "I love watching you unravel. I love . . . I love . . ." With three more short and quick thrusts, he found his release.

We both hissed as he pulled out of me, feeling the immediate absence of the other.

He murmured words like *beautiful* and *perfect* and *mine* until we both fell asleep, our spent bodies intertwined.

THE WUNDERKIND (FIRST DRAFT)
"PILOT" 10/8/07

EXT. PARK—EVENING

There is a strong breeze. Summer is disappearing. They sit on swings. He faces forward. She faces him.

POPPY

Kissing you was a mistake. I'm sorry.

ARLO

What if it wasn't? What if I love you?

POPPY

I never asked you to.

Poppy stands and walks away.

POPPY (V.O.)

Waiting for him to decide if he loved me hurt more than leaving ever could.

April 17, 2020
Vera S.
Is this angst earned?

THE WUNDERKIND by Vera Stein.

I detangled myself from Eli as the sun began to warm the bedroom with morning light. Careful not to wake him, I slid out from under the covers, clutching my phone to my chest.

Gingerly, I walked out to the kitchen, my body stiff from our activities and the kind of sleep that leaves you sweaty and disoriented. After slipping on a T-shirt and Eli's robe, I sat down at the kitchen table with a granola bar and one of Leonard's scripts.

As I flipped through the pages, I checked my phone and found a stream of notifications. I had vague memories of missed calls and text messages from yesterday, but I couldn't imagine even speaking to anyone then, let alone anyone who didn't know Leonard.

There were nine missed calls and sixteen text messages. All from Brody.

The messages were all some form of a request to talk and there were no voicemails. How had we worked together for so long and he still hadn't managed to remember that one of my major sources of anxiety was missed calls with accompanying we-need-to-talk texts and no other hints of what might be going on? It was emotional clickbait.

Just as I was weighing my options on how to respond, my phone rang again.

Brody. Of course.

And because I knew he would just keep calling until I answered, I found myself picking up.

"Hi."

"Vera," he said, and then took a pause. "I really did not expect you to answer."

"I had a feeling that you would keep calling until I did."

"Yeah, I'm sorry for the nonstop calls. It's just . . . I didn't know how to say this over text." He paused for a second and cleared his throat. "And everything else too. I can't blame you for not wanting to answer. I get it, but I need you to hear me out."

"Okay," I finally said after letting his words sit in silence. I was in no hurry to meet him halfway.

"I have two offers for you. First, I got a backer for my production company." He went quiet for a moment, likely waiting for congratulations that would not be coming.

"Right," he said to himself. "And I need you. The job would be sort of a creative director with some day-to-day responsibilities until we've expanded a bit more."

What.

"Vera, this is the job you were made for." His tone was heartfelt now and I could practically hear his longtime acting coach, Rolph, telling him to dig deeper. "*You* set the tone. The pay is fair. Good, even. Full benefits."

I didn't say anything, and he took my silence as indifference. If only that were true. My greedy little mind was whirring. Was this really happening? I couldn't say yes. But what if this was the moment I'd waited years for? The moment I'd promised myself would make everything worth it?

"The second piece to the offer is that I've found our first acquisition. Your first duty would be to sign off on it."

I sighed. "Sounds like you're back-seat driving the job I haven't even accepted."

"Aren't you going to ask me what the project is, Vera?" There was an amused lilt in his voice, and I hated how easy it was for him to feel familiar again. "I can hear you rolling your eyes," he said.

With a huff, I gave in. "What project is it, Brody?"

"*The Wunderkind*," he said simply.

My mouth dropped and the phone slithered down my shoulder and onto the table.

The volume was turned up enough that I could still hear him speaking, but my brain couldn't translate what he was saying into anything meaningful.

I'd been staring at my half-eaten granola bar for a long moment when he finally paused. "Vera? You there? Vera?"

My hand trembled as I picked the phone back up and held it to my ear. "You—you can't buy a script that doesn't exist, Brody."

He was quiet for a beat. "I had it recovered," he finally said. "After you drove off, the laptop fell off your car just outside the gates. When I came to see you, I had brought it with me, but then . . . then I don't know. I guess after how everything went down, I thought keeping it to myself would punish you in some kind of way—"

"That's—"

"Fucked up," he said. "I know. I felt awful about it, which is why I found the most expensive IT company out there and had them take a look to see if they could recover the files."

"Did they?" I asked quietly, trying to hold on to some bit of indifference but failing hugely, even though I already knew the answer.

"Vera, it's so good. I could practically hear you reading it aloud to me in my head. It's everything you said you would write back in college. It was like we were sitting in your dorm all over again. We could attach two fresh faces with incredible chemistry to play Poppy and Arlo."

I hated myself for it, but my chest swelled with pride. It wasn't just about the script being good. It was that Brody thought it was good.

My god. I deserved an ass kicking for even caring.

He chattered on about casting ideas and taglines and alternative titles. And all I could think was that I had to get off the phone before I agreed to something I might not be ready for—or that Brody couldn't actually deliver on. Because that had been the last twenty years, hadn't it? Brody dangling a carrot in front of me so that I would stay the course.

"I need to go," I blurted.

"What— Oh. Okay. But please check your email, Vera. There's a formal offer letter there."

A formal offer letter? I didn't know Brody was even capable of using that kind of business jargon. "Sure."

I was already pulling the phone away from my ear when he said, "You promise?"

"Okay."

I hung up before he could say another word or, even worse, before I could.

His attention was a flowering weed. So beautiful. So invasive.

Brody was right. The offer was more than fair. It was nice-place-without-a-roommate money. It was eat-out-as-much-as-you-want money. It was buy-a-new-car-with-seat-heaters money.

Marlon circled at my feet as Eli walked into the kitchen, rubbing his eyes. Wearing gray sweatpants slung low on his hips, he kissed me on the top of the head before starting his morning espresso ritual.

After he was fully caffeinated, he sat across from me. "I think I'm going to pick up some boxes tonight. Maybe start taking over a few things this weekend."

The house. I nearly forgot.

He waited for me to weigh in with my plans too. But all I could think of was Brody's offer and Leonard's box of script drafts. Pages upon pages that he'd pored over for decades.

Maybe it was overly sentimental, but I couldn't help but wonder what pieces of my life would be forgotten as trash when I was gone. I wanted to think that I could have Eli and my unbelievable opportunity, but that felt so naive now. What was I going to do? Disappear into the desert and write? If I wanted to be in the film business, I needed a foot in the door. I needed to be in the Hollywood bubble, and working for Brody as more than an assistant could be the opening gambit I'd been waiting so long for.

What would Eli say? I couldn't stay here only for him, could I? It couldn't be that simple.

"I got a job offer," I said.

His gorgeous face lit up, and his joy for me was a stab to the gut. He was plainly happy for me. He didn't know that Brody was the source of the offer or that it meant I would have to leave.

"Vera, that's great. You never mentioned that you were looking, though." There it was. Just the slightest bit of hurt that I hadn't shared something with him. "Is it something you're excited about?"

I nodded slowly. "It's an industry job. Something creative."

He was taken aback, but not in an insulting way. "We have to celebrate. Tonight! I'm taking you out."

This felt too good. I enjoyed this too much. The thought of him being excited for me. The thought of us sharing our lives in this way. "Eli." I reached across the table for his hand, which he freely gave. "The offer is in LA. With Brody."

He stilled for a moment before running his tongue along his lower lip and nodding to himself. "Okay."

I pulled away, letting go of his hand. "That's all you have to say?"

He leaned back in his chair with an air of indifference, hands braced on his thighs. "What more do you want me to say, Vera? Your mind seems to be made up."

"It's not entirely," I said softly. I wanted his input. I wanted him to tell me it was okay.

"Make up your mind and then we can talk," he said in a chilly tone. "I'm not your boss. I can't counter the offer."

"I wish you would tell me what you think."

"Does it matter, Vera? I think I've made it perfectly clear what I want. But right now, you springing this on me and then waiting for my response like it's some kind of test . . . it's not fair. You want a reaction from me? Why? Because you need me to be the reason you stay? The reason you say no to Brody, who has never, *ever* been a good employer or friend." His voice dropped. "Or lover. I've asked you to move in with me, for Christ's sake."

"You *left*," I reminded him. "Nineteen years ago, you left. So excuse me if my first inclination isn't to throw myself on the tracks for . . . whatever this is. I don't even know if you're my boyfriend, Eli."

"Vera." He sighed heavily. "*Boyfriend* is too simple a word for what I want to be to you." He slid his chair back. "The real question is: What do you *want* to be to me? What do you want us to be? Because right now you throwing out Brody's job offer as casual morning chitchat feels like you're waiting for me to jump first instead of just deciding what you want and where we fit into your life. So what's it going to be? Tell me what we are."

My throat was sandpaper and the only word I managed to get out was his name. "Eli."

With downward-turned lips and a soft voice, he said, "You couldn't take a risk if it was going to save the world. You want to know why it's easier to tell me about this job offer and wait to see what I do or say?" He stood then, his eyes hooking into me. "Because it's safer. It guarantees that only one of us has to put their heart on the line."

"That's not fair," I told him. "The last few months have been one giant risk. I left everything behind when I came here."

"Coming here wasn't a choice. It was a last resort. But congratulations, Vera. I'm so glad Brody finally woke the fuck up and offered you the job you deserved years ago. I hope this Venus flytrap he's set for you pans out."

"Eli," I called, my shoulders sinking, but the door to his room was already slamming shut. My eyes began to brim and tears spilled down my cheeks.

I looked down at my phone to find a text from Brody.

Brody:

Did you see the offer letter? Come into town for a few days and we can discuss. I'll set you up in the pool house.

CHAPTER FIFTY-FOUR

"Mr. Turner will be with you in just a few minutes," said Holly. Or maybe it was Molly.

Brody had hired three new assistants since I'd left and they were all girls under the age of twenty-two with names ending in *Y* who wore clothing so trendy that it was ugly in an ironic way. (At least, I thought so.) Or maybe I was just uncomfortable with how reminiscent it was of something I would have seen in a dELiA*s catalog in high school.

"Does he have you call him that?" I asked.

She blinked at me blankly. "By his name?"

"Well, yes, but *Mr. Turner*. He doesn't go by *Brody*?"

"I was raised to respect my elders," she said.

I choked back a laugh. What would Brody say if he knew one of his little hottie assistants referred to him as an elder?

I sat at the kitchen island, waiting for Brody, and I tried not to judge the disorganized piles of PR packages. It required even more effort to not sort them myself.

Brody had sent a black car service to pick me up and drive me back to LA. If his attempt at wooing me saved me gas money and let me nap for the whole car ride, then consider me reluctantly wooed.

It had been six days since my argument with Eli and some part of me held on to hope that his anger would pass. But when bedtime came, he closed his door for the first time in weeks, and I retreated to my own room. The longer the wall between us stayed up, the taller it became. We barely spoke for the next few days as he shuttled boxes in and out of the apartment and I was left to imagine what a future without him would look like.

I hadn't decided on accepting Brody's offer, but Eli seemed so sure that I would. The more distant he felt, the more likely it seemed that I didn't have anything to lose in coming here. But I couldn't help but wonder if I would always regret not hearing Brody out.

Then there was Leonard and the box of his scripts.

So here I was.

A hand settled on my shoulder and there was Brody, hovering behind me. "I'm so glad you're here," he said.

I swiveled around. "Thanks for having me, *Mr. Turner*."

He rolled his eyes. "The staffing agency has them call me that. Makes me feel old as fuck."

"Brody, we *are* old as fuck."

He shook his head. "I pay good money for those microneedling sessions." He stepped back from my chair so that I could stand up. "Come on. We have a lot of work to do."

"This isn't me accepting your offer," I told him as I followed him into the more comfortable of the living rooms, furnished with cream sofas with modern lines that were actually comfortable.

It was so bizarre to be back here again. Like revisiting a childhood home and finding you don't fit inside of it in the same way you once did. And yet everything was eerily similar, especially Brody in his athletic shorts and T-shirt with the sleeves cut off. He'd obviously come straight from working out.

He sat down across from me, his elbows braced on his knees. "I want to talk about *The Wunderkind*."

"Yes, I too would like to talk about how you broke into my laptop and read my work without my permission."

"The laptop you left on your car before driving away?"

He did have a point there. I leaned back against the sofa and crossed my arms, refusing to smile or give any indication that I was warming to him.

"I want *The Wunderkind* to be our debut project, Vera."

"Brody, I've been dabbling with that script for twenty years. Why now?"

"Well, first of all, you never let me read it, and second . . . it's not bad."

"That's it?" I asked. "*It's not bad*?"

He shrugged. "Well, yeah. But it feels right too. You've been working on this project since we were in school, Vera. It feels right that the first project out of the gate should be one you've dedicated half of your life to. It's the right thing to do."

Half of my life. Jesus Christ. That sounded bleak. This didn't feel the same as the effusive praise from his phone call. This felt like Brody trying to make up for something that could never really be recovered. Time. *The right thing to do.*

And then something that scared me almost as much as losing Eli struck me. I hadn't read *The Wunderkind* in full in *years*. Just bits and pieces here and there. What if it was awful? What if this was my big chance and I wasted it on some script I started when I was twenty-one and never let go of because I was scared that I would never be able to create anything else?

"I need to read the script," I told him.

"Of course," he said, and leaned toward the coffee table to grab a spiral-bound printed copy, which he handed to me. "I want you to be sure, okay? But my investors are also in a hurry to announce while I'm in the run-up to *Cactus King*. They want to capitalize on the publicity. We'd like to—"

"I get it," I said. "Just give me the afternoon."

He stood. "I guess you know where everything is, so make yourself at home."

I glanced around at the plush sofas and the artfully placed overpriced bottled water on the coffee table. I didn't feel . . . clear-headed here. "I think I might need to . . . get out of the house. Away."

"Ruben can take you anywhere you want to go," Brody said, seemingly unbothered. "Do you have a place in mind?"

INT. MONTAGE—DAY

The summer season is ending. The ice cream shop is closing for the year. The boardwalk is quiet. Seasons change. So do Poppy and Arlo. Poppy has become distant. She has missed calls and text messages from him. She sees him walking alone one day while she drives home. She wants to call his name. She doesn't.

POPPY (V.O.)

Some people don't ghost you. They haunt you.

CHAPTER FIFTY-FIVE

I ♥ Ramen was my mom's favorite place for us to be—as she called it—alone together.

It had opened in the shopping center near our house when I was in middle school. Mom and I always bypassed the booths and tables, opting instead for the little bar meant for single diners. We would each bring a book or a magazine and sit in silence while we waited for our food. Alone. Together. Ruby was baffled by the experience and always tried to start up a conversation, missing the point entirely.

Tilly, the older woman who owned the restaurant with her husband and their two daughters, sat at the hostess stand wiping her dry-erase seating chart. "Where's your mother?" she asked without even bothering to say hello.

The same soft, rehearsed expression I'd grown accustomed to using when I broke the news about Mom settled on my face. "She passed away earlier this year."

Tilly nodded slowly, her usual frown growing deeper. The staff here had known Mom was sick since it was one of the only places we still made an effort to go to toward the end and they always went out of their way to make sure she was as comfortable as possible.

"You know, any time she finished a book, she always left it for me to read," Tilly said. "Sometimes, she'd highlight passages and write in the margins too."

"She did?" I asked. I vaguely recalled Mom talking to Tilly about her books, but I hadn't realized she'd passed them along to her as well.

Tilly nodded and pointed to a shelf full of dilapidated paperbacks behind the counter. "My daughter Sue always said that your mom's notes and highlights were like reading a book with a friend. I let solo diners borrow from the shelf if they want."

"She would have loved that," I told her.

Tilly led me to the usual spot where Mom and I sat. The last two seats at the end of the bar nearest the wall.

I ordered a milk tea and a bowl of ramen with extra fish cakes and then I took out the script and began to read.

At first, I started with a pen in my hand, but after it took me fifteen minutes to read the first two pages, I forced myself to put it away and just read. The itch to change every little word and piece of punctuation was intolerable. I had to sit on my hands at one point.

My food came and I slowly ate my ramen as I continued, thankful for something to occupy my hands and hoping to find a spark of inspiration.

The script was . . . fine. It was an unmarked file, so all of the notes and edits I'd made over the years were gone, but I didn't need them to guide me. Because with each passing page, I felt more and more distanced from *The Wunderkind*. And not just the script itself, but the person who wrote it. It was the same feeling I would get in middle school or high school when I found a relic from a long-lost hobby or interest and felt embarrassed for even liking the thing in the first place. It was like rediscovering your toys and realizing that they were only ever just overpriced chunks of plastic.

I was wholly disconnected as I bit down on my lower lip, my brain doubling over a very shitty metaphor about pigeons and doves.

My phone lit up with a text from Brody.

Brody:
How's it going? Like falling in love all over again?

My fingers hovered over the screen as I contemplated my response. I was only forty pages into the hundred-and-two-page script.

Of course Brody loved the script. Now, seeing it with new eyes for the first time, I could plainly see that *The Wunderkind* was about him after all. It was about us. And it was written by the girl he met in college. The girl who made him feel like he could do anything.

The screenplay was from the girl's point of view. Poppy. And yet every page lived in service of her love interest—an overgrown Peter Pan who had once felt whimsical to me . . . but now . . .

It all came down to this: I wasn't twenty-one anymore. I wasn't the girl who was so obsessed with the feeling of being in Brody's orbit that I had to write about it. I remembered those emotions, of course. But twenty-one felt like a universe away. Hell, I wasn't even the same Vera I was ten months ago. And just reminiscing felt like taking ten steps backward.

At the time, this story was the quirky fantasy version of falling in love that I'd told myself. The version that twenty-one-year-old me had romanticized. This wasn't a story I knew how to tell anymore. It didn't feel true anymore.

Behind me, the bell above the door rang and Tilly greeted the incoming diner.

I was flipping through the next few pages, looking for anything that felt salvageable, when someone sat down one chair over from me. I glanced at them quickly before turning back to my work, but then . . . my brain stuttered and I looked up again. A kelly-green sundress lined with embroidered margaritas and open-toe slides encrusted with huge chunky gems.

"Ruby?" I asked. Of all the places in Southern California, my grandmother was *here*. We lived in the same retirement community and I'd managed to avoid her for weeks, but somehow here we were in LA just one place setting apart.

She scoffed and shook her head. "Would you believe that I came all the way out here to spend time alone thinking at the one place you and your mother always forced me to sit with my own damn feelings? And as my luck would have it, I'm not alone at all."

I nodded. Of course, *she* was the inconvenienced one. God, something about her made me revert to an enraged fourteen-year-old. "Right. I guess there's no use in pointing out that I was here first."

She sighed and untied the silk scarf she was wearing over her hair and then put on her reading glasses to peruse the menu.

I forced my attention back to the pages, even though there was no use. As Ruby placed her order and shuffled through her purse to find her compact mirror, I read the same scene heading over and over again.

I made an attempt at the next line as I sipped some of my broth.

"You sound like a farm animal when you slurp like that."

Instead of responding, I slurped again, but louder.

The waitress brought Ruby a yuzu lemon drop martini and I managed to make it through a few more pages, even though I hadn't formed a critical thought since she'd walked in.

After I pushed my bowl of ramen to the side, I felt Ruby watching me as I dug out my credit card for the waitress.

"Well," she finally said, "aren't you going to tell me what you're reading?"

Without looking up, I said, "I thought you came here for some quiet time."

"The quiet is boring." She paused for a moment before swiveling her body to face me. "I could never understand it. Why you two would go to the trouble of going out to dinner only to sit together in silence."

"Haven't you ever had that with someone? A person you could do nothing with."

She shook her head. "I don't like the quiet."

"What about Hollis?" I asked.

She drummed her nails on the countertop. "The woman invented stoicism. But she doesn't seem to mind when I fill the silence with chatter."

"Sounds like you've met your match," I told her as the waitress came back with the check.

"I fear that is the truth." She sounded despondent. Regretful.

"It's an old screenplay of mine," I said, holding up a page. "Brody's starting a production company and he wants to option it."

She grinned tightly, doing a poor job of hiding her delight. "Well, it's about time that job paid off."

I shook my head, unable to hold eye contact with her as I said, "I'm not going to say yes."

With that, she slid off her stool and came to sit next to me. "Vera."

She rapped her knuckles on the counter. "You're not getting any younger, dear. This business is tough, especially for a woman of your age."

I wanted to respond with a quip about how out of touch she was, but I couldn't in good faith. The film industry had progressed, but not so much that she was entirely wrong. Still, I was angry at her for pointing out the truth. This could very well be my only shot.

"I started writing this when I was in college," I told her as the waitress brought my card back, and I thanked her before signing the receipt. "I want to tell stories, but I don't think this is what I want to say anymore. And I know that you know this industry, and that you have opinions, but I think I need to do this on my own terms. I took my time getting here. I don't want to throw away my first impression on something I don't even connect with anymore. Something I'm not really proud of."

She inhaled through her nose for a long moment. "Forgive me. Perhaps it's gauche, but I believe there's something to be said for taking every job. Every deal. It gets your name out there, Vera." Her voice was desperate now. "This could be that for you." She shook her head. "As someone who has seen the underbelly of this town firsthand, I'm offended that you would turn your nose up on a perfectly good offer."

I opened my mouth, ready to defend myself, my temper beginning to rise.

She held up a hand to stop me. "I know you think I don't understand you, Vera. And I know I wasn't the ideal grandmother. You've made that *very* clear, and you're not entirely wrong."

She paused, waiting for me to correct her, but that wasn't going to happen.

"I was never very good at comforting. Even with your mother. Lord, she had such a soft heart. I didn't dote on you like I should have. But I did push you in the same way I wished someone had pushed me."

"I'm not you, Ruby." It was a phrase I'd said so often that it might as well have been carved into my forehead.

She chuckled. "You know, when your mother grew up, I thought that was it and I was done being a mom. I thought it was just something you could clock out of, but then you came along and your mother's health . . . Well, I took on a role with you I'd never planned for."

"You resent me for it," I said softly. "It's more obvious than you think."

She blinked a few times, holding her eyes shut for a moment, before saying, "There was a time when that was true. Vera, I clawed my way through life. Through this business. No one wanted to see women succeed back then, especially not one who was a single mother. I was as much of a set piece as the goddamned trees."

"I know it wasn't easy for you back then. And I know you think I'm throwing a perfectly good opportunity away by not taking the offer. But I've waited all this time to see my words come to life. And now that it doesn't feel so impossible, I want to know that I'm doing this on purpose. *The Wunderkind* does not give me that feeling. It's a thing I never knew how to let go of until it was forcibly taken from me. And if I hadn't driven off with my laptop on my car that day, I don't think I ever would have moved on to the next thing."

"The next thing?" she asked, one brow arched, her interest very clearly piqued.

"It's in the baby stages, so don't get too excited." Just talking about it out loud made me feel claustrophobic. "I shouldn't have even said anything." Whatever this project was that I'd started in Leonard's workshop, it was still only mine and I wanted to be greedy with that feeling. "But I also really like my job at Starlight Palms. More than I ever expected to, honestly. Being outside of . . . this place and this business . . . it's nice. It feels like I'm pulling inspiration right from the source instead of eating prechewed food and spitting it back up again."

"How poetic," she said with a snort before sighing and reaching over to place a hand on my thigh. "Vera, I need you to understand. I always wanted more for you. Better. We try to raise children using the same rules we succeeded by, but by the time they need those rules, they're obsolete. As much as it pains me to say it, maybe the roads have changed and my map is out of date."

I glanced over at her, doing a poor job at hiding my surprise to her admitting that she might not always be right.

"Just because something is offered doesn't mean it's worth taking."

I hadn't expected that from Ruby at all. Her voice was this constant presence in my head telling me to take a leap. Jump first. Look later. But for the first time in my life, my grandmother was telling me to trust myself.

She swiped her finger along the sugared rim of her glass and licked it clean. "I sure as hell signed on for way too many duds with far too many skeevy men calling the shots and not a single one of them made me the big star they promised I'd be. I don't know what the whole history behind you and Brody is, but it's clear that there is one."

"He's not skeevy," I told her. "Well, not for the most part. He's a man-child. And one that I don't want to take care of anymore."

The waitress brought Ruby her ramen and she ordered a vodka tonic. She sipped the broth and indeed did so without slurping.

"Your turn," I told her. "What has you looking for a quiet place to think?"

"Hollis asked me to marry her." She took another sip of the broth as though she'd told me she'd just gone to the grocery store.

"So you said yes and promptly came here to celebrate by yourself?"

"That's not all."

"Okay . . ."

"Leonard's lawyer called." She placed her spoon on her place mat and smoothed the napkin over her lap. "Leonard asked that I be in charge of the posthumous management of his works . . . his scripts. And the nonfiction book he wrote decades ago about crafting dialogue."

"What about his nephew?" I asked.

"Any profits will go to the family, except for a small management fee. But his nephew is a dentist who lives in Utah. He was more than happy to hear that the responsibility did not fall to him."

"Wow. I . . . um, found a whole filing cabinet full of unfinished projects in his apartment."

She laughed. "I'm surprised he didn't request that they be burned."

"Technically, they were marked as trash, but I . . . I couldn't let that happen."

"Well, that's good, I suppose. Since you'll be hearing from his attorney soon as well. The second piece to Leonard's wishes was that when I'm no longer around, he would like for you to take over the job." She rolled her eyes and laughed to herself. "At my age, it seems silly to even pass the torch to me, if I'm being honest."

"He did it for a reason," I said. And if he had included me in his end-of-life planning, his will was very much up to date. He could have easily revised his wishes regarding Ruby and the management of his works at any time. But he hadn't. After the years of scorn and vitriol between him and Ruby, Leonard had still chosen her. "Are you going to finally tell me why the two of you stopped talking all those years ago?"

She took a long sip of her drink before turning to me. "Take this as a lesson," she said, "that the longer you let something sit, the bigger it becomes. Because what I'm about to say out loud is just . . . well, it's embarrassing how long we let this keep us apart. I caught him with his mouth full," she said, "of my date at an awards show in the eighties."

"Oh." I wanted to laugh, honestly.

"That wasn't what really set me off, though. It was that Leonard knew I was being used as a beard, and he didn't just tell me. I would have happily played along! But instead, I let myself be charmed by the most charismatic man." She shook her head.

"Would I know him by name?"

She laughed to herself. "Oh, every person in this country knows him by name."

"What! Are you serious? Who was it?"

She zipped her lips and shook her head.

"If I guess his name, will you tell me?"

She shrugged. "What I will say is that he was a perfect gentleman, so I should have known better than to think he was straight."

"Jack Nicholson?"

She took a moment to examine her nails, which I took as a clear *Guess again*.

"Okay, fine, I'll save my theories for later. But how does Hollis fit into all of this?"

"We walked out of the lawyer's office this morning and I spent the whole ride home airing my grievances. I'm sure you think there's something meaningful behind Leonard and his will, but it's just him getting the last word, I assure you."

"Or maybe it was Leonard's attempt to acknowledge how important you were to him. And who knows how long you'll be managing his properties? I don't think he was considering time when he made this decision. Knowing Leonard, this was all about symbolism. No matter how wide the chasm between you both grew, he trusted you. And now you have his will to prove it."

The waitress brought her drink and Ruby nodded a thank-you.

"That's what Hollis said. And then she asked me to marry her." She closed her eyes as though she was remembering the moment. "'Marry me for a day or a thousand,' she told me. 'I just want the paper trail to say that you and I loved each other.'"

"And you chickened out again?"

Her gaze cut over to me. "I think I prefer the quiet."

"Why not say yes, Ruby?" I asked. Now the tables were turned and I was the one who couldn't make sense of her decision—or indecision. "You love each other. The stars have aligned. The timing is right. Finally."

"It's *too* perfect," she said, her voice small as she nursed her drink. "I can't stand the thought of it being over. Whether it's me who goes first or her. Both possibilities hurt too much. I don't want to be a widow, and goddamn it, it's selfish, I know, but I get jealous at the mere thought of her living without me. Not because I'm jealous of *her*. I would choose Hollis's life over mine every day if I had to. But I am jealous of all the people who would still be able to enjoy her company. The only way this whole story ends is when one of us dies, and that's not somewhere either of us can follow the other to."

"And how does a signed piece of paper change that?" I asked, the thought of Eli and his offer to move in with him tickling the far reaches of my brain. "Love has got you fucked either way. You might as well call her your wife."

Ruby pursed her lips, eyes trained ahead on the rows of liquor bottles behind the bar.

"There's no happiness without pain," I said, speaking to myself as much as I was to her. "And I'm starting to think that saying what you want out loud—putting a name to it, letting it be something you stand to lose—makes the joy of having it so much sweeter."

"When did you become so emotionally intelligent?" She sighed. "I'll have to find the perfect shade of ivory. I will not risk looking putrid on my wedding day." Then she tossed me her keys. "And you're driving us home. I am, as the kids say, wasted."

CHAPTER FIFTY-SIX

As I drove us back to Starlight Palms in Ruby's car, she explained that Leonard had indeed chosen a natural burial. It would take forty days for his body to be composted into soil.

Today was day six.

He had requested that Ruby and I be present when his soil was spread. I could do that for him.

All good stories have a wedding and a funeral. It seemed that my time at Starlight Palms would have both.

Hollis sat waiting on Ruby's couch when we returned.

"Yes," Ruby said the moment she walked in the door, like she was announcing a ceasefire.

Hollis hardly noticed me as she stood and berated Ruby with questions about where she'd been and told Ruby how she had been so, so worried and that if they got married, Hollis was too old for this kind of worrying.

Ruby walked to Hollis and enveloped her.

"Hold on. Yes?" Hollis asked. "Did you just say yes?" Briefly, she looked over Ruby's shoulder to me and I gave a nod and a small smile before seeing myself out.

With Marlon at the boarders', I came home to an empty apartment. The furniture was still there, but every sign of Eli was gone. The only thing out of the ordinary was the slim white box on the kitchen table. Atop it was an envelope addressed to me. Eli's harsh and angular handwriting had practically cut through the page. I ran my fingers along the back of the paper and felt the indentation of his letters there as I began to read.

Vera—

I've just finished clearing the apartment of the last of my things. Like I said before, the place is still yours if you need it.

I haven't been my best self for the last week or so. I know that.

You infuriate me. The way I feel about you infuriates me.

I don't know how to have anything in between or casual with you. I don't know how to tell you to go back to LA and explore this opportunity with Brody. That would be the mature thing to do. That would make me the bigger person. You're supposed to let something go so that it can come back to you.

But like I said when I followed you to New Orleans: I want to be everywhere you are. I want to be the only person you ever wake up next to again. I don't know how to feel any other way. I don't know how to do this halfway. I want something you can't give right now.

I don't trust myself to be here when you get home. I don't trust that I will be the person who tells you to spend time on yourself when you could be spending it with me. But you deserve to figure things out without me complicating it all. You've taken care of everyone but yourself for so long, Vera.

You deserve to choose yourself and I think both of us need you to make that decision without me.

This whole letter feels wrong. I want to stomp around like a caveman and keep you to myself. But I'm scared that if I try to do that, there will be nothing left of you to have.

So maybe I'm weak to say all of this in a letter instead of to your face. But when you're ready, so am I.

—Eli

PS—I decided to give you your Christmas present a few weeks early. If you decide to give it back to me, I'll throw it in the pool.

I stared at his letter for a few minutes, rereading bits and pieces.

I wanted so much of what he wanted. But I didn't know how to have it. The temptation to just drive straight over to his house and tell him I was ready was a bottomless ache. But I couldn't cheapen his letter like that. If I went back to Eli, I needed him to know I meant it. I needed to know I meant it.

Decomposition Day 9

He gave me a brand-new laptop and I couldn't even bring myself to peel the cellophane wrapper off the box.

I didn't trust him not to throw it in the pool either, so I left it on the kitchen table, and it haunted me like creaking floorboards in an old house. The only way to stop your mind from playing tricks on itself is to ignore the sound all together.

Decomposition Day 11

I sat at the kitchen table with a half-eaten bagel. I'd seen Eli around the main building, but only in spare glimpses. It had me wondering if he was avoiding me or if I saw him so much before because he had always sought me out. Either way, it seemed unfair that he would ask me to take time to myself when he had the nerve to walk around with that honey-blond hair falling in his eyes, overdue for a haircut, and the veins in his forearms twitching as he shoved his hands into his pockets.

I licked the Nutella off my butter knife and then used it to open the plastic covering of the laptop box. The lid of the box slid off with a satisfying pop. It was the nicest laptop I'd ever had.

No, not had. Because this couldn't actually be mine. I'd find a way to give it back to Eli without him throwing it in the pool.

I peeled back the interior packaging to find a brushed gold laptop. My fingers hovered above it, but I put the lid back on the box before I could let myself get too familiar with this laptop that definitely did not belong to me.

Decomposition Day 14

It was Saturday and Ruby had an appointment to go wedding dress shopping at ten in the morning, but I woke up at four and couldn't go back to sleep.

I tried sitting on the couch and watching old episodes of *Gilmore Girls*, but eventually I wandered toward the kitchen and I couldn't do that without walking past the laptop on the table.

As I made my coffee, I watched the box like it might move if I looked away.

When my cup was done and doctored to my liking, I sat down in front of the box and tried to sip my coffee, but it was too hot.

"Fuck it," I muttered, and slid the lid off the box.

I cracked open the laptop and was immediately prompted to choose my settings and preferences.

As the sun began to break, I found myself staring at the empty laptop. Before I could talk myself out of it, I uploaded the photo I'd taken in New Orleans of the Touchdown Jesus statue in St. Louis Cathedral in the Quarter and made it my screensaver.

I finished my cup of coffee and relocated to the couch, where Marlon curled up on my feet.

Soon, I was signed into my inbox and penning an email to Brody. When I left LA, I'd told him I needed time.

I didn't need any more time.

Brody,

First, thank you. Your offer meant a lot to me. But I have to say no.

Please understand that I'm not saying no so that I can take this project elsewhere or anything like that. I need to say goodbye to *The Wunderkind*. It's not a world I know how to live inside of anymore.

I'm scared. This might be the biggest mistake of my life. But I have to trust that my best is yet to come.

—Vera

Decomposition Day 16

I bought screenwriting software. It was on sale, and I decided that even if I never used it, I was at least stimulating the economy.

Ruby found her dress. It was the first one she tried on, but of course we had to go to four other stores and try thirty-nine other dresses before she knew the first one was the right one. Considering the story of her and Hollis, I found that rather poetic.

Decomposition Day 17

I opened the software just to make sure it worked. It did. The page was as blank as I expected it to be.

Later that night, I began to transcribe Leonard's drafts. I didn't know why, but it seemed like a way to warm my creative muscles. It felt like I was teaching my body how to write again. Of course, Ruby and I would never try to sell anything of his that he hadn't explicitly decided was finished, but I didn't want to risk the papers getting destroyed. Especially now that I knew what the fuck the cloud was.

Sort of.

Decomposition Day 24

Tess:
The renovation is done. I've decided I don't have to kill my family. Besides, they never use flattering pictures on those true crime documentaries.

Vera:
congratulations on choosing a crime-free life.

Tess:
Hey now, I said nothing about going cold turkey. Just laying off the murder.

Tess:
Is the blank page still taunting you?

Vera:
the page is no longer blank, but it is still taunting me.

Tess:
You're such a good girl for Mommy.

Vera:
you are probably the closest thing I have to a daddy.

Tess:
Now go write Daddy some more words. And what do you think about making the trip to LA for a housewarming? I guess it's more like a house reheating. A house microwave. You can spend the night. We can get high after the kids go to bed.

Vera:

can we watch *Donnie Darko*?

Tess:

You and that fucking movie.

Vera:

I'm starting to doubt your commitment to Sparkle Motion.

Decomposition Day 28

"*This* is the kind of thing I want to write," I said as I dug another pickle from the very fancy jar Tess had been sipping from. She'd hosted her house reheating the weekend after Thanksgiving, and we were subsisting on leftover finger foods and charcuterie accoutrements.

"Absolute drivel that makes no money and the only people who like it just pretend to understand it?"

"You don't understand my creative vision," I said as we watched the credits for *Donnie Darko* roll. "I want to make the kind of thing that you see when you're nineteen and still quote random lines from because you can't get it out of your head, so you make your best friend watch it with you twenty years later."

She sighed and yanked the remote off the coffee table, which cost more than the value of my earthly belongings and which Tess said was originally chipped when it arrived, so she strong-armed the manufacturer into replacing it before she had to tap into a kid's college fund, which she was not beyond doing.

"I'm turning on *The Princess Diaries*," she said, before chugging pickle juice straight from the jar. "My brain needs a detox. I'm way too high for Jake Gyllenhaal in a scary rabbit costume to be the last thing I see before I fall asleep."

Decomposition Day 31

This morning before work, I began inputting the notes I'd compiled for my own project and since I wasn't done, I put the laptop in my tote bag so I could continue during my lunch break.

Ruby brought by the draft of the wedding invitations she had commissioned.

She stood behind me as I studied the line drawing of the original Starlight Palms sign that framed the words on the invitation.

"I approve." A slight feeling of melancholy settled in my chest. The sketch reminded me so much of the wedding chapel where Eli and I got married. "It's perfect."

"Good. Now, I need you to gather some quotes from a few different printers."

"This feels like it should be paid labor," I joked.

She shook her head and took the invitation from my desk before heading toward the door. "I've never been married, but I'm pretty sure that maids of honor are not typically compensated for their efforts."

I looked up just in time to catch her before she disappeared down the hallway. "You're having a bridal party?"

"Not a party," she said. "Just you. Hollis has her niece."

I swallowed back whatever feeling was ballooning in my chest, pressing tears into my eyes. "Well, in that case, I better send over some quotes for my services as maid of honor."

She puckered her lips to temper her smile and shook her head.

At lunch, I stayed in my office and pulled out my laptop. I finished adding my notes and now there was just the handful of pages I'd already written.

I started typing and allowed myself to tinker with words and phrasing. Before I knew what was happening, I ran out of prewritten pages and I just kept . . . going. I kept going for so long that I didn't hear the knock at the door or notice the broad figure standing in the doorway with his hands in his pockets.

When I finally paused for a second, the clacking of the keys broke long enough for me to realize that Eli was there.

He ran a hand up the back of his neck and then against the grain of his hair. My fingers tickled with the memory of how good his hair felt brushing against my skin.

I slammed the laptop shut and shuffled papers on top of it like I'd been caught. "Hi." So smooth.

He motioned with his chin. "I take it I won't have to throw that into the pool?"

I stood up and brushed the crouton crumbs from my salad off my dress. "You shouldn't have done that, Eli. It was too generous."

He shrugged. "I hope you like it. I wouldn't have thrown it into the pool if you needed to exchange it, but I guess I forgot to include that in my note."

"Haven't you ever been told that it's not fair to buy people extravagant gifts because then they feel like they need to buy you something equally as extravagant in return?"

He rocked back on his heels. Eli Buckley was fidgeting. Eli Buckley was not a fidgeter. "That sounds like a made-up rule."

"Thank you," I told him again.

He bowed his head once in lieu of saying *You're welcome*. "I came by to let you know I'm going by the apartment. I accidentally had a package delivered there this afternoon. So just in case you see me lurking."

"Thanks for the heads-up. Marlon will be happy to see you lurking."

"I've missed him," he told me, his eyes cutting down to the floor and then back to me.

"He's missed you too."

Decomposition Day 34

The invitations were ordered. Hollis took care of the cake. And I'd written twenty-six pages of words. Not necessarily good words. But words.

The story was heading in a weird direction, and I had to turn off the voice in my head that said no one would ever want this, especially someone who was trying to decide if they could make money off it. It was the same part of me that had absorbed all the closed-door discussions I'd seen Brody sit through about strategically choosing the next project and answering creative questions with business solutions.

So I pretended I was writing a story to entertain myself. Like I was reading a book I couldn't put down. I was the creator *and* the audience.

I couldn't let myself consider what came after typing *The End*, but I couldn't ignore the fact that for so long, it felt like I had deferred my dreams. That *The Wunderkind* would still have its moment when the time was right. It was what I would console myself with when I was feeling restless or left behind. But maybe I had to kill that dream to make room for a new one.

Decomposition Day 41

Leonard had donated most of the soil created by his body to a nature preserve near Palm Springs, but he had requested that those who would like to memorialize him take the Palm Springs Aerial Tramway to the top of Mount San Jacinto State Park and scatter a small amount of soil there so that he could always overlook the town he'd loved for so long.

"Are we even allowed to scatter remains in a state park?" I asked as Ruby and I rode the tram.

Ruby lifted her chin proudly. "We scattered your mother's ashes in Disneyland and managed not to get banned. I'm pretty sure sprinkling some dirt on a mountain is fine."

I sat back and nodded. We would meet Leonard's nephew and his family at the top, scatter some soil, and then eat lunch at the restaurant up top. It wasn't a bad way to celebrate a life.

Over the last week, as I continued writing into the new year, I toggled between writing and transcribing Leonard's work anytime I felt stuck. What he wrote was so far off from my own work, but sometimes I would read something that would spur a new thought or send me down a rabbit hole. In a way, it felt like being back in his writing workshop again. It made my heart ache as much as it comforted me.

When the tram stopped, Ruby took my hand to steady herself and I guided her through the doors.

It was at least thirty degrees cooler up here, and I was thankful that we'd all bundled up before leaving. Most would have considered it to be a nice, cloudless day, but it was absolutely frigid by Southern California standards.

We followed the off-loading crowd up the steps. Hollis and I let Ruby lead the way.

I saw him before he saw me.

Eli.

All the way up here in the clouds stood the man with a fear of heights.

I couldn't imagine what Eli must have done to survive the tram ride, and I immediately felt a pang of guilt that he'd made the trip on his own.

Towering over the other visitors, he stood just off the path, wearing dark jeans and a black jacket. His hands were clasped behind his back as he searched the crowd.

As the throng of people thinned and we followed the flow of foot traffic closer to him, he finally noticed me. My lungs burned against the cold, dry air, and I almost felt lightheaded at the sight of him.

"Dr. Buckley," Ruby said. "So nice to see you here."

"No name tag?" I asked. "I thought name tags were funeral protocol."

He shook his head, a familiar smile twitching at the edges of his mouth. "I'm not here on business."

"Leonard would be happy to see you here," I told him.

He nodded, and we stood there in silence as Ruby connected with Leonard's nephew Caleb—who she seemed to be somewhat acquainted with—and his family.

Eli and I took up the rear as our tiny group wandered toward a small wooded area near the steps trailing down to the lookout point.

Leonard's nephew seemed eager for anyone but him to take the lead, but no one else seemed to notice his spike in anxiety, so I stepped up and put on my activities coordinator hat.

"Maybe we could all scatter our soil," I offered, "and then reconvene to say a few words."

Caleb gave me a grateful nod and handed each person a small silver tin containing soil.

His young girls, including the one who had been in Leonard's lap at his living funeral, immediately ran off, giggling, while his wife and then Caleb himself followed close behind.

Ruby bit down on her lip until they nearly disappeared, her eyes glassy. Hollis pulled her close and the pair took their time looking for the perfect spot.

I stayed where I was and opened the tin in my hands. I didn't know what I expected to find, but the small mountain of soil was completely normal. Unremarkable.

Eli stood a foot or two from me, his own tin in the palm of his hand.

With Ruby and Hollis heading toward the cliffside and Leonard's family heading deeper into the woods, I decided that this was as good a spot as any.

As I dipped my finger into the dirt, Eli's voice disrupted the quiet. "You said it was nice of me to come for Leonard."

I took a small bit of dirt and sprinkled it at my feet. "It was," I said.

"Leonard was a great man. One of my favorite residents, honestly, even when he was a pain in the ass, but Vera, I didn't come all the way up here in that death trap for him."

A very small but powerful sliver of bravery forced me to turn and look up to him.

"I came here for you."

"But you hate heights."

He opened his tin and squatted down, dumping it all in one go before pressing it back into the earth where it belonged. "Yes, but not as much as I wanted to be here for you."

I swallowed back a lump in my throat as I continued to sprinkle my soil among the trees. "I'm glad you're here," I finally said.

He stood up, suddenly much closer to me than he had been before, his mouth opening as if he was about to speak.

"All right," Ruby said as she tiptoed around the forest floor like it might contaminate her. "Let's get this mushy stuff over with so I can have a lemon drop martini for lunch."

"And something to soak it up," Hollis added quietly.

Caleb and his family reemerged, the four of them rosy-cheeked and holding hands.

We all took turns telling stories about Leonard. Hollis shared about the time she and Leonard were on set in West Texas and went to a local bar and pretended to be rodeo workers. Caleb and his wife talked about their wedding and how Leonard had hired a barbershop quartet to surprise them but didn't realize that the singers were also dancers . . . of the adult variety.

Eli mentioned the time Leonard called the resident emergency number and requested a house call . . . for his bird.

Ruby told everyone about the time Leonard had rescued her from a meeting with a handsy producer at his house. Not only did Leonard swoop in to save her, but he also brought a dozen eggs and on their way out he tucked them under the driver's seat of the producer's unnecessarily fancy car.

I told the story of meeting Leonard and how he convinced me to list a coffin for sale on Facebook. Caleb laughed so hard he cried. And the girls laughed along too just to be in on the fun.

And then that was it. The soil was spread and our memories were shared.

"Before we head over to the restaurant, I have a letter from Leonard. His lawyer said he wanted me to read it at a gathering of his loved ones, so I guess—" Ruby stopped abruptly, collecting herself for a moment as Hollis rubbed a circle across her back.

Ruby nodded and unfolded the letter. "'You didn't think you'd heard the last of me, did you?'"

We all laughed and I wiped away stray tears.

"'I might have had my living funeral, but that was just the dress rehearsal. This is opening and closing night all in one. Now, if you followed my instructions, you're at the top of the tramway with dirt that I made myself. Free-trade, organic Leonard dirt.'"

There were a few more chuckles as a warm hand wrapped around mine. I looked down to see my and Eli's joined hands and then up at him, but his gaze was straight ahead on Ruby.

"'If I'm right and I died of natural causes at the ripe old age of eighty-four, then my death came as no surprise. In fact, most would say that you couldn't ask for anything more in terms of a grand exit, and I think I'd have to agree. I wasn't stolen away in my youth. I'm one of the lucky ones.'"

Ruby took a deep breath, and I wondered if she was thinking about how long of a future she and Hollis had to look forward to. Then she stepped toward me and held the letter out. "Read the rest for me, would you?"

I nodded and held the letter in my free hand. Eli didn't make any motion to let go and sharing this physical contact with him felt like he was holding my actual heart in his hand.

"'I'm sure some of you are surprised to see my decades of funeral planning be set aside, but as I felt my body drawing closer to the end, I looked for hope. And in searching for that hope, I settled on this: Death cannot exist without life. It's a lesson I learned as a young writer. There were many times when I had to go through the pain of writing things that would never get any camera time or even be read by anyone besides myself. But all the drafts and wasted pages existed so that other work could be created and shared. And my greatest hope is that my life follows that same path.'"

I saw the next few words before I said them out loud, and there was no hiding my choked sob.

Eli squeezed my hand once. Twice. In time with the beating of my heart.

I took three deep breaths and continued. "'Like the soil you've spread, it would be my greatest honor for my death to create new life.'" I folded the letter back up. "'All my love, Leonard.'"

Hollis shook her head and dabbed under her eyes with a knuckle. "He just had to make us all cry one last time."

Ruby laughed and leaned her head against Hollis's shoulder. "He always did bring the drama."

And if Leonard had a headstone, those are the words that we'd engrave on it.

THE WUNDERKIND (FIRST DRAFT)
"PILOT" 10/8/07

INT. ART MUSEUM—DAY

It's winter. Everything is gray and cold. Not a tourist in sight. Poppy misses Arlo every day, and she's tired of living without him. She parks her car illegally and then runs past the ticket stand into the museum, searching for Arlo. He is working as a security guard now. She finds him in the Impressionist room. Their eyes meet. They are drawn together.

POPPY

I didn't write a speech. But I'm here.

ARLO

(smirking)
You're late.

POPPY

What if I love you too?

ARLO

What if?

They kiss. A single security guard awkwardly claps.

POPPY

This is probably a mistake.

ARLO

Let's make it anyway.

October 14, 2019
Vera S.
Can it really be this simple? Maybe.

<u>THE WUNDERKIND</u> by Vera Stein.

Caleb and his family were the first to go. His girls were restless and they had a long drive home. Hollis and Ruby found a spot at the bar, where they watched in silence as the tram went up and down the cliffside.

So that left me and Eli, who was wringing his napkin until his knuckles turned white.

"What'd that napkin ever do to you?" I asked.

He gave a dry chuckle. "I just realized that I have to go back down the mountain. I was so concerned about getting up here that I just . . . forgot I had to go back down."

"How did you get up here, anyway? You could have waited for us to get here so we could all go up together."

"I wanted to be here for you," he reminded me. "That didn't involve you coaching me through a panic attack."

"You made it up here, though," I said.

"Yeah, well, I had to close my eyes and stand in the dead center of the car while I recited the Hippocratic Oath under my breath over and over again."

"The Hippocratic Oath?"

"It was the only thing I could think of that didn't involve singing. But maybe that would have been better. The family riding up with me probably thought I was a serial killer."

"Do you want to get it over with?" I asked. "Going back down?"

His fist closed around the napkin once more and he nodded.

We went by the bar to say goodbye to Ruby and Hollis.

As I hugged my grandmother, I bent down and whispered, "Michael Douglas?"

The only answer I got was her eating the olive out of Hollis's martini.

There wasn't a line to go back down, so Eli and I had the tram car to ourselves.

He immediately stepped into the center, facing the mountainside, and gripped a handrail.

I stood directly in front of him and let my hands cover his.

The tram lurched forward, and his throat bobbed as he clenched his eyes shut.

"Ignore the windows," I told him. "Just look at me. Listen to me."

He breathed in through his nostrils and opened his eyes, glancing for a moment at our touching hands.

"I didn't take the offer from Brody," I told him. "And before you say anything, it wasn't only about us. In fact, it was hardly about us."

"Okay." His voice was full of trepidation, but his breathing had leveled out.

If I could distract him from the fact that we were suspended in the air and get these words out that had been building inside of me for the last forty days, then this could be a win-win. "Sometimes I get so sad when I think about all the time we missed and how unfair it is that we can't pick up where we left off that morning in Vegas. Did we miss out on an entire life together? It hurts to wonder."

The quiet devastation on his face made it clear that I wasn't the only one of us to consider that same thing.

"But we couldn't have had this back then. If we hadn't exploded that morning—if we hadn't fallen apart—it would have only been a matter of time. And fuck Leonard for always being right, but maybe this"—I motioned to the space between us—"couldn't exist if things had been any different. Maybe the only way for us to have a second chance was for us to fail so miserably the first time."

The car jerked and he pulled me to him, and his body hunched over mine so that our foreheads were pressed together.

"Breathe," I reminded him. "Just breathe and listen to my voice."

He nodded, and I waited a moment for the rise and fall of his chest to slow down before I continued.

"For years, I've thought that my life was only before and after. That there was this younger version of me who was so much more capable of living the life she wanted. And then there's me. Vera in the now, who's just trying to survive and make up for lost time. But with you, I'm the Vera I was *and* I'm the Vera I am. And you make me feel like I'm the Vera I could be."

He allowed himself to let go of the rail completely to slide a strand of hair behind my ear. His lips parted, words on the tip of his tongue.

"Wait," I said. "I need to say this and I need to say it before you do, because . . . because I've been chickenshit. You might be scared of heights—"

"It's not the heights I'm scared of, love," he whispered. "It's the falling."

I nodded, because I understood. I understood completely. "Me too, Eli. I used to believe that patience was a virtue. That if I just waited patiently and quietly for someone else to come along and make the first move, I would be rewarded." I shook my head. There was no going back now. "Patience isn't a virtue. It's an excuse. Which is why I can't let myself wait any longer. I need you to know that I love you and I want to show you all the big and little ways I can love you every day."

He exhaled a long, shaky breath, but I'd never seen him look so certain—so determined. If Eli could be up here with me, I could walk right off the edge with him.

"We're both scared of falling," I said. "But it's not the ground that worries me. It's you. It's us. I don't know if I'll ever stop being scared, but you're worth the risk, Eli. So, I love you. I love you and I'm not scared to say it first—actually, yes, I am scared. But fucking hell, I'm doing it anyway."

His wide eyes searched mine and then he leaned down so close to me that each of his words brushed against my lips. "I loved you then, Vera. I didn't recognize it for what it was at first. But I loved you then and I love you now, and if you'll let me, I want to love you tomorrow and the next day and the next day after that."

"I need you to kiss me," I told him, my rib cage swelling to accommodate my love for him. "You can't say something like that and not kiss me."

I barely got the last syllable out before his fingers were tangled in my hair and he was crushing me against him, our mouths urgent. All heat and tongues and teeth. His hand snaked around the back of my neck, his kisses marking me and claiming me as though he'd been kept at arm's length and finally, finally he was allowed to give me the full force of his affection.

I moaned into his mouth as my hands moved from his face to his neck to his shoulders to his chest, as if my fingerprints could soak in this memory.

"Please watch your step as you exit the car," the automated voice said.

I leaned back and Eli looked me over frantically, his thumb caressing my cheek, like he had to be sure that this was real. That we were real.

"We're back on solid ground," I said. "You survived."

He looked from side to side with amazement. "Do you think they'd let us go again?"

I laughed as the doors opened and I pulled him out onto the platform.

"Where should we go?" he asked.

"Home," I said without any hesitation. "Let's pick up Marlon and let's go home."

"Home," he echoed. "Brigid has been on my ass about giving you space, so she'll be happy to see you when she comes for dinner tomorrow." Eli took my right hand, his finger twisting the ring on my finger. He tugged on the metal band slightly, and then looked down to me through his dark lashes.

I gave him a nod, and he slid the ring from my right hand and moved it to my left.

The ring was as plain as it had always been, but this somehow felt different from Vegas or even the night in New Orleans when I wore the ring on my left ring finger. This time I wouldn't have to take it off at the end of the night.

Eli kissed the ring. The ring that had for so long reminded me of an ending was now our new beginning.

Ext. Palm Springs Aerial Tramway Parking Lot—Evening

The perspective pulls out for a bird's-eye view of the parking lot and then the city, mountains, and endless desert. Vera and Eli are two people—two specks among many—who have found each other. The moon is a disco ball in the sky.

In cursive script, the title curls out across the view and reads: VERA STEIN IS ~~FINE~~ GREAT.

THE END

ACKNOWLEDGMENTS

If you've made it this far, to the acknowledgments of this book, thank you. Some books happen in an instant and others sprawl out across years. I don't have much patience with the latter and rarely stick with an idea that doesn't feel immediately right. But Vera was different.

I've been sitting with Vera's story since 2017, when Sierra Simone texted me an article about Denville Hall, a retirement home in Northwood, London, for actors, members of the entertainment industry (including circus performers!), agents, and spouses of any of the above. In that moment, I knew there was a story there, and I wanted to write it immediately, despite the fact that I was wholly unprepared.

Vera came to me in bits and pieces. Little did I know in 2017 that I had so much life to live before I could fully tell her story. Since then, I dabbled in screenwriting, I turned forty, I came to the conclusion that I would never be a mother, I moved away from my immediate family for the first time ever, I was diagnosed with endometrial cancer, I had a radical hysterectomy, and I became a caretaker for both of my parents at different times. It was a challenging period, but these were also the experiences that have made me the most *me*. Through it all, I have never been more certain of myself and, in the end, more prepared to write Vera.

Not every writing experience can be like this, nor do I want it to be. The emotional and physical toll is too high, but I am deeply grateful for the people who have surrounded me in the years it took to bring this idea to the page.

John Cusick, thank you for responding to that first email about Vera with this brief but electric response: *JULIE, I am so psyched to hear this. We can get you into the adult space, and I do think your readership will follow you there. The proposal is on my Kindle and I will read today if I can. Apologies for the brief email, but the short answer is YES YES YES.* John, you have guided me through so many career pivots, including the move into adult books, with such grace. You are a friend and partner for the ages.

May Chen! I love you even though you hate every title I come up with. (Don't worry. You're in good company with Sierra. *Creatures of Habit* lives on in my heart.) But seriously, thank you for giving me the space and time to work on this book and for telling me it was okay to slow down even when I was sure that cancer was, like, seriously no big deal and I was certain I would have this book to you in just a few weeks. (Reader: The book did not arrive in a few weeks. Turns out cancer is a big deal even when it's not.) I'll never forget meeting you at that Harper BEA party in 2019, when you asked if I'd ever considered writing adult books. It turned out to be a great pickup line because here I am.

Julie Paulauski and DJ DeSmyter, thank you both for tolerating me and my not-so-subtle bossiness and for always being game to consider my ridiculous ideas. You are both gems of the highest order. Ella Rumsey, thank you also for keeping the wheels spinning!

Justine Gardner and Hope Breeman, I am so grateful for your copyediting prowess and for constantly having your eyes on the timeline, because goodness knows I don't. (Thank you also for the occasional LOLs in the comments. Getting noncopyediting comments from a copyeditor is like being the teacher's favorite but better.)

Kerry Rubenstein, when I say your patience knows no bounds, I truly mean it. Thank you so much for helping Vera find the perfect cover. I cannot thank you enough for your willingness to listen and partner with me on this, because I am fully aware of what a handful I am. And thank you to Matthew Laznicka for your incredible, inspiring art.

I have the best friends and colleagues. Thank you to Sierra Simone, my fellow overnight-long-haul-trucker-not-so-essential-vampire-worker BFF, for the initial spark for this idea and for being one of my emergency contacts. Flavia Vazquez for always gassing me up and loving me even when I frown about making social media content. Ashley Lindemann, my birthday twin, for being the best office cuddle bug, maintaining The Calendar of Things, and adopting me as one of your beloved Sims.

Thank you also to my mom and dad, Bob and Liz Pearce, both Trevino families, Ashley Meredith, Kate Fasse, Ashley Brown, Juliet Johnson, Julia Whelan (my Palm Springs expert), Nisha Sharma, Erica Russikoff, Carley and Jess at Under the Cover, Natalie C. Parker, Tessa Gratton, my Supper Club pals, Amy Wilson, Mary Kole, and last but never least in my heart: Mr. Simone.

Ian, when I think of all the things the last few years have brought us, I am well aware of how easy it would have been to let it all push us apart. But not only did you stick around, you dug your heels in and brought us closer together than I thought was possible. I love you and the life we've built even when it's hard.

ABOUT THE AUTHOR

JULIE MURPHY splits her time between North Texas and Kansas with her husband, who loves her, and her cats, who tolerate her. She is the author and coauthor of over twenty books for all ages, including *Dumplin'* (now a Netflix original film) and the Christmas Notch series cowritten with her best friend, Sierra Simone. When Julie isn't writing, she's hunting for the perfect slice of cheese pizza, discovering a new hobby that she will soon discard, and planning her next travel adventure.

then